MW01641408

QUEEN OF THE BAY

J. CLARE

QUEEN OF THE BAY

This is a work of fiction. Unless otherwise indicated, all the names, characters, businesses, places, events, and incidents in this book are either the product of the author's imagination or used in a fictitious manner. Any resemblance to actual persons, living or dead, or actual events is purely coincidental.

All statements of fact, opinion, or analysis expressed are those of the author and do not reflect the official positions or views of the CIA or any other U.S. Government agency. Nothing in the contents should be construed as asserting or implying U.S. Government authentication of information or Agency endorsement of the author's views. This material has been reviewed by the CIA to prevent the disclosure of classified material.

ISBN: 979-8-9874759-0-4 (paperback)
ISBN: 979-8-9874759-4-2 (eBook)
ISBN: 979-8-9874759-5-9 (hardcover)

Cover design and the *Then and Now* graphic, Katelin Spector; book design, Maureen Campanile; Marina House, Devon Felt; regional maps, Autumn Birt; Carter coat of arms, Emily Quinn and The Carter Family Tree. Broadside 1880 .C35. Special Collections, University of Virginia.; sextant line art drawing black and white, Pete Klinger / Alamy Stock Vector; Galleon, Oleksandr Chaban / iStockPhoto.com; uncredited images in the book are courtesy of the Spanish Princess and the author

Published in the United States by Old Dominion Press, Commonwealth of Virginia

Printed in the United States
2023---First Edition

SPECIAL SALES
Old Dominion Press books are available at special quantity discounts when purchased in bulk by corporations, organizations, and special-interest groups. For information, please email sales@OldDominionPress.com.

PUBLISHER'S NOTE

To put yourself in the mood as you read *Queen of the Bay*, we recommend you play the cited music when a scene references a song. A playlist is provided on our website (www.OldDominionPress.com) with links to free playable versions.

Since the manuscript was originally written to serve as a screenplay, you may want to envision whom you would cast for the roles. We'd love to hear your thoughts on this via our publisher's social media fan pages.

Clues to the underlying mystery are scattered throughout Book One, and you may have questions. To that end, we maintain a Q&A page on our website with answers we receive from the author. Feel free to submit your questions via the mechanisms listed on our website.

DEDICATION

For Emilia, still in the womb when the ink went to paper. For you at the appropriate age, that you may know and embrace your American history. There is so much more I'd like to tell you, but I can't.

To my mother, a great *Lady*. I pray they've upgraded to digital eBooks in Heaven. I think you'll love this. Maybe a hardcover edition will be available in the New Earth, and you can tell me if I got it right.

Revelation 21:1

And of course, to Ollie, my love, how could I have done this without you . . .

ACKNOWLEDGMENTS

To the many people and organizations that supported this endeavor with your research, editing, artwork, beta-reads, etc. Thank you! You know who you are (and to Nina, who is no longer with us). I'm indebted to you all.

To the Agency's Publication Review Board, whom I affectionately refer to as my political minders, thank you for your timely review. By doing that, it encourages the rest of us to do what is right. Although I am unable to tell the whole story, you encouraged me with what remained.

THE KING'S RANSOM BOOK SERIES

Book I: **QUEEN OF THE BAY**
Book II: **THE KING'S RANSOM**
Book III: **LADIES OF THE REALM**
Book IV: **THE CODEX**

**Queen of the Bay* is the first book in a four-book series. Though the main storyline of each book will be wrapped up at the end, a significant part of the historical mystery will not be resolved until the end of Book Two, and the final mystery until Book Four.

CONTENTS

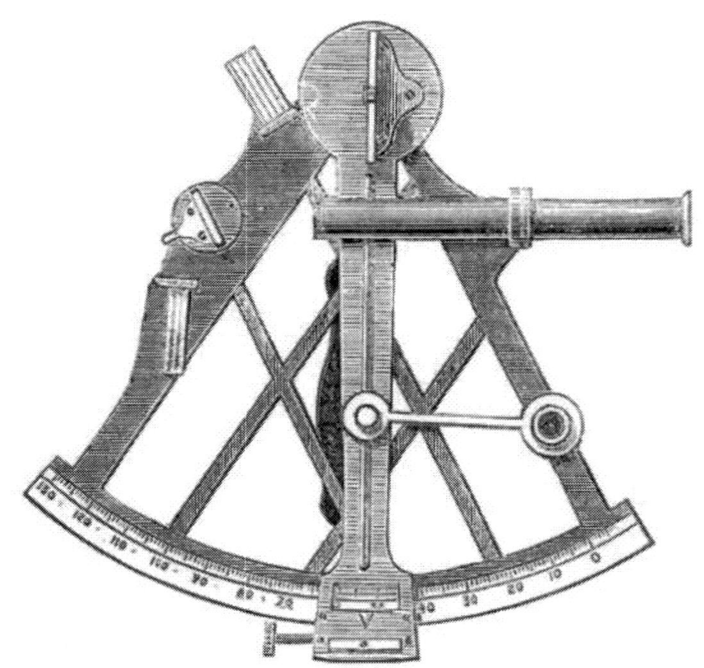

CHARACTER MAP

Then and Now

Then (1607):

Captain John Smith: Of Lincolnshire, England, Smith, a Puritan, rose from humble and hardworking farming roots to be considered one of America's most colorful persons of the last four hundred years. In his fifty-one years, the Admiral of New England transcended roles that included sailor, pirate, soldier, mercenary, slave, prisoner, explorer, politician, fisherman, author, and knight. Nearly executed by Christopher Newport for mutiny on their voyage to America, Smith landed at Cape Henry on April 26, 1607 and eventually became the governor of the Virginia Colony at Jamestown until his departure in August 1609. He was the first Englishman to map the Chesapeake Bay area, having led the exploration of it and its major rivers.

King James: James VI and I (James Charles Stuart; 19 June 1566 – 27 March 1625) was King of Scotland as James VI from 24 July 1567 and King of England and Ireland as James I from the union of the Scottish and English crowns on 24 March 1603 until his death in 1625. The kingdoms of Scotland and England were individual sovereign states, with their own parliaments, judiciaries, and laws, though both were ruled by James.

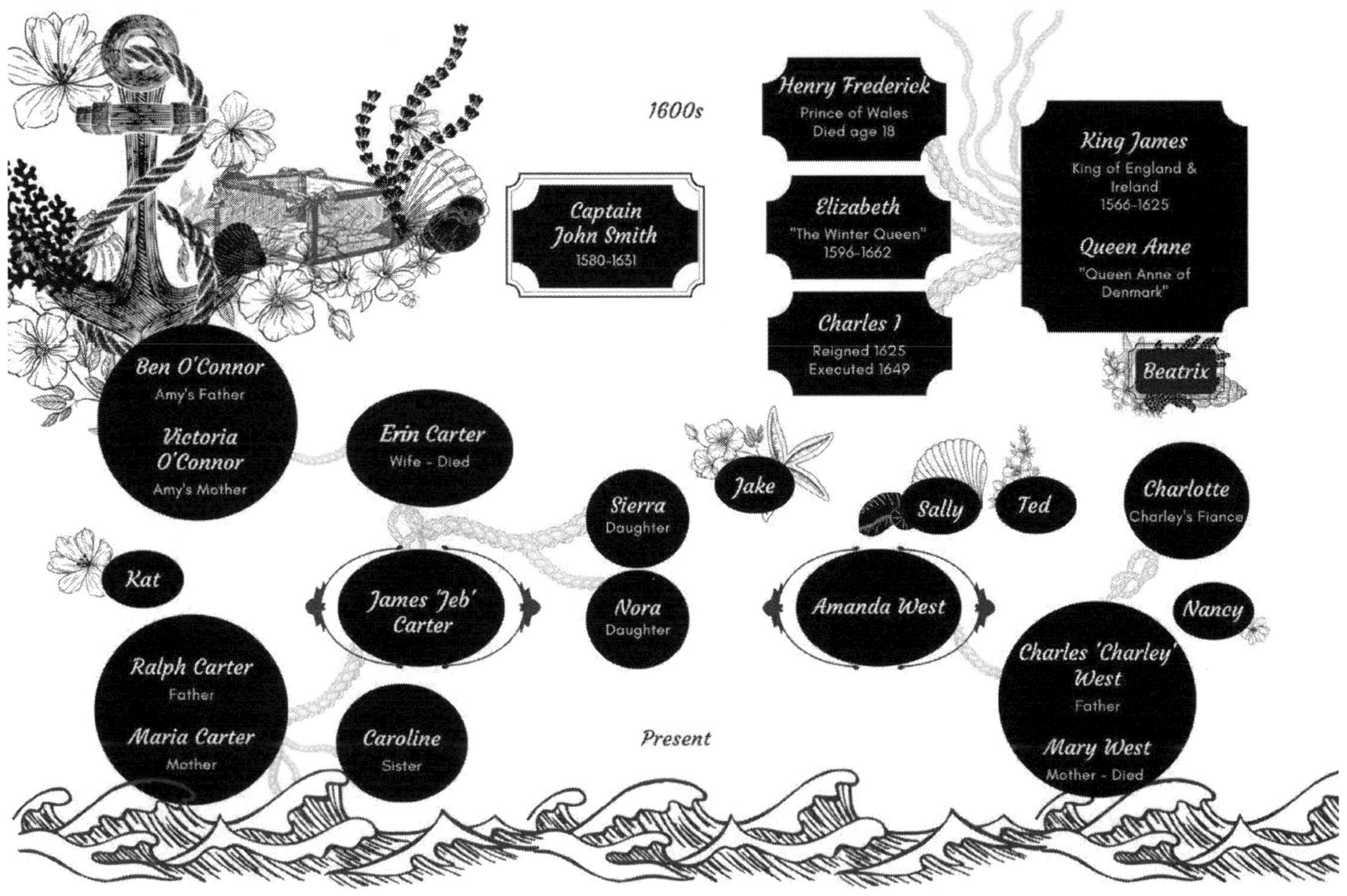
1600s
Captain
John Smith
1580-1631
Henry Frederick
Prince of Wales
Died age 18
Elizabeth
"The Winter Queen"
1596-1662
Charles I
Reigned 1625
Executed 1649
King James
King of England &
Ireland
1566-1625
Queen Anne
"Queen Anne of
Denmark"
Beatrix
Ben O'Connor
Amy's Father
Victoria
O'Connor
Amy's Mother
Erin Carter
Wife - Died
Sierra
Daughter
Jake
Sally
Ted
Charlotte
Charley's Fiance
Kat
James 'Jeb'
Carter
Nora
Daughter
Amanda West
Nancy
Ralph Carter
Father
Maria Carter
Mother
Caroline
Sister
Present
Charles 'Charley'
West
Father
Mary West
Mother - Died

Queen Anne (aka Anne of Denmark): Queen consort of Scotland, England, and Ireland by marriage to King James VI and I.

Beatrix Ruthven: Lady-in-waiting to Anne of Denmark

Christopher Newport: An English seaman and privateer. He is best known as the captain of the *Susan Constant*, the largest of three ships which carried settlers for the Virginia Company in 1607 to what would become the settlement at Jamestown.

Thomas West: Third Baron De La Warr, governor-for-life of the Colony of Virginia.

Now (Twenty-First Century):

James (Jeb) and Erin (deceased) Carter and his daughters, **Sierra** and **Nora**

Amanda West

Charles (Charley) and Mary (deceased) West: Amanda's parents

Ralph and Maria Carter: Jeb's parents

Ted and Sally: Amanda's work colleagues and friends

Kathi (Kat): Owner of the Yokel coffee shop

Charlotte: Charley West's fiancée.

Prologue

JAMESTOWN VISITOR CENTER

Excerpt from a Placard for Anne of Denmark

"Queen consort of Scotland, England, and Ireland by marriage to King James VI and I. Shortly after a proxy marriage in Copenhagen in August 1589, Anne sailed for Scotland but was forced by storms to the coast of Norway. On hearing that the crossing had been abandoned, James, her fiancé, sailed from Leith with a 300-strong retinue to fetch her."

Excerpt from a Placard for King James

"He considered his voyage to fetch Anne the one romantic episode of his life."

1609 - Visit with a Queen

Although the world typically passed by her unmeddled, Anne of Denmark had a knack for reading people. She received news that Captain John Smith had returned from the Americas and was scheduled to brief King James and his Crown ministers. She rarely joined her husband for meetings, but Smith's dealings with the native tribes of this new world intrigued her. With the King's increasing interest in the colony's health—and even keener interest in the Captain's exploration of the Chesapeake Bay—she wanted in on the game.

Smith was already present when Anne arrived in the Royal Map Room, a lofty court, fashioned by Doric-styled columns and decorative cornice moulding. She positioned herself to the side. Not a chance they'd allow her a front-row seat with James, but she maintained a direct line of sight to London's most glamorous society figure. The thirty-year-old captain was dashing. And a bachelor, or so it seemed.

It helped that no one dared turn their back on her, even if she was only a queen consort.

Not that she cared for her titles. She still liked to think of herself as a Danish princess, cherishing the memories of her early years when she was carefree and hopeful. Days that came screeching to a halt at fourteen when she was married off to James.

Maybe she was delusional back then. To think that she could marry for love when, in reality, she'd been sired for political brokering.

The Captain didn't ignore her during his briefing. He granted her genuine smiles, ones that acknowledged her own predicament.

Smith outlined the progress and financials of the fledgling Jamestown settlement. Anne yawned. She came to hear about relationships, and the Captain didn't disappoint. A momentary look of melancholy crossed his face as he spoke of the Powhatan tribe.

His stories and his eyes kept her in the moment, but when the Captain returned to the mundane aspects of the settlement, her thoughts drifted back to a time when she'd been infatuated with James. She laughed at her girlish self and the fantastical image of James she'd created without ever having met him. Artificial love? Forgivable. She muddled through life like all the other aristocratic Ladies. Or, as she and her best friend, Beatrix Ruthven, liked to call them, the *caged* Ladies of the Realm.

It didn't take long for reality to set in once they'd married. The breeding part was not effortless, but she eventually bore James a son named Henry. Soon thereafter, James stole off with him, placing Henry outside her care, in the custody of the Earl of Mar in a far-off castle in Scotland. "Scottish tradition!" is what James called it. "Ignoramus" is what she called him.

What a grand start to their marriage. She was still young at that time, and James should have realized she was a mama bear at heart. To have poked her in that way summoned all her ire. And if James found reason to execute her? Why should she care? Henry had become her only love, and he was gone!

Could she forgive James? Only in that she understood him. He was politically controlled—like everything else in their lives. The cycle was continuing with her beloved daughter Elizabeth, now thirteen.

Anne had similar tendencies of her own at that age: make-believe love. Like Anne, Elizabeth would have little choice in whom she married. A decent proposal had arrived from the Spanish court, putting forward Victor Amadeus I, grandson of Philip II of Spain. Not a bad catch, if only love was at stake. The young man was fiery and full of passion!

James's choice for her? Louis XIII of France. Talk about politics!

The Captain granted her his eyes once again. What did he see in her? Probably what most outside the palace walls thought: *Queen Anne lives a life of privilege.* She did, but to her, it felt more like prison. Except for Beatrix, her ladies-in-waiting were nothing more than guards. Maybe Anne exaggerated their role, but at their best, they were her political minders.

Beatrix was more like a kindred sister, one who empathized with her in their doomed plight, and she could trust Beatrix with her most guarded secrets. But Beatrix wasn't in attendance today.

It was through Beatrix that Anne had received an illicit morsel of gossip; a secret she now suspected was intended only for her . . . and not the king. Alongside the formal proposal from the Spanish prince came an unofficial snippet masked as hearsay, making the case for a union between the two empires.

Although Anne lived separately from James, she still garnered significant influence; a fact of which the Spanish were well aware.

In truth, James had come to respect Anne's resolute stand against his bullying ways. Her sway over the petulant man explained their motives for another leak—*La Estrella*—a revelation she believed so outlandish, it could never be put to paper. The canard purported the device as the greatest navigation achievement in maritime history. The advantage it could provide to the Spanish Armada gave merit to their merger proposal. But who'd ever believe such a story from a Lady? The King's courtiers would only slander her, mocking, "Fool's gold!" James didn't need to know. He only needed to be influenced.

Anne's vision swept from the Captain to the King. Now at the ripe old age of thirty-five, she and James had reached a steady state in their relationship: fulfilling their duties and remaining at peace with one another. Maybe not a romantic love, but at least they'd attained mutual respect for each other. Her special love would remain for the children. That was enough.

James was exiting the Map Room with his court in tow when Anne gave him her sly, subtle eye roll, the one she used to tell him she owned him and all his little secrets. No one else had seen it but James. Apparently, he had more pressing matters. A lunch party. The knowing wink he returned said the status quo suited him just fine.

Two of her Ladies, adorned in court-appropriate dress, had joined her in the Royal Map Room. Behind their backs, she referred to these two as the *Earl's Little Knives.* Many knew about the ornate knife set she'd received as a wedding gift from a particularly dreaded earl. They were always ready to seize upon her missteps. She suspected they reported to Robert Carr, Earl of Somerset. The dog!

Let them watch me. The Captain holds the clues. Now was time to play offense.

Anne approached the center of the room—the map resting on the large oak chart table. She caressed the map's oily parchment between her fingers. Narrow windows adjacent the fireplace illuminated *his* subject—the charts, documenting his exploration of the Bay. She stood, her back to the light, illuminating *her* subject—the Captain—and tapped the glossy wood.

The Captain pivoted gracefully, one set of fingertips remaining on the table. "Excuse me, Your Highness?"

Her heart skipped a beat. The man moved smoothly, and she suspected him to be a fine dancer. Not typical for a soldier turned explorer.

"Fascinating," she said, and she meant it. He was just that: fascinating. All of him. Guilty thoughts she labored to exterminate.

She turned slightly but wouldn't face the man. He performed his duty well, aligning his feet with hers and giving his eyes. He was confident, but not arrogant.

She'd chosen one of her favorite Danish dresses for the occasion, one of rich black embroidery—the bodice distinguished by a scoop neckline and tight sleeves. Not her finest, but one that brought back better memories.

"Thank you, ma'am." His buttery voice sent shivers down her arms, spoken with a tone that conveyed more than deferential respect. Maybe he appreciated her knowledge of the arts and sciences.

The Queen straightened. "You may not be an admiral yet, but you will be."

His brow furrowed.

She closed her eyes. Light conversations drifted in from outside the Map Room, echoing up the long court hallway. Her hearing was so much better than her eyes. So good in fact, she once thought she could make out a person's heartbeat. Maybe she couldn't hear Smith's heartbeat, but she could hear his breathing and it had changed.

The man is no fool! He probably suspected her trap after that dose of flattery.

But it wasn't a lie. She'd already been privy to talk of Smith's promotion within the Royal Navy. And another expedition—this one to a place to be called New England. Her husband's courtiers made the colossal mistake of underestimating her—the Lady of fashion. They dismissed her as frivolous, tolerating her presence only for her beauty. It made her that much more powerful. Like it had today.

She wondered what the Captain thought of her minders. They weren't so bad looking either . . . and astute. When she opened her eyes, she was determined not to glance back at her Little Knives. *I'll take a different approach.*

Narrowing her brows, Anne whispered into his ear. "I sense you know something. Something you would have liked to inform the King, but failed to do."

He controlled a flinch.

She gently grazed his arm where his loose sleeve covered bandages. "What happened?"

He inhaled a startled breath. She already knew the answer. No one in the prior meeting had noticed or conveyed any sympathy.

"A gunpowder accident on a shallop. That's why I've returned to England." The man explained further details of the mishap. Her empathetic approach was working now; he was talking.

"I'll see that the King grants you the finest care." She lifted her chin. "From his own doctor, if necessary."

"Thank you, ma'am."

"You did not want to come back?"

"No, ma'am."

She gestured to his bandaged arm. "May I see?"

He cocked his head, an understandable surprise. Why would a queen care to look at his wound?

She reached for his arm, pulled back his sleeve, and carefully undressed the bandages near his wrist.

"Yes indeed, you've made a horrid mess of this." She maintained a gentle grasp on his wrist, avoiding the discolored skin. Like her own mother, Sophie, Queen Consort of Denmark and Norway, who'd nursed all her children, she was truly a mama at heart. *Parenting is not something to be delegated. That's the way these stupid English do it.*

The man's eyes were unlike any she'd ever seen. In her mind, they held images of all the places he'd been and the cultures he'd experienced. She'd heard the stories of Smith, captured by the Turks, and sold into slavery. How he'd escaped by killing his owner and traveled across Russia, Poland, Europe, and North Africa. Now he'd been to the Americas. She felt like she was seeing the world through his eyes. Better yet, she held his pulse.

She inhaled deeply. The scent of the salty sea hovered about him like a perfume. Then she picked up a whiff of lavender. She tilted her head back and rolled it in a circular motion, doing nothing to hide sighs of pleasure.

His soft, radiant blue eyes came to hers, and she gave him a flirty smile. "Where were you twenty years ago?" she whispered.

His pulse remained steady, but his face reddened. She tapped him gently. "Don't mind me, Captain, you're too young for me."

Better the facade of a flirt than to say he was too old for her daughter Elizabeth. He'd figure Anne for the hypocrite that she was. At least, that's how she felt about herself. She was the daughter of a king, the sister of a king, the wife of a king, and the mother of a future king. If Elizabeth married well, Anne would be the mother of a queen. Now that would be a full house!

He stiffened and his eyes widened.

Enough play time. She needed to get back on mission. "There have been rumors, Captain."

His pulse quickened in her grip.

Does he know about La Estrella? A discovery like that, if it was true, would be critical to the Crown and its survival. He should know that if he failed to report it, he'd be executed. Certainly not what she wanted. She'd never met a more mysterious man, one that drew out so many of her conflicted emotions. All pricking at her conscience.

"You have some enemies, do you not, Captain?"

"I know not of what you speak, ma'am." He stutter-stepped backwards.

She was loving this now. Smith certainly had his enemies. His own ambitions had created fierce resentment from other leaders of the colony, notably Captain Christopher Newport. During their voyage to the Americas, Newport had charged him with mutiny. They'd nearly executed Smith upon arrival at Cape Henry, but the royal orders, once unsealed, revealed the Captain to be a leader.

Had one of his enemies discovered the secret? The thought wrote itself across Smith's eyes.

Anne rebuked herself for the torture. *I'm better than that. Remember where you come from.*

"Are you married, Captain?"

"I think you know me not to be, ma'am." His tone was steady, but her question taunted him, his half-truth blaring.

She narrowed her gaze. "Yes, I *see,* Captain."

Smith's brow tightened and he cleared his throat. "Your Highness, what do you see?"

Anne's chest constricted. He was trapped . . . just like her. Was his predicament, whatever it may be, by choice?

She removed her hands from his wrist and restored the bandage.

She could only hope the white ceruse on her skin hid any reddening of her eyes. It was fine for Smith to see it, but not her Little Knives.

Return to mission, Anne! She tapped her chin. It hadn't been her intent to intimidate the Captain. The rumor about *La Estrella* was ringing true, but not how she envisioned Smith's involvement. He was no traitor! But who from the expedition had sold out to the Spanish? And what of the secret map—the one copied from Smith's own charts and exfiltrated out of England? It had already become known in circles as the *Don Pedro de Zúñiga Map*, named after the cunning Spanish ambassador.

Was Smith abiding by a higher moral standard?

"I see you're protecting one secret for the sake of another, and you value the secret of the heart above it."

He jolted slightly, not missed by the Little Knives.

Anne's gaze drifted towards the ceiling. How *deep* was this man's love?

Anne returned her eyes to the explorer. "What are your inclinations towards the daughters of Lord De La Warr? I recall receiving another one here just this season. I think it was Anna."

Smith's face froze. She'd made him uncomfortable again.

The Crown had recently appointed Thomas West, Third Baron De La Warr, as the governor-for-life of the Colony of Virginia. The lord had received Smith several times at his estate, primarily to exchange information regarding the colony. One daughter had taken a liking to him, and during one visit, the baron actually apologized for her smothering attention. Another fine tidbit passed along by her loyal Beatrix.

"No . . . you need not answer that, Captain. It will be better to see you at tonight's soiree."

He crooked his head. "Soiree?"

This caught the attention of her Little Knives. Any mention of a party—an occasion to show off their dresses—would launch them like fireworks.

"Yes . . . hosted by the French ambassador. I'll ensure you receive an invitation."

"Thank you, ma'am." Anne detected some dread in his voice.

Anne threw a cackle in her tone. Not so much for the Captain, but for her Little Knives. "I will take far more pleasure in observing your thoughts in action, Captain."

"Indeed, Your Highness." His pleading eyes met hers. "Might I take your leave?"

She gave a slight nod and kept her eyes on him as he fetched his charts. He rolled them tidy and provided a genteel neck-bow. His muscular legs looked as if they would send him running past the guards posted outside the Map Room. Her Knives would see that too. How unfortunate.

A younger version of herself longed to run with him, like the way she'd chased Henry when he was a boy. She had once outpaced his nursemaids and saved him from drowning in the palace lake.

She wanted the Captain to know he could trust her. Instead, she'd planted paralyzing fear in him.

Anne gazed into the empty room and laughed. She'd gained the upper hand by reading him, while others in the Map Room had only listened. Despite feeling cloistered in the palace, this experience left her exhilarated. Like she was thirteen again.

He was already present when the Queen arrived at the soiree with her Little Knives. Beatrix was also in her party, thank God! She'd do her bidding.

Smith provided numerous courtesies and danced with all the ladies needing a partner. He flashed charismatic smiles, trying to give them all something, but not too much. He avoided creating jealousies amongst the debutantes seeking his attention. Although charming, he was perfunctory.

Anne remained stoic and poised. A role that came easily was now a necessity as she labored to hide her girlish pleasure in the man—as graceful a dancer as she'd presumed. She danced vicariously through the debutantes and fought back jealousy. Through Beatrix, she requested the string quartet play a sad song—"Amarilli, Mia Bella"—and watched him. She confirmed her suspicion—he was ailing of a broken heart; she was certain now that this love protected other secrets.

The Queen needed a private moment with the Captain, nearly impossible in a setting like this. More than anything, she wanted to be asked for her hand in a dance. Outrageous! He'd never violate that code of conduct.

Anne nudged Beatrix and whispered, "Tell him he must dance."

Beatrix startled and narrowed her eyes.

Anne understood her friend's subtle rebuke and softened her tone. "The Queen kindly requests the honor of a dance."

While the quartet paused, Beatrix performed her duty, crossing the floor to engage the Captain. When she returned, Anne said, "I want something sprightlier."

The Captain came from across the embassy's great hall as the music began. He bowed and led her to the floor.

As they danced, Anne spoke in snatches, cognizant of the eavesdropping couples who passed by them. "You need to trust me, Captain."

He responded to everything with a slight head shake, rarely more than a twitch.

"I know it wasn't you," she said, referring to the secret map. She teased him a little too. "Relax, won't you!" They glided to the other end of the hall. "Dance with me like you danced with the debutantes."

That earned the Queen a veneer of a smile.

She muffled a giggle. "I understand that too." Anne gave him a lopsided version of her own. "Which is why I trust you."

His small twitch told her she was on-target. Only Beatrix should learn what this real man was doing to her. She thought about her sons, Henry and Charles. *If only they could come under the Captain's influence . . . but that would take a miracle.*

"Hold to your values, Captain. You will come out right in the end."

To herself, Anne spoke the same. *Hold to your values.* The Captain didn't hide his, and his transparency went against the grain of how she outwardly lived. She suspected his Puritanical outspokenness had provoked a murder attempt on his life. Her most hidden values—her Catholic leanings—if made public, would put her own life at risk.

Anne surmised how the rest of the evening would play out. Her Little Knives were already bragging about how their Queen had toyed with Smith and his unusual behavior. The wife of the Spanish ambassador would replay the society talk to her husband on their carriage ride home.

Anne already knew the Spanish Crown had tasked Zúñiga to

collect observed anomalies with regards to the Captain. The ambassador would add a brief paragraph of the innocuous incident to his monthly communique back to Seville . . . and she was fairly certain the government in Seville would not acknowledge the value of the observation.

Anne may have, at one time, had it in for her King James, but she was never disloyal to him or to her Crown. Through Beatrix and another trusted Lady, she had some influence over the English spy network. She offered a few pounds, targeting specific information from Spanish sources. She longed for a favorable outcome. Not only for the protection of her Crown, but her belief in the Captain. A man she wished to save from false accusation.

The timing of her visit with Smith and what followed proved that the Spanish acted immediately. Anne learned they'd ordered construction of a new galleon. A fact that was hard to hide with well-placed sources in Seville, always eager to trade tidbits of information for Spanish reals. They built it to the exact specifications of one previously deployed, the *Santa Margarita*—gone missing in 1607. It would rejoin the Columbia convoy, Spain acting as if they could hide the loss of their first *Santa Margarita*. In addition, the vacant shop of a particular watchmaker turned scientist-astronomer was searched for schematics containing designs for a rather unusual device. His papers were collected and burned. All the bronze contraptions found in his shop were melted down.

CHAPTER 1

(Current Timeframe - August)

Marina House

The sand gave way beneath Amanda's feet as she climbed up a small dune berm. It was behind her now, along with the girl, and a majestic home stood before her. She paused in the yard to take in the breadth of it—the iconic manor that had once been her home.

How long would she have until the girl became suspicious? Amanda's adrenaline kicked in. She'd conscripted Sierra for a clandestine mission and kept the girl unwitting of her true intentions. What harm could come of that? Sierra had served impeccably as Amanda's eco-tour guide, navigating the two aboard paddleboards along a tidal creek, then a river, and finally a bay. They'd stopped for lunch right on the beach in front of the house. Amanda wondered now if she'd violated any laws. How could it? This wasn't official business.

Memories shot at Amanda like cannons fired from the third-story widow's walk—what her mother had first called it. The unusual feature distinguished the estate from any other in the Northern Neck. It was on it where her parents formally introduced her to the Chesapeake Bay.

Her father had blindfolded her at the driveway entrance before pulling onto the property. She was twelve at the time. He and her mother led Amanda from his truck and into the home. The wood floors were solid, but irregular, and held a hickory scent. They placed her hands on a stone wall. It was cool to the touch, and she followed its curved shape. Metal on metal screeched. "That calls for some oil," her father said. A damp musty stench enveloped her, and she realized he'd opened a large, heavy door.

They went through a passageway and were soon standing on what felt like cobblestone. "Careful now, Izzie." His voice echoed, carrying forth her given name. "You'll need to hold the handrail. We're going up." Her father led her by the other hand, her mother's steps trailing closely behind. The rail was cool, and the stairs felt like metal grates as they rose in a circular pattern.

When she'd thought they'd reached the pinnacle, another door creaked open. She smelled fresh salty air. It was warmer at the top. Rays of sunshine hit her face, and what felt like wood planks supported her feet. Her parents were on either side of her when they removed the blindfold.

She remembered gasping. The expansive water view was stunning, a panoramic postcard wouldn't do it justice. All of it—breathtaking—abetted by the property's location at the tip of Windmill Point.

Her father waited until she caught her breath, and then, with a dramatic voice, he said, "My dear, behold . . . your realm."

She took in more of the view, and then he pointed southeast.

"The Atlantic Ocean is less than fifty miles from here. You'd be seeing it, but for the curvature of the Earth."

Her mother spoke with a tint of rebuke in her tone, "Charles, why so serious with the girl?"

The yard below her was magnificent, and all its possibilities stole the moment. Amanda recalled squealing with delight.

"It's the water you must come to love, my dear," her mother said.

Her father eyed her mother with admonishment, raising an eyebrow, the picture of his expression still vivid. "Now look who's talking?"

Her mother slugged him right in his bicep. He took less than a second to neutralize her, wrapping her in his arms. Amanda remembered wiggling out from between them, racing down the spiral staircase and into the green and plush yard. After her father's overseas Navy deployments, here . . . she finally had a yard to call her own!

She turned and looked up towards the widow's walk—the wrap-around deck at the top of the tower. Her parents were still embraced. "We'll play soccer here, Daddy!" she yelled at them.

"Have you forgotten me?" her mother teased.

"No, Mama!"

"You're not being truthful, young lady." Her eyes were playful. "But just remember, I play a mean croquet."

It was true. Her mother was vicious at the game and knew how to take advantage of the water hazards—a trick Amanda later learned to employ against her rivals.

They left the tower, and not long after, came to the back porch entrance. Her father had a flashlight in his hand. He left Amanda's mother along a porch rail, then bounded down its stairs to where Amanda stood in the yard. He waved the flashlight up and down, pointing from the top of the porch down to ground level. "Extra insurance against the storms."

Her father spoke to her like he was the realtor and Amanda the client. Like he still had to sell it to her!

Her mother remained on the wrap-around porch with a look of utter contentment. "Go on, you two."

Amanda's father led her by the hand to a small doorway at the side of the house. They entered it and found themselves in a roomy crawl space. It enclosed a stone cellar with an access door. He opened it and sprayed the space with flashlight beams. "This can serve as a storm shelter." He turned around and pointed the light to the floor joist above them. "They built this with turn-of-the-century lumber." His voice remained adult-like. "It's why the farmhouse has survived so long, battling all those hurricanes and nor'easters."

"But, Daddy, it looks like a castle." The girlishness in her voice embarrassed Amanda.

He lowered his head as they exited the crawlspace and pointed towards the rooftop. "You mean the turret?"

She nodded.

"The farmhouse was built around what once was a stubby lighthouse." His explanation for the widow's walk. "A caretaker's house was attached, but they expanded around it. The beacon's nearly two miles offshore now . . . at the tip of the Windmill Point sandbar."

Her father gained sight of her mother. Her lips were pursed, and her father narrowed an eye. It was the end of his adult-like realtor's voice. He got down on a knee, put his arm around Amanda, and they eyed her turret. "Okay, Princess, then for you, yes, this was first a castle. Positioned here to fight off those nasty English invaders."

"But, Daddy, I thought we were English?" Amanda felt the need to play along. Her parents were constantly embarking on some sort of history lesson. Acknowledge something, and they'd shorten the lecture.

"Yes, but then we became Americans, and those darn English conscripted our sailors on the open seas. An affront to our liberty!" He gestured toward the waterfront. "They came right up the Bay."

She knew he was testing her and belted out immediately, "The War of 1812!"

From that point on, to Amanda, the Marina House was first and foremost a castle, then a lighthouse, and finally, in its current form, a rustic farmhouse.

He didn't mention the threat of waterspouts, but she'd learned soon enough when spring arrived. She'd witnessed several from the house over the years. The narrow funnels falling from the sky mesmerized Amanda, and as long as they stayed clear of the Marina House, she'd never run to the cellar—which she eventually learned was really the base of the lighthouse.

The sloping yard she now crossed held memories of their family croquet games, just the three of them. Practice sessions before invasions of her Aunt Nancy with her raucous boys. Football and rugby were their sports. Amanda would often invite a girlfriend over to join her, so as not to be dominated by all those boys. Whoever she invited inevitably fawned over her ruggedly handsome cousins.

Amanda would never admit it to anyone, but she did the same, although vicariously through her friends. The boy-cousins were romantically off-limits to her. Maybe that's why she had so much fun with them.

When her cousins got the better of her in their sports, she'd turn the tables by switching either to kickball or soccer. She had a special rule. "If you kick the ball into the water, you're out!" Their foot control with the ball was abysmal. When they launched the ball into the drink playing soccer, her side earned a penalty kick.

Amanda swatted away a horse-fly, returning her to the moment. She was halfway across the lawn when a strange thought hit her, how those boy-cousins reminded her of Sierra's father—a man she'd nicknamed Paddleboard Guy. He had a similar temperament and confident ruggedness. Eerily not that different from her own father.

Earlier, before setting out on her tour with Sierra, the man had tested her patience. This caused Amanda to tussle with him, forcing him to relinquish his daughter to guide them. It was the only way he'd release a paddleboard. Nothing had gone right with the man, irritating her from the start, like a pinched sciatic nerve.

She smelled the freshly mowed grass, and an image of her father's face appeared again. Playing catch with her in the yard—countless hours in the springtime. What else would he rather be doing? Not like he had a son. Right? And her mother on the back porch, yelling out pointers and words of encouragement.

Amanda paused another moment and eyed the porch. She saw herself during those final autumn days, doing her homework, swaying from a porch swing. Her parents would join her on the adjacent one. They'd watch the sky melt into a spectrum of colors, scarlet and crimson-orange hues dominating the sky.

Her parents were counting the days. They rarely missed a sunset together out on the porch, her father's muscular arms wrapped around her mother. He doted. If his Mary was chilled, he'd rise instantly and fetch her a blanket. If her tea was low, he'd refill it. If it cooled, he'd dash off to reheat it. The marina business suffered due to his diverted attention, but he didn't care. The look on their faces and the sound of their voices during that season? Even now, it was still etched on Amanda's heart.

Although the farmhouse was old, it was in immaculate shape,

another reminder of Amanda's father, skilled in so many areas. When the charter business slowed in the winter, he went to work on the home, providing him an additional excuse to be near her mother.

His attention towards Amanda hadn't waned either during that time. He may have not been fully himself, but he still cared for his only child. He helped her with her homework and was there to cheer her on in her many sports. Until she got her license, he taxied her about, especially if her mother was fatigued. He took an interest in her friends—asking about their college plans, who they were dating. Boy discussions always pulled him in—typically when he thought she was speaking privately with her mother. He'd suddenly appear. She'd try a different tack, talk like there was nothing to hide, in a normal tone, like an essay she'd been assigned for homework. He still stayed tuned. No denying it.

He never told Amanda she couldn't date, but neither did he encourage it. "It'll all work out," he'd say. Amanda could still hear the confidence in his voice every time he'd say it.

Well, if he only knew now. "Dad, things didn't work out!" And under her breath, "I hate you for it."

She'd never cared to ask him about any particular boy. None had ever measured up to her father. Not even close! He was the measuring stick and it stretched long.

Amanda sneaked around the back of the farmhouse. She found the side door by the kitchen unlocked. Her parents had only ever threatened to lock the doors during zucchini season, a time when neighbors left behind their abundant extras. She entered quietly and then yelled out, "Anybody home?" Maybe her father's fiancée had taken residence? What if they came face to face?

Amanda wondered how she would confront the woman. "But for the grace of God," Amanda said to herself, worried now she'd kill the woman if she caught her wearing her mother's ring. She didn't feel like she deserved God's grace today, especially after how she'd been acting. Her behavior towards Sierra's father had been unbecoming, and Amanda had no doubts about her weakness now, how easily she could fall trap to a violent encounter.

Her pulse nearly exploded with each beat, and she felt ready to pounce, but the house was eerily quiet. She inhaled and dropped her shoulders, scanning the kitchen for evidence of booze. Then a gander at the dining room dry bar. *Completely empty! Has he kicked the habit?*

She moved quickly, heading upstairs, noting changes as she went. There were few. The furniture was the same—all antiques used by her parents to facilitate history lessons. The family pictures with the three of them remained, but those with only her father and mother were gone.

She searched her father's room in the obvious places. Dressers and the keepsake military boxes that contained his naval memorabilia. While she didn't recall her parents maintaining a safe inside the house, she remembered there being one in the marina office.

She headed down the hall where her bedroom had been. She took barely a step into it, sucked in a quick breath, and froze. The room and its contents hadn't been altered since her leaving nearly ten years ago. It was clean, dusted, and nothing displaced.

The past suffocated her. Amanda's stuffed bears remained on her bed—just as she'd left them. A stack of DVDs lay on a desk—*National Velvet* on top. *Black Beauty* and *Seabiscuit* would still be in the stack as well. Her books were all there. Sir Thomas Malory's *Le Morte d'Arthur* caught her attention. In it, she'd learned the rules of chivalry. She cursed under her breath. *Rules that Dad abandoned!*

Her many trophies were still on their shelves—the cherished sailor's championship cup at the center. She paused in front of her favorite sailing shot. The photographer had caught her dramatic lean over the water with the tiller and mainsail rope in hand. She'd led her school to the national championship that year. Alongside was a picture of her and her teammates hoisting the Mallory Trophy. With the Naval Academy serving as the venue, the east coasters gained a significant advantage over the perennial favorites, Point Loma High School of San Diego.

Now, while Amanda looked at herself in the picture, she saw only a half-smile, nothing more than a facade to cover the turmoil of her emotions. Her mother's health had been in decline while she celebrated.

Amanda passed her hand over a stuffed brown dog and headed to the attic. She'd save the guest room for last. Maybe her father had stored the ring in the Jamestown chest? She only knew it by that name; it was what her mother called it.

The box had ornate inlays with maritime iconography,

astronomical symbols, and charts. Her mother encouraged her to explore it, to learn its contents, but didn't provide details. When Amanda asked about certain documents and artifacts it contained, her mother would only respond, "In *time*, dear. In *time*."

A blast of hot air smothered Amanda as she flipped on the light switch. She scampered up and down the rustic attic catwalk. Nothing seemed out of place but for one box—the chest was missing. Why wasn't the chest returned to the attic after her mother's passing?

During her waning days, her mother requested the chest be brought down to the guest room, where she spent her final months of hospice. She liked the view of the marina from there, enjoying the sight of her Charles returning from his charters, preferring sunrises over sunsets.

"In time" had never transpired between Amanda and her mother and discussions regarding its secrets ceased.

She'd left for school at her mother's insistence and was mostly absent until the final days leading to her death. Her gut tightened, and she struggled to breathe. It was a wretched memory. Who was really to blame? Her mother? Father? Maybe herself.

To be back in this room after all these years. Her mother died here. The memory flattened her like a rogue wave.

She scoured the room, checking under the bed, in drawers, and the closet—no sign of either the chest or the ring. She stared at the bed and froze. The flash of lightning from the west and the boom of thunder didn't budge her. Amanda was quick to calculate the distance of the approaching storm—five seconds per mile between flash and clap. Boats were returning to the marina . . . her father's boat included. She could recognize it miles away.

She recalled the day her father found her in this same bedroom months after her mother's death—home on her summer break. The day he kicked her out of the house for good. This memory clawed at her like the gale force brewing in the distance. He was drunk and had returned from the marina. They'd already had harsh words in his office at the dock. She'd been on her knees crying with her arms wrapped over the bed.

"Get out!" he screamed.

She lifted her eyes. Her stomach twisted. "What?"

His breath reeked of liquor. "Get out, I told you. You'll never be who she was!"

Amanda rose and faced him. What had become of him? The finest gentleman she'd ever known. An officer of officers.

His eyes were red. "You'll never rise to her level!"

Tears streamed down her face and confusion set in. "Huh . . . ? Daddy, you need help."

"Get out of here," he snarled. "Your mother had big hopes for you, but you've turned out to be a failure!"

"You're drunk!"

"She did everything for you, and just look at yah . . ." His growl sickened her. "Get out!"

She tried to soften him. Calm him down. "Go to bed, Dad." It didn't work.

He spoke in a tone she'd never heard from him, like arsenic on his tongue. "I'll go to bed when I feel like going to bed! You don't tell me what to do!"

Amanda pushed her way past him. "I'm getting out, Dad." She glanced over her shoulder. He collapsed on the bed, draped his arms over it, and sobbed.

The scene was pathetic, and from the safety of her bedroom she could hear him slapping the bed.

She waited until his groans faded before returning to the doorway. "When you wake up from your drunken stupor . . . I'll be gone."

Amanda was true to her word. Before he slept off the booze, she packed her essentials and left in the middle of the night. She arrived at dawn at her Aunt Nancy's in Arlington. She'd never gone back . . . not until today.

Dealing with most criticism came easy for Amanda, even the harsh words from jealous rivals during her school years and at work. But her father's words were different. They were all the harsher from the one person she'd held most dear. The person who knew her best. The person she most admired. The person who was supposed to love her the most. Words from others rolled like water off a duck's back. Snide, vulgar remarks on the soccer pitch amid a tight game? Those words did nothing. But those words from her father? She couldn't shake them. They gnawed inside her.

A rapping on a door below shook her. The memories stopped cold, and she released a shaky breath.

"Anyone home?" the voice yelled. "Amanda? Amanda? Where

are you?"

Amanda hurried down the stairs. "I'm coming, Sierra!"

"What are you doing here?" Sierra's eyes were wide when they came face to face.

Amanda exited the side door and pulled on Sierra's arm. "I came in to use the bathroom," Amanda responded matter-of-factly—as if she owned the place.

Sierra spoke quickly, "We don't have much time. We need to pull the paddleboards from the beach and shelter-in-place."

"Hang on . . . wait here a moment." Amanda raced to the corner of the house and peered down towards the Marina. Nearly everyone disembarking the *Queen Mary* was heading to their vehicles—all but one. The clean-cut man with salt-and-pepper hair was heading straight toward the house. His stride was confident, and he carried himself like a military officer.

Panic slapped her in the face. It was her father.

And he wasn't drunk.

Letter

One Week Prior

What had set her on such a crazy course when life had been orderly and manageable? Amanda turned back the clock in her mind to the prior Saturday at her condo. She rarely took naps, but on that day, the letter she'd found in her mail slot left her exhausted.

Amanda had just returned from a soccer clinic, one she'd volunteered at on a whim. Her alma mater, Marymount University, had mentioned the opportunity in a newsletter. A Special Olympics clinic.

She was amazed how they did it. Though Amanda worked in the Intelligence Community—known as the IC—those alumni people tracked her better than most first-world surveillance services. Their newsletters would find her around the world, at nearly every overseas station where she'd deployed. For now, she was on home leave, and they'd found her new address at an upscale condo complex in Northern Virginia.

The day of volunteering had brought back some of Amanda's fondest memories from her collegiate years in Arlington. Not so much her time spent on the soccer pitch, but her volunteer activities.

It was hard to call it volunteer work when the athletic director declared the events *team activities*. The university hosted an annual Special Olympics invitational basketball tournament, and their Division III teams were expected to support it.

Team event or not, Amanda wondered if she'd finally found her calling. The school's men's and women's basketball, lacrosse, and soccer teams adopted a Special Olympics team for the day, cheered them on, and provided a little coaching. They created a raucous environment for the visitors and their parents with elaborate banners, cheers, and color commentary. It was just plain fun for everybody!

She'd volunteered at other events in later years when she wasn't overseas. The big Special Olympics track and field meet at a historic boarding school in Alexandria was one. The school reminded her of her own high school, beautiful stone buildings surrounded by leafy old-growth trees and expansive green space. The difference here was the blue blood money.

What she most remembered was how she clicked with the athletes. Mostly those on the autism spectrum. The way they thought and their drive made sense to Amanda, especially the long-distance runners. She appreciated those with antisocial tendencies. They didn't ask too many probing questions. They'd probably figure her out if they did.

For the more social athletes, she had to be on guard, learn how to deflect. Undoubtedly they would ask, "Are you married?" or "Do you have a boyfriend?"

"No, but how about you?" she'd respond. That normally worked. The athletes loved talking about themselves and rarely did anyone listen like Amanda. She enjoyed their stories as she shuttled them between their events: the dashes, the shot put, the high and long jumps, and then the relays.

It didn't always work. Some would lock on to the subject. The obsessive compulsives. The ones she most related to. Those individuals needed to drill down into the topic. Amanda was a puzzle, and they couldn't leave the pieces scattered about. Where was the logic and reason in all that?

"Why not, Miss Amanda?" That's how she preferred to be addressed. No reason to lob her last name about. A practice avoided at work where a secure information system shrouded it behind a pseudo-name.

"I'm not sure I want to get married." It was the only answer she could arrive at without lying. So what if she was in her late twenties and single?

If a parent or guardian was in earshot of the conversation, they'd attempt a rescue. "Maybe Miss Amanda hasn't met the right guy," spoken in a tone intended to dampen the inquisition.

About nine times out of ten, if it was a male athlete, they'd respond with utmost earnestness, "I'll be your boyfriend," and the more bold, "I'll marry you!" They'd jump up and down. "Will you marry me, Miss Amanda?"

Although they were serious, most would laugh like it was the funniest thing in the world. She'd join their laughter and the topic would soon be forgotten. It was time for their next attempt at the high jump, and Amanda would rile the crowd to cheer for her charge.

The personal questions weren't nearly as dicey as those which related to her work. Those questions didn't come up too frequently, but when they did, she'd notice the ears of the parents perk up. Some were just curious. It was the Washington Metro Region, after all. Maybe *Miss Amanda* was an aid to some big wig senator . . . or maybe she worked in the current administration? For those who based their self-worth on what they did for a living, mostly the dads, it was an important question.

Over time, she learned to describe her job in the most unremarkable terms. "I do logistics."

"What's that?" they'd occasionally ask.

"I move stuff around to people who need it."

Never would she tell them she managed the procurement and delivery of technical operations gear to worldwide CIA stations and bases around the world. All sorts of cool spy gadgets, from signals-collection gear that could eavesdrop on phone calls to miniature cameras and listening devices. She delivered media forensic tools which parsed the content of smartphones—tradecraft that aided vetting and assessments of walk-ins at US embassies. Walk-ins who'd come to volunteer the secrets of their country to the US Government, mostly for money. She'd ship commercial equipment too, stuff that could appear in plain sight. Like GPS trackers or high-end binoculars. Whatever Tech-Ops requested, within reason, she located and delivered.

For Amanda, the excitement in the job was long gone. She only thought of the spy gear now as just some other widget that needed transport from a nondescript CONUS warehouse to a location overseas. She was kept at arms-length on how the gear was used, typically by Tech-Ops officers. They, in turn, aided case officers who conducted HUMINT operations. The case officers managed human assets, real people who had access to information that could benefit the good ole USA. Sometimes the gear supported covert action. The tip of the spear stuff and all tightly compartmentalized.

Ninety percent of the time, her blasé answers ended the questioning about her job. Occasionally, a parent would chime in, "Who with?"

"State." It was her government-sanctioned lie. Amanda's official cover. Not as sexy as the officers who operated overseas with non-official cover (or NOCs, as they were called). Amanda's black diplomatic passport allowed her to travel with official cover, a get-out-free jail-card. Not so with the NOCs. Get caught conducting intelligence operations using non-government cover, like an aid worker, and you were toast.

"State Department or Department of State?" That question invariably indicated the parent was privy. Heck, it felt like half the Washingtonians worked in the IC, especially in the Virginia suburbs. Amanda wasn't naïve. She knew real State Department employees answered one way and sloppy Agency officers answered another.

Amanda dished her sly smile, the one that said, "You're obligated to protect my paper-thin cover."

They typically returned it with a knowing wink, and the questioning ceased.

When she pulled the mail from the letter box at her condo, the envelope begged for her attention. *Wedding invitation?* The bills and junk mail could wait. But not the vintage-looking envelope, postmarked from Jamestown. The ornate stationery looked like something you could get off Etsy—hand crafted and old. But it looked more authentic than fake. Its texture was silky smooth and slightly oily, unlike anything she'd ever touched.

The handwriting on it was exquisite. This was no form letter, and who'd use 1907 Jamestown commemorative stamps? A small laminate protected two aged stamps, affixed with scotch tape. For good measure, a standard first-class stamp was canceled next to it.

She entered her condo and tossed the rest of the mail to her kitchen counter. The stamps still held her attention, and she did a quick Google search on them using her smartphone. *Wow! Rare!* But it had to be a fake because eBay showed similar stamps for sale for over $1,000.

This was by far the most elaborate scheme she'd seen to grab her attention to a solicitation letter. The envelope deserved to be opened simply for its creativity. Maybe a timeshare down in Williamsburg was offering a free weekend getaway to make their sales pitch?

She emptied the contents of the envelope onto her kitchen table. Out came several newspaper clippings and then a smaller envelope secured with an exquisite wax seal. It didn't take long before all her good feelings and the happy faces from the soccer clinic were launched into space like an NRO satellite.

She turned over the clippings, the ones showing advertisements. Now the newsworthy side of each cut out provided a consistent message. No doubt about it. Multiple sources all in agreement. An engagement announcement. News that sucked the oxygen straight from the room. Her father was engaged!

The blood drained from her face, and the room began to spin. She fought back some nausea and her breathing turned erratic, feeling as if she was suffocating. It was impossible to continue reading the clippings; the black dots in her eyes were playing all sorts of tricks.

Amanda stood carefully, grasped the top of her chair, and stabilized herself. She paused for several moments and took a quick inventory of nearby hard edges, barely able to recognize herself in the wall mirror. Her granite countertops gave her no comfort; if she collapsed now, she'd strike an edge on the way down.

She held her hands out and took small shuffling steps towards the kitchen sink. The cold floor granted some relief to her feet. She righted herself at the counter and made a quick grab of her cupboard door. She reached for a glass mug. It toppled back towards her, crashing off the counter and on to the floor.

Why didn't I hear it?

Amanda looked down to see a large glass shard had barely missed her foot. "Argh." Even to her, the gut-wrenching groan sounded like a desperate animal fallen into a pit.

She pushed back the faucet's lever and sucked in several mouthfuls of water. Her breathing steadied.

Placing her hands over the edge of the sink, Amanda's gaze drifted through the window above it. The black dots lessened. The floor was almost level. Why did it feel so hot? She checked the thermostat. Everything appeared normal, but her condo should've felt like an igloo compared to Virginia's sticky August weather.

Amanda retrieved a water bottle from the refrigerator and returned to the table. She glanced back at the remains of the mug—a glass shard sticking straight up. She returned to it and tossed it into her wastebasket. The smaller glass pieces on the tile floor could wait.

She eyed the documents scattered on the table. *From Dad?* A roundabout way to communicate with her? *How twisted!*

As much as Amanda hated him, the deed didn't fit his style. It also made little sense. While her father practically gave up life after her mother's death, she picked up the pieces of her own and chose to live.

But now? Remarry? So what if it had been ten years? How could he do it? Treason to her mother's memory. *How could anyone follow in Mom's footsteps?*

Worse, was he choosing a relationship with another at the expense of a relationship with his own daughter? Who was this woman? Another alcoholic? Someone who could nurse him along in old age?

Maybe the fiancée was a gold-digger? Amanda always suspected her mother was well off—family money—but she'd said nothing directly to Amanda. Her mother seemed to go out of her way to hide affluence. She'd made no promises to Amanda, only that her father would take care of her. Really? *If Mom could've only envisioned the man he's become.*

There'd never been a silver spoon for Amanda. After she'd exhausted a small trust fund to pay for some of her college expenses, she'd learned the art of frugality, navigating the world on her own. Both figuratively . . . and literally. She raised her eyes to the black-framed photographs which hung from the walls. There to remind her just how far she'd made it. And survived.

There were shots from Tripoli, her first overseas assignment. Some of Rome. The mountains of Uzbekistan. Bangkok. Quite a few depicting harsh desert landscapes. She'd made the mistake of acquiring her gun qualifications right out of school, not realizing it made her eligible for the less desirable assignments—those in the war-zones, some lousy sandboxes. On several occasions she'd covered for a fellow logistics officer—often at the last minute. Even if it was just a short two-week gig, it permitted them a home visit for training. The pictures still reminded her of her courage to live. Unlike her father. But now she wondered, *who's really living?*

From the newspaper clippings, her father appeared to be living quite robustly. Had he plucked up the pieces from their shattered life? If so, he wouldn't have sent a letter like this. He'd never taunt her. *Or would he?*

Absent from the pictures on her walls was anything that resembled Virginia's Tidewater Region. She'd framed and hung photos from her exotic Caribbean vacations, but only if the shots didn't remind her of home. But sometimes they did. Like the way Cedar Island appeared on a low tide—the Little Bay waters transformed to emerald green.

After inspecting each of the newspaper clippings, she set her sights on the small envelope with the seal. She caressed the seal ever so gently and sniffed it. *Authentic?*

Imprinted on the seal was an unusual coat of arms, the Spanish Cross of Burgundy, and a sextant. It was strangely familiar. *Mom's seal?* Even the fragrant scent of the wax matched the scent of her mother's.

Amanda fetched a large magnifying glass from a kitchen drawer. She hovered it above, and the seal came into focus. The detail was so exquisite she could discern lettering on it. *Mom's sextant?*—the one she remembered as a young teen. *No! It can't be!*

Her phone sat on the counter. She reached for it and took several pictures of the seal. After inspecting the picture quality, she stood and retrieved a small toolbox from the upper shelf of her laundry closet. She pulled a spackling knife from the box and meticulously wedged it under the seal. The seal released from the bottom half of the envelope and remained entirely intact.

"Whew," she breathed. The seal was far more valuable intact, and she could put it under a microscope later.

A thick, weathered piece of paper fell from the smaller envelope and skidded across the table. She grasped the ivory-colored material between her fingertips and massaged the oily texture. *Lamb skin?* Decorative calligraphy inked the vellum:

"Dear Lady,

It is High Time you claim what is rightfally yours.

Time is of the essence!"

Amanda gritted her teeth. Where was the signature? *Why not put* something*? Even the Unabomber signed his letters.* Amanda shook her head. The spelling was atrocious. The glass from the sliding patio door reflected the scorn on her face, three times paler than before.

What a cowardly act! A juxtaposition from what she garnered from the newspaper clippings, further eliminating her father as the sender. Not to mention, he wouldn't have misspelled *rightfully*!

But one thing became clearer in the days that followed—whoever sent it meant for the seal to be the signature. Maybe they weren't as cowardly as she first thought. For the faintest moment, she'd wondered whether her mother was speaking from the grave.

SPOs

Amanda's thoughts were on the letter as she looped back from the W&OD horse trail and towards the compound. She passed her hand along a twelve-foot fence, topped with razor-sharp barbed wire and sensors throughout. It surrounded the facility where she worked. She eyed the interspersed closed-circuit security cameras, knowing several of the security guards who monitored them. Had it not been for the fact the compound was in the middle of the Northern Virginia suburbs, she knew some might mistake it for a prison. For Amanda, it contained work full of intrigue and sometimes adventure. But today, and on her run, she couldn't focus on her job.

She sucked in the warm air through her nose, trying—and failing—to ignore the mandate of the letter. Several words in the overt text alarmed her, and she suspected that underlying it all was an encrypted message. She kept thinking it was a prank. Apparently, though, the Jamestown stamps were not.

It didn't take her long to list them on eBay. Someone snatched up the pair immediately at a *Buy It Now* price of $2,000. Now she wondered if they'd been worth a lot more. And, strangely enough, the stamps were headed back to a post office box in Jamestown. The deposit to her PayPal account arrived immediately after the sale. Coincidence? Amanda didn't think so. If it was an attempt by the letter's author to make up for Amanda's pain and suffering caused by the news of her father's engagement, it wasn't helping. But it gave Amanda another idea—a plan she was now formulating on how to spend the windfall.

The security fence she passed at a measured clip provided some amount of comfort. She could hide behind those fences and the well-armed guards, within the walls of the Agency, from a life she left behind. The one with her father and his designs on her life. It all became worse after her mother died. *She would've protected me!* The thought of the letter still made her blood boil.

If the newspaper clippings provided the gunpowder, the sealed note was the fuse and match. It was time to act. She couldn't ignore it. If the sender's intent was to launch her like a mortar, they succeeded. Amanda had yet to tell anyone, but she vowed to speak with Sally, her closest—and possibly her truest—friend. She'd keep the fact of the inner sealed envelope and its contents close to her chest.

The newspaper clippings will be enough for Sally. Even she didn't need to know all of her familial dysfunction.

Over the years, Amanda had grown confident in her ability to keep her past—tangled with all of its emotions—latched and buried in the deepest part of her soul.

As she approached the compound's gate, she silenced her angry thoughts. *Better I use the energy for my final kick.* A familiar face was manning the entrance—one of the Security Protective Officers—a SPO.

Bill provided a friendly nod. She made it a habit to learn names of the SPOs, the guards who helped protect the Agency's secrets and the denizens who worked inside its buildings. Most employees made no attempt to learn the names of those who worked a mostly thankless job. But that wasn't Amanda's style. Like her, she figured they had bad days too and wished they'd chosen another profession.

She flashed her badge and granted a smile. He waved her through, and she maintained a full stride until she crossed the hydraulic security barrier.

She caught her reflection in one of the large, round traffic mirrors. It was hard not to miss the woman in the racing-red running shirt. Amanda did her best to wear modest attire; if she turned some heads along the way, well, that was on them. She clicked the stop button on her watch, slowed to a trot, and turned back in the direction of the guard shack. She stopped, hands on her waist, to catch her breath. "Top of the morning to you, Bill!"

"You too, Amanda!" He was always careful not to use her last name. "Did you run an extra mile for me?"

"Yes, like I do every morning," she heaved.

He pointed at his watch in a silent question and she looked down at her own.

"Not bad for the conditions."

The SPOs were tough, fit, and carried guns. They never ogled her, far too professional for that. If she caused Bill's fifty-plus-year-old heart to skip a beat whenever she ran past, it could only be good for him.

They were always checking up on her safety since she ran the trail alone. One time, in June, she came by the guard shack, expecting her daily lecture. While she circled back and slipped in behind Bill close enough to count his missing gray hairs, a fellow SPO said to him, "Don't worry, she's got legs." He looked over Bill's shoulder, giving Amanda a small wink. Enough for Amanda to know that he was pulling a prank on Bill.

Bill slipped that day, completely unaware Amanda stood directly behind him. "Her legs are obvious."

The other SPO flashed a mischievous grin. "No, not in that sense. Athletically." He was younger than Bill. One who'd seen her kickboxing in the gym.

She tapped Bill on the back of his shoulder, and he turned around. His face flushed red.

"I'm sorry, Amanda," he flustered. "Did I ever tell you I have daughters of my own?"

Her face brightened. No reason to hold a grudge against the man who protected her every day.

On that day, after she'd showered, she loitered by the front entrance command post before returning to her office. Bill had come inside and sat behind the reception counter. She learned about the man's wife, his daughters, and their school progress. His appreciation for her interest, which was by no means fake, was written across his face. Family life was a foreign concept for Amanda. In some ways, she thought of herself more as an orphan. Bill's life revolved around those of his girls.

"We just care to know you're safe out there," Bill said.

She issued a quick shrug. "I know."

"You really ought to find a running partner."

She reached into her gym bag and pulled out her MACE canister. "This is my partner."

He dismissed it with a slight throw of his head. "A fellow SPO told me you were in his M4 re-qual class."

"Yep, this past spring."

His eyes narrowed just a little. "Said you were pretty good with a gun."

"Thanks, Bill." She teased her eyes to the nearby magnetometer. "Obviously I can't bring it to work."

Sally

Amanda met Sally before noon at the front entrance of their office building. Sally had come from the opposite side of it, all three floors dedicated to the Open Source Center (OSC). They headed out through the pedestrian gate. Their destination, a French bistro, was a half-mile walk to the trendy suburbia town center.

The Agency building they exited had a storied history, housing the oldest entity of the CIA—the Foreign Broadcast Information Service, precursor to the OSC. The building was soon to be demolished; taller high-rise buildings had sprung up all around it. With the extension of the light-rail Metro line and a nearby station, the economics for a three-story building faltered.

Sally wasted no time asking about the PCS—a Permanent Change of Station. "So, did you apply?" She referred to the logistics position in Vienna, Austria.

"Yep. Why not? Nothing to lose." Amanda tried to hide the strain in her voice.

The two matched strides. "Everything to lose. I know you better, girl." Sally dispensed a quick glance. "You make a great show of acting like a career woman."

Amanda tossed her head back. "Not this again." She'd already served four years in the field and was nearing the end of another home tour. She felt like a yo-yo.

"Okay . . . I'll drop it." Sally wiped her forehead. They continued for several strides before she spoke again. "I wouldn't be doing this but for your prescription of Vitamin D." She squinted and pointed up. The sun poked out from behind a cloud. "I prefer these walks in the winter."

"I take it that hot-n-humid isn't your thing," Amanda teased. "I think it helps your entire constitution." She took a deep breath. "Last winter you said you wished our walks were in the summer."

"Here we go again." Sally shook her head and dispensed a friendly swat with the back of her hand. "I think I have a hankering for some onion rings."

Amanda sighed. The thought of anything fried made her stomach roll. She was going to mention French onion soup as an alternative, but bit her tongue.

"No need to panic. I only said I had a hankering. I like the diet stuff you have me on and I appreciate what you've been doing for me. I've been feeling much better the last few months."

Amanda shrugged. It was odd for her to think she'd done good for anyone. Her volunteer work with Special Olympics? Selfish! She was the one who came home with the self-satisfied buzz.

Sally arched her shoulders back. "I feel more confident."

They continued their walk into the town center along a pedestrian bridge. It took them over remains of the historic Washington and Old Dominion Railroad. Sally complained for nearly fifteen minutes about an overly ambitious project-manager, one of Sally's peers in the OSC. She'd barely taken a breath until they were seated in the cafe.

Amanda kept the "Mmm-hmms" going. The culture was different between the organizations, but not that different. *Humans there too*, she thought.

She kept nodding, but her eyes drifted and her fingertips tapped the table. Sally was finally ready to move on. After several long moments, Amanda glanced at her friend. "How are things on the guy front?"

Sally startled, and after a brief beat, shrugged. "Which guy? You know me better than that."

"Right. How many *shallow* fish do you have on the line right now? Three? Four? I think it was *five* by my last count."

"Coming right back at you, girl." Sally's tone turned feisty. "With your good looks, you should be pulling along a dozen. But no, what does Miss West do every time?"

When Amanda opened her mouth to speak, Sally's palm came up. "No, no, no. Don't answer that. Let me tell you how she finds the most creative ways to dump a guy."

Amanda crossed her arms. "It's not dumping if there aren't attachments to begin with."

"You're the master of excuses. I've known you for what, six years?" Sally shook her head. "I don't recall you ever entertaining a real date."

"That's not true. So unfair." Amanda's stomach tingled.

"Okay, then, what happened to that guy in your office? What's his name? Paul?"

"Right. Paul. Nice guy, but he wasn't into spelunking." Amanda flashed a mischievous grin. "I agreed to a date and provided him with the link to *Cave Adventures*." Amanda raised her nose. "I suppose he didn't like what he found."

"Of course." Sally cocked her head. "I'm sure he discovered everything he dreaded. You knew he had a fear of snakes and heights."

Amanda felt naughty and her words were tentative. "Bats and spiders too?"

Sally shook her head. "I inspected the website—noticed the small print at the bottom of the page. Possible sightings of copperheads and timber rattlers!" She threw her hands up. "By my count, that was his eleventh attempt asking you out and I don't believe you've ever been spelunking!"

"He failed to call my bluff." Amanda threw in a small shrug. "The tour included rappelling, and I was really looking forward to that . . . would've been a great day."

"The one snake he should've feared most?" Sally shook her head. "*Amanda West*. Always ready to strike if a guy gets too close."

Amanda faked a quaint smile. The truth in Sally's sarcasm stung. *If only she knew me in high school. My friends considered me carefree and loving.*

Sally's eyes narrowed. "How's it you put such a spell on these guys?"

There was no reason to touch that one. Amanda let her eyes drift away.

Sally worked through the latest on her five current potentials, or as the two would say, "fish nibbling the line," before Amanda proposed a sixth.

"I think Ted McCormick would be good for you. He's really nice." She tapped her finger on the table. "Met him playing softball." Sally would know she meant the Agency's coed league.

Sally bit down on her spoon. "How many times has he attempted to ask you out?"

"Six . . . maybe seven," Amanda stated frankly.

"I think I remember this guy. At one of your games." Sally released a deep breath. "Tall, dark, and handsome. Does he still like you?"

Amanda smirked. "It ain't happening, so let's get that out of our heads."

"Oh, so you say he's nice, but not good enough for you, but maybe roadkill suitable for me?"

"Sally!" Amanda glared. "Ted's different . . . more than nice. He's stable. Rock-solid. I'm just not ready for a serious relationship. If I was, I'd consider Ted." She sucked a large breath. "Whereas you always seem to attract the wrong type of guys. Ted's the opposite. He's totally the *right* type of guy."

"What ails you, girl? You don't accept designs of love in reverse."

"Nope. Not now. Maybe never." Heat climbed up the back of her neck.

Sally's eyes sharpened. "If not now, when?"

Amanda threw a sideways look that said she'd rather not be badgered. She regretted it instantly. Why energize Sally?

"The clock's ticking, Amanda!"

That knocked Amanda off balance, but her voice was firm. "I don't want my life being designed by anyone but me."

"Ouch. Wowww. I see I've hit a nerve."

Her friend nodded and rubbed her cheek for several moments. Sally's dark brown eyes demanded Amanda's attention. "Are you going to let your father hold you hostage for the rest of your life?"

Amanda huffed. "So you think you know me? Fine . . . okay, I'm a bit oversensitive right now. But not what you think." She paused, feeling much hotter than before. "I need your help."

Sally scanned Amanda's expression. It was hard to hide secrets from her friend.

Several moments passed before Sally said, "Okay, you're serious."

Amanda's words burst, "I need to do some spying on my father!"

Sally flinched. "What brought this on?"

Amanda reached into her purse dangling from her chair, retrieving the envelope—the ominous letter. She moved her salad bowl aside and organized the newspaper clippings in front of Sally. "I received these last week." Amanda pointed at the face of a man pictured in one of the clippings—an engagement announcement. "That's my father." A silhouette of a person is all that stood next to the man—the figure of a woman surgically removed. Amanda snarled, "The fine work of an Exacto knife."

Sally's head snapped back. "You? Did you do this?" She fingered the hole in the clipping.

"No!" Amanda stiffened.

Sally snatched a different clipping. "Who sent these?"

"I don't know!" Amanda didn't hide her anger. "Look here." She slid forward another clipping. There was a small rectangular hole in it. "Whoever sent it was careful to remove the woman's identity."

"You looked it up online, right?"

"I tried. I bought a digital subscription to the most likely newspaper. It was a guess, but I don't know when they made the announcement."

Sally's eyes showed genuine concern. "Have you spoken to your aunt?"

"Yes. She confirmed it." Amanda folded her arms and pulled her body tight. "He's engaged."

"You make it sound as if he died. Did she send the letter?"

Amanda's emotion spilled from her voice. "No, and she couldn't have hid that from me if she did."

"How about his fiancée?" Sally poked at a pickle. "Any details?"

"No." Amanda shook her head and took in a deep breath. "She's staying true to form and insists she won't be a go-between."

"Good for her, forcing you to set things right."

"Don't start that with me, Sally." She leaned forward. "I need to head home and break into my father's house."

"What!"

"Mmm-hmm." Amanda nodded. "I want to find my mother's engagement ring. She always wanted me to have it, and I certainly don't want it going to this fiancée of his."

Sally's voice rose. "What if he's already given it to her?"

Amanda let some moments pass before saying, "I'll kill her, but only after I cut off her finger."

Sally looked like she almost believed her.

Amanda reached for Sally's hand and lightened her tone. "I'm kidding." If only that were the truth. She'd maintain the facade, but she knew in her heart she already despised the woman. Was hatred really any different from murder?

"Hope so, otherwise you'll lose your clearance!"

Amanda guffawed, and the two glanced about. A few nearby heads turned. She turned serious again as she whispered, "I'd like to recruit another member for our team."

Sally leaned forward. "Now wait a minute, Amanda, I'm not breaking into anyone's house."

"It isn't breaking and entering when it's your own house and the doors are left unlocked. But don't worry. I won't be asking that from you and *Ted*."

Sally brightened. "Ooooh . . . this is getting better."

"I thought sooo." Amanda lowered her voice and leaned in. "I need Ted's help with cover. He's a pro with disguises—works in the Office of Technical Services. I'm heading home—small-town America. Everyone knows everyone. I'll likely be recognized without good cover."

Sally sat back and crossed her arms. Amanda knew her friend was holding her tongue.

"If I'm caught, I'm going to need Ted to act as my fiancé. I'll need you to coach him."

"I'm only going along with this because it sounds so fun. Sometimes in life you ought to take a lesson from Sally and just roll with it. Where's this place again?"

"The southern tip of the Northern Neck . . . White Stone."

Sally stiffened. Her panic perplexed Amanda.

"You said *southern* and *white* in the same sentence. Do I need to worry?"

Amanda chuckled. Her friend was hiding something, and it had nothing to do with race. Amanda waved dismissively at her. "You'll be with me and Ted . . . but I get it."

She, in fact, didn't get it, but she wouldn't pry. Amanda saw real trauma behind Sally's eyes. Certainly, her friend had a past as well.

Ted seemed shocked by the proposal he received an hour later. Amanda sent it via chat over the Agency's internal secure network. She offered him not just a single outing, but an all-expense paid weekend at a five-star resort in the lower Northern Neck, with two catches. First, that Sally would accompany them as a chaperone, and second, it would be all business. She needed his help with disguises, and as necessary, playing the part of her *significant other*.

Her phone rang. It was Ted. "A front-row seat to observe your antics?" His tone hinted at a question. "What do I have to lose?"

"Was that an insult or a compliment, Ted?" He should know she needed his help. Logistics officers weren't trained in his field of expertise. That thought made her mad, too. *I could do so much more here.*

"Come on, firecracker. You should've taken it as a compliment."

"So you'll do it?"

"Yes, of course . . . the Queen has spoken."

CHAPTER 2

Irvington, VA

Birthday

Saturday, 2nd Week of August

Jeb poked his head into his daughters' bedroom. It was still dark and his two girls, Sierra and Nora, didn't budge. He remained for several cycles of the strobing channel marker at the mouth of Indian Creek. It illuminated their faces in the gentlest light. Their sun-kissed wavy hair fanned out over their pillows. He breathed easy and deep. *Angels.* God had given him two angels; they were his only remaining purpose for living.

James Carter, better known as *Jeb*, would let them sleep in this Saturday morning. His mother could drop them off later at the Shop on her way to the farmers' market. He exited the Bay House through the back stairs. No need to wake his parents, who slept in the first-floor master bedroom. He grabbed the bag of birdseed at the foot of the stairs, exited the garage, and laid the bag in the back of his truck.

He needed the girls at the Shop; today was sure to be busy, but he cherished a ritual he performed in private every year on Erin's birthday since her passing. Jeb had told them, "It'll be all-hands on deck." He didn't want to mention it would be their mother's birthday. *Why keep reminding them*?

He, of course, could never forget.

Jeb covered the short distance to Irvington in fifteen minutes. He would have driven faster but for the fear of striking a deer. Lately, turkey had become a hazard too.

Dawn was threatening as he pulled into the Shop's driveway. He parked in the small gravel-grass lot in the back and set about refilling the birdfeeders. They were behind the Shop, halfway down the backyard to his small waterfront. He'd brought the feeders—Christmas presents he'd given to Erin—from their previous home in Richmond. She'd been an avid birder who relished the bird counts at Christmastime and Presidents' Weekend, making them family affairs.

A friend told him the birds improved the Shop's ambiance. He didn't care—he maintained the feeders for Erin. The birds certainly brought back memories. Too many to count and too many daggers piercing his heart.

Sun slivers poked through the trees on the opposite side of the creek, but instead of the dawn holding promise, it held the day's heat and humidity.

The cacophony increased in intensity, intermixed with mockingbirds, the forlorn cries of mourning doves, and tweets from cardinals and wrens. Ospreys squawked. His lost love would've identified twenty different species. Maybe the fluttering of their wings would bring *her* back. The screech of a great blue heron echoed across the water. *Erin, I got that one.*

Jeb opened the shed's roll-up door and the sun's rays burst in, chasing away the dark corners. The tiger maple grains from his handcrafted paddleboard reflected the light as he pulled off the tarp. He kept it on sawhorses in the rear of the shed. It didn't need to be buffed, but he did it anyway, rubbing in a circular motion, the shoddy rag absorbing his tears.

A teal-framed picture of them standing on a paddleboard together looked down from the workshelf. He was holding Erin's waist, peering over her shoulder. She pushed him immediately after the shot, and unable to escape his grasp, fell into the water with him. He could still hear her squeal.

Jeb lifted his eyes to the picture. *Why you, Erin? Why not me!*

He never had the chance to give her the paddleboard. It was to be a Christmas present, long before he even considered an eco-tour business. He'd never actually tested it, either. Would she have cared how it performed in the water? *Probably not.* After all, it was Erin who'd introduced him to the sport. She would've cherished the paddleboard, even if it had to be made into a bench seat for their deck. She would've used it as a conversation piece to tell her friends stories of the many years she stuck with Jeb, her high school sweetheart, who'd eventually become a contracts lawyer.

It was such a different world back then when he paddled with Erin—simply for pleasure. Now, he paddled for work and her memory.

Jeb groaned as he rubbed and polished the shellacked wood, sweat pouring from under his sleeveless shirt. His painful reverie was jostled by a craving for coffee. Dark, black coffee . . . Kat's coffee. He preferred it on Erin's birthday. It was another way to remember her.

He placed the tarp over the board and made his way to the outdoor shower. After cleaning up, he completed his transformation with a brightly colored sportfishing shirt, embroidered with the Shop's name and its logo.

Jeb looked out the window of the shop's front door. Time to get moving. He took a deep breath and glanced down the street. The village was coming alive, and he grasped the cold door handle.

You can do it, Jeb . . . just for one day. Fake it!

Launch

Saturday Morning, Northern Neck

Amanda cracked open the blinds. When they arrived last night, she hadn't noticed the picturesque marina that was now staring up at her. She wasted no time in heading out for a quick exploration of the resort property. The air was tepid. A few young boys crabbed from a bulkhead. Resort staff were preparing for the hubbub of activities that would soon commence. Platters with sternos were set in place in the breakfast room overlooking Carter's Creek. A boat-hand scrubbed the floor of the small ferry. Resort staff flipped lawn chairs upright and wiped off the dew. The bocce court was tidied. Someone else was raking the horseshoe pit.

Not long after returning to her room, a light knock sounded from the door. Amanda stepped towards it and glanced back at the bed. Sally's head was still wrapped underneath a pillow.

Amanda cracked the door open. "Hi, Ted," she said, peering out.

"Good morning. Are you ready?" His cheery tone matched hers.

"I am, but we need to give Sally a few minutes. Why don't we head down to that coffee shop in town?" Amanda stepped into the

hallway and shut the door. “She’ll be ready when we get back. How’d you sleep?”

“Fantastic! I’ve already walked the property. The place is amazing!”

“Me too. Did you find the saltwater pool?”

“Yes, and I walked the docks by the marina. There are some impressive boats!”

They were several strides down the hallway before Amanda stopped abruptly. “I think those would be called yachts unless you were referring to that center console with the outriggers. Over a thousand horsepower hanging off the back of that thing.”

She doubled back towards the room she shared with Sally, pacing nervously back and forth in front of it.

Ted remained firmly planted. His head tracked her as he spoke. “Whatever you say. You must’ve paid a pretty penny for the room. Thank you!”

Amanda stopped pacing and sighed. “You’re welcome, but as I said, this is business, and it’s time you and I get to work.” She scraped her hand through her hair. “How am I looking?”

Words seemed to escape him, nothing more than a few incomprehensible mumbles while rubbing the back of his neck.

Amanda darted into her room, leaving Ted to loiter in the hallway. She picked up a pillow from the sofa and lobbed it at Sally, her head still under the sheets. "I asked him how I looked and he didn't answer. What's he not saying?"

Sally's face emerged. "He's being polite. You think he'd call you a hot mama to your face?" Then she mumbled something about Amanda's figure.

"Why on earth would Ted think that?" She inspected herself in the mirror. The tight-fitting black tank top she wore with white shorts and designer sandals seemed blasé.

"He's a man." Sally's eyes widened. "That's your problem, Amanda. You don't see yourself like these men do."

Amanda huffed. "It wasn't intentional and I've never been a mama. Not even close."

Sally stiffened, so Amanda remained silent.

"There's a difference between us," was all Sally would say on the topic, and then she pursed her lips. Amanda knew the look—Sally deep in thought, like she might have something profound to say. "I sense an awakening. Hometown girl is blooming."

Where was the truth in that? She'd been back only a night. Amanda shrugged.

Sally spoke softly, "He's shy. I like that."

"I told you!" Amanda didn't hide her enthusiasm.

Sally raised an eyebrow. "Are you having second thoughts about taking a pass on the man?"

"Absolutely not! Trust me, Sally. I'm plowing a clear path for you." Amanda blew her friend a kiss and returned to the hallway.

Ted was staring at the ceiling when Amanda found him, and when he looked at her, he bit his lip. "Ummm . . . you *better* tell me you packed some items from the list I provided."

"I did," she said as she put on an oversized sun hat, followed by a pair of sporty sunglasses.

Ted winced. "No, no, this won't do. The only thing that works here is the hat. We need a large pair of sunglasses with very dark lenses. You need to ditch the shorts."

"Ugh . . . It's summer. I don't want to wear pants."

"Suit yourself. Want to be recognized or not? Where's the sun shirt I told you to pack?"

"I'll be right back." She re-entered the room and closed the door.

She returned to the hallway wearing a sun shirt and dark gray cargo pants. The bottoms were raised above her ankles, suspended by a button.

Ted nodded. "Those glasses work. The frames obscure your face." His eyes rested on her top. "The shirt is out. Your tank top bleeds out from under it."

He was choosing his words carefully. What had Sally mumbled? "Your shapely figure screams out." The thought sent heat to her cheeks. *Oh my* . . . What was it about being back in the Northern Neck? Feeling more comfortable in her own skin?

The sensation took flight, replaced by a nervous pout, and Amanda looked down at her feet.

"Let me see the pants when you drop them below your ankles," he said.

"Ted!" she said in mock disbelief.

"You know what I meant."

"Gotcha."

She looked down and unfastened the pants' knee-buttons, dropping the hems to the tops of her feet.

"Better. I don't see your ankles. I can envision your legs by inspecting your ankles. I'd suggest some tennis shoes to hide your feet. One or two sizes larger than what you have on. Pad them if you have to." He paused, crossed his arms, and set his chin in the palm of his hand. "Please turn around . . . slowly."

Halfway through her rotation, she glanced over her shoulder. "You're looking at my butt, aren't you?"

"Umm . . . yes. Thanks for mentioning it. I was pondering how I might explain this to you. I would've appreciated Sally's help with this one."

She turned and faced him. "Are you trying to tell me my butt is fat?"

"No, only that it's distinguishable. Do you know the story of Harlon Block and the flag raising at Iwo Jima?"

"No."

"But you know Joe Rosenthal's famous picture, right?"

"Of course. I run by the statue at the finish line of the Marine Corps Marathon."

"Back in 1945, when Harlon's mother first saw it in the newspaper, she alerted the military of their misidentification of one of the flag raisers."

"What? She recognized her son's butt?"

"Exactly!" Ted's eyes lit up.

"That would make sense given the thousands of diapers she changed . . . I suspect you're wondering if a father might recognize a daughter's butt?"

"Correct," he nodded. "What else have you brought along that can help hide your figure?"

Amanda left him again in the hall and changed. She returned wearing an oversized opaque sun shirt with flowers, a pair of baggy, military-style cargo pants, and Converse sneakers. She expected him to say something, but his face said it all. He continued to hesitate, so she spoke for him, "Hideous, isn't it?"

"Yeah, but I wasn't going to say so. Everything now appears to be well hidden."

"You mean my butt?"

"Yes. The shirt does an adequate job of concealing your fine-looking butt." His tone was matter-of-fact. "Where'd you get the pants?"

"I already owned 'em. I wear them on the shooting range."

"Makes sense."

The two walked to Ted's SUV through hanging air. Amanda chewed on her lip. "There'll be thunderstorms this afternoon. When I was in high school, I could set my watch by them."

"Lighten up." He offered a smile. "You'll be fine."

"Thank you. I have a lot on my mind. I need to arrange for a boat. But first . . . oh please . . . coffee."

Their drive to the Yokel was short, most of it within the resort property. While they passed the Frisbee golf course, Amanda motioned towards it. "Hey, this might be fun for you and Sally this morning."

"Sitting by the pool is more my style." He popped up in his seat. "Didn't you say you kept your hair down in high school?"

"Right."

"Bundle it up. Keep it under your hat. Did you remember the insert for your shoe?"

"Right here." Amanda retrieved the orthotic device from her purse, removed her right shoe, inserted the device, and replaced the shoe. "Voila!"

The street parking in front of the coffee shop was full. She pointed to a parking lot across the street. “Pull over there.”

“We can’t park there, it’s a church.” Ted frowned.

“Doesn’t matter. Nothing going on today but the farmers’ market. This isn’t Northern Virginia. Just pull in and point the car facing the coffee shop.” She exhaled slowly. “I want a moment to catch my breath.”

Sundial

Jeb exited the Shop’s front door and stepped onto his porch. A young boy with large glasses meandered up the sidewalk. He made his way directly into the Shop’s yard, taking a liking to a sundial in the middle of it. His mother’s focus was elsewhere. Their minivan was parked in front of the Yokel, and her back was turned as she unbuckled the last two of her posse from their seats.

The drivers were distracted today, and the boy had looked like he’d dart off anywhere. Without breaking stride, Jeb scooped the boy up in his arms and continued down the sidewalk towards the coffee shop. The last thing he wanted burned on his conscience was to have ignored a child in danger. He glanced at the lad, who stared back at him with wide-eyed surprise. Jeb allowed himself a small smile. “I think we need to get you back to your mother.”

The boy’s gaze returned to the sundial and fixated on it.

Nearly halfway to her car, Jeb observed the boy’s mother, panicked and scanning for her son.

“Win! Winston! Where are you?” When she turned around and looked up the sidewalk, her eyes locked with Jeb’s—and then moved to the boy. “Ohhhh!” Her eyes came back to Jeb. “My son likes to wander.”

Jeb swallowed.

He nodded to show some understanding. “Yes, I see he likes his independence . . . inquisitive type.”

She exhaled. “Thank you.”

Jeb moved his eyes from her and looked off into the distance. The air stirred, and he sensed he was being watched. It was the weirdest feeling. After a long interval of silence, he lowered the boy to the ground.

The woman crouched to her son’s eye level. “Oh, Winston! You can’t be running off like that.” Genuine desperation filled her voice.

She reached for her son's hand and looked back up at Jeb. "We're from out of town . . . visiting my parents."

Jeb softened his eyes. "I see you have your hands full." He fought the temptation to turn and determine who was surveilling him, but that would be rude.

"Yes, my husband had an early tee time with my father this morning at the Eagle," she said, referring to the nearby golf-course. "My boy's a runner."

Jeb cocked his head. He hadn't seen the boy running. *Why call him a runner?*

"No worries, ma'am," Jeb fibbed. He hesitated, unwilling to express his concern. "He came right up the sidewalk." The urge to scan his surroundings grew stronger.

The woman flashed a nervous smile. Jeb didn't know what to think. He thought he was good at reading people, but he wasn't connecting. Something about the way she said "runner." He tried to convey understanding, but she was embarrassed. *Maybe she's upset because a complete stranger picked up her son?* But Jeb wouldn't have done it any differently.

She pointed at the coffee shop. "Do you have any recommendations?

"Yes, ma'am," he nodded, glad to see that she'd composed herself. "Other than the coffee? Kathi's Chesapeake cinnamon buns. I'd suggest you order an extra one for your husband."

"Thank you . . . I'll do that." She turned around and pulled her toddler from the car seat. Grasping the hand of another child who had climbed out of the van, she shut the door and turned around.

Jeb hadn't moved. "Do you need a hand?"

"I'm okay. I do this all the time." She smiled and put Winston in front of her. They shuffled their way into the shop—her toddler on her hip as she gripped the hand of her middle child.

Jeb followed and opened the door for her. Maybe it was the woman who was being watched? Not him. *Who cares about me?* A simple small-town guy minding his business.

"Thank you," she said.

"Glad to help, Ma'am."

She continued with her troupe to the restroom and shut the door.

Jeb eyed Kat behind the counter and he took a few deep breaths. The eyes which he'd felt on his back were gone. For good measure, he glanced back over his shoulder. Nothing suspicious.

Blink

Amanda and Ted remained in his Explorer while she inspected for locals: anyone who might recognize her. She caught his glance in her direction.

"Time for a tradecraft lesson?" Ted asked, his tone upbeat.

"Okay, why not?" Her eyes remained focused on the street scene.

"Look at that man walking with the boy." Ted flicked his wrist up the street towards an outdoor shop. Several paddleboards leaned upright on its front porch and a kayak hung from the ceiling.

Ted's focus wasn't obvious, and Amanda wondered if that was the tradecraft lesson.

"Now, tell me what you see. What can you learn about this person in a *blink*?"

Amanda thought she'd play along. The thirtyish-looking guy's stride was confident and punctuated with an athletic grace. He approached a minivan while holding the boy, whom Amanda estimated to be fifty pounds. But the man? Sturdy! As if he was holding a feather.

The man's eyes were set within a well-tanned face. He wasn't ready to release the boy. Bits of conversation floated in through the open window—the boy's name was Winston.

As the man looked away, a lump formed in her throat for which she couldn't explain—an odd sensation as if she'd peered into another world.

The man set Winston on the pavement and the mother said something about the boy being a runner—a special needs code word. Amanda rubbed her chin and whispered under her breath, "He doesn't understand." Her chest tightened. The mother blushed. *He embarrassed her! What an idiot.*

Amanda continued to track them as the man held the door open for the family at the entrance to the coffee shop. *He's wounded*, she thought. *Why take it out on the woman?*

Fingers snapped in front of her face.

Amanda winced. "Uhh."

"Yeah . . . I didn't want you to be so obvious," Ted said.

"Was I?"

Ted chuckled.

The family entered the coffee shop, and Amanda turned to Ted. "Strange. I'm not exactly sure what I saw." She didn't mention the pain she saw in the guy's face as he held the boy.

"The guy came off as a bit of a jerk. Why dump all the kids on his wife? She looked like she could've used a hand, but he just followed them inside." Her conscience pricked her. *Where'd that come from?*

Ted tilted his head. "Right, maybe they weren't married."

Heat rose up Amanda's back. "No, I think they're separated. He's probably returning the boy after his visitation for the week."

Ted tapped the steering wheel. "Did you spot a wedding band?"

"I wasn't looking close enough. I thought the woman blushed, but I think she was just mad at him. He acted so confident and in-control, but he didn't have a clue . . . just steamrolled right over her."

"Wow, all that in a flash?"

"Yes." Amanda's tone was confident. "The boy has special needs."

"Oh?"

Amanda's anger leaked. "Absolutely! And the man's in denial about it. Maybe even ashamed." *Probably why he's so quick to dump his family, the jerk.* Amanda tried to put a clamp on it, but she said it anyway, "He reminds me of my father."

Ted flinched.

Amanda eyed him. "I'd rather not go into it. Sorry for mentioning it."

Ted rubbed his hands together. "Okay, that's the lesson. I don't know if you're right or wrong about your observations. I noticed the man *wasn't* wearing a wedding band. You need to realize how quickly people make snap judgments based on what they see in a blink."

Amanda nodded. She'd paid good money for his expert advice. Time to listen.

He continued, "From their clothing, they appeared to be from two different worlds. The guy seems to be in his element. She doesn't. I think this was a chance meeting." He set his hands on the steering wheel and eyed her. "There are some situations where our intuition leads us down a wrong path and, at other times"—he inhaled deeply—"it's dead-on accurate. I know you're nearly covered head to foot, but for starters, you need to throw off the intuition of people who know you."

"Okay, I get it. Thanks." Amanda took several deep breaths. *Relax*, she told herself. *You need to get Dad out of your mind. And that man!*

She glanced at Ted. "Now, I have a lesson for you. Do you get hit on by all those cutie young case officers at the Farm when you teach your class?"

Ted's eyes widened, then narrowed. "No, I don't think so."

"Do you think I was flirting with you back at the resort?"

"Huh? No!" Ted's head shook in panic.

"Correct . . . but I was close." Amanda's words came out sweet. "I think your problem is that when a girl does flirt with you, you miss it, and then she's discouraged."

"What are you saying?" Ted shot up in his seat. "Where's this going?"

"Nowhere with us. This is business, but I want you prepared in the event you ever do get a hint from *another* woman."

He blinked, and shifted in his seat. "Okay."

"Yep, no charge, Ted. Thanks for helping me out here."

He dropped his shoulders.

She continued, "I'm ready to test this getup. What should I do with the glasses once inside?"

"For this first go around . . . keep 'em on. I'll check your gait when we walk in.

Ted watched her cross the street, pleased on one hand, worried on the other. *She's still nervous. I think she's going to trip.*

The Yokel and the Shop

Jeb sauntered into the Yokel, hoping to enjoy the calm before the morning storm. Shuffling feet and voices of the woman herding her crew into the bathroom trailed behind him. He scanned the premises. The patrons were cheery and talkative and not in any sort of rush. Typical for a Saturday.

As usual, Kathi stood behind the counter, dirty blonde hair tied in a ponytail. Her hazel eyes were sizing up her patrons as they entered.

Jeb knew her as Kat. She was the owner-manager of the Yokel. He never called her Kat in front of outsiders. It was an unwritten code. She'd become a surrogate mother to his girls and his close friend and confidante.

Nearly a quarter of the pedestal tables were occupied. The chairs were unremarkable, cherrywood backs with taupe vinyl seats; but the tables had some flair. Their artistry was embedded into their custom-made tabletops—a reflection of Kat's free spirit. Not all the tops were complete, but the ones that were showed colorful mosaics of the area's attractions made from ceramic, glass, and marble.

Jeb was as regular as they came at the Yokel. He glanced to his right, curious to know whether his table was taken. Not that he was going to stay. The table's mosaic featured Historic Christ Church, of Georgian design. It was one of the best-preserved colonial churches in America. He held some pride, knowing his great ancestor built it. Robert "King" Carter. In his time, one of the wealthiest men of the Colonies.

The regulars, during the offseason, claimed their favorite tables as their right. Jeb was no different. During the summer, they relinquished to the tourists, who made up half of the shop's patrons this morning. Some were early risers trickling in from the Ebb and Flow, which was less than a mile up the tree-lined street. Visitors from the resort kept the Yokel bustling during the tourist season, coming for Kat's famous cinnamon buns and coffee. The other half were locals, a bit more serious, several here for the farmers' market.

He'd badgered Kat on countless occasions regarding the table tops. "When're you going to do a fishing scene? That's what people care about."

"No, they don't," she teased.

"I'll commission it." He was completely serious. "Whatever I pay, I'll still double my money on it." He twiddled his fingers. "I'll bet you could make more off these table tops than selling coffee." That hit a nerve.

"I get plenty of offers for 'em." She folded her arms in front of her chest. "I can't stand the thought of losing one of my babies." He realized then, like him, she struggled to break even every year. Her business, like his, was about the lifestyle.

A few months later, he arrived at the coffee shop to find a beautifully framed mosaic of a wetlands marsh landscape sitting on his favorite breakfast table. "What's that?" he said, pointing across the shop towards his table.

"Go see for yourself," she told him.

As he got closer, with a coffee in hand, he absorbed the full masterpiece. In the background, it showed an angler, upright on a paddleboard, fighting a leaping fish. He spilled his coffee.

"I guess you like it." Kat came running with a small towel.

Jeb looked down at the mess, the brown liquid splattered over several table legs.

"How much do you want for it?" He pointed at it and felt his jaw still hanging. "Name your price, Kat."

Kat's eyes lit up, and she released the towel on him, swatting his backside. "I'll be adding the extra coffee to your bill." Her voice was firm and even a little angry. He knew what she meant. Her child was not to be bought or sold, and he didn't push her further, accepting the gift.

He'd hung the mosaic on the predominant wall of the Shop, where no one would miss it. Twice, he'd been offered over five figures for it.

Jeb enjoyed watching Kat's business instincts in action. Many patrons came seeking ideas for weekend activities. If she encountered a young family, millennials, or Gen-Z'ers, she'd recommend a paddleboard tour—good for both herself and Jeb. She could count on Jeb to bring them back, famished. No doubt, it wasn't halos she saw hovering above these sweet children and restless teenagers, but dollar signs. Jeb trumpeted the Yokel's menu while out on the water with clients, and when they returned, they rang up large tabs.

As Jeb approached the counter, Kat caught his eye and gave him a friendly nod. She jabbed, "Jeb, the guys are starting to pay attention to that daughter of yours."

Jeb leaned into the counter. "You mean Caleb? I know he and Sierra spend a lot of time together in the Shop, but you're probably misreading things."

"No, not just Caleb." She shook her head. "I see *them* take notice when she comes by to pick up your sandwich."

His stomach tightened. He knew Kat meant the high school boys who frequented her shop.

"Ahh . . . Yes. What should we do about it?" He spoke from the side of his mouth—clearly he wasn't comfortable with the topic.

Kat sighed. Her voice softened. "You've got to get over it. How many years has it been now? The girls need a mother . . . and you—you need a wife."

Jeb didn't think twice about changing the subject. "Hey, Kat, I made an incredible discovery this morning down by the creek. The osprey pair with the nest out back. They're breeding a second time this season."

Kat's face betrayed her confusion.

"Rare. Never noticed it before," he continued. "The first batch was out of the nest by Memorial Day Weekend. If the current pair of chicks aren't flying before Labor Day, they'll probably die."

She folded her arms, glaring knowingly. "Mmm-hmm. Might be a lesson in that story . . . *Jeb*."

He blew out an exasperated breath. "They need a better father . . . and to your second point . . . I'm fine!"

Kat pulled out a small mirror from under the counter and pointed it at him. Melancholy still wore down his face. He flashed her a smile as artificial as the fishing lures he sold in the Shop.

Jeb didn't consider himself perfect, but he was conscientious and attentive. Although he became a bit distracted during the summer, he always recalibrated in the fall when his tours tapered off. His accountability partner, Charley West, had been a good influence on him—helped him manage his grief. But since Jeb had started his own business, no longer serving as a mate on Charley's boat, they spent less time together.

Kat re-stowed the mirror, but her stare demanded more of an explanation. He'd stick around for a longer discussion this morning. Jeb glanced to his left. Winston and his family were exiting the bathroom. Just as Jeb stepped back from the counter to let them go ahead of him, he felt an elbow hit his chest. A ghastly glob of a woman grabbed his arm and moved right past him. *Who does she think she is?* She now stood in front of him. *All the nerve! . . . Brash.*

He was taken aback by her abruptness—not typical of Kat's customers, especially the locals. This lady? Definitely not a local. But still! Even the tourists slowed down in the Northern Neck.

The woman turned around, looked at him, and then mumbled something. Jeb shrugged. He couldn't make out her words and most of her face. *Typical urbanite east coaster. Probably visiting from*

Washington . . . possibly New York. What's up with the limp? She must be hungover—that would explain the sunglasses. And the large sun-hat. Stupid! Probably with a bridal party. If she's the bride, I feel sorry for the groom. I can only hope she's not part of my morning tour!

He stepped aside and turned to Kat, who was wide-eyed. Jeb wanted out—and fast. The day was hard enough to get through as it was without a pushy tourist in the mix. Erin was still on his mind. Kat would've helped him regain focus, but their conversation was cut short.

Kat observed the awkward lady when she entered the shop. How could she not notice the oversized sunglasses and the way the woman mostly stared at the floor as she approached the counter? When the woman finally looked up, Jeb's eyes knocked her flat. No wonder she tripped, pulling Jeb backwards by grabbing his arm. She steadied herself, readjusting her hat and sunglasses.

A tall, good-looking man, who lingered by the entrance, accompanied the woman, but strangely kept his distance.

Kat's conversation with Jeb hadn't tapered off. If it had, she would've politely signaled Jeb that she needed to move on. He could come back later for the village gossip.

She glanced over Jeb's shoulder. The mother of three stood shell-shocked, incredulous at what had just transpired between Jeb and the New Yorker.

Jeb moved off to the side, and Kat's eyes locked with his. Her voice was tender. "I'm sorry." She cocked her head and mouthed, "Erin's birthday." She closed her eyes and nodded. "Are you going to be okay?"

She opened her eyes to find sadness and irritation had filled Jeb's. He answered in an upbeat tone. "All good."

She wanted to shriek but breathed in a heavy sigh that said, "Honestly?"

"Thanks for remembering." He provided a small nod.

It was something. Jeb should know he didn't need to fake it with her.

His tone was still hollow when he said, "I'd appreciate it if you'd keep an eye out on the girls today."

Jeb hadn't placed his order yet, always taking his time. It would be a busy weekend, but she sensed he wanted a few more minutes of chitchat. The clumsy woman still stood next to him, and apparently didn't have a clue. She was shaking as she looked at Jeb—out of nervousness or anger? Kat couldn't tell, but the woman had cornered Jeb, whether she realized it or not. Jeb needed a rescue and Kat would do it just like a mother dolphin would shoo her calves.

"The usual, Jeb?"

His answer was always the same. "Yes, thank you, no need to fix something that isn't broken." Jeb contorted his face into a fake smile.

You are broken, Jeb. I wish you'd let someone help you! Kat tried to catch his eyes, but he looked away.

The rude woman stepped in front of Jeb, blocking Kat's view of him.

"I'll get out of your *customer's* way," Jeb said, his tone dripping sarcasm. "I'll send Sierra up for it. Morning's tour will be arriving soon." As he departed, he passed a young boy and touched him on the head. He glanced back over his shoulder, "Take care of this one."

Jeb rarely asked for favors on behalf of her customers. Something was stirring with him. She just couldn't put her finger on it.

Sailor's Delight

Amanda's heart rate doubled when she entered the coffee shop. The guy she'd seen outside was at the counter and dawdling; she didn't want to expose herself any more than necessary. This was the type of public setting that Ted had warned her about, but it'd be an excellent test for her to gain confidence in her cover. *If an old friend recognizes me*, she thought, *I'll abort.*

As she approached the counter, the man in the loose-fitting fishing shirt glanced at her. His mournful look so startled her, she stumbled right into him and caught herself on his arm. "Oh, I'm sorry," she said, and then tried to change up her voice, attempting a Bronx accent. "I just need to order a coffee." *Awkward.* Amanda grimaced. *That didn't come out right.*

The guy was perturbed. Amanda was equally alarmed. It was the man from the street, *the one who abandoned his family.* But now, face to face, she captured his soulful eyes. They resonated with her, deep down. The rich, even tan of his face accentuated their startling blue color. For a moment, she was mesmerized. *Ignore them.*

His face turned blank.

Not working. We're not connecting. Some new local code of conduct? I need to keep things moving. Whatever. Definitely the "jerk" I spotted outside.

Her anger towards the man burned, stabilizing her. Anger was her comfort zone, but she'd never admit it was an addiction. For only a moment, the man's face—his look of sadness—reminded her again of her father. The look he wore after her mother's death, which led to his drinking. Amanda forced herself to stop shaking.

The man completed his order and the lady behind the counter faced Amanda. He'd called her Kat and she acted like the proprietor. Her tone was sharp. "And what can I get you this morning, miss?"

Amanda took a long breath. *A lousy way to treat a customer. Stay angry, Amanda. It works.*

She glanced back towards Ted. "What should we order for Sally?"

Her eyes chased the man. Kat had called him Jeb. He left the coffee shop and shook his head as he approached the sidewalk. *What a turd*, she thought.

Ted was at the entrance looking like he'd seen a ghost. Amanda waved for him to join her.

He came, but it took him a moment to find his words. "I'll take an egg and cheese sandwich . . . I'll split one of those Chesapeake cinnamon buns with her."

Kat's sympathetic eyes followed Jeb, then turned to Ted.

Wow, the jerk has her snowed . . . just like my dad, a cesspool of self-pity.

"Regular coffee?" Amanda asked Ted.

"Yes." He was stiff, his eyes still wide.

Amanda directed the order to Kat with a touch of sass—something the real Amanda would never do. If these people were buying into her uppity out-of-town persona, she'd adopt it. "Okay, we'll take one cinnamon *roll*, an egg and cheese sandwich, and two regular coffees. For my coffee, I'd like a double espresso latte."

Kat was confident the goofy girl had never looked at her large menu affixed to the wall behind the counter. She knew the type and ignored the slight—*calling my famous cinnamon bun a "roll"!* She controlled her tone. "Coming right up." But to her barista, she whispered with a sarcastic snarl, "*Sailor's delight* for the lady. Two regular coffees. I'll take care of the bun and the sandwich."

Sailor's delight wasn't on the menu, but her barista got the point and prepped a dark, heavy brew with a good dose of salt. It was an insider's joke, used when the staff encountered a snooty up-stater, or even worse, a New Yorker. Memories of a former President who occasionally escaped the White House for a golf weekend at the resort didn't sit well with Kat. Locals, like her, weren't happy about the visits—regardless of their political affiliations. The security detail snarled the few road arteries coming into the region, shutting down the bottom half of the peninsula. That wasn't the worst of it. The Yankee entourage that trailed him soon discovered the lower Northern Neck, and since that time, a few New Yorkers still lingered. Unfortunately for the goofy lady, Kat suspected her of being one.

The New Yorker and her companion found a table in the corner—the map table. Kat's mosaic displayed the key features and landmarks of the lower Northern Neck, all in colored glass. More favored by tourists than the locals.

The mother of the three children approached the counter. Kat smiled at her and lowered herself to eye level with the five-year-old. "How would you like a chocolate-covered croissant, sweetie pie?"

He nodded, but didn't smile. His hands were fidgety. The credit card machine caught his attention.

Kat looked at the mother. "It's on the house. Apparently, your boy had some effect on the man you walked in with. Are you doing better?"

"Yes," she responded. "How d'you know?"

"You seemed a bit flustered when you came in."

"Yes, I guess I was . . . Who is he?"

"James Carter." Kat didn't hide the pride in her voice. "Most people know him as Jeb. He has that effect."

The mother's voice was sincere and hinted at embarrassment. "Yes, I'm not sure what happened."

"Right . . ." Kat nodded. "He doesn't know who he is, and the effect he has on people." Kat felt her angst with Jeb bubble in front of the woman, but at least she'd put a positive spin on his personal issues.

Kat noticed the New Yorker in the corner flinch. *How could she have heard me?* Now, to continue her blubbering about her good friend would be a betrayal, so she stopped.

A few minutes later, she delivered the couple's order. The man thanked her.

The New Yorker raised her head. The eyes behind the glasses were almost perceptible. "Do you know where we might rent a watercraft, possibly a jet ski?" The woman's voice was calm—the snootiness, absent.

Kat forced a friendly reply, "Not around here. You can always hire a charter . . . but unlikely without a reservation. You might want to check with Ingram Bay Marina up by Wicomico Church."

The front door opened, and Kat turned to greet a familiar face. "Good morning, darling. Your father's sandwich is on the counter."

"Thank you, Aunt Kathi." Sierra's eyes sparkled as she eyed the bag.

"I added a Chesapeake cinnamon bun for you and Nora." Kat enunciated the name of her trademark buns. She turned to the gentleman and winked, hoping he'd convey the previous slight to his annoying companion. "Oh, have you considered a paddleboard excursion?"

"Uh, no . . ." the woman answered slowly. But then said, "Well, that might work. Who around here rents paddleboards?"

"See that young lady?" Kat tossed her head towards Sierra. "Just follow her. Two doors up."

Options

Amanda slapped the table. "It's brilliant."

Ted startled. "What's brilliant?" He reached for a napkin and mopped his sloshed coffee off the table.

"Paddleboards." Amanda kept her gaze on the young lady as Ted wolfed down his bagel sandwich. As soon as the girl disappeared, Amanda dashed to the front counter and snatched a brochure. The front cover displayed a smiling family of five paddleboarding on a creek. She quickly learned the Shop offered paddleboard excursions, rentals, eco-tours, and skinny-water fishing trips.

"Why not a jet ski?" Ted asked when she returned to their table.

Amanda placed her index finger on Ingram Bay shown on the mosaic. "Too far to the north . . ." She lowered her voice and pointed to Windmill Point. ". . . of my target."

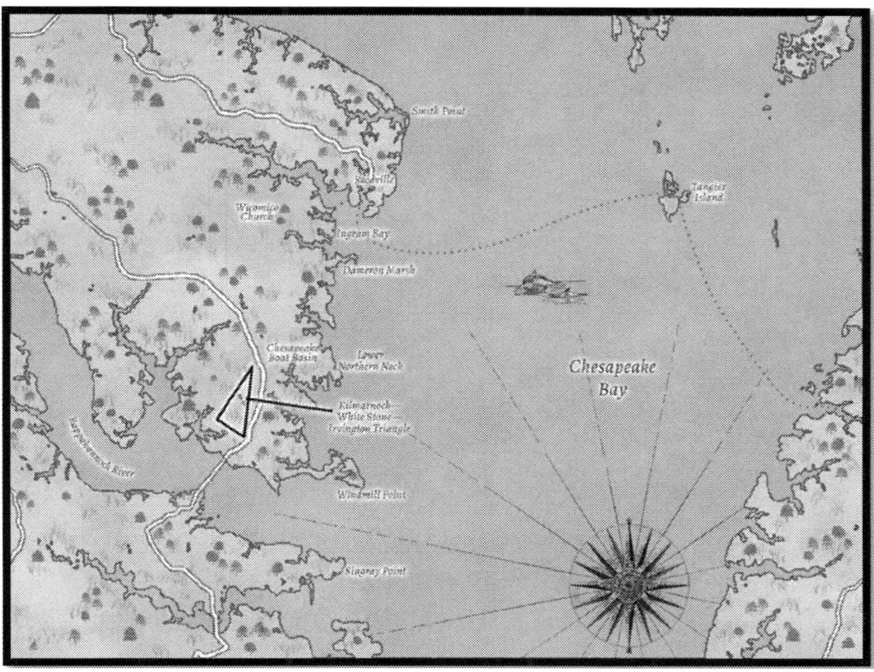

"I'm surprised the area doesn't have a strong rental market for jet skis?"

"Most of the 'come heres' already own 'em. Did you look down Carter's Creek this morning? Nearly all the docks dotting the waterline have a jet ski on a lift, a boat . . . or both."

He eyed her. "I notice they come in pairs."

His innocent observation salted a wound. He was right. Jet skis were typically bought in pairs . . . unless the model was large enough for two people. Why go out alone? *So much of my life is going out alone.*

She whispered across the table, "Pulling up on a jet ski might draw attention, but who's going to notice a girl on a paddleboard?"

"Mmm," he grunted with satisfaction while looking out the window. "You're not a girl . . ." he mumbled, "and you garner notice."

She slapped Ted's hand. "I heard that!" Her eyes returned to the young teen loitering at the counter. Amanda noted the girl's confident interactions with several customers and the coffee shop's staff.

She looked back at Ted. "If questioned, I'll just say I was tired and needed a break. I can hang out on the beach till the coast is clear and make my move."

Ted took a swig of coffee. "That'll work. What's the worst that can happen?" He exploited her pause and kept his voice low. "You're caught on your own property breaking into your own house and prowling around."

"It's my dad's house," she spat out.

"Did he ever legally kick you out? No. And based on what you told me previously, you just never returned."

A jolt of anger braced her. "Doesn't matter. I want to follow my own timeline and I don't want to be surprised by his fiancée. I only care to know what happened to my mother's ring."

Amanda placed her finger on a village to the north. "Reedville has a quaint waterfront lined with historical Victorian houses built by famous ship captains. The Fisherman's Museum here showcases the area's three hundred fifty plus years' history since colonization."

Ted massaged his chin. "The detail in this thing is exquisite. I've never seen anything like it."

She pointed at the passenger ferry route to the famed Tangier Island. "You and Sally might like this."

He nodded. "Yeah, but let's take care of you first. I'll help you secure the board and then we'll be off. Sally's coffee is—" He stopped mid-sentence, his mouth hung open as he gawked out the window.

Amanda followed his stunned gaze. *Sally's riding a beach bike!* She pulled right up the sidewalk and to the front of the shop. Ted's eyes were still tracking her. She wore a bright yellow fitted sleeveless top with an olive-green Athleta skort. He studied her as she deposited the bike in a stand and entered the shop.

Sally approached their table. "Howdy." She handed Amanda her keys. "I was on my way to your Jeep, but I saw the courtesy bikes at the front entrance." She giggled like a young girl. "I'd forgotten how much I loved riding."

Sally's joy was contagious. Amanda couldn't help but smile back at her. A self-satisfied smile.

"We were just getting ready to head back." Amanda handed over Sally's coffee. "We didn't want it to get cold."

Ted and Sally shared a shy glance, and Amanda smiled as her friend blushed.

"Thank you." Sally turned her gaze to the menu behind the counter. "I think I want to try one of their fruit smoothies." She then pointed out the window at a three-foot-tall ornamental pair of boots that stood at the front entrance. "Those are really cute. Half the businesses here have them."

"Watermen's boots," Amanda said with a hint of pride as she stood up. Ted's gaze was still on Sally, and Amanda glanced between them before saying, "Do you mind if we run a quick errand nearby?" She waved the brochure. "It shouldn't take long."

Sally shrugged. "Sure."

Amanda made her way to the door as Ted reluctantly followed. He looked back at Sally standing at the counter. She turned her head and smiled. He snapped his head back as if caught. Amanda whipped her focus towards the sidewalk as he fell in behind her.

Amanda's chest lightened, and her breathing eased.

Confidence? I'll take it.

CHAPTER 3

The Fort

Although Jeb occasionally used his own ramp to launch tours on Carter's Creek, he rarely did so in the summer. His summer groups preferred tours out near the creeks emptying into the Bay. It was cooler. Today would be no exception. Caleb, his teenage help, would be on hand by noon to help him with the afternoon tour. Sierra, his older daughter, was now being called upon more frequently to man the Shop. That's what he called it, "manning the Shop."

Kat often teased him about it, but earlier in the summer she'd called him out on it, seizing a quiet moment at the coffee shop. "Jeb, this has nothing to do with help."

"What do you mean? I need them . . . both girls."

Kat's face turned serious—like his mother's when she needed to make a point. "Be honest with me. You know what this is really about."

Jeb shifted his eyes toward the street. He wished a customer would pop in the door—then he could run. No luck. He returned his focus to Kat. "You seem to know, so why not just tell me?"

Kat clicked her tongue and set her elbows on the counter. The face-off continued.

"Say it, Kat, just say it. This seems more about you than it does me."

"James Carter!" She clapped her hands and stood up straight. "This has nothing to do with me."

I've unleashed a fire-breathing dragon! He took a step back.

Kat continued, "Ever since you've come here, you've smothered them . . . the girls. You've made that Shop of yours into a fort . . . more like a castle . . . and people like me serve as your moat."

"Is that what you think?" A blast of heat hit Jeb's face. It wasn't the truth that hurt him. It was the confrontation. He'd never seen so much fight in her.

She exhaled. "Ok, I'm sorry. I've come on too strong."

Jeb drew his head back. "I'd say."

Kat's tone softened. "Jeb, it's not just your shop. It's the school, the Bay House, your parents, Erin's parents." She pushed herself up from the counter using one hand.

Jeb braced for another zinger as Kat narrowed an eye.

Her voice was certain, "Face it—you've cocooned them."

He threw up his hands. "Cocooned?" He slapped his chest. "I'm protecting them!"

Kat lowered her voice, and her tone held little emotion. "All right, bubble wrap, then. Jeb . . . Sierra has been eligible for the junior high summer camp for the past two years. Why didn't you let her go?"

"How could that camp compete with what we have here?" Jeb's voice pleaded. "She'll spend more time outdoors with me here than she would that entire week at camp."

"That's not the point. She needs to meet new people. Make friends her age."

Jeb pursed his lips.

"How about your sister? How many times has she offered to take them away for a day at the museum?"

He didn't answer. As much as he loved his sister, Caroline, she could be flighty and flirty. And in his book not the best role model.

"Sleepovers? Ever let Sierra or Nora go to a friend's house?"

"No. Why?" His words were quick. "The Bay House is paradise. My mom loves to entertain their friends."

"You're in denial. I suspect you maintain some checklist to vet anyone who might claim any influence over your girls."

Jeb removed his gaze, letting a few moments pass, then returned his eyes to Kat. He felt the fight leave him. "It's what Erin would've wanted." A heaviness hit him. The sorrow for Erin was one thing. To exasperate his girls was another. But an admission to Kat could breach a dam.

"Yes, but not necessarily in the way you're doing it. I understand your motives."

Erin wanted to raise them with strong traditional-family values. *Isn't that what I'm doing?*

He remained defensive. "How about Captain West? Charlotte? Don't they count for something? They're not family."

"Barely . . . I suspect he's been vetted."

Jeb took a seat across from the table and relaxed. "More than that, Kat. Charley's a role model for me."

She chuckled. "A role model. What does Charley know about raising kids?"

This time, her words went too far—Kat was referring to Charley's prodigal daughter. Charley had pulled him from the abyss after Erin's death. *She needs to show Charley some respect!* What did she have on the guy, anyway?

Captain West had hired Jeb as his mate for three seasons—significant therapy happened on Charley's boat. *So what if his daughter had left him?* By Jeb's estimate, Charley and his wife had been exemplary parents to the girl and his wisdom on parenting was sound. He took responsibility for her departure, fully transparent with Jeb regarding who he became after Mary's death. Charley continued the healing process by sharing his mistakes with other grieving widowers.

"We share the same values. Values that Erin and I agreed upon."

Kat stepped out from behind the counter and took a seat opposite him. Her voice softened. "I can see that . . . and I know how much the two of you have gone through together." She took his hand between both of hers. "Jeb, I just want you to recognize that your girls are growing up. You can't control everything and everyone around them. Give them the opportunity to make some mistakes . . . I'm not saying big mistakes . . . just loosen up a bit. If you don't, you're going to suffocate them."

Jeb thought long and hard about what Kat said in the days after that conversation. He committed to make some changes. Instead of Sierra trailing him on nearly all his tours, he'd let her tag-team with Caleb in the Shop. Sierra, in turn, could mentor Nora. He had other motives for it as well. If Sierra and Nora could learn to man the Shop alone, he might one day free Caleb to run tours on his own. *Change is good*, he thought, *might even grant myself some freedom.*

But I'll never free myself from Erin.

Map Room

Jeb returned to the Shop with only moments to spare before the arrival of his first clients. Two women entered—the bride and her maid of honor, here for their scheduled Hens and Roosters Tour. He breathed a sigh of relief. They were pleasant, and he was glad to learn he wasn't dealing with the rude creature he'd clashed with in the Yokel. Had she reappeared as the bride, he wondered if he'd feign sickness and cancel the tour.

The Hens and Roosters Tour was one of Jeb's most popular excursions. Since the resort hosted so many destination weddings, he tailored the tour for the bridesmaids and groomsmen. The first half of it, for the Roosters, typically launched at daybreak. He'd guide the men on a fishing excursion on well-equipped paddleboards. Boards he'd outfitted with small coolers and pole mounts.

Jeb tapped his in-depth knowledge of the area—combined with a check on the weather—to deploy only where the water was smooth. If a northeast wind blew over the Bay, he'd launch from the protected tributaries of the Rappahannock River, also known as creeks. Sometimes he'd launch from the back of his property into Carter's Creek. For southerly winds he'd shuttle the parties to the north of Windmill Point and fish the protected creeks emptying into Little Bay.

For the Hens, he employed his most stable and comfortable paddleboards. He facilitated what he considered a *social adventure*, guiding talks during the tour focused on the Virginia plantation history, sea life, and romantic pirate stories. Although he borrowed some material from Michener's classic novel, *Chesapeake*, he told his own stories passed down from his mother—vignettes of the mysterious Captain John Smith and his exploration of the Bay.

At least one Hen from every tour would blurt out, "That guy who married Pocahontas."

This would elicit some cackling from one or two other Hens. "No, you've mixed up Captain John Smith with John Rolfe."

If Jeb sensed a Hen overplayed her hand, belittling a fellow bridesmaid, he'd cite some other factoid, such as, "John Rolfe was a wealthy tobacco farmer," or even, "The marriage was a second one for both Rolfe and Pocahontas."

It might garner a jab by the injured Hen. "See there, *smarty pants*? You probably didn't know that, *did you*?"

If a Hen deemed Jeb had interfered, she might say, "What else should we know, *Mr. Carter*? Why not tell us about *yourself*?" Every eye of the party would immediately turn on him.

He'd avoid the bait. "Rolfe married again and had even more children." He'd stroke his paddle through the water and move along the history trail, maybe even jump right to the Civil War.

The bride-to-be in front of him was a peach—*lucky groom,* he thought. *First-class treatment for this one. Game on.* It was time to help her create some memories she'd never forget. He hastened to his business, offering the ladies coffee and tea, and then guided the advance party to the Map Room to discuss a myriad of options for their tour. His clients nearly always accepted his recommendation. The remaining bridesmaids trickled in and he greeted them with similar courtesies. His girls assisted with the coffee machine, then returned to their stools behind the counter.

He pointed at the oversized floor-to-ceiling map. "With light winds this morning, I'd suggest we launch from Foxwells and paddle the canal to Cedar Island. You're likely to observe nesting ospreys and a few bald eagles. We'll pass one of their nests early in the tour. If we move out quickly, we may even spot an otter family."

The Hens were giddy with excitement. He exhaled and dropped his arms. They were hooked.

Doll House

When Amanda and Ted first arrived at the Shop, she'd paused at the sundial. The hardscape was in the design of a world globe—half of it, showing the Atlantic Ocean side. "Breathtaking," she said to Ted.

"Yeah . . . I'm not sure I've seen anything like it." He gestured towards the colored pavers. The detail of the varied coastlines was just enough to give the scene an idyllic ambiance.

Amanda dropped to her knees and honed in on one corner of the dial's bronze octagonal plates. *In a blink!* That's what Ted had said. That she'd see things in a *blink*. She suspected the thick layer of pollen hid something beneath it. She wet her thumb and rubbed. An image came into view, and she gasped. She glanced over her shoulder. A passing car had masked her puff, and Ted hadn't noticed her startle at the sight of the diminutive coat of arms—not much bigger than a quarter. Where had she seen it before? And when? *A childhood memory?*

Ted was on his way to the porch, and she stood and joined him. The assaulting questions could wait.

As they approached the door, Amanda tugged on Ted's arm. "Hold on a second." She gestured towards the large window.

Amanda peered into it, and they remained unnoticed. The girl she'd seen at the coffee shop—and a younger one—graciously serviced a group of young ladies. Jeb led the dizzy women to a large room with maps and began some presentation. Amanda was certain they stopped listening to him after less than a minute. She too became transfixed by the fluidity of his body—big and strong—moving about as a dancer as he pointed towards the large map.

"Are those his daughters?" Ted asked.

"Amazing." A powerful sense of déjà vu swept over her as she looked at Jeb.

"Who? The man?"

"What? No! Of course not. The girls are amazing." Amanda tore her eyes from Jeb. "The guy is a jerk, Ted. Those girls must be from his first marriage." *I'd like to meet the woman who's raising them . . . despite the jerk.* The last part was a lie. More worrisome for Amanda was how quickly it came.

The memory came at her like a fast ball. She was five and standing in front of her doll house—a gift from her parents, hand-crafted by her father in the Victorian style. It had a high-ceiling grand-room, like the way the Shop looked through the window. The ladies? Her royal subjects. And those girls? They reminded her of her dress up dolls. The man? She smacked back that memory as fast as it'd come.

Ted chuckled. "So, you think he's burned through two marriages?"

"Yep. I know the type." She thought about her father—the Naval officer. He was polished on the outside . . . but it was all for show. What type of man would reject his only child?

She felt lightheaded. That would explain the weird memory. *Probably dehydrated.*

The Client

Jeb looked over to his girls. "Sierra, I'll need you and Nora to man the Shop." As the Hens exited, he said, "We should be back by noon."

"Got it, Dad." Sierra drew out her words. "I already checked in with Aunt Kathi. We'll be fine."

"I'm sure you will, and I'm expecting Caleb before noon. Kathi will be watching that too." Jeb projected a serious look.

"Oh, Daaad, Caleb's just a friend." Sierra gestured with a dismissive wave; it did nothing to assure him.

The door chimed, and Jeb lifted his gaze from Sierra. A lady with large glasses limped in, trailed by a lanky gentleman with dark hair. Jeb felt his entire chest collapse. *The whack. Please, God, spare me.*

Jeb turned and headed towards the back door.

"Excuse me!" The lady's voice bellowed.

Jeb stopped and turned around. The woman had raised her hand, and she was shaking it in the air as if demanding to be called upon.

Jeb blurted, "Oh, you." He couldn't hide his disdain for her. He redirected his eyes to her companion and repaired his customer-service smile.

The woman's tone matched his own. "Yes, me."

Jeb held his gaze on the man and ignored her. "How may I help you?"

The man froze, having taken only two steps into the Shop.

With an odd limp, she flew across the floor and stepped in front of Jeb, blocking his view of the man. "*I* need to rent a paddleboard," she said.

Jeb strode to his left and addressed the man, "Would you mind coming back at noon? I've got a tour heading out."

Her man still seemed shell-shocked, but it didn't matter. She wasn't Jeb's problem. He continued on his track to the exit.

The woman side-stepped, and now she was directly in front of him. Her cheeks, rage-red.

Okay, Jeb reasoned, *she's on an authority kick.* Her face came within inches of his.

"Yes, I would mind," she snapped. "I was hoping to head out this morning."

He caught sight of her lips, spitting on him when she spoke. Her mouth and cheeks were the extent of what he could discern from her face. And the lips? *A disservice to the woman.* Lips like those belonged to Julia Roberts.

Jeb took a step back and scanned her from the top of her silly sun-hat down to her black sneakers. Her baggy army-green cargo pants were hideous. *The New York style? A rapper? Probably covered head to foot with tattoos.* He stared into her sunglasses and wondered if she'd read his thoughts. If she'd been a tiger, she would've growled.

Jeb looked at the man and threw up his arms with an expression that said, "What's up with her?"

A speech for his girls rattled in his head: *How not to behave in small-town America!*

He tried to keep his tone a notch below annoyed. "Sorry, miss, I really can't help you. I'm not letting my boards go out without a guide." He forced his most professional, practiced smile. One that wouldn't come close to reaching his eyes. "If you were a repeat customer, then, yes, sometimes we rent our boards . . ." He shrugged. "Our practice is to send them out with a guide."

He took a step to the right. His line to the door was clear. The Hens had pulled their vehicles onto the street, prepared to follow his truck and trailer. For a beat, she seemed defeated, but then she matched his step with a side-step to her left and she was in his face again.

The tall man backpedaled. *The guy seems alright.* A healthy response to Miss Crazy. But if the roles were reversed and she was Jeb's girlfriend—or wife—he wondered what he'd do. But Erin? Never had he known a woman more polite and gracious than his Erin.

The customer's tone softened slightly, but not enough to lower the temperature in the room. "Any chance you have a guide coming in later this morning?"

Jeb glanced at his daughters, craning their necks as if watching a NASCAR race and anticipating a smash up. *They're enjoying this!* Sierra maintained the brakes on a smile, but Nora? The whites of her eyes showed.

He rubbed his neck. "Nope, sorry, miss. Single-threaded today." Jeb tried again to get around her and out the door.

"Daddy, I can do it!"

He glanced over his shoulder. Sierra was up from her stool and she unleashed a dangerous smile. One that might energize the woman.

Jeb's words came fast. "Nope, you're not insured." Sierra's smile evaporated. She'd helped him on numerous excursions, but she'd never led one.

He directed his gaze to the woman. His conscience pricked him over the half-truth—his insurance didn't restrict his children as guides. *She won't know this.* Besides, Jeb was desperate to rid himself of the spectacle.

"She looks like she can do it," said the woman. "And as for the insurance, I'll sign a waiver."

Jeb grumbled and ground his teeth. "She's never conducted one on her own." He tried to ignore her lips. It was easier to deal with her when she was mad, but Sierra seemed to have softened the woman's razor-sharp edge.

He turned around, fully intending to quiet Sierra. Then he'd be able to regain control. Sierra's countenance had tanked. An apology was in order, and he took a step in her direction. But it was too late. The woman pounced—sidestepped again and blocked his path to Sierra.

"You ought to have more confidence in your daughters." She pointed at Sierra. "I noticed her earlier, at the coffee shop. She comports herself well."

Jeb crossed his arms and shifted his weight to his heels. "I think I remember *you* earlier, too. You don't *comport* yourself well. Now yes, where was I? Oh yeah, about to place my order when an elbow slugged me in the chest, and your *personage* pushed me aside."

The woman looked at Jeb and then to the girls. Nora came off her stool. If he embarrassed this woman in front of his girls, she deserved it. *Good riddance!*

The woman guffawed. "Personage?" This time, he felt the woman's spit and wiped his face.

His thoughts screamed. *How can I get rid of her?*

It wasn't his style to pick a fight with a customer; in fact, he couldn't recall a single incident in which he'd ever done so. *Why does she ruffle me?*

The man was still frozen in place and bewildered. But her laugh? Vaguely familiar. He caught a whiff of her. She actually smelled nice. *Try to think the best in people, Jeb.* It's how he was raised.

"I tripped coming up to the counter," the woman argued. "I apologized, *mister.*"

Jeb glanced at her companion. Her man was still tongue-tied, but he mustered a nod.

She continued, "A proper *gentleman* would've caught me. Might have shown some concern."

Gentleman? A needle prick went right to his ribs. "Didn't hear you," Jeb fibbed. She had said something. He just couldn't remember what. "You must've been mumbling."

His words failed to placate her. She spoke slowly and deliberately while she gestured to Sierra. "I'd like a private tour conducted by this guide." She sucked in a deep breath and straightened. She punctuated her words, "I believe . . . her name . . . is . . . Sierra."

The tall man's eyes widened further. Nora gaped.

Sierra jumped out from behind the counter, grabbed Jeb's arms. "Let me do it, Daddy! I can take her!"

Why? It had to be the craziest thing he'd ever heard from his daughter. Not her desire to lead a tour, but to take the lunatic woman. If only Sierra had said she'd drown the woman, he'd be celebrating.

The man extended his palms, flat and pointed up in a way that said, "I know nothing."

Wow! Jeb thought to himself. *Even her boyfriend fears her.*

Jeb returned his attention to the woman-blob before him and struggled to find her eyes. His gaze drifted to the front window. The Hens waited in their cars along the street.

He gave an exasperated sigh and closed his eyes. "Okay, lady, it'll be off the books. Please sign the waiver, but I won't be charging for the tour."

"Now you just wait a minute, *mister*—"

When Jeb opened his eyes he found her finger wagging in front of his nose. At least now she wasn't spitting at him.

"I'm paying full price. I won't permit you to insult your daughter." The bit of the woman's face that was visible had reddened.

A flash of heat raced up the back of Jeb's neck to his ears. Why was she making it so personal? A complete stranger!

Like a bull ready to charge, he flared his nostrils. He thought about picking her up and carrying her out of the Shop. Her man had nothing on him. He'd do it gently, but she needed to get out! Instead, Jeb massaged the back of his neck. He wanted to laugh at her, the large-framed glasses and ridiculous sun-hat; but then he felt sorry for her. *She must hate herself and her small life.*

He walked over to Sierra, put his arm around her, and whispered, "I'm sorry. You'll be fine. Knock it out of the park."

He turned and faced the lady. He thought he might stare her down, but it was futile.

She took a step towards him. "So is that a yes?" She was holding back a victory smile.

"Yes," the word came, too painful to let it linger on his lips.

He raised his voice and peered over his shoulder. "Sierra, have the lady fill out the paperwork. I'll leave the paddleboards at the launch. Take the radio and make sure you walk through *all* the safety procedures."

"Oh, Daddy, thank you!" Sierra bubbled. Her arms fastened around his neck instantly.

He whispered in her ear, "Okay, okay, let's be professional about it."

Jeb didn't know what to feel, jammed between his ecstatic daughter and the crazy lady. The Hens were still waiting too.

He turned to the woman. "Ma'am, I assume you have a vehicle? You'll need to drive your guide to the launch after you finish the paperwork. Sierra will provide safety instructions."

"Yes, we can do that." The woman nodded and folded her arms in front of her chest.

Jeb pivoted and made a notation on the Shop's whiteboard. He glanced back at her. "I trust you won't be kidnapping my daughter."

She grunted.

He decided he'd snap a photo of their vehicle tags on his way out—just in case. He didn't trust NY-crazy, but the timid guy? He might have bird legs, but something about his demeanor suggested he was a straight shooter.

Now the woman flattened her lips and shook her head like she still wanted to fight with him.

Jeb cringed. He also suspected she was still trying to embarrass him in front of his girls. *This must be her victory dance.*

He issued a stern look to Sierra. "Please call me on the radio when you arrive at Foxwells."

"Yes, sir." Sierra fought back a widening smile. He cringed at that, too.

For the benefit of the woman and her boyfriend, he said more loudly, "Keep an eye out for the storms."

He rubbed Sierra's head lightly with his fist as he held it close to his chest. He kissed the spot where he'd rubbed and whispered, "Take it easy out there. She doesn't look fit."

He brushed back Nora's hair from her face and gently kissed her forehead. He brought his face close to her ear and spoke softly, "After Sierra leaves, lock up the shop and stay with Aunt Kathi until Caleb arrives. I'll let her know. If you want to return to the Bay House, just call Gramps or Grans."

"Daddy," Nora said looking towards the woman, "I can show Grans how to run the Shop with me."

"Ooh." Jeb tilted his head back. *Why didn't I think of that?* "Okay. Sure. If that works, go ahead."

Jeb faked a step in the direction of his exit. The woman didn't stop him this time. He sighted a few of the Hens hanging out of their car windows. He flashed her a plastic smile and proceeded.

He peeked over his shoulder on the way out. Nora and the woman exchanged beaming smiles. He had to wonder.

What did I miss?

Sierra watched her father exit the shop. A caravan formed behind Jeb's truck, pulling their trailer of stacked paddleboards. The woman waited until they were all gone, and then turned to Sierra and removed her sunglasses.

Wow! What a pretty face. *And the eyes!*

The lady glanced at Nora, and Nora's expression went slack with awe.

The woman turned from them and browsed through the aisles, inspecting the Shop's merchandise—heading first to the fishing tackle. Her companion made his way to the fish tank.

Sierra resumed her spot on her stool. *I'm going to lead my own tour!* Chills ran down her arms. She took a quick breath and exhaled slowly. It seemed to help.

She relaxed, but what was it with her sister? Nora's eyes were huge and followed the strange lady, who was now sifting through an apparel rack.

With a shake of her head, Sierra let out a sigh. Loud enough that it should've gotten the attention of her sister, but Nora remained mesmerized by the woman.

Sierra leaned over and whispered, “Stop it.”

“Stop what?” Nora whispered back, holding her gaze on the woman.

“You’re staring.”

Nora ignored her.

“Why are you staring?” Sierra gently slapped Nora’s hand as the woman continued to browse.

Nora fidgeted. “I don’t know.”

Sierra hissed through her teeth, “You’re going to make her uncomfortable.”

“I don’t care,” Nora said, still staring.

The woman looked up from a clothing rack. She’d pulled a hot-pink ladies-styled fishing shirt off the rack with the Shop’s logo. She smiled at Nora. That seemed to set Nora at ease.

The lady raised the dangling price tag closer to her face. “Your prices are reasonable, but I’m surprised you don’t charge more.”

Sierra simmered. She’d helped her father set the prices. “Thank you, ma’am.”

“What’s up with the tarpon?” The woman’s voice held both challenge and curiosity as she eyed the Shop’s logo: a tarpon leaping out of the water with a hook in its mouth.

Nora held her mouth wide in disbelief. Sierra was equally startled. No first-time visitor had ever called out their tarpon. *And Dad has never identified it on the website!* He didn’t advertise it with his customers, either. Maybe if the Shop was in Florida, an angler might suspect a tarpon. But Virginia’s Northern Neck? *Who is this lady?*

Sierra crossed her arms in front of her chest. “How’d you recognize a tarpon?”

“Uhhh . . .” the woman stuttered. “It doesn’t look like any other fish I know.”

Sierra wondered if Nora had picked up the stranger’s insinuation. Now the lady looked embarrassed. Like she regretted crossing some line. *Yeah! She should be.* She’d encroached on family honor, accusing Sierra’s father of exploiting a cult-like fish for marketing the Shop. The woman would’ve been better served had she gone for his throat!

But how would she know both? The tarpon, which had been a

secret only between the three of them, and the fact she crossed a sacred angler's line?

"I'm Amanda, by the way." She smiled again. The woman's eyes danced between Sierra and her sister. Nora remained paralyzed. It was no wonder. Everything about the lady's expression was warm and genuine, even if she dressed funny. *Bizarre was more like it!* Heavy cargo pants in the middle of the summer? *She must be burning up.*

"This is my friend Ted, but he won't be going. It'll just be you and me on the tour."

"Okay, Ms.—sorry, what's your last name?" Sierra asked, but she still wondered about the tarpon.

"Just call me, Amanda, that'll be fine, thank you."

"Okay, Amanda. You already know I'm Sierra. This is my sister, Nora."

Sierra was about to dig a little deeper. But Amanda took over. She made a quick step in her sister's direction, like greeting a puppy on Christmas morning. "How do you do, Nora?"

Amanda took off her sun hat. *Looks like something Grans would wear, fishing off the end of the dock.*

"I'm just fine." Nora struggled to speak.

Amanda dug her fingers into her hair bob and scratched it as if it was foreign. Then she tossed her head causing her hair to fall across her shoulders.

"You're prrrrreeeetty!"

So what, Nora! Sierra wanted to scream at her sister. *Who cares if the woman is pretty?*

Amanda's eyes brightened, and she threw her head back.

"And feisty," Nora added. "I like you."

Amanda's cheeks reddened. She waited a moment. "Thank you." She touched Nora's shoulder. "I like you too."

Amanda exhaled deeply. "I thought you two needed a bit of girl power back there. Someone to stick up for you."

"Yes! Thank you." Sierra struggled to say more. A flood of emotions crashed about within her chest. The woman may have touched a nerve with her, but she'd also helped her gain some freedom. *Amanda may be strange, but she's nice.*

Did Dad get her wrong? He's not acting right today.

Nora filled in the pause, "I'm ten, and Sierra is thirteen."

"Oh." Amanda bounced a glance between the two of them. "I would have guessed you were twelve and Sierra was fourteen."

Sierra eyed her sister—Nora was pleased with the response. Sierra, however, scowled. "You tacked on two years to Nora's age and only one to mine."

The man piped in, "She's got you there, Amanda."

"Yes, she does." Amanda's face reddened again, and she burst into laughter. She was laughing at herself, and it was infectious.

Ted and Nora joined in. Sierra tried not to laugh. It was her joke, after all, even though she'd been serious.

Amanda looked at her watch. "We need to get going, but first, I'd like to know about the fish." She raised the shirt in her hand. "The tarpon?"

The girls clamored over each other to speak, while Ted moved in closer to hear. Sierra took a step back, letting Nora tell it. Might as well. She'd learn more by watching the exchange between the woman and her sister.

"Now, where did he catch it?" Amanda asked.

Nora answered, "We told you, Miss, it was up on the marsh."

"What marsh?"

"Dameron Marsh."

Amanda's voice was full of challenge. "And he pulled this beast in while standing on his paddleboard?"

"No, Miss. It was hooked while he was fishing off his paddleboard. They were in the shallows. He jumped in the water and wrestled it in."

"Hmmm . . ." Amanda squinched her brows. "In the Northern Neck?" She spoke as if accepting defeat, trying to be gracious. She took her time before continuing. "I thought you were going to call me Amanda."

"Yes, Miss, —" Nora responded.

Sierra finished by saying emphatically, "We'll call you Amanda!"

"In that case, I'd like to buy the shirt." Amanda waved her hand towards the racks. "Ted, why don't you find one for yourself? It's on me."

Amanda's voice softened. "Nora, I believe you can ring these up yourself. Right?"

Nora brightened and nodded.

"I thought so." Amanda winked.

If Sierra was being honest, Nora's infatuation with the strange woman grated on her nerves. *First my dad, now my sister. Both are loony today.*

Paddleboard Guy

Amanda surprised even herself with her aggressive behavior directed towards the *paddleboard guy*. Unlike her. Why, she wondered, had she compulsively come to the girls' defense? And why had her task turned more into confronting the man than renting the paddleboard?

I don't think the man could see my eyes. He'd searched for them. *How funny!* She couldn't have kept up the tantrum had he seen her eyes. To be somebody she was not. Hide her weakness—her insecurity.

She'd have time on her tour to gain a better understanding of the father's rigidity. He was overprotective in one regard, but loose in another. Where was the girls' mother? Why did he leave Nora in the care of the coffee shop lady? She couldn't be his wife. She was at least ten years older. Wouldn't the girls' confident nature be the product of a healthy marriage? But he wore no ring. *If I was his wife, I'd demand he wear a ring!*

Why was he so resistant to Sierra taking out customers, but then trusted two complete strangers to drive his daughter to the launch? Amanda glanced across the aisle. Her faux fiancé thumbed through some t-shirts. *Of course Paddleboard Guy should trust me, but why Ted?*

"What do we have here?" Sally entered the shop holding her smoothie.

"Over here," Ted said, waving his arm to beckon her. "Come see this."

Sierra followed Sally as the three stood in front of the saltwater aquarium.

"Ooooh, look at that one. Cute," Sally said, pointing to a halfbeak.

"We fill it with fish we've netted from our nearby creeks and bays," Sierra explained.

Amanda stood back and continued to marvel at the girl. *I'm watching a younger me.*

Sierra continued. "My dad uses the tank to explain the interplay of marine life in the Bay." Sierra pointed to the placard above the tank: The Chesapeake Bay—*Northern Atlantic Ocean's Greatest Estuary!* She turned dramatically, opened her arms, and directed them to the large map on the wall. "The Bay serves as the nursery for many of the ocean's fish."

Ted gave her his full attention. "Go on."

Amanda glanced back and forth between the Map Room and Nora, who was ringing up her cash purchase. Nearly checked out, she said, "Nora, why don't you show me some of the fish in the aquarium."

"I'd love to, miss."

"Amanda, remember."

"Yes, Miss Amanda," Nora said with a sheepish nod.

Amanda absorbed the girl's large soft eyes. Like those of the Paddleboard Guy. Nora's sister resembled someone else. Still, no question, the jerk was the father of both.

In the excitement, Nora didn't notice that Amanda provided only a *W* for her name on the waiver. Nora just filed it along with hundreds of others.

Nora grabbed Amanda's hand and guided her to the aquarium. She began pointing. "This one here is a mummichog, that's a silverside, here's a killifish."

"What type?" Amanda asked.

Nora tilted her head. "Oh, yes. A *banded* killifish. Here's a striped killifish."

"Do you have a bull minnow?"

"Yes." Sierra pointed to one hiding behind a small stack of oysters. "They make excellent bait," she said, earning a glare from Nora.

"Bay anchovy?" Amanda asked, looking at Nora.

"Right here!" Nora yelled back, glancing at her sister with a look that said, "I have the floor*."* She continued, "That's a fiddler crab," pointing to what appeared to be a one-armed crustacean on the sand mound.

On closer inspection, Amanda spotted the much smaller second claw.

"How cute!" Sally squealed.

"Male or female?" Amanda asked while raising her index finger towards Sierra and keeping her eyes on Nora.

"Male!" Nora nearly leapt off the floor. "My dad put a diamondback turtle in here—once."

"And what happened?" Amanda's voice filled with anticipation.

The girls looked at each other and responded in unison, "The fish disappeared!"

Ted burst into laughter. The girls eyed each other, rather pleased. Once he calmed down, Ted said, "I expect this thing's always changing."

"Yes," Sierra said, "Caleb and my father are constantly experimenting with it. A lot of folks visit just for the tank."

Amanda looked at Sierra. "Caleb?" The girl blushed and Amanda added, "No need to answer that."

"What can you tell us about that beautiful hardscape out front?" Amanda asked.

"My daddy built it," Nora effused.

Amanda tilted her head. "And your sundial? Where'd that come from?"

Sierra's brow tightened slightly like she was suspicious. "My grandmother."

Nora remained excited. "Queeny! She gave it to me and my sister."

Sierra's glare squelched Nora's enthusiasm.

Amanda drew her attention to Ted and Sally. "Okay, you two, I need to ferry you along so I can return here for my tour with Sierra." Amanda looked at Sierra. "I'll be back around ten. Will that work?"

"Yes, that'll be fine. Don't forget your sunscreen and water shoes," Sierra said.

Amanda exited the Shop with a spring in her step. As soon as they were out of earshot of the girls, Ted said, "Why do I feel like you speak their language?"

"Maybe it's because I do." She smiled back at him. "I feel sorry for those girls."

"How so?" Ted was bewildered.

"Apparently that jerk of a father was quick to dump the duties of his shop on them." But her gut said something different.

Ted chuckled. "You're the one who talked him into it! He must trust you . . . you seem to have made quite the impression."

She really didn't know what to say. Her stomach knotted. The girls pulled at heart-strings she didn't know existed, throwing her emotions into turmoil. And now she'd be co-opting Sierra for nefarious purposes. *Who's the jerk, Amanda?*

Ted's keys came at her; she snatched them from the air and eyed them. "Huh?"

"I'm riding the bike back." Ted placed his hand on the handlebar.

Sally grasped the other side. "That's my bike!"

"You can ride on the handlebars." Ted spoke matter-of-factly and looked at Sally with a growing smile.

Sally's eyes came to Amanda, who nodded back with encouragement.

Amanda trailed them slowly. Sally cackled with delight, riding on top of the handlebars as Ted pedaled. Amanda waved to the driver of a golf cart behind her, gesturing for them to pass. When Ted made eye contact with the cart's occupants, his pedaling increased—not quite enough to keep up—and the bike wobbled.

Sally's cackling crescendoed, "Go, Ted! *We* can do it."

Amanda didn't account for the bonus entertainment that she herself provided the pair before they embarked on their own course of activities. As Ted recounted Amanda's run-ins with the Shop owner, she laughed along, but deep down, she felt embarrassed. Who knew what further characterizations of her idiosyncrasies they'd talk about during their day together? But it was all for a good cause. *I deserve whatever they say about me.* She still pinched herself. *Both missions on track!*

She imagined patting herself on the back, and her confidence soared, all but for a strange feeling.

Something in the air didn't feel right.

CHAPTER 4

Briefing

Sierra fidgeted about the Shop for nearly an hour in anticipation of her client. She spat commands to her little sister in rapid-fire:

"Fold this—and fold that."

"That shirt isn't hanging right."

"The fish need to be fed."

"Where's the pointer? I need the pointer!"

"Sweep, sweep, sweep—we need to sweep."

Some fishermen came in to buy some tackle. Sierra fumbled with the card reader, and Nora had to complete the sale.

The anglers exited, and Sierra exhaled a sigh of relief. "Thanks, Nor." Their eyes met. Sometimes Nora could be so kind. She gave her a tender hug . . . her little sister was growing up.

Nora climbed onto her stool. "Try taking slow deep breaths, like this . . ."

Sierra was practicing the technique when the bells on the door chimed. Amanda bounded through the entrance—right on cue.

"Ready?" The excitement in Amanda's voice was compelling.

Sierra eyed her. "Yes."

Amanda wore a different outfit—nearly as hideous, but without the glasses. In lieu of the cargo pants—baggy gray sweatpants.

Sierra grabbed the pointer from under the counter and led Amanda to the Map Room. She explained the geography of Fleets Island and how it formed the southeast tip of Windmill Point. "To the south of the peninsula," she pointed on the map, "the Rappahannock River empties into the Chesapeake Bay." She showed a narrow peninsula shaped like an *S*. Her pointer landed on the northern curvature gap of the *S*. "This is Little Bay—picturesque with deep water." Amanda nodded, and Sierra continued, but she caught Amanda's continued glances towards Nora. "It's a mainstay for weekend sailors who like to drop anchor for the night."

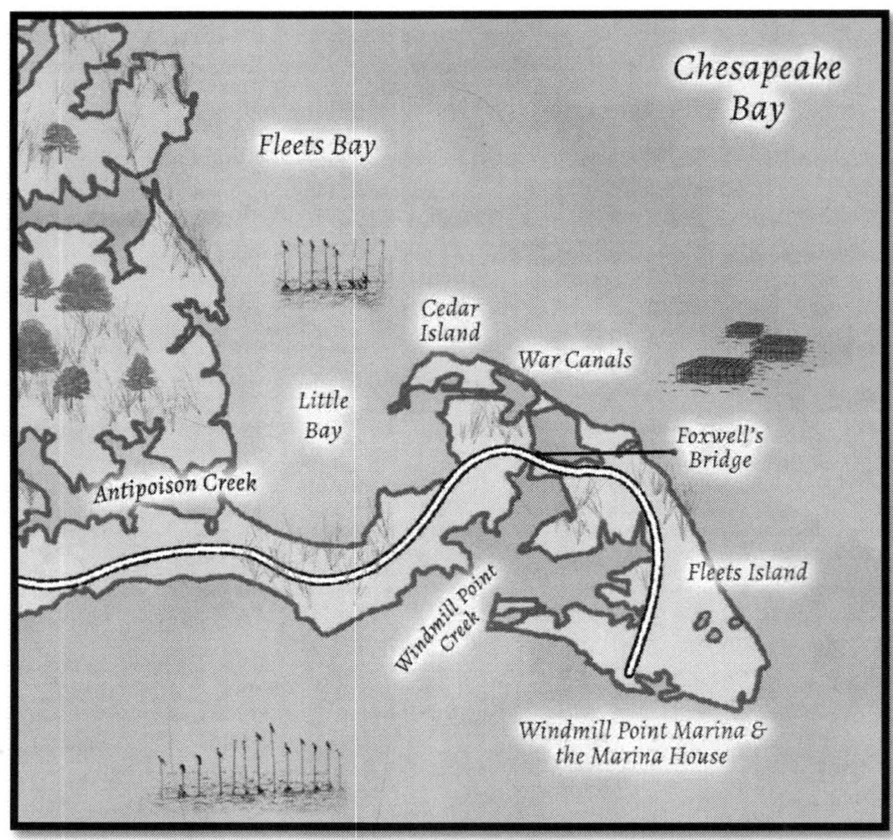

Sierra explained the effect the winds would have on their tour which could lead to trouble.

Amanda's eyes bounced between Sierra and Nora. Once Sierra finished the presentation, Amanda headed straight to the counter.

"Hi, Nora. So you're in charge now?" Amanda's voice was sympathetic.

Nora's voice cracked. "I think so."

Sierra entered behind the counter and gave her a small hug. "Just go to Aunt Kathi's."

Nora's tone was resolute. "No. Caleb will be here soon."

"Fine . . . but lock the door till he shows and put out the closed sign."

Nora reconsidered. "Maybe I'll go."

"Good." Sierra rubbed Nora on the back and looked at Amanda. "I'm ready. Let's go."

Amanda glanced compassionately at Nora as they left.

I think Nor has this woman wrapped around her pinky!

Amanda pointed to a Jeep parked street-side. Its aquamarine color stood out. "That's mine. Hop in."

Sneakers

Sierra seemed pleased with the Jeep, but Amanda said little as they motored out of town and headed east along the peninsula. Had it not been for her secret agenda tied to the tour, she would've engaged the girl more. Instead, she was making Sierra uncomfortable. Amanda was paying good money and wanted to make the most of it. It was critical they paddle a course that took them by the Marina House and much of her attention was consumed in how she'd broach the subject with Sierra.

Amanda snatched glimpses of the water on both sides of the road through breaks in the cornfields. *Good year*, she thought to herself, absorbing the slightest changes on their route, whether a newly constructed home or one gone into disrepair. She knew exactly where the paddleboard-kayak launch was, but she let Sierra guide the way and talk about the sights as if Amanda was seeing them for the first time.

On nearing Foxwells Bridge, Amanda asked, "Would you consider a counter-clockwise loop around Fleets Island?"

Sierra bit her lip.

"You think I ignored your presentation back at the shop?"

The girl shrugged.

Of course I ignored her . . . I was enamored by Nora. Amanda slowed down as they approached the bridge.

"Stop here for a moment," Sierra said. "It's safe. I'd like to check for my dad's tour."

Amanda stopped the Jeep at the center of the small bridge. They peered north and spotted a group of paddlers.

"They're moving at a snail's pace." Sierra pointed. "They're making a bee-line to that beach."

"Yes, I can see how tempting that would be."

"He's made a safe bet for them given the southeasterly winds." Sierra fought to hide the tremble in her voice. "I think we should do the same."

Amanda was too afraid to mention the threat of a storm. The side of the island where she wanted to go was doubly exposed.

Not long after arriving at the launch, Amanda shed the sweats and the oversized sun shirt to reveal a stylish black top and white shorts. She replaced her floppy hat with a sports cap. Sierra stared in disbelief. Her father had gotten this lady totally wrong—the toned woman appeared fit and had beautiful skin. Sierra seriously doubted her CPR training would be needed. Trying to cover for her caught stare, she said, "You're not wearing a swimsuit."

Amanda looked down at her Converse sneakers. "That's right. I don't plan to get wet except for my feet."

"I'm sorry. I forgot to offer you a pair of water shoes at the Shop. Are you going to keep those on?"

"Yes," Amanda said firmly, earning a nod from Sierra.

"Another point for her," Sierra spoke to herself. *She's no idiot—I'll save my lecture about rusty nails, broken bottles, and razor-sharp oyster shells.*

They found the three paddleboards partially concealed near the launch. "Belle of the Bay sandwiches for lunch!" Amanda yelled as she returned to the Jeep and grabbed a bag. "Sparkling water and chips too."

"You can put them in my cooler." Sierra pointed towards the rear of her board. "It seals watertight if you want to bring your phone."

Amanda's eyebrows rose. "My board doesn't have one?"

"No. It adds weight. We try to keep the client boards as light as possible. This one is a fishing paddleboard. I store my mobile radio in it."

Amanda pouted and joked, "You're not taking me fishing?"

Sierra returned a wry smile as she called out over her mobile radio, "*Paddleboard Alpha*, this is *Paddleboard Charlie*, come in Alpha."

Some moments passed before her father's voice crackled back. "I've got you loud and clear, Charlie."

"We're ready to launch." Sierra suppressed her excitement. So what if this was her first solo? She was going to be a professional.

"Roger that, *Paddleboard Charlie*. Be safe!" Her father's tone was encouraging, but even beneath the radio static, his voice sounded off— sad. Sierra remembered her father's strange behavior earlier. *Maybe it wasn't Amanda who caused it.*

Sierra stowed the radio along with the lunch into the cooler and sealed the lid. "If this were a fishing excursion, all the boards would be outfitted like mine." She grabbed the board using the center handgrip, tilted it, careful not to drag the fins, and gently set it into the shallow brackish water. Amanda followed cooperatively, appearing relaxed, but then straightened.

Girls Go-a-Paddlin'

Amanda waited until she was settled with her board halfway beyond the creek's edge before attempting a new tack. "Why is it you call me a client instead of a customer?"

"It's just the way my dad does it . . . how he trains us. He says customers buy products, like our fishing tackle. *Clients* are buying *us* and an experience. Customers come and go, but with *clients*, he wants to create enduring relationships."

Amanda muzzled the urge to howl in laughter. Not about the first part of what Sierra said, but the last—the man's concept for creating enduring relationships. *He's horrible with people!* Amanda nodded like she was pleased but only to soften Sierra.

"Why don't we start in Windmill Point Creek? I appreciate the recommendation you made at the Shop, but now seeing this in person, it's enticing." Amanda pointed towards the aperture to their south, concealing her intentions to proceed into the river and follow the shoreline east past her father's property. Her conscience needled her. The day had become confusing. Nora's big beaming eyes wouldn't let her go . . . and now Sierra, one with the water. *She reminds me of myself sixteen years ago.*

Sierra's reluctance to change plans was obvious. Amanda tried a subtle smile. "We'll have the added benefit of avoiding your father's tour."

It worked, and Sierra relaxed. "Okay, but I need to warn you, if those southeast winds pick up, it'll be a difficult paddle on our return. You may be thrown off your board." She wiggled her torso. "If you ever feel wobbly, just drop to the Indian position." Sierra demonstrated a squat with her knees protruding to her front.

"Okay, I'll remember that." Amanda attempted the same move, dropped to her board, and quickly returned to a standing position.

Sierra's approval showed in her eyes. "Did you play sports growing up?"

"I did. Many. Softball, basketball, soccer, skiing, and sail—" Amanda caught herself and swiftly added, "How about you?"

"Soccer." Sierra's smile gleamed.

Amanda hid her relief—preferring to avoid a sailing discussion and its ties to her local roots. "Then we have some common ground. Soccer and now paddleboarding."

"You seem fit. A natural balance on the board. We should be able to slog through the chop once we get to the Rappahannock."

"Thank you, Sierra. I feel comfortable." Amanda pushed herself free from the shore. "Let's give it a shot."

Sierra chased her into the flat waters of Windmill Point Creek.

Amanda took slow deep breaths of the salty air and closed her eyes. The rhythmic sound of a paddle stroking through the water intensified. Sierra was soon at her side.

"Do you like it? Most people don't like the smell of the mud flats."

"I do," she said in a long breath, not divulging the scent was pulling something wonderful from the depths of her core. She played dumb and asked Sierra what created the smells.

The prodigy spoke about the myriad life forms in the tidal marsh ecosystem—living and dying. Amanda may have seen herself in this young girl, but she soon accepted that Sierra understood the marshes and flat-water better than herself.

In high school, Amanda's focus had been on the deep waters of the Bay—the underwater contours and the trenches. Information which proved invaluable to her father and his fishing charter business. Larger species, like rockfish, cornered the baitfish along the ledges and fed.

It was her mother who encouraged her to study the fishing logs and notes they'd bought from Capt. Kip when they purchased his marina. The marina at Windmill Point had passed through many hands. After the market collapse in 2008, her parents acquired the property—and what would become their new home—for pennies on the dollar.

Capt. Kip's fishing logs contained decades of detailed data that included his catches correlated with salinity readings, water temperature, school migrations, and a species' predominant size. He could accurately predict when a particular fish species would have a banner year in the Northern Neck or when to expect a species drought. Although her mother encouraged her to absorb the logs and help her father's fledgling charter business, Amanda suspected her mother had purchased the logs for a different purpose.

These thoughts of her own mother aroused Amanda's curiosity about Sierra's. Sierra continued to mention her father, but never her mother. Amanda willed herself to be patient. *Tread carefully.*

Sierra had plenty to say about her father. *Fair game*, Amanda thought to herself. Follow-up questions ensued. Mostly about his business. His tours. Never anything that dug too deep into the man himself. *Why would I care?* Only to understand how he could be the father of two delightful daughters.

Their time turned even more relaxing, and while Sierra was more protective with what she said about her father, she was effusive with anecdotes of Nora, the girl without guile. Sierra spoke as if she were the proud mother. Amanda pegged Nora as the innocent girl she once was—and wished to return to—until life became complicated.

As they paddled towards the Rappahannock, Sierra's tone turned professional, like a museum docent. "The creek we're in now leads to the Civil War canals. That's where my dad took the Hen party. It connects the Rappahannock with Little Bay."

Amanda played along. "Is that so?"

"Yes, during the war, the South dug the canals to evade the Union blockade at the mouth of the river. The Confederates unloaded goods from their plantations onto barges where we are now, and then pulled them through the canals to Little Bay." Sierra waved her hands towards the east, beyond the river's mouth. "Once in Little Bay, they'd reload their cargo onto waiting ships and make a clean escape to the Chesapeake Bay."

"Interesting. Where'd you learn this?"

"From Gramps and Grans . . . and, of course, my dad. This is the way he tells the story to his clients. He's probably already told it to the Hens today. The canals are narrow and straight beyond Foxwells."

"What does he call them when he's not with his clients?"

Sierra's eyes narrowed enough to alert Amanda she'd slipped.

The girl hesitated before saying, "Slave canals. They were dug by slaves during the War of Northern Aggression."

Amanda chuckled and rolled her eyes.

Sierra snapped her head. "What did I say?"

"It was your reference to the *Union*. I do know a thing or two about the rape and pillage of plantations that occurred here during the Civil War. Does your dad still side with the South?"

"No, of course not! Our family fought on both sides." Sierra's tone was matter-of-fact. "We have roots going back to Jamestown."

Amanda shuddered. *Jamestown?*

"What's wrong?" the teen asked.

"Nothing . . . please go on." Everything was wrong. Thoughts of her mother . . . her father. So much of her own history connected to Jamestown. The strange letter. *My ring!*

Bewilderment clouded Sierra's face. "He avoids certain topics to not offend the clients."

Amanda wondered if he was code-switching, but she put a lid on it.

"We attend a diverse church. There aren't many like it here in the Northern Neck."

"How so?" Amanda narrowed an eye.

"Most churches here are either all white . . . or all black."

"Does your father take you?" She would have preferred to call him the *jerk*, but for the girls. It didn't make sense. Maybe Ted was right. *I've got him all wrong . . . and why am I working so hard to dislike him?*

"Not really. Mostly my grandparents, Gramps and Grans. He used to take us. We were more active in our church before . . ." Sierra missed a stroke.

Amanda could barely detect the incoming tide from her strokes. She pulled gently on her paddle and waited until Sierra was back alongside her. "Before what?" They glided in unison, but Sierra avoided her eyes. "I'm sorry. I didn't mean to pry."

They continued to paddle in silence. Sierra's countenance remained flat. They neared the creek's mouth, and Amanda freed Sierra from her gaze.

Amanda thought about her mother. Some dizziness hit her, and she dropped to her knees. Sierra's eyes would be on her. *Why hide my sorrow?*

Sierra's speech sounded very adult-like, and Amanda wondered who the girl mostly conversed with. Adults? Her good mother . . . Grandparents? Uncles? Aunts? Possibly all actively involved in her life. As an only child, it wasn't so different from Amanda's world. She had her parents all to herself.

Amanda recalled the day she'd been invited to dinner at the nearby retirement center, one of the finest in the Commonwealth. She was in high school at the time and remembered how uncomfortable she'd felt. A neighborhood friend of her mother's, who had recently moved into the facility, invited Amanda and her mother. They ate in the formal dining room. It was a rare outing in which her mother wasn't shy about wearing her ring.

An all-black staff served them, as if they were living out a scene from Margaret Mitchell's *Gone with the Wind*. The antebellum South! The worst part? Some of the staff had been her friends since middle school. Even now, the pit in her stomach ached.

A former Virginia First Lady sat opposite her at an adjacent table. Her son-in-law, now a US senator, was dining with her. Amanda's mother stood, grabbed Amanda's hand, and introduced Amanda to the fine Lady—a woman whom her mother had never spoken of. The Lady's face brightened, like it was the highlight of her year. How would the two—her mother and the Lady—have known each other?

The First Lady looked directly at Amanda while saying, "So, you're *Isabella*. I've heard so much about you, dear."

Amanda froze. Her mother stood proudly, but said nothing to help Amanda make sense of the moment.

Fortunately, her mother's friend spoke up. "Yes, Anne. This is the one, but please, let us not disturb you." Amanda considered it a polite rescue.

The First Lady stiffened. "This is no disturbance." Her rebuke directed towards Amanda's host was accompanied by a quick glare before a soft smile returned to Anne's face. "Quite a pleasure to have met you in person, Ms. West. I hope you enjoy your meal here." The woman's gaze moved to Amanda's mother. "Looks like you've done a fine job with this one, Mary," she spoke like they were old friends. Then the Lady's eyes fell to her mother's ring. "Let *me* not interrupt you all any longer."

Even now, Amanda wondered why the stranger doted on her. Even more so, addressed her by her formal name? *No one calls me Isabella!*

And her mother? The weird deference the woman showed to her mother! It should have been the other way around.

When had her mother and the Lady met? The annual Holly Ball? It was the Northern Neck's oldest social function, stemming from the area's colonial-era candlelit balls, conducted after Christmas. Her parents attended with her, both of them exceptional line dancers. It was an occasion for which her mother felt comfortable wearing the ring. Like herself, Amanda's kindred debutantes claimed descendancy from Virginia First Families, and she'd been crowned queen her senior year of high school. But even after all these years, something still didn't make sense: her meeting with the First Lady occurred long before Amanda attended her first ball.

Another image of her mother from the Holly Ball blasted Amanda like a lightning bolt. A glimpse of something else she'd noticed her mother wearing—but only for an instant.

"Are you okay?" Sierra's voice startled her.

Amanda fought to dam the river of memories as she felt Sierra's stare. *I'm being rude.*

Unable to staunch the flow, Amanda blurted, "My mother died when I was a teen."

Sierra dropped to her board, and Amanda caught her eyes. They were mixed with fear and gratitude. Grateful the silence had been broken, but afraid to speak. *Did her mother run off?* That would make sense, wouldn't it?

Amanda let some moments pass. The dizziness was gone.

Sierra seemed to gain some confidence and finally spoke, softly and carefully. "How'd she die?"

Their boards nearly touched. "Breast cancer. Much too young, and when I desperately needed her."

"How old were you?" Sierra's eyes mirrored Amanda's pain.

"Eighteen." Amanda inhaled a large breath. "My first year of college."

"I was eight."

The ache shooting through Amanda's chest doubled. *This isn't what I bargained for today.*

"I'm sorry."

She searched Sierra's eyes. The girl barely breathed.

Amanda spoke gently, "Sierra, if you ever need someone to talk to, I'm available. I'll give you my number after the tour. Text me, and we can chat."

The tension was gone from Sierra's voice. "Thank you." She raised herself.

Amanda followed her lead and stood up on her board. They'd drifted out of the channel, and the sandy bottom crept up beneath them. The water was clear, and several needlefish darted back and forth.

Sierra spoke with a tinge of bitterness, "My dad won't allow me to have a smartphone."

Amanda sunk her paddle through the shallow water and into the sand. "Why?"

"He says it will distract me from my studies."

"I'm sure of that and a lot of other things," Amanda said with a lighthearted laugh. "I may have to side with your father."

Sierra's brows furrowed.

What just happened? Amanda wondered. *I need to hate that guy.*

Amanda suspected Sierra was equally relieved to move off the subject of their mothers. "May I play the devil's advocate?" She hinted at a smile, but the girl was slow to respond.

Another strange feeling passed through Amanda. She cared that the young girl would trust her. *Why am I having these feelings?*

When have I ever cared about a child . . . a teen?

"Most of my friends have smartphones," Sierra said.

Amanda maintained her gaze.

Sierra dimpled a smile. "Okay . . . what do you advise?"

"Have your pleas been emotional?"

Sierra frowned, confused.

"We'll fix that," Amanda continued, not giving Sierra a chance to respond. "He won't know what hit him if you approach him rationally . . . and from his *own* perspective."

Sierra flinched, and Amanda regretted her words. She'd misplaced her anger from her own father to Sierra's. "I'm sorry. I didn't mean it like that."

"Oh, no. That actually makes sense." Sierra's genuine smile heartened Amanda. At least something was making sense to somebody.

Why, she wondered, did it feel like all reason and logic were spiraling out of control? On a day when she needed to be in command of both!

Lunch on the Beach

The pair paddled in unison for several more minutes and exited the channel. They were now in the Rappahannock River, and the view was expansive. To their left, the river's mouth spanned six miles wide as it emptied into the Bay.

Leaving Windmill Point Creek behind, the ladies continued a counter-clockwise course around the island, hugging the shoreline east towards the tributary's mouth.

"I'm sorry about this chop. The southeasterly wind brings it from the mouth of the Bay," Sierra stated flatly.

"No reason to apologize." Amanda pursed her lips. The paddling had become laborious. The increased struggle was evident in Sierra's face. Amanda bent her knees, helping her cushion the roll and pitch of the board. "You warned me."

"The Bay is absorbing the energy from these winds unchecked."

"Yes, I can see that, but the water is being oxygenated. That's a good thing, right?"

Sierra tightened her eyes and wrinkled her nose. "Yeah . . . not just for the fish, but also for the grasses and other sea life. Where'd you learn this?"

Amanda paused before answering. "I might've paid attention in a science class . . . but I wouldn't swear to it . . . I was distracted by the boys." She added a wink.

Sierra nodded but her nose wrinkled all the way to her brow.

"Where'd you learn it . . . your father?" Amanda asked.

"Yes, but Grans too." Sierra raised her fists, one hand holding her paddle, and gestured dramatically. "She makes this funny speech about the wind, the waves, and the water."

Amanda startled, but quickly recovered her balance. Her own mother spoke similar truths. She had never known her mother to be more passionate about any subject.

Sierra pointed with her paddle. "It will be clear sailing once we round that jetty."

Around the jetty? Amanda knew exactly what was around the jetty, and she shuddered. They were only moments away from sighting her home. A home she hadn't seen in nearly ten years. Her heartbeat quickened.

When the country home on the rise came into view, her memories ran rampant, the weight of them coming down on her like Niagara Falls.

"What do you say we stop for lunch?" Amanda looked straight across the yard to the marina. *Good timing*. Her father's charter boat, the *Queen Mary*, wasn't in its slip. She pinched herself.

It did nothing to help her nerves. She could only hope the girl didn't notice she was trembling.

Sierra's stomach growled. Even her arms felt sore. "Yeah, we can do that." She hid her relief. The lady, who'd walked into the Shop limping, initially appearing overweight and out-of-shape, wasn't fatigued. *Dad was so, so . . . wrong about her.*

"Beach up by that house over there?" Amanda pointed towards a picturesque farmhouse. "Nobody seems to be home, and we can stay hidden behind that small dune."

Sierra was relieved. "That'll work."

"You're not worried about trespassing?" Amanda teased.

"As long as our feet are in the water, we won't be trespassing. If someone complains, we'll pick up and move to the next beach."

"Great, cuz I'm starving."

"Me too." Sierra's tone filled with trepidation. What had Amanda packed for her? She'd seen the Belle of the Bay on the menu at the Yokel, but had never ordered it—a portobello mushroom sandwich with roasted peppers and avocado. *No way!* She remembered the chips and sparkling water. *I've survived on less.*

After pulling the boards onto the beach, Amanda handed out the sandwiches. Sierra took a small bite, eyed the sandwich, then sunk her teeth into it. "Wow, this is really good!"

Amanda twisted her face. "To the hungry soul, every bitter thing tastes sweet."

"No, I'm serious." The sandwich was sticking to her bones.

"It's very healthy. What do you normally order? No, let me guess . . . chicken tenders?"

"Close." Sierra spoke with a pinch of shame. "I like the chicken sandwich." She was afraid to mention it was the fried variety.

Sierra remained attentive to Amanda's lecture on the health properties of the peppers and the avocados. Why not? The lady across from her was fit and beautiful.

"How about the mushrooms?" Sierra asked.

"Well, those are healthy, too. Low in saturated fat, an excellent source of magnesium, and even selenium."

Sierra brightened. Her father was no health nut. Not by

intention—he juggled too many balls. *Mom would've kept this part of our lives in order.*

Sierra wiggled her shoulders when she said, "Your skin is so clear," but didn't say she thought Amanda's skin radiated.

"Healthy foods will help you with that. You need good *oils*." Amanda's tone was understanding. "The sun will also help your complexion, but you need to be careful."

How many times had her father said the same thing? Sierra had her mother's fair Irish skin, and she rarely ventured out on the water without a sun shirt.

They dabbled their toes in the water while they ate. On several occasions, Amanda glanced over her shoulder back towards the farmhouse. Whether there had been any activity, or not, Sierra ignored it.

Amanda reached for her sneakers. "Do you mind waiting here for a moment? I need to relieve myself."

"Sure. When I need to go, I just hop in the water."

The woman made a funny face.

My method isn't good enough for her?

"Okay, I'll be right back. I'm going to see if I can find a bathroom." Amanda donned her shoes and dashed up over the small berm and across the lawn. The limp was gone.

Sierra turned and looked over her shoulder, but the lawn's steep grade shielded her view of her client. Something didn't feel right—Amanda had been too abrupt.

A faint rumble sounded in the distance. Sierra sent her eyes to the horizon. A storm was approaching from the southwest. Predictable. With eighty percent humidity, the midday thunderstorm developed over the Bay and was right on schedule. Where it would hit was anybody's guess.

What does Grans say? About feeling a storm in her bones?

No doubt, Sierra felt this one in her bones.

Escape

The sand gave way beneath Amanda's feet as she scrambled up the small dune berm. It was behind her now, along with the girl, and a majestic home stood before her. A large, gently sloped yard was all that lay between her and the Marina House.

How long would she have until Sierra became suspicious?

The weekend was going from bad to worse. Why did it have to be a girl like Sierra placed in her path? She couldn't have been in the house more than fifteen minutes before hearing Sierra's knock. Now she realized she'd need hours inside scouring for the ring.

And now the sight of her father! She peered again around the corner of the Marina House towards the docks. His gaze targeted the sky and then his attention turned to a customer who'd lowered their car window to talk with him. The distraction was a godsend and could buy them time to escape.

Amanda's gut twisted. She kept her head low, scrambled back to Sierra, and grabbed the girl's arm. "Let's relaunch." Amanda glowered at the beach. "We can try to get ahead of the storm."

Fear filled the girl's eyes. "We can't retrace our path. The winds and waves will make it impossible to return to the creek."

Amanda tugged at Sierra and began sprinting across the yard. She looked back over her shoulder. "Didn't you say we could return via the slave canals?"

Sierra caught her breath, "Yes, but the storm will overtake us before we reach the entrance."

Amanda grabbed Sierra's shoulders. "Are you scared of the storm?"

"No. But I have respect for it. I know what to do if we're caught in it out on the water." Sierra looked up towards the darkening sky. "It's not the storm that kills you, but *how you respond to it*."

Amanda stiffened. How often had her mother used those exact words? As a competitive sailor, they never took chances with the weather. The mast of a sailboat could act as a lightning rod. It wasn't unusual for a sailboat to be struck by lightning. Although her father avoided storms, she'd still weathered through several with him. Far more than she cared to count.

"Sierra, would you feel safe in *this* storm out on the water?" Amanda looked into the threatening sky. *We need to get off the beach!* The guilt of what she was doing made her nauseous. She fought for breath as they hid behind the berm. Amanda didn't doubt herself. Lightning striking a beach was the worst of killers.

"Possibly. My father told me what to do in cases like this. He'll be very upset with *me* if he learns we didn't shelter in place."

"If you feel comfortable out on the water, I'll take the heat with your father. He doesn't need to know we stopped here. I need to get away from this house. We'll find another one."

Sierra shrugged. The fight was gone.

Amanda nodded. "Okay, I owe you."

"I just want to get off the beach," Sierra said, while Amanda grabbed Sierra's board and pulled it into the water.

"Yes, feet off the sand!" Amanda yelled, returning to her own board. *This is crazy.*

In the urgency to launch, Amanda wondered about the radio. Maybe a callout would be prudent. *No, I don't want to explain it to the jerk.* Sierra was still flustered, and the radio remained powered off in the cooler.

This whole thing is crazy! How did I end up here with this girl? A fresh dose of anger pumped through Amanda's veins.

But this time it was directed at herself.

CHAPTER 5

A Storm

Jeb parked in the rear and burst into the Shop. "Have you heard from Sierra?" he said, dripping sweat.

Caleb jolted and pushed himself up using the counter. "No sir, I haven't seen her, sir."

"I meant on the radio." Jeb tried to slow his words. "She's leading a tour."

"Oh." Caleb's eyebrows rose a notch. "No, sir."

Jeb pulled out a small towel from under a workbench and wiped his face. "She called out when they launched but I haven't been able to get through to her since."

"Storm? The storm, right?"

"Yes, Caleb. I'm concerned." Jeb set his smartphone on the counter and adjusted the radar map on his weather app.

"They've issued small-craft warning alerts," Caleb said.

Jeb lifted his eyes. He wouldn't hold back the fear. "I cut my afternoon tour early." For a moment, he felt the room swaying.

"Yeah, that family didn't seem too happy when they returned. You missed them by ten minutes."

"We were beach hopping after launching from Little Bay," Jeb said, and then more sternly, "You need to understand something, Caleb. In this business we never take chances with lightning."

"I know what you're going to say."

Jeb waited, beckoning a response by raising his brows.

Caleb stood taller. "If someone gets struck, it's not only a tragedy—the business will go up in a puff of smoke."

Jeb nodded again. The muscles in his face strained. On any other day, he would've wrapped his arm around Caleb's shoulders. The teen was earning more of his trust. As Kat had accused earlier, Caleb was vetted. "For heaven's sake," she told him, "you've practically raised him as your own these last three years."

"Knowing Sierra, the radio is probably turned off in the cooler. Saving the battery." Caleb glanced over his shoulder. "Oops." His eyes came back to Jeb, and the teen gritted his teeth. "I missed that she was out."

The call-sign *Paddleboard Charlie* was boldly inked on the dispatch whiteboard with Sierra's name assigned to it—in her own handwriting!

Jeb's convention for the call-signs kept the tours organized regardless of who was leading them. Written in blue dry-erase ink, the morning's tour was designated *Paddleboard Alpha*. Jeb's afternoon tour received the suffix, *Bravo*. Sierra's tour, scheduled last—*Charlie*.

"Where'd they launch from?" Caleb asked.

"Foxwells. I returned there *before* and *after* my afternoon tour . . . should've seen them in the slave canals this morning." Jeb held back his other concerns. *More freedom for the girls?* It made his stomach queasy.

He didn't trust the lady with the limp. A Jeep was parked at the launch, not the client's car he'd seen earlier at the Shop. He found—

and retrieved—one of the three paddleboards he'd left at the site. Untouched!

Did the crazy woman bail on the tour? Maybe she was leading interference for the guy? Jeb didn't like where his thoughts led him, and he wouldn't dare tell Caleb. Jeb's chest squeezed tight, and he could barely breathe. He didn't know what was worse. The storm threatening its rage outside? Or the one within?

Would Sierra push back if she suspected foul play? Maybe something else transpired. Would the couple have attempted to double on a board? The woman did seem helpless. Either way, where had they gone?

Time stood still. He must have closed his eyes because he felt Caleb nudge his shoulder. Jeb shook his head. "I should've sent her out with a phone."

Caleb gave nothing away with his eyes. "I always go out with mine."

"I know, Caleb, but Sierra doesn't have one, and neither does the Shop." He couldn't fully express his concerns to Caleb and now felt small in the young man's eyes. He should've planned for a situation like this—protected Sierra better. And even worse, Caleb would've cared for her more! The kid was so conscientious. Beyond his years. *Had Caleb only arrived earlier! I could've sent him out with that nut job.*

Thoughts of the woman rattled about his head. *How'd she do it?* He gave in far too easily. His heart sank again. *I've never done that for anyone . . . except Erin.* Fell into a trap. *Rashest decision I've ever made!*

Jeb glanced about the Shop. *I wonder if she stole anything?*
Maybe my daughter.

Bones

Ralph's phone buzzed. He wiped his hands on his shirt before answering. He and his wife, Maria, were staking tomatoes in the garden.

His son's tone on the other end of the line was tense. "Hey, Dad. I'm on my way home." Jeb spoke fast. "I haven't heard from Sierra in a couple of hours and I'm worried."

"Where was she last?" Ralph glanced in Maria's direction. She pulled off her garden gloves and stepped closer to him. He toggled his phone to speaker mode.

"She took two clients out today on a private tour from Foxwells." Jeb sounded anxious.

"When did she start doing that?" Ralph's eyes locked onto Maria's.

"Today, but it doesn't matter. I'll explain later. Do you see the storm?"

Ralph stepped towards the yard's edge by the rip-rap. He stood on a large boulder and had a clear view of the sky. What he saw sucked the air right from his chest. His arms dropped limp to his sides. After a few small waves slapped the rip-rap, he raised the phone and spoke without any emotion. "Yes, about ten miles southwest." His eyes widened. "It's a bigun." Now, Ralph wished he hadn't said it, because when he glanced back at Maria, her face was colorless.

"I've been tracking it via my radar app. Would you mind readying the boat for me? I'm about five minutes out."

"Of course!" Ralph's shoulders straightened. "I'll join you." He ended the call and pocketed his phone.

Maria stood rigid on the patio-deck, facing the Bay. She was trembling as she looked to the west. "I see it in the skies . . . blowing through the trees . . . and on the water!" She reached for him and clasped his hands. "I feel it in my bones."

Their eyes locked as he took her hands in his. Goosebumps struck his arms. He recognized her words . . . spoken like his own mother . . . a retelling of a family tale. They closed their eyes, and he offered a brief prayer. Maria stopped trembling, as he turned toward the dock. She pulled him back.

"Thank you," she said.

He gave her hand a quick squeeze.

"I love you." Her lips came to his for a moment. "You're a good man, Ralph Carter."

Then she pushed him away, and Ralph hustled to the dock.

He wasted no time lowering the thirty-two-foot *Galleon* into the water using the heavy-duty electric lift. The boat's two three-hundred horsepower outboard engines were revving by the time Jeb's truck pulled into the driveway. Ralph spotted his son heading towards the dock in a determined jog, his tormented eyes on the horizon. Deploying the boat would be more for show than anything else. With so many square miles of open water to search and Sierra not wearing a beacon, the chance of finding her out in the storm was doubtful. But at least they could put themselves in her likely vicinity once the storm passed, their visibility restored.

Ralph flipped on the marine radar unit and stepped outside the pilothouse. The wind whistled by his ears, and the open-array antenna rotated above. He rarely used the radar, but these conditions warranted it. The sky was darkening. He reentered the pilothouse and cast his eyes on the display. Distant flashes in the sky correlated with the returns on the radar. He hadn't underestimated the storm and could see it was localized. It was packing a huge punch and bearing down on them. More concerning was whether his son would overreact.

Jeb detached the dock lines, jumped on board, and stuck his head in the cabin's door. "I've never been more grateful for this pilothouse."

Ralph acknowledged Jeb with a wink and maneuvered the sleek vessel away from the dock. Once clear of the pilings, he hammered the throttles, launching most of the boat into the air.

"Whoa, Dad!" Jeb's hands raced to the console grips.

"It's my granddaughter. What'd you expect?"

Jeb slammed his hand down. "She's my daughter, Dad! My precious daughter!"

"I'm sorry, son. I'm not making light of the situation. I know you're worried."

"So, why did you do it?" Jeb yelled over the roar of the engines.

Ralph navigated into the deep-water channel. "To lighten you up."

"It's not working." Jeb gestured to the ominous sky and the lightning to their south.

"I have faith in her." Ralph nodded towards Jeb. His voice was reassuring. "You've taught her well."

Jeb stared blankly towards the horizon. "Well, you shouldn't have faith in me. I should've never let her out on her own!"

He'd seen Jeb tortured like this once before . . . nearly five years ago. The day he'd watched his son from the airport terminal. Jeb was on the tarmac, escorting Erin's coffin from the plane. Ralph felt his stomach knot. He reached over and grabbed Jeb's shoulder. "You're alright! She's alright! Positive thoughts, okay?"

Jeb turned pensive, as if in a daze. His eyes remained fixed on the horizon as the first raindrops splattered on the windshield. "There's going to be hail in that storm. I can see it . . . This boat's gonna take a beating."

"Who cares?" Ralph tapped gently on the console. "She can handle it. Don your preserver if you're worried."

"I think we should head towards Windmill Point . . . try to hug the shoreline. Knowing Sierra, she would've sheltered in place."

"And what if she didn't?"

"I suspect the winds will sail them our way." Jeb glanced at the speedometer. "And for heaven's sake, Dad, don't run 'em over!"

Oyster Cages

Amanda and Sierra launched from the beach and frantically paddled mere minutes before being overtaken by the storm. The winds picked up and thrashed cold rain at them in horizontal sheets. They were completely blinded except for some visibility to the north, opposite the direction of the incoming torrent. Whitecaps rose ominously, jettisoning them around the tip of Windmill Point. Few houses existed along the stretch due to the shoreline's low elevation, which was mostly strips of sand. Their bodies had become sails to the wind, so they abandoned their standing positions and attempted to paddle Indian style. It was hopeless—the wind and waves slapped them off their boards. They lost their ability to navigate, and the winds hurled them northwest towards Fleets Bay.

Amanda wiped her face and looked towards the west. It wasn't fear that gripped her, but guilt. The shoreline was so distant now. *Blown this far out? How'd that happen so fast?* Finding shelter in a home now was out of the question, much less regaining the land. She only hoped Sierra wouldn't notice their plight.

"You'll need to get low and flat on your board. The lightning's getting closer!" Sierra yelled, edging herself back onto her board. She pulled out her anchor rope and tossed an end to Amanda. "Tie this on so we don't get separated!" she pointed to the bungee straps on the back of Amanda's board. "Stow your paddle."

Amanda marveled. Panic hadn't overtaken the girl.

Amanda was content to follow Sierra's lead—to a point. She wondered whether the girl would maintain best water safety practices under the changing conditions. *Strange. This girl is so in her element. As if she was made for it.*

The storm's menace continued as they skirted the coastline, floating like bobbers in the chop. "Are you getting cold?" Sierra called out.

Amanda flashed a smile that probably came off more like a grimace. Her teeth chattered. "I think we lost twenty degrees." The chill had set in some time ago, and she would have preferred not to think about it. *My little adventure is going from bad to terrible. How will I explain this to Sally and Ted?*

"We'll get the heat back once this passes. We can drag behind our boards. Safer from the lightning, too, just as long as you aren't touching the bottom. Don't let go of your board!" Sierra said, then added, "Make sure your tether is attached before hopping off."

"Good point." Fear and doubt laced her voice, and she could barely hear her words over the howling winds.

She admitted to herself that she hadn't considered the risk of losing her board, and by the looks of it, a very expensive one. As a sailor, in the event of capsizing, she'd been taught to stay with the boat. *Makes sense. But this isn't sailing!*

Bolts of lightning shot down around them like Neptune's trident. A chill passed through her arms, and her heart pounded wildly. The lightning spread across the surface of the water, a complete discharge. *Would the girl know this?* Amanda had rarely seen the phenomenon. If it could kill fish near the surface, how about them? She wondered whether Sierra realized the imminent danger. Better she not. *Why panic over something we can't control?*

The duo, both tethered to their boards, and the boards tethered to each other, dropped into the water. It felt at least ten degrees warmer than the air and the pounding rain.

"I'm glad I left my phone!" Amanda yelled, trying to relieve the tension. She no longer shivered, and the color of Sierra's lips returned to normal.

"Why?"

"It'll *survive* in the Jeep!" she said, instantly regretting her word choice. Her cap tore loose in the wind. "Ahhh!" She batted at it with her hand, but it was long gone.

The storm brought darkness, and with it, hail. Amanda tried to duck as cold pellets peppered her head and shoulders. "Ouch, ouch . . . ouch!"

"Amanda!" Sierra yelled, "Try pulling your life jacket over your head!"

Both removed their safety preservers and attempted to shield their heads with the buoyant foam. As the raging chop played unmercifully with the paddleboards, the tethers—attached to their ankles—toyed the ladies like a yo-yo, jettisoning them back and forth while they stared up into the storm. They synchronized gasps for air in the troughs of battering swells.

Amanda coughed up a mouthful of saltwater. "This isn't working!"

"Same here! I'd rather breathe."

They re-donned their life jackets while still being pulled on their backs, and covered their faces with their arms.

"A little better," Amanda said between repeated "ouches."

The frozen balls splashed amidst the swells. While Amanda was more demonstrative, Sierra was wordless. For a moment, Amanda heard Sierra whimpering through the pelting, but the wind soon drowned her feeble sounds. *Oh God, what have I done?*

"The hail is hitting my legs!" Sierra cried.

"I'm so sorry, Sierra. I shouldn't have put you through this!"

Sierra struggled for air between wave crests.

"Sierra, what's that?" Amanda eyed an obstruction in the water, battered by the surf, ominously growing larger as the boards dragged them swiftly towards it. It wasn't far from where she'd seen one of those horrible lightning strikes.

Sierra struggled for a breath and looked up, her face ashen. "The oyster floats!"

Over an acre's expanse of cages, seeded with oysters, lay ahead. The bay's chop crashed irregularly against the steel support structures, and froth soared high into the air like a battered rocky coastline. Now, the pain from the pelting hail seemed insignificant as the gusts dragged them closer to what Amanda feared would pulverize them.

The boards whipped wildly about in front of them—the wind claiming all its authority. They instinctively attempted to unfasten the tethers from their ankles, but to no avail. The boards yanked at their legs forcing them precariously on their backsides in the violent surf.

Amanda cried out, "Oh God! Protect her! I don't care about me . . . just protect her, dear God!"

A bolt of lightning illuminated the cages, enough to see they had only mere moments before being hurled on them. The blackened sky and the salty foam spun in her eyes. She was on the verge of a blackout. *Not a bad way to go I guess. Death will take me unaware.*

Another blinding flash of light split the darkness. Was it that or her own blazing anger? Anger towards her father! Was he to blame for this? There were pains of guilt, too. Strangely, both emotions were overtaken by concern for the girl struggling to survive next to her. Amanda opened her eyes.

A wave of compassion swept over her, and a blast of adrenaline came in its wake . . . a strength and passion Amanda didn't know existed. She dove into the water and searched for Sierra, clambering in all directions with outstretched hands. Amanda found Sierra's leg and traced down it, before Amanda's board yanked her away. She came up for a gulp of air and returned, finally finding Sierra's tether. Amanda followed it to Sierra's ankle and removed it.

Amanda thrust her head to the surface. "Swim!" she yelled before the force of the two paddleboards yanked her back down, as if they alone controlled her destiny.

Amanda struggled to surface for a long half-minute. The boards' erratic movements fighting each other transferred to her leg. Her lungs craved for air when her head finally popped up out of the water.

"Stand, Amanda! Stand!"

How long had the girl been screaming? Amanda attempted to turn her body erect, and by doing so, felt the sandy bottom hit her feet. The water was only four feet deep near the cages. *I should've known this*, Amanda scolded herself. She drove her body down hard, and fought the tension from the yanking boards. She planted her feet on the bottom and launched out of the water.

Sierra was now doing the same, but without the struggle of the boards at her ankle. *She's safe, God! That's all that matters now. She's safe. Thank you, God!*

Sierra maintained her position, bobbing up and down.

Amanda continued to bounce off the bottom, but fought to prevent the boards from smashing against each other. She gingerly meandered away from the cluster of metal floats towards Sierra.

Amanda sucked in a deep breath and exhaled. She felt lighter and glanced towards Sierra, who must have been thinking the same.

The girl spoke, "I want to re-tether."

A wave slapped Amanda in the face. "Alright . . . good. Anything to worry about ahead of us?"

"Pound nets, but they're a good ways off." Sierra located her tether and refastened it.

The bungee pulled Sierra more viciously after she bounced off the sandy floor, so Amanda had to drive down to compensate. It gave the girl an extra breath on each bob.

Once beyond the floats, they resumed trailing the boards, their bodies floating flat on the water while they gripped the boards' tails. Their pace accelerated.

With the squall subsiding, Amanda looked over to Sierra and smiled. Fear still held its grip on the girl, and Amanda extended her hand.

Sierra took it and relaxed, holding back tears.

Dolphin Dance

Within a half hour, the storm had fully passed, and the waves diminished. When the sun returned, it wasn't long before the ladies were upright on their boards. Amanda paddled alongside her guide, reached over, and put her arm around her.

"I'm sorry." Amanda felt the urge to retch. She fought back the desire to explain her panic and reasoning for leaving the Marina House. Why involve the girl in her own conflicts? *What a lame excuse.* Her insides weighed her down.

Sierra's palm covered the lower half of her face as she sniffled.

"Sierra, you did a good job." Anger flickered in Amanda's tone—anger reserved for her father . . . and possibly Sierra's own father. *What was that idiot thinking?* But then she saw reason. *No, not him.* "I'm to be blamed for this."

The girl wouldn't face her.

"Please, Sierra, don't hold this against me." She looked intently into the girl's face, searching for forgiveness. "Will you promise me that?"

It didn't come.

They paddled effortlessly in silence north to the edge of Little Bay and the Antipoison Creek channel. The water darkened as they approached an underwater ledge—the sandbar dropping to over thirty feet.

Sierra broke the silence. "I need to call my dad. I'm sure he's worried." She kept her face turned away and wouldn't let her eyes meet Amanda's. Several long moments passed, and the water exploded.

Sierra screamed, "Amanda, look! Dolphins!"

Amanda aligned her sights to Sierra's target, then waited for the next burst to appear. Several dolphins breached and chuffed, sounding through their blowholes.

"Awesome!" *How did she spot them before me?*

"They must've found the mackerel!" Sierra yelled as they neared the frolicking pod.

Dolphin pairs jumped straight out of the water and collided vertically. *Chest bumps?* Amanda thought about all the strange phenomena she'd seen in the Bay, including a few whales, but nothing like this. The chest bumps were not a coincidence. It occurred repeatedly with countless pairs.

Sierra drifted into the middle of the display while Amanda remained outside of the pod. She kept her eyes fixed on the girl and gaped in awe as the dolphins encircled her. From the tip of her toes to the top of her head, her body tingled. How many minutes had it been since staring down death? Now this wild feeling of freedom and ecstasy. *What's going on here?*

Sierra stopped paddling, pivoted on top of her board, and acknowledged each pair as they leaped completely out of the water. She glanced towards Amanda and silently mouthed the word "Wow!" while spreading her arms.

The dolphins leaping close to Amanda deserved similar praise. Still holding her paddle, she clapped. Water exploded behind her; she'd missed a pair.

They stowed their paddles, and the performance continued for ten more minutes. They added "oohs and aahs" to their applause for the breaching pairs as if they were watching a fireworks display. Amanda remained breathless and shook her head in wonder.

Sierra eventually pulled out the mobile radio from the cooler, powered it on, and called out, "*Paddleboard Bravo*, this is *Paddleboard Charlie*. Do you read me, *Paddleboard Bravo*?"

She waited a few seconds before hailing again. Several moments passed and Sierra shrugged.

"Now I'm wishing I—" Amanda spoke, ready to mention her smartphone, but a male voice crackled over the radio and cut her off.

"*Paddleboard Charlie*, we read you. This is the *Galleon*. What's your twenty, over?" Amanda recognized the relieved voice as Sierra's father.

"*Galleon*, we're not far from the pound nets off Cedar Island, over." The poor girl trembled.

She's afraid of him. Amanda knew the feeling all too well. *But it wasn't always like that . . . only after Mom died.* Her body convulsed. *Why am I so consumed by him? My father! This could've been a great day, but I've made a wreck of it!*

"Roger that, Sierra. We'll be right over." The father's tone turned stern. "Just hang close to those nets. Over."

Sierra's shoulders sagged. "My dad's on his way. We need to paddle over towards the pound nets."

Amanda understood. Sierra was afraid of a tongue lashing by her father . . . She might even fear being embarrassed in front of Amanda. Well, that certainly wouldn't happen on her watch. *If that man crosses the line again, I'm going after him!*

A self-satisfied smile settled upon Amanda's face, but it didn't last. She sighted the pound nets and bit her lip as she paddled alongside Sierra. *I need to take responsibility for this.*

Pound Nets

The nets had been a staple for Jeb with his family tours. An invention from the early 1900s, they were emplaced with loblolly pine stakes along the edges of the Chesapeake Bay shoreline where the water depth dropped steeply. The ones near Cedar Island captured numerous cownose rays and stingrays as a byproduct. If the waters were smooth, he'd bring the clients carefully alongside the heart of the nets. They gawked from their front-row seats—hundreds of wild rays thrashing before them. He often wondered what would happen if someone accidentally fell off their board and into the pen. How would his insurance company view that mishap? They certainly wouldn't be keen on it. It was a calculated risk, and thus far, paid dividends with satisfied customers.

Jeb's pulse beat in his throat. Even though he and his father stayed dry in the *Galleon's* pilothouse, the V-shaped hull took a beating. Fortunately, their course towards Windmill Point put the bow head-on into the five-foot waves. The lightning was nerve-racking, a feeling of foreboding. *I failed Erin! Now Sierra? What was I thinking?—that woman! Whoever she was, paralyzed my good judgment.*

Had Sierra found refuge, she would've already called on the radio, or from a landline. She must be adrift.

After Sierra's radio hail, a wave of relief hit him, but it was short-lived. Anger worked its way into his bloodstream, and he tightened his jaw.

His father squeezed his shoulder. "She's alright, son. She's tough and smart. She'll be alright!"

Jeb remained silent, vowing self-control. He wouldn't vent his ire at Sierra. *I failed her.* He still needed to take care of the clients. *I'll maintain a good bedside manner—I don't want to be sued.* There was absolutely no reason for them to have been out on the water. *Adrift! Should've never happened.*

The limping lady seemed like the type of person who'd sue him. As soon as he could settle with the clients and get them on their way, he'd have words with Sierra. Privately. He wouldn't embarrass her in front of Gramps and Grans . . . and especially not in front of the clients. He was better than that.

But I want to know what happened!

The water turned flat. Amanda looked up and took in their current surroundings, reliving a pleasant memory; Cedar Beach was at her portside. The beach island had been a Sunday hangout with her high school friends. A time for summer volleyball, cookouts, and swimming. Exclusive. Accessed only by boat or jet-ski.

Amanda estimated the storm passed by them fifteen minutes before it struck the *Galleon*. The paddlers loitered around the pound nets, but Sierra showed no interest in small talk about the rays. The enthusiasm, which infused the start of their day, was absent. An uncomfortable moment was approaching with each crash of the *Galleon* battling through another wave to their north. From the core of her being, Amanda longed for redemption, but Sierra was mostly ignoring her.

"Sierra, I have a question for you." Amanda steadied herself by holding a tall piling. "What would you've done had the water been cold, say fifty degrees? Like, what if our tour had been in November . . . or December?"

Sierra flinched. "We would've never ventured out in cold water."

"Even though we both had life preservers on?"

Sierra's voice was robotic, and her face set. "The danger is the cold water. Our bodies would be in shock had this been November. It wouldn't be long before we'd be dead of hypothermia or cardiac arrest. If my dad had fitted us with dry suits, that'd be different."

"Where did you learn this?" Relief filled Amanda's voice. The girl was talking. *It's not all about me. She's worried about her father.*

"My father, of course—and Gramps and Grans are constantly lecturing us about water safety." Sierra's voice trailed off as she dragged her paddle.

"Yes, but from whom did you *first* learn this?" Amanda said softly, echoing Sierra's melancholy.

"My mother." Sierra's voice came firm.

Amanda's eyes locked on the girl's. "Yes, I know." The approaching vessel, now hurtling towards them, drowned her words. The pair instinctively dropped to their knees, anticipating a sizable wake.

Sierra's eyes moved towards the vessel. Amanda blew out a thick breath. The awkward moment was averted. How could Amanda explain it to her? That her own mother held a weird obsession about survival in cold water versus warm.

Amanda had an uncanny sense the girl was being groomed under a regimen of culture, history, and life experiences not so different from her own at the same age.

The day's additional strange coincidences didn't help her suspicions, but those thoughts were sidelined. It was time to face Paddleboard Guy.

Rescue

The boat came off plane and edged alongside them, having produced the smallest wake. Amanda recognized Sierra's father. *Ugh.*

An older man, wisps of gray hair escaping his cap, pulled back on the throttles. *Must be the grandfather.* He extended his head through the pilothouse window. His cheeks were fat and friendly, and he grinned a toothy smile. His wink said it all, "What, you didn't trust me?" The man's eyes were like those of his son's, electric blue, but the grandfather's were vibrant and full of joy. *Nothing wasted on that man!*

Amanda absorbed Jeb's demeanor. His attention was fixated on his daughter. Amanda's pulse quickened, and she readied herself for battle.

She felt the eyes of the grandfather on her. He had the oddest expression. She met his gaze, and he flinched. He cocked his head to the side and then seemed to pull back in surprise.

Amanda didn't know what to think as she blew the salt water from her mouth.

The older man moved his gaze to Sierra.

Sierra's gaze bounced between the men, as if seeking affirmation. Jeb ignored his daughter, while the grandfather, whom she presumed to be "Gramps," nodded towards Sierra and mouthed the words, "It's okay, it's okay."

Jeb pulled off his shirt, tossed it aside, and dove off the stern. His head popped up alongside Sierra's board, followed by his broad shoulders.

Sierra's face was tight and pale, showing a good dose of fear. She slid off her board and floated. Jeb grabbed her head in his arms, bringing it close to his chest. He brushed her hair back and kissed her forehead, treading the water and remaining silent. Seawater dripped down his face—*or were those tears?* Amanda's heart did a funny thing, and she hid her face behind her hair.

Gramps, too, was absorbing the moment between Sierra and her father. Amanda parted the hair in front of her face and smiled at him. Surely, he sensed her embarrassment. He returned a look of understanding, but didn't break the silence.

Amanda willed herself not to be softened by the girl's father, but she was failing. Maybe he didn't have ice water running through his veins after all. *Didn't my daddy once love me like this?*

Jeb hadn't really noticed the woman when his dad pulled the boat up alongside the two. He only saw the girl with strawberry blonde hair and vibrant green eyes. *Erin!* Erin as she looked as a teenager. The time he first caught sight of her in a lake in Pennsylvania. He'd never forget Erin's green eyes and the fiery Irish girl he'd quickly fallen for. Jeb succumbed to relentless teasing by his cabin mates that same night. He told them, "I don't know who she is, but one day, I'm going to marry that girl." It wasn't until the second week of summer camp that he finally got the nerve to say a word to her. His group was right behind the girls' team on a high ropes course. He told her, "Never forget to double-check your safety carabiner." She carefully turned around to face him, her eyes almost perfect circles. He'd never felt so awkward and dumb in his life, but he'd done it. He'd finally spoken to her.

"Mind your business," she snapped and turned her back to him.

He nearly jumped off the tower.

She turned back around and beamed at him. "I think you're cute."

He lost his balance and barely caught himself.

She giggled. "Don't be scared of me. I don't bite."

From that moment on, his confidence soared. She helped him overcome his fear of girls, but she warned him, "James Carter, it's fine for you to speak with me, but I don't want you getting any ideas for any other girl at camp." Her green eyes fired at him like lasers. "Do you understand me?" Her voice was firm and sincere. He'd never forget her special serious tone, and whenever he heard it, he always snapped to attention. "Yes, ma'am."

Now, seeing Sierra in the water, he remembered the last time he saw Erin alive. They were both so full of life and still very much in love, enjoying a vacation without the kids—a real second honeymoon in St. Croix. He was climbing the ladder of their snorkeling excursion catamaran. Jeb removed his mask and glanced back at her. He could still make out her green eyes—at a distance and through her mask, but he saw them. He saw the storm, too, not that different from today's, and moments later, the thud.

His heart pulled like the weight of a boat anchor. *When will this day end, Lord?* He felt guilt for being alive. His father's hand rested on his arm, and Jeb blinked back the vivid images. Anger worked its way back into his bloodstream. Anger about the mishap. Anger at himself for letting Sierra go out alone with clients. But Sierra was alive and looked no worse for wear. Why did she look scared? *Scared of me? If only she knew how much I love her . . . how I cherish both her and Nora.*

He tossed off his shirt and dove into the water. The hug came naturally. Sierra needed to know how much he loved her. Never to be afraid of her father . . . as much as she might feel like she was in trouble.

This was his doing. *In a rush to get out with those Hens I gave in to that crazy woman.* Loosening the reins had been reckless.

Jeb released Sierra, freeing his arms, and gently rotated in the water. A woman bobbed in the water and faced him, not that he could see her eyes. Those were obscured by her lovely veil of hair. He couldn't find his voice. *Where's her man?*

Sierra piped up, "Daddy, the lady from the shop . . . my client."

Jeb's eyes remained wide. Not really sure what to say. Then she parted her soaking hair, revealing amazing eyes. Intelligent and dangerously beautiful.

He swam to the stern. His father dropped the ladder, and Jeb climbed back onto the Whaler. The two trailed behind him, pulling their boards. He looked down, aghast. The paddleboards were cracked and splintering apart. How had they been able to stand on them? They'd been upright on them when the *Galleon* approached. Jeb lifted what remained of the paddleboards from the water and stowed them. Finally, he hoisted Sierra onto the deck, rubbing her head reassuringly as she passed on her way to the pilothouse.

The woman followed. He directed her to the ladder at the stern and extended his hand. When she met his grasp, he felt the softness of hers. His pulse quickened, and grasping her wrist, her pulse radiated to his other hand—strong and steady.

How could this be the woman from the Shop? Warm-blooded with a pulse? That woman had no figure. This one did, and it was well proportioned. He didn't remember her hair with any distinction. This lady's beyond shoulder-length hair, no longer obscuring her face, framed a portrait he hadn't previously noticed. One that looked better without makeup. If there had been any to begin with, it was all gone now. He resisted the urge to gape. *Beauty comes from deep within the soul*, he spoke to himself. *Don't be a fool, Jeb. This woman doesn't have one.*

The loose-fitting sun shirt was soaked and tight over her sports bra. He expected she'd be covered in tattoos, but he didn't spot any. Little else was left to his imagination, creating a small rush of embarrassment for letting his gaze linger.

Their eyes met, and his jaw loosened. Her eyes pierced and probed him, almost as if she was trying to surveil his innermost being. They were even deeper and more beautiful than what he'd seen while in the water. *What does she want?* He gave in to them a moment longer. *What does she want to know?*

He spoke in a friendly tone as if he'd never met her, "Hi, ma'am, I'm Jeb Carter."

Her tone held hurt. "Yes, I *know* who you are."

What was that supposed to mean? He barely recognized the voice, but it was her—the lady that cut in line at the coffee shop.

The lady that co-opted Sierra for the tour.

"I didn't introduce myself back at the Shop." He removed any hint of friendliness from his tone. *This is business.*

Her words were sharp, "You should have."

Yeah, he would have, but he'd been in a hurry. He mustered a plastic smile, just barely short of a smirk.

Her eyes weren't letting him go. He relented with a small nod. *Come on Jeb, lower the temperature. Don't let her get to you.*

"Humph." She raised her head a little like she'd won.

"I'm sorry about the mishap." Jeb put some apology in his voice. Not too much. She still needed to know he was annoyed. "You can dry yourself off in the cabin, and we'll get you safely back to your vehicle."

He grabbed a towel from under a bench seat and handed it to her.

She snatched it from his hands. "What mishap?" Her voice was feistier now, like how it had been in the Shop.

Jeb paused. *Let it go. Don't take the bait.* Her words said one thing, but her soft smile communicated something else.

She didn't give him a chance to respond. "Mr. Carter, I've had a remarkable adventure . . . and your daughter? Magnificent! A wonderful tour guide. I'll be paying an additional tip."

He matched her gaze. *They shouldn't have been out in the storm. She's setting me up to be sued. Don't admit negligence, Jeb.*

From the corner of his eye, he caught Sierra covering her mouth. He dared not look away from the woman.

"Mr. Carter, if you're alluding to the squall, I'm to be blamed—not your daughter! I pushed her when she advised against it." Her voice pleaded, "Please don't be angry with her. She practiced good judgment and provided safety instructions at every step of our tour."

The woman gripped both ends of her towel draped about her shoulders.

He was forced to align his feet with hers, facing her head-on.

Now her tone was laced with a touch of snarl. "Do I make myself clear, Mr. Carter?"

Jeb held his breath. He wanted to look away from her intense gaze, but with her fists grasping the towel by the sides of his face, he couldn't. He wondered if she was doing it intentionally. Why did she demand his eyes? And why had this suddenly become private—kept out of view of his father and daughter?

He finally sucked in a deep breath and sealed his lips. He'd have words with Sierra later.

Her gaze slackened, and this time his own penetrated to her soul. As fiery as this woman was, she was also lost and lonely. The woman dropped the towel and began to wring out her hair without releasing him from her sight. The smallest smile turned at the corner of her lips. His heart rate quickened again. *That shouldn't be happening. Get a grip, Jeb.*

His father yelled, "Hold on!" He launched the *Galleon* up on plane and made a tight turn north, back towards the Bay House.

The acceleration sent both Jeb and Amanda back a step. He bent his knees and recovered his balance. She grasped the handrail with one hand while her other smacked flat onto Jeb's chest.

She didn't appear to be in any rush to move it; her warm palm lay flat on top of his heart like a defibrillator paddle. He grasped her wrist and daintily lifted her arm away from him. More for show than anything else. As he moved her hand to the rail, he inspected her pulse again. Why not? Her beats came hard and fast beneath his thumbs. He wondered if his had stopped.

She glanced over her shoulder and cowered a little. "Sorry." What was it about her eyes? Every time she looked at him, they penetrated the deepest parts of him.

"No worries, ma'am. I think we can blame that on my father." Jeb kept his voice flat and arrested the urge to smile.

A sense of relief overwhelmed him. The woman was now taking in the sights of Little Bay, cutting him loose from her stare, and every other intoxicating thing about her.

Upon entering the pilothouse, Jeb found his father tapping gently on the console and whispering sweet words to his boat.

A few minutes passed, and the lady entered the cabin. She brushed his shoulder on the way, and grasped a console handle to steady herself.

Did she really bump me? Maybe his mind was playing tricks on him. He wasn't about to face her again. Jeb exited and found Sierra on the bench seat. He sat beside her and wrapped his arm around her.

His little girl was no longer just a little girl. Kat was right.

Trauma filled Sierra's eyes, and she shook in his embrace. It startled him. What had that lady put Sierra through? She's barely a teen! Who was the adult out there? Was the woman that stupid to challenge a storm? *Maybe she never ventures outside.* An ounce of common sense was all that was needed.

His anger boiled. *If she bulldozed me, how hard would it have been to overwhelm Sierra?*

He glanced over his shoulder. The woman was still in the pilothouse, immersed in conversation with his father. Her demeanor held no remorse, her manner exuding confidence, as if she owned the boat. As if she owned the whole Bay! More not to like about her. Her tanned legs? *Artificial!* he lied.

He dared not deny the woman's beauty, but what scared him was that she'd manipulated him without it. She was hideous at the Shop and he couldn't see her eyes, but still . . . she had her way with him. Most of all, he was angry about giving in to her wishes.

The way he'd yielded to Erin.

Chapter 6

Snowy Egret

Maria paced in the comfort of the Bay House as the brunt of the storm pounded the roof and decks. The sound was deafening. Nora shrieked each time the house shook from a nearby lightning strike. The lights flickered several times, and hail pinged off the windows and gathered on the decks.

The marine radio—stationed in the breakfast nook—pulled the tumultuous electrical storm from the atmosphere directly into the house. Maria would've preferred to turn off the crackling radio to prevent a power surge from blowing out its speaker, but she was desperate for any news from Ralph.

It had been nearly an hour since her husband and oldest son had sped off in the *Galleon,* navigating directly into the squall. And now Nora sat in the corner of the breakfast room whimpering.

Maria went to her and cradled her in her bosom. "Nora, we must be mindful of the salvation that may come from a storm."

Nora raised her chin, perplexed. "But Grans, my mommy died in a storm."

"I know, dear, but we must never lose hope. Your great-grandmother taught me this truth."

Call-outs from Sierra and Jeb finally crackled from the radio. *Sierra is safe!* Ralph would've alerted her otherwise. Right? *He should've called!* Maria took a sharp breath. *What distracted him from making a quick call?*

She grabbed her phone off the kitchen counter. "No!" she set the phone down. "I'd be a distraction." *He'll think I'm a worrywart.* She sighed. *It's in your hands, Lord.*

Maria waited ten minutes after the storm's passing before stepping out onto the porch. She inspected first for hail damage. She breathed a sigh of relief. Some limbs were down and scattered about the property, but nothing too serious. She'd check the rest of the island later with Ralph.

Their stately residence, a landmark of Bayberry Island, was situated at the mouth of Henry's and Indian Creek. Like many of the homes that dotted the western shore of the Bay, the family knew it as the Bay House, but this one was much more than that and came with a pedigree—a famous builder's dream home, an aesthetic masterpiece, and nearly invisible from the water. For such an expansive structure, with commanding views of the entrances to the creeks and the vast Chesapeake, it was a wonder how the effect had been achieved.

Maria planted her feet in the eat-in kitchen, stationed in the most strategic location of the entire house—behind the sink and the broad bay window. Her position commanded the best views of the southernmost tip of the property. From it, she could keep tabs on the deep tidal lagoon where the girls swam. She could monitor activity on their long dock, punctuated by a *T*, extending to deeper water, where the *Galleon* was usually stowed on its lift. From the builder, she'd learned the house was designed around the kitchen and its view. She never doubted it.

She looked down at her slip-on walking shoes. The pinewood floors showed their age—worn by the sand tracked in from her grandchildren. *No shame in that*, she thought. Maybe it needed a quick sweep. These were bittersweet years—time granted with Sierra and Nora born through tragedy. She wondered if she and Ralph would look back on the years and call them "golden." They were both still active and in good health, their lives filled with service and relationships.

Nora cried out from the porch, "I see them!"

Maria looked up. The *Galleon,* still on plane, approached the mouth of Indian Creek. Sierra sat with Jeb at the boat's stern. "Thank You, God," Maria sighed.

Wait, there's someone else. A woman. The party glided to the dock, soaked and rumpled, but all accounted for. The strange lady strode confidently, coming off the dock and making her way towards the house with Sierra.

Maria couldn't place the familiarity. Even a feeling of resonation. *How odd.* Ralph was a few steps behind the stranger and looked perky—the same look he wore when bringing Maria a big striper catch for dinner.

"Your Gramps looks like a retriever wanting to show off a bird in its mouth," she said to Nora, but when she glanced towards the porch, Nora was gone.

The visitor's mannerisms resembled a snowy egret absorbing her surroundings—intentional in her movements, turning her head slightly, as if to capture new images without depending on her peripheral vision. As she came across the beach-yard, she paused the entourage several times to take in the beauty of each additional view.

Maria cracked open the window. Their voices trickled in, happy and eager.

Halfway to the house, the stranger stopped, allowing Ralph to explain the work he'd contracted for installing rip-rap, preventing erosion of the petite peninsula. His efforts had saved a small beach on the property, which the stranger pointed out, and he acknowledged.

"Miss Amanda, Miss Amanda!" cried Nora, racing across the sand toward the woman.

The woman turned around and absorbed the collision around her waist, wrapping Nora in her arms.

Jeb seemed to stall his return, acting like some loose end needed to be dealt with on the boat—the *Galleon* already tidily perched on its lift. Only after Maria came out of the house to greet Amanda and escort her inside did he cease loitering.

Dinner at the Carters'

Amanda was shocked by Nora's greeting, nearly knocked over by the girl's exuberance, but she wasn't surprised by Sierra's glare. Guilt pricked Amanda's side. *I don't deserve Nora's attention . . . especially after nearly killing her sister.* But then Sierra shrugged and a curious smile took over.

Nora stepped back and looked up. "I did it, miss. I did it!"

"And just what did you do?" Amanda beamed in return.

"I ran the Shop for a whole two hours before Caleb came . . . all by myself!"

Fear pulsated from Amanda's core. Sierra reflected similar concern, but not judgment. Only surprise.

Amanda glanced over her shoulder towards the dock. Paddleboard Guy was dawdling with something. This never should've happened! As safe as Irvington was, this young girl shouldn't have been left alone to tend a shop. Who knew what type of strangers might walk in off the street, see a vulnerable girl, and take advantage? Teenagers would be tempted to shoplift, too.

"I sold over two hundred dollars of merchandise!"

"Why didn't you lock up and go to your Aunt Kathi's? I remember your sister telling you to do so."

Nora remained exuberant. "But I wanted to show you, miss, that I'm a big girl. I could do it on my own."

Amanda willed herself to calm down. If Jeb discovered the mishap, he'd probably blame her—Amanda now endangering both his daughters in a single day. The wild feelings she'd experienced with him on the boat? She brushed those aside. Her stomach stiffened, and she lowered herself to a knee and hugged Nora. "I am proud of you. You don't need to do anything to prove you're a big girl for me." She leaned back from the girl and gently tapped her own chest. "I know what's here. Please don't think you need to prove anything to me."

"Oh, yes, miss . . . but I can do it." Nora's voice pleaded.

"Yes . . . but your safety comes first." Amanda blinked back the sting of tears. She considered returning to the dock to face Jeb and confess her wrongdoings, but Ralph's hand came to her shoulder. Sierra's eyes were wide and her face pale. Amanda looked towards the house. An older woman peered out at them from behind a window.

The woman then appeared at the door and found her way to Amanda on the porch landing. Her eyes were warm and welcoming, and a feeling of affirmation swept through Amanda.

Nora was the first to speak. "This is our Grans."

Amanda looked at Grans with a nervous smile. Amanda eyed the outdoor shower, but immediately found herself being pulled into the house, Nora gripping one hand and Grans the other.

Saltwater residue clung to Amanda's skin. A new old feeling. It didn't really bother her. "An immersion in that water will heal you," her own mother had told her. That was her mom's remedy for poison ivy. "Just jump off the dock! That will take care of it." Her mother was right. But now? Amanda glanced back towards the water when she entered the house. Jeb was lingering at the end of the dock, and if he was going to return her to her Jeep, she could at least clean up. Maybe he'd loosen up without the audience of his girls.

Once inside, the older woman offered the use of their roomy bathroom across from the kitchen.

"Feel free to freshen up," Grans said, as if the woman had read her mind. "I can pop your clothes in the dryer while you shower."

The bathroom had a view of the lagoon. She suspected, based on the house's layout, every room had a water-view, whether it was the lagoon, the creek, or the Bay. Having settled herself, she peeked through the blinds. Jeb had returned from the dock and carried the paddleboards on his shoulders. His shirt was still off and draped around his neck.

A stab of guilt hit her. It was wrong to stare. Recalling a scene from the *Sound of Music,* she misquoted Baroness Schraeder, mumbling over the running water, "I'd hardly be a *woman* if I didn't notice *that man*."

She took her time in the shower, hoping to erase the memory of the storm. As good as the sticky salt felt on her skin, it felt even better rinsed off. It didn't come off immediately, much like the guilt still clinging to her body. The image of the lightning bolt spreading over the surface of the water was clear in her mind. *It must've hit the oyster floats!* Had they reached the iron structure a minute earlier, they'd be dead.

She kept showering. The Carters' water was soft—not unusual in Virginia's Tidewater Region, and a better excuse for the long shower.

She turned off the faucet, and a few moments later, gentle taps reverberated through the door.

"Fifteen more minutes left on the dryer." It was Maria. "I have a bathrobe for you."

Amanda extended her hand around the door and received the robe, white and emblazoned with a crest—royal blue shield with gold leaves. At the top of the shield stood a dog. Below the canine was the iron hood of a knight. Two small ship wheels were in the upper corners, and a larger one placed at the lower center. She couldn't read the Latin insignia at the bottom, but guessed it to be the Carter family coat-of-arms. She rubbed the embroidered gold leaf.

Having donned the robe, she exited the bathroom and crossed the hall into the spacious kitchen.

Grans was slicing an onion as she raised her head. "Darling, you must stay for dinner. Now that these boys have gone through quite an adventure to pluck you out of that Bay, you owe it to *me* to enjoy a meal." Her voice was adamant, and she vetoed all suggestions that Amanda be promptly returned to her vehicle at Foxwells.

Amanda responded graciously, "Yes, of course, Mrs. Carter." But it was odd. *Why do I owe her anything?*

The girls hovered on stools alongside the kitchen island and monopolized Amanda's attention—mostly Nora. Sierra was reserved, while Nora couldn't keep her eyes off Amanda.

Amanda barely noticed that Jeb had returned from showering. He'd not said a word and sat in a wicker lounge chair in the corner. He refused to meet her eyes, and for that, she kept her back turned to him. Moments later, sandals smacked across the great room and up the stairs, his steps more akin to stomping.

Nora broke her stare, and the grandmother touched Amanda's

arm. "Amanda, please call me Grans. That's what the girls call me. We're not too formal around here."

"Thank you, Mrs. Carter—I mean Grans. How about you, Mr. Carter? How d'you prefer I address you?"

"Out of respect to you, please call me Ralph. You're not a little girl."

Grans stiffened. "Now, Ralph, you're just making me look bad in front of this fine young *lady*."

Ralph responded slowly, "That's my point, *Maria*. Amanda here is a fine young *lady*."

"Amanda, please don't mind my old curmudgeon." Maria's eyes flashed. "Call me Grans."

"You can call me anything you like." Ralph winked at Amanda.

Maria held up a knife. "See there, Ralph, you did it again. Making me look bad in front of our guest."

Amanda alternated her glance between them. "I'll call you Ralph and Maria."

Ralph nodded with a self-satisfied smile. "That suits me fine. I like the way you put *Ralph* before *Maria*."

Amanda hadn't seen the move coming. She'd hoped to have stopped the squabbling between the two, but he wanted to keep it going.

Maria must have noticed Amanda squirming, because she chose to end it. "Oh, you'd never think we've been married for over forty years!"

Ralph walked over to Maria, wrapped his arms around her, and nibbled under her ear.

"Now, Ralph, you just stop that. I need to get dinner moving." She wasn't really fighting him off. "Amanda, I hope you like fish. These boys have been catching a slew of Spanish mackerel this summer, but if you don't, I'd be glad to throw a burger on for you."

Spanish mackerel? Amanda's insides warmed. "The fish sounds wonderful, and if you'd like, why not let me help you with the salad?"

She was equally relieved there'd be no reason to ask Maria if the meat was organic.

Amanda gazed across an expansive great room. On the opposite side of it, an enormous stone fireplace rose to a cathedral ceiling. Jeb was sitting in what looked like a home office on the second floor, the door partially open. She took a deep breath. He was wearing a T-shirt which labored to contain his form. She hadn't noticed his physique at the Yokel or at the Shop where he'd been wearing a loose-fitting shirt. She battled to reign in such thoughts, even to chastise herself. She'd never fallen for a guy based on his looks, and it wasn't about to happen now.

The sulking man confused her. Why was it that even his stomping up the stairs carried fluidity and lyricism? His quirky madness made him that much more alluring.

The rattling dryer stopped, and before Amanda had a chance to fetch her clothes, Nora raced across the hall right past her. She was waiting in front of the dryer with the small clothing bundle when Amanda arrived, and then she meticulously handed Amanda each article, curiously eyeing each as she did.

Amanda rubbed the top of Nora's head. "Thanks."

She returned to the bathroom and changed, carefully hanging the bathrobe on the door. The inside of the belt showed embroidery. Something she'd missed when she first put it on. Staring up at her was a sextant. At the other end of the belt, the Spanish Cross of Burgundy within a miniature coat-of-arms. She gasped. The floor shifted, and her vision clouded. She took some calming breaths while tightly holding onto the sink counter.

Nora waited for her, and she didn't have time to inspect it thoroughly, but she made a quick analysis. Not her mother's sextant and not the one from the letter's wax seal. But it was a sextant!

Amanda returned to the kitchen with a fake smile. When she learned Ralph was offering fresh crabs, it became genuine. He led her and the girls out to the dock where they pulled in their crab pots. The activity gave her moments of normalcy, a reprieve from the weird synchronicities of the day.

After a steam crab appetizer on the porch, Maria stepped to the opening of the great room. "Jeb, dinner!" She set down a plate of sliced lemons. Pointing at the chairs on the opposite side of the table, she said, "Girls, I'd like you to sit over there. Amanda, why don't you sit here next to me."

Apparently, the men knew their places. Ralph found his seat at the head of the table, with Maria to his left. The girls sat across from her, Nora perky as ever. Jeb returned, bleeding apathy, and found his perch at the other end of it. He was to her left and plopped his elbows on the table with a thud, causing her water glass to rattle.

She resisted the urge to pour it on his head.

He rested his chin beneath his fists, and his elbow sat inches from her fork. It would've been nothing to knock his elbow off the dinner table. Fein an accident. *What a sight that would be!* To finally get his attention.

Ralph cleared his throat to get everyone's attention. It seemed as if they were all to join hands. Maria grasped Amanda's tightly, but Jeb broke the chain, not offering his right hand to Amanda. Ralph paused, eyeing Jeb curiously, and then plunged ahead into a beautiful prayer, thanking God for keeping them all safe in the storm. He offered kind words of gratitude directed at the women for the meal preparation.

They dug in and plenty of conversation ensued. Jeb still wouldn't make eye contact. Only the girls were able to dampen the awkwardness. The thought of accidentally touching his foot frightened her. But just her luck, it happened.

Jeb flinched.

"Sorry."

He exchanged his scarce words with grunts. The only consolation for Amanda was his aroma. If he'd come down with a heavy dose of cologne, she was sure she would've smacked him. A whiff of that would've given her a headache. At most, he had a touch of aftershave—another reminder of her father. But what really struck her was a subtle scent of lavender. She remembered it from her run-in with him at the Shop. Jeb was a *salt*—a natural—one with his element, comfortable in his own skin, even if he was acting like a child.

When Maria served the plates of mackerel, Amanda begged the garlic aroma and onion marinade to drown her thoughts of the man at her side. Why did Maria put her so close to him? Maria should've understood the tension long before dinner.

I need to dislike this man. He overreacted and he's passive-aggressive. She was sorry that she'd inconvenienced Jeb, but not remorseful. *For the distress I caused his daughter?* Agony!

I miscalculated the effect of the winds. Should've known better. The nuances of the storm patterns and the contours of the shorelines were long faded from her teenage memories. Still, she deemed Jeb's response unmerited. Didn't she deserve a chance to be seen differently?

Ralph seemed to be entertained by the whole affair. *What would he have been doing otherwise?* Amanda learned he was semi-retired. The rescue was a good excuse for him to show off his boat. He hadn't appeared scared. He looked at Amanda when he spoke. "I've instilled water safety skills in all my children and grandchildren. I can't count on my hands the number of times I've been caught in the middle of a thunderstorm. I was confident in Sierra. I knew she'd keep you low and flat."

Maria grunted and softly bumped Ralph with her elbow.

Ralph cleared his throat. "We've both preached water safety here, Amanda. I worried you might've gotten cold, but with the water at its warmest this time of year, you two had a simple solution."

Amanda nodded.

Sierra lifted her fork. "That's exactly what we did, Gramps."

"With the predominant winds, I knew they'd blow you back to shore. Then you'd scamper to one of the summer houses along the shoreline, take refuge, eventually get a call out." Ralph grabbed his granddaughter's hand. "Sierra, even if you had to break into a house, no one would fault you for it. I would've taken care of any damages."

Maria patted Ralph's hand while glaring at Jeb. "As you can see, Amanda, he trusts the instincts of his granddaughter."

Amanda caught Jeb's expression from the corner of her eye. He wasn't amused.

Ralph put his hand on top of his wife's. "That's right, Maria. She's growing to be a fine young lady." He glanced at both Sierra and Amanda.

Sierra cracked a small smile while Amanda grinned nervously and wouldn't let her eyes venture to Jeb.

Ralph fixed a hard stare at his son.

Maria looked at Sierra. "I think it's been an exciting day for Gramps."

Sierra remained solemn, looking at her father.

This time Amanda turned to look at Jeb. He stared towards his parents and returned to his meal.

"Jeb, you're so quiet tonight." Maria's tone was light, but some sarcasm leaked through. She looked up from her salad. "Might you be a bit more engaging?"

Heat hit Amanda's face.

Jeb looked up from his plate, acknowledged her for a quick second, and then returned to forking his leftover mackerel skins.

"Mother . . . the fish is spectacular." His sarcasm was palpable. "Thank you for the meal."

Maria glared at her son and then eyed Ralph.

Ralph's eyes bounced to his plate, then the sink, and then to Jeb and the girls. Maria seemed to absorb every squinch of his face. She tightened her eyes slightly and barely nodded.

It reminded Amanda of the way her own parents had communicated. Without words. It was cute. Even mysterious.

Maria said, "I'm glad you like it because I'm going to leave you all to clean up while I drive our *guest* back to her car."

Jeb straightened his posture, looked straight ahead, but said nothing. Amanda thought she'd seen a trace of disappointment, like maybe he had been expecting to ferry her back to her Jeep.

Nora was disappointed and whined. Ralph was quick to tamper her complaints and added, "I'm doing my part, too, Nora. Skillet duty for Gramps."

Sierra watched her father with concern.

All conversation ceased, like a dead-air moment during a radio broadcast. Amanda was so uncomfortable, she felt obliged to speak, making a good show by describing the approaching *Galleon* coming to their rescue and how pretty its lines were in the water. Ralph perked up with his proud retriever look, the one she'd heard Maria teasing him about.

"I felt like I was being rescued by a knight riding in on a black stallion," Amanda continued, stealing a glance at Jeb upon the word *knight* while turning to Ralph with a playful look.

"Ahhh," Maria said sweetly, then leaned over and gave Ralph a small kiss.

Ralph teased back with a pout. "But she's light blue."

"Looks black in the darkness of a storm!" Amanda said, and garnered a few chuckles—but not from Jeb. He continued to keep his head down and poke the remnants of the fish, now mostly skin.

Sierra seemed to have picked up on the awkwardness, because she moved the conversation to earlier phases from their tour. Before the storm. When Sierra raved about the healthy Belle of the Bay sandwich, Jeb woke up from poking his fish. He smiled at his daughter and nearly moved the same expression to Amanda, only to pull back and return to his coldness.

Amanda felt as if her chair's seat had transformed to a plate of needles. She wondered if Sierra would mention her excursion into the Marina House. Sierra didn't, and Amanda sighed with relief.

Amanda thought she might actually understand Jeb's icy reticence. She understood what triggered hers, but could only guess at his. He was a man gallantly trying to hold it together after losing his wife. Unlike her father!

He failed . . . and he failed me.

Amanda found her way to the restroom before departing with Maria. She needed a moment to inspect the bathrobe. Would it contain a second crest? Hidden behind the belt?

To her dismay, the bathrobe was gone.

Crab Pots

Jeb wanted to think better of this Amanda person, but something had gone terribly wrong. His top-of-the-line paddleboards were destroyed. On their return to the Bay House aboard the *Galleon*, he'd searched Sierra's face. It told the story of great trauma, a vulnerable, innocent girl, taking on a storm in the wild. He still felt his insides ripping apart.

The woman acted as if nothing had happened at all. Like she and Sierra had merely been out for a walk in the park. Maybe Amanda's natural response to shock was to ignore it? Just like she ignored the paddleboards?

Jeb avoided talking about the topic with Sierra in front of Amanda. If things had gone as bad as he suspected, he'd be held liable, and frankly, he didn't trust her. She seemed aggressive and ready to attack.

He wanted to believe there was something good about her. After all, he felt something the moment he'd grasped her hand and looked into her eyes. He couldn't deny the spark. He'd been glad she returned to her nasty ways though, when she got in his face and yelled at him. Her feisty behavior was a godsend, helping him suppress the other strange feeling.

Deep down inside, though hard to admit, he liked the way the woman stood up for Sierra. He wondered whether he was working as hard to dislike her as she labored to dislike him. *James Carter doesn't make enemies* . . . but with that woman, it happened in an instant.

Jeb took his time tidying up the *Galleon* before returning to the house with the shredded paddleboards. *What's the rush?* The woman may have duped his father, but his mother would annihilate her. She'd see right through the game she was playing. It wouldn't take his mother long to figure out that the woman had nearly killed her granddaughter.

Jeb loaded the truck and expected to find Amanda on the front porch, awaiting her ride back to Foxwells. He stepped inside to learn she was showering. *Why inside?* They had an outdoor shower.

Jeb dashed upstairs and did the same. He was in the habit of using an English variety lavender soap bar—something Erin had insisted on early in their marriage. She said it would help his skin. Even after her death, he hadn't deviated from the practice. Why fix something that isn't broken? He applied a touch of aftershave for the girls. One touch. They'd all be celebrating their mother's birthday as soon as the client was returned to her vehicle. As in years past, he'd help them bake a cake, but the girls had forgotten all about the tradition.

They were all talking when he headed downstairs. His mother invited Amanda for dinner! When has that ever happened? He gritted his teeth. The woman asked about being returned to Foxwells. *Great!* But then his mother squashed her request. *What's Mom thinking?* Heat raced up the back of his neck. He prepared to rush forward, grab the woman's hand, and lead her out of the house. When he came around the corner, he found her standing in the kitchen practically naked. Wearing one of their family bathrobes! It did a poor job hiding her legs. Legs that made her taller than his mother. Elegant legs that didn't hold a limp.

She blushed.

He took a seat in the corner, the farthest distance away from her, and picked up a boating magazine. Anything to keep his eyes off the intruder. She kept her back turned to him.

The girls hovered. Nora's behavior was the scariest of all. On an evening when she should've been remembering her deceased mother, she was entranced by this whack from New York.

Jeb caught his mother's eyes while Amanda's back was turned to him, the girls commanding her attention. He didn't wish to be rude.

Mom just needs to know I want her out! He pointed to Amanda and then the front door.

His mother shook her head and grimaced.

Jeb resisted the urge to slap his hand down on the side-table. He needed to cool down, and the best place to do it was in his home office. The dryer buzzed. *Great! At least now she won't be half-naked when she sits down for dinner.*

He took some angry breaths through his teeth, then bounced up from his armchair, strode across the great-room, and fled up the stairs.

Jeb closed the door to his office—then on second thought, opened it a crack to listen to the activity below in the kitchen.

The Shop had been left totally abandoned—a busy summer weekend to boot. Caleb would be gone, and the teen wasn't in the routine of locking up for the night.

Fortunately, Jeb's security cameras allowed him to monitor the Shop from his laptop, and he could lock the doors remotely. Irvington village was bustling, and the tourists were grabbing his flyers. Hopefully, they'd discover they could book tours online. But now he desperately wanted to get to the bottom of the mishap with Sierra.

His father offered to pull in some fresh crabs from the crab pots at the end of the dock. The woman practically slobbered over the offer. "Oh no, Ralph, that's far too much trouble."

Really? Gimme a break!

Jeb perked up as he watched the scene unfold from his perch. His mother waved her head at his father with a look that said, "Too much for one night."

Ralph raised a finger. "Just an appetizer." He then grabbed Amanda's hand and dashed out the door with the girls in tow.

Jeb popped up from his chair and quickly descended the stairs. The eat-in kitchen would have a better view. He could barely hear them out on the dock, but his eyes were enough.

His girls became the "crab experts" and instructed Amanda on all the in-and-outs of the pots, the bait, and the acceptable sizes. Nora clamored the hardest for Amanda's attention. Sierra was a bit standoffish, but occasionally, it was as if she couldn't help herself and would jump into the fray. She pointed to a crab loose on the dock. "It's a keeper!" she cried. She placed the tip of her flip-flop on its shell and grabbed its two back swimming legs. Before long, the crab was paralyzed. Amanda looked impressed, and then Sierra tossed it into the bushel-basket.

Once they completed their hunt, Ralph led them off the dock carrying the bushel-basket, and they followed him like he was the Pied Piper. Jeb scurried back upstairs and resumed his perch.

His father glowed in Amanda's attention as he cleaned and steamed the crabs. They laid out newspaper on the picnic bench in the screened-in porch, set out several ramekins of melted butter, and sat down with nearly a dozen crabs. Jeb slid his chair closer to the hallway to get a better look. Nora claimed the honors of teaching Amanda how to eat a Chesapeake Bay Blue Crab. The woman showed no skittish tendencies. Jeb wondered if she were placating Nora, because once Amanda was set loose on her own with a crab, she was in another world. She was a natural with the whacker, wasted not a second going for the meat of the back claw. *I guess they have crabs in New York.*

Jeb arrived at the dinner table to discover that Amanda was placed to his immediate right. *Why did Mom do that? What if we bump legs? I can't avoid looking at her. Does the woman really need to know how angry I am? It's Erin's birthday! We should be celebrating Erin's birthday!*

The grip Amanda had on Nora made his skin crawl. She was the scary influential type Jeb needed to shield from his daughters. As best he could tell, she was unmarried and professional. Investment banking up on Wall Street? How was it she wasn't married? *She's plenty attractive—no denying it. Probably divorced.* Her work was her god. Jeb's dislike of her had nothing to do with whether she was a professional. That didn't bother him. It was about her moral compass. Where did the needle point? To what extent would she go to serve her god, whether that be work or herself? *She's angry, too.*

Jeb perceived the dinner became more about his mother than anything else. She was enjoying the sway she had over the woman—almost to the point of control. *Mom's totally in control . . . No doubt about it.*

His father's behavior also annoyed him. He catered to Mom, the two of them acting like a tag team. Why did they seem to feel so obligated to entertain the woman . . . almost as if trying to make her part of the family? She was a foreigner and the worst kind. *Maybe she's convinced Dad she's a mermaid.* Unfortunately, the first time his father had ever seen her was when she came out of the water by the pound nets. *If only he'd met this woman earlier, like me, he'd know differently!*

Jeb stole a glance at Amanda, then quickly looked away. He'd been lying to himself. *I'll admit it. I was looking for her tail too when I pulled her out of the water.*

Amanda was uncomfortable when they sat down to dinner, and he didn't want to make things worse by expecting her to hold his hand during his father's prayer. He wouldn't deny the tension. *I'm certainly not helping her.*

Her presence next to him was tortuous. The way she breathed bothered him. She took deep breaths throughout the meal—her chest rising and falling. He wasn't annoyed. That's why it bothered him! The woman was fouling his thoughts for Erin.

He fought back a weakness that had overcome him: empathy for Amanda. There was more to what she was dealing with than just the awkwardness of the setting—dinner in a stranger's house. There was something deep down wrong with her. *Like me.*

She laughed at his father's corny jokes. Not all of them. *Something about the laugh?* It was a laugh that seemed to want to break out of a prison and live. A yearning laugh that was always sincere and considerate. His father was trying to loosen her up. If she didn't like a particular joke, she didn't flatter him. It had to be good. In one case she gestured, pinching two fingers together, saying, "Ralph, it would've been great, but your timing was off by an intsy wintsy bit."

His father told funny stories about Jeb's girls, and he heard it again. A restrained and testing laugh. If the girls weren't embarrassed, the woman would break out into a robust laugh, and they'd join in. It was infectious, and Jeb fought back the craving to participate. Her laugh scared him. It reminded him of the way he could laugh with Erin. And the way Erin could light up a room.

He wished he could laugh again. People used to think he was funny. The life of the party. No one said that anymore.

Jeb stole glances at the woman. Amanda savored the fish, seeming to hide quick breaths between bites. *She can't be that great of an actor. Mom would've known if she was faking.* Would've carted Amanda home an hour ago if she'd caught her. *Why can't*

Mom just make her go away?

He felt her knee hit his own. *Was it me or her?* The thought was horrifying, creating a twisted feeling that bordered on betrayal.

Amanda's feathery voice anytime she spoke to Nora wasn't helping. Jeb wondered if it was fake. Worse, if Amanda ever spoke to him in that tone, he worried he'd melt.

When Sierra talked about their lunch on the beach, she seemed afraid and confused, as if she were hiding something. Amanda squirmed. *What really happened out there?*

My own daughter ate a healthy sandwich? The poor thing must have been starved. *Whose fault is that, Jeb?* He'd sent her out without provisions. *What was I thinking?*

Nora was keen to hear the story of the storm and how they survived it. Jeb's attention fixated upon the account of the two as they struggled to get air between the swells. His insides tightened on Sierra's vivid portrayal of herself gasping for air, even if she'd overdramatized the recounting for Nora. Neither Amanda nor Sierra spoke of the danger the paddleboards created when being caught up in the wind and waves. Based on how they tethered them, he wasn't surprised at all to find them shredded. He nodded to himself on hearing their decision to stay tethered and not separate from each other, but he winced at the image of either one being hit in the head by a paddleboard.

"Seems you only had a choice between two terrible options?" His father spoke as if wanting to divert the topic. He suspected his father protected Sierra. And maybe the mermaid too.

"That's right, Gramps," Sierra said. "We could've ditched the boards and swum to shore—we had our preservers. Could've camped overnight on Cedar Island."

Ralph raised his fork. "You would've landed with a few sea nettle stings and then been devoured by mosquitos and no-see-ums."

"We would've survived." Sierra's tone rang with confidence. "I could've built a fire."

"I'm glad you took the second option . . . expedient . . . maintained your comms . . . quick rescue . . ." Ralph's palms came down flat on the table. "And now you're here."

Jeb grimaced at his father's words. It was great that he'd dwelled on the sunny side of life, but no one acknowledged the serious implications the whipping boards created—a deadly force. Both

Amanda and Sierra remained oblivious to it, and Jeb wouldn't mention it, unwilling to raise the specter of Erin's death.

Sierra mentioned an unusual encounter with leaping dolphins. Nora asked Amanda to retell it. Jeb suspected that both Sierra and Amanda were prevaricating, as if something about it embarrassed them.

Jeb's mother was clearing the table when Amanda told her version of it. His mother jolted slightly, stopped what she was doing, and sat down. She let out a tired sigh that Jeb doubted was genuine. Of all the dramatic stories being told, his mother paid closest attention to Amanda's account, but attempted to hide her focus.

The saving grace to it all was that the girls remained chatty during the meal and prevented gaps in the conversation. Amanda was keen to dote on them and stay in front of any prying questions. By the end of the meal, he'd learned very little about the woman, while she'd harvested a windfall of knowledge about them.

Most excruciating of all for Jeb was the fawning attention Nora paid to Amanda. *It's her mother's birthday, for crying out loud!* That's where the focus should've been—on Erin. *Nora has forgotten her mother.* The thought weighed on him the entire evening.

I've failed as a father and a husband.

Play-by-Play

Maria insisted on returning Amanda to her Jeep at the launch site at Foxwells. Amanda remained stiff and guarded on the drive—worried that Maria would ask probing questions. She didn't, and Amanda wondered if the woman was intentionally trying to keep her at ease.

Amanda found Ted and Sally lounging with drinks on the veranda overlooking Carter's Creek when she returned to the resort. They seemed relaxed and more comfortable with each other.

"Did you find the ring?" Sally asked the moment she and Amanda had retired to their room.

"We'll get to that," Amanda answered. "But first I want to hear how things went between you and Ted."

Sally narrowed an eye.

"Really, Sally. I promise. I'll get to it. It's a saga."

That seemed to sway her. "Well, after dropping off the sandwiches, we went up to Reedville and took the ferry over to

Tangier Island." Excitement filled her voice, "Girl, did you know they still speak the Queen's language over there?"

Amanda nodded. "I recall meeting some of the old-timers, watermen who'd come by the marina to drop off their catches. It sounded like *Elizabethan English*, but I was a teenager. What would I know?" She attempted a southern drawl, "My diddy called it *Eastern Shore* ray-ed neck."

Sally chuckled. "Ted lost his lunch on the way over. Other than that, we had a great time."

"What else? What'd you do after?" Amanda asked.

She listened to the full account of Ted and Sally's day. Amanda surmised Sally was playing things down, but Amanda let it go. No point in claiming a victory. Not yet, at least.

Amanda infused some optimism in her voice. "I have big plans for you two tomorrow."

Sally answered with a smile.

Amanda went on to describe the events of her day. She downplayed the story of Jeb's role in the rescue.

Sally eyed her funny. "Girl, what am I missing here? Explain again how you came out of the water?"

Amanda took a deep breath. "You know . . . they just helped us onto the boat. A minor detail."

"Well, I want to know the details *here*." Sally thumped her fist on the coffee table between them.

Amanda recalled the image of Jeb coming out of the water shirtless revealing his bronze and chiseled physique. *Mention this to Sally?* No way! She'd erupt with excitement as if she were Mt. St. Helens.

What appealed to Amanda more was that she doubted his muscle tone was the fruit of a gym or steroids, rather believing he'd developed it through the daily grind of his paddleboard business. A tormented man like Ben Hur—from a novel she'd read in high school—whose character was refined through adversity.

"This story gets even better at the Carter dinner table." An easy smile grew on her face. "The grandfather is adorable."

"It's not what I asked. Now just tell me what happened when you got into that boat." Sally's eyes narrowed. "What are you hiding?"

Amanda explained how Jeb dove in and swam over to hug his daughter. "It was strange."

"He sounds sweet." Sally's tone was soft.

"Yes, it was that too, but why dive in for her? She was still on her board. It was odd and sweet at the same time."

"Was it for show?" Sally suggested.

"No . . . awkward. I had to hide my eyes."

"No, girl. You did that because you didn't want him to see that you were touched!"

Amanda flinched, and she felt a tug on her heart. Sally was right, but Amanda wasn't about to admit it.

Amanda described how he assisted them onto the boat, at which Sally pointed out, "Girl, you're still glossing over something. Just walk me through this last little bit like you're a sports commentator, breaking down the play."

"Alright, Sally, here it is. Sierra was already up in the boat, and then the *Shop guy* turned to me. He reached out his hand and helped me climb the ladder until I settled myself."

"Settled?"

"Hmmm . . . actually, he kept his hand on me until I could carry my weight. Now *there*, are you satisfied?"

"No. What was going on with the eyes? Where were they set? In play-by-play, you have to call the quarterback's eyes."

Amanda deadpanned. "I don't remember him having any."

Sally slapped her palm down on the bed.

Amanda ignored the gesture. Her voice stayed steady, emotionless. "I could feel my hair standing on the top of my head . . . but completely explainable. I climbed aboard in a grounded state."

Sally narrowed an eye. She knew the basics of electricity from her job, but that wasn't the problem here.

Amanda lightened her tone and plowed on. "He was on the boat. A different charge potential."

Sally wasn't buying it, and not a chance Amanda would mention what happened when he grasped her hand—the electricity that ran through her body and made her spine tingle. And why tell Sally she thought the guy was half-dead? She remembered her hand flat over his warm chest without ever feeling a beat.

"Wrong!" Sally slapped her hand down again. "You forgot he'd just come from the water, and your hair was wet. Both of you were grounded."

"Ugh." Amanda threw up her hands. "Whatever, Sally."

"Hah, I thought so!" Sally nodded her head in triumph. "You can't hide the goods from me!"

"Sally, the guy's a complete jerk." Amanda pursed her lips. "It was nothing. There is nothing!"

"But you say his daughters are sweet and unspoiled. How can a *jerk* raise sweet girls?"

"I don't know . . . maybe the girls are still benefiting from the memory of their nurturing mother. Maybe the grandparents have taken over. All I can tell you is I think the guy's a *jerk*." Amanda placed her hand on her cheek.

Sitting so close to Jeb at the dinner table had nearly paralyzed her. No way should Sally know about that, and that she'd practiced controlled breathing to help her relax and take control of her overactive imagination. That's all! No spark. Just her imagination.

She placed her hands in her lap. "Not once did he address me by my name—not once! I sat there for over an hour, and all he could do was look down and poke at his fish. He acted like a baby. If not for his mother's insistence, I doubt he'd have come to the table . . . pathetic. He's all about playing victim Olympics."

"Amanda, your words say that, but everything else about you says something else. You'd make a horrible poker player."

"Hey, I'm good at poker." Amanda was defensive. "We should invite Ted for a game . . . hustle some dough out of him."

"Mean, girl." Sally pursed her lips.

It worked. Mentioning Ted seemed to get Sally off her trail.

Amanda silently exhaled a breath of relief as she pulled out a deck of cards. She felt her heart pulling in so many directions. Paddleboard Guy did one thing to her, and Nora, the sunbeam of light, another. And with Sierra? Complete remorse!

Amanda thought she'd seen a glow from Jeb when he pulled her from the water. Looking straight into his eyes, she hadn't felt invisible to him. Yes, he turned ice cold, but a flicker radiated from his deepest parts. During their meal, again, as Sierra spoke of lunch, his smile was like the sun poking through the clouds, but then gone.

"I created trauma for that girl—real trauma!" Amanda said while she dealt the cards.

"Does he know?"

"Who knows what she's told him."

"You'll make it right, won't you?"

Amanda looked up from her cards. "Yes, in all my power, I'll make it up to her."

Sally's eyebrows rose a notch. "To her . . . but not him? Her father? He would be traumatized too."

Amanda put her cards on the table, and she directed her gaze out the window into the night. A few fireflies flashed about. The crazy pull of Paddleboard Guy crashed against the animosity she had for her father. Her words came out wounded, "No, I can't."

Amanda felt Sally's stare, but she wouldn't look at her. Amanda moved the discussion on to Nora. She couldn't keep from talking about the young girl. Sally's eyes widened as Amanda went from one story to the next. Only a snap of Sally's fingers forced her to take a breath.

"Maternal instincts. You do realize that's what's going on here?"

Amanda jolted upright. "No!"

Sally bobbed her head.

Amanda's voice cracked. "Doesn't matter . . . he's in the way."

Her words didn't make it to Sally's eyes.

Amanda spoke further of her impressions of Sierra, but was careful with her body language and her choice of words. Sally was in awe of the dolphin story, but Amanda didn't disclose the entirety of their dance around Sierra. How could she? It bordered on the paranormal . . . but in a bizarre, regal kind of way, as if the beautiful creatures were honoring the child.

Sally was already prone to prod at Amanda's eccentricities, but always for fun and sweet jesting. So why tell her?

It would be like filling up a water pistol, handing it to Sally, and saying, "Here, shoot me in the eyeballs."

CHAPTER 7

Sunday

Grumpy

Jeb arrived at the Shop early and grumpy. He craved a reset before facing his clients. He'd secured a decent booking overnight, so his day was now full. A Hens tour in the morning, and a Family Reunion tour in the afternoon.

He unloaded the remains of the two paddleboards from his truck to the rear of the Shop. The boards were shattered in several locations, and he still wondered how they'd been able to stand on them. He salvaged them for the hardware and rigging—saving a cooler and pole mounts. All the tethers were fine. The centerboards and tail fins were severed at the bottom of the board—*probably saved the girls from a slashing!* He deliberated whether he should file an insurance claim, but quickly resolved that nothing good could come from the carrier learning a storm overtook one of his tours.

Jeb threw the remnants of the boards onto the free-standing surplus rack. *They should've never been out in the squall!* He still wondered how the client had taken advantage of his daughter, but he hadn't pressed Sierra on the matter. The woman hadn't acknowledged—in any way—the dismembering of two prized paddleboards. Worse, she hadn't acknowledged the danger she'd put Sierra through. That neither suffered any injury was beyond reason—even the *Galleon* incurred hail damage. *Dad should've been incensed at that idiot woman!*

Jeb fetched his usual from the Yokel, but kept his chit chat with Kat brief. He needed to sort some things out in his head. Maybe that was his problem—thinking. And *thinking* it was all in his head. Not a chance he could admit that to Kat.

Seeing his favorite table occupied, he headed back to the Shop. Better to eat his smoked salmon bagel in the privacy of his office, anyway. Kat was bound to probe.

Jeb set his sandwich down on his desk and unwrapped it. A caper escaped, but he ignored it.

He took solace in not having vented his anger with Sierra. Erin would be proud. Even his actions towards the woman were restrained. *But why did I act childish? Why feel sorry for myself?* He understood his overreaction and dread for Sierra, but what of the childishness? The spark to his heart created another anxiety. Or was it guilt?

Cream cheese irritated the corners of his mouth, and he dabbed it clean with a napkin. Yesterday was Erin's birthday. He'd failed to celebrate it with the girls, running nonstop from sunup till sundown. The calamitous events of the afternoon derailed his plans to quietly honor it. Honor her! Only after Amanda's departure could he relive in his mind the days spent with Erin on her birthday: in high school, once married, and then with children. He fell asleep longing to go back.

As for his childishness, he admitted it was selfish. Jeb eyed the caper and smashed it. *I've been unchivalrous. If I run into her again—and she admits responsibility for Sierra's peril—I'll apologize.*

Hens

Jeb refreshed a browser tab—the one fixed to the local weather. His morning Hen's tour was soon to arrive. The wind prediction was similar to Saturday's, so he'd recommend the same tour from yesterday: the war canals and the beautiful little sand spit beaches along the way to Cedar Island.

The bridal party trickled in, and after offering coffee and tea, Jeb began his presentation in the Map Room. Using a long pointer, he showed the predominant winds and exactly why he recommended a particular route. He promised numerous ray and eagle sightings. He pointed out the beaches, evoking "oohs" and "ahhs" from the ladies. Directing them to the aquarium, he introduced them to the smaller fish they would see in the tidal pools.

"I'll adjust the tour to your own pace," he promised them.

A cute brunette stepped forward. "Do we need to worry about snakes?"

He wasn't sure if she was serious or simply wanting attention. "They'll be more scared of you than you should be of them." Jeb's canned response. Maybe it didn't ring true for the brunette because she ran her tongue on the inside of her lip.

Had it been an early spring tour, he'd advise them to be aware of aggressive snakes due to their mating instincts. Jeb had his own memories as a boy of being peppered by angry moccasins while paddling a canoe. He was safe in the canoe, but their heads striking up against its sides sounded like hail.

Once out on the water, Jeb would point out and describe marine life. They'd spot pufferfish, his favorite, for their large, bright green eyes. If they made good time, he'd guide them to a pound net and the oyster floats. He'd pull up the miscellaneous crab pot to provide a lecture on the history of the contraption and the original patent.

He traced the planned route on the floor-to-ceiling wall map. The women were mostly wide-eyed, sweet, and young. He had a good feeling about this group. The bridesmaids were excited to celebrate, and Jeb perceived the bride had found a good match. Why else would they be happy? The tour would be easy. Just get out there, keep 'em together and socializing. Nature would take care of the rest.

"If we maintain a good pace, we'll reach Little Bay and the mouth of Antipoison Creek by 10:00 AM. I'll treat you to one of the most exclusive and popular beaches in all the Northern Neck. Cedar Island!"

"We'll do it," the bride said enthusiastically from the back.

"Why do they call it anti-poison creek?" It was the brunette again.

Jeb normally saved this story for the tour, but since she brought it up, he delved right into the history. "You said it like how it was originally meant, kind of like an anti-venom."

"Aahhh!" cried the Hen. "Does that mean snakes?"

Jeb winced. *Not again!* But the round-faced girl deserved his attention. After all, they'd paid good money for the tour, and her flirty tease deserved a genuine smile. "No. I only wanted to note that the locals pronounce it like *anna-poison.*" He gave her his attention.

Nothing forward. Just enough so she'd know he took her seriously.

She took a stutter step backwards. A small smile worked at the corners of her mouth, and a dimple showed.

He sent his attention to others in the party. "The creek received its name from Captain John Smith. A stingray had barbed him, left a nasty wound, and the local Indians advised him to bathe in these waters." Jeb pivoted and pointed at the map. "While exploring the mouth of the Rappahannock River on July 17th, 1608, he was barbed right here." He tapped at a spot. "Who wants to guess the name of this geographical feature?"

The bridesmaids were right on it. "Stingray Point!"

"Right! We have a bright class this morning." His smile was automatic and worked with the ladies.

"Stingrays?" a Hen squeaked. "What if I fall on one?"

"We should come across a few, but it's very unlikely you'll fall on one." His sincerity came through in his tone. "They're graceful swimmers. Enjoy the moment."

Jeb guided the women to his small indoor training pool. The custom pool, which he designed, was installed to provide his clients a feel of the paddleboards before ever launching out on the big water. It was rectangular and had handrails on both sides. Those who wanted to check their balance and positions on their board before departing, did so. "We'll deal with the risk of falling in my next lesson."

A scuffling of footsteps sounded from the front porch . . . and then the door chimed as a party of three entered.

Jeb recognized the man, and lingering behind, mostly obscured, was Amanda. She was wearing another big ugly hat and large framed sunglasses. She took them off once inside. Jeb kept his attention on the bridal party. The last thing he needed was the pull of her eyes, and better she not suspect he noticed her. Notice her? His body shuddered with guilty confusion.

He still assumed the man to be her significant other, but today he appeared to be with someone else—a beautifully dark-complected woman—classy, and inconspicuously absorbing the scene in the Shop. Something in her face looked familiar. The thought quickly passed as he braced for Amanda.

Jeb readied himself to be friendly and address her by her name. How many times had the girls cried out at dinner "*Amanda* this!"

and "*Amanda* that!"?

Now, he couldn't get her name out of his head. He sized up her significant other, the string bean with chicken legs. He appeared to be a standup guy, but why would she go for a guy with chicken legs? Jeb's conscience pricked, thinking so uncivilly of a man he considered a proper gentleman, a man who could accurately read a situation.

Jeb stepped towards the tall man, careful to avoid eye contact with Amanda. "I'm Jeb Carter. What can I do for you?" He extended his hand. "I remember you from yesterday."

"Hi, I'm Ted. We're hoping to slip in for a tour today." Ted touched the second woman's shoulder. "Sally and me."

Jeb paused, not sure what to think. He preferred that Amanda be spoken for, but that's not how this looked.

A plan quickly took shape.

He put his arm on Ted's shoulder and directed him into the Map Room where the bridal party was still assembled and watching the fish in the large aquarium. Talking slowly and emphatically, he said, "Oh, I'm so sorry, Ted, but these ladies have booked an exclusive tour. I just don't see how we could fit *you* . . . in with *them*."

The cute brunette was the first to notice Ted, followed by the rest of the Hens. They'd turned their attention from the aquarium and took no consideration of his skinny legs. Surely they would make room for the slim, tall, good-looking Ted.

Jeb intentionally left Sally out of the picture for fear the tagalongs would be dissed by the Hens. Sally's inclusion wouldn't become known until they all arrived at the launch site—and Jeb was confident he could schmooze things over with the other ladies. He'd keep them distracted with a bit of charm until the entire party settled on the water. *The outing will work for everyone!* More than anything, he'd do it, even if it was smarmy.

I'm the mature one here.

Leave it to Amanda to approach him and apologize!

When Sally woke with the idea that she wanted to go paddleboarding with Ted, Amanda did everything to dissuade her.

"It'll be miserably hot . . . You'll get tired . . . The bugs will eat you up, and I know how much you hate 'em."

Sally stiffened. "No, Amanda. I think Ted will love it."

There was no stopping Sally from suggesting the idea to Ted when they met up in the resort's lobby. He jumped at the prospect, knowing that Amanda needed the morning to herself for another incursion onto her father's property.

Amanda told them, "I can't risk you two getting into trouble with me on this one."

"Hey, we'll only be a phone call away if you need us . . ." Ted reassured her, "and besides, I like to immerse myself in the local culture wherever I go."

Although Ted was sincere, Sally was acting coy. Amanda suggested they use the courtesy boards at the resort, but Sally insisted that Ted deserved a full-fledged tour from the Paddleboard Guy.

Amanda groaned. "Suit yourself, Sally. I think you're making a big mistake."

"We'll be the judge of that," Sally retorted.

Later, when Amanda arrived at the Shop with her friends, she paused on the porch before entering. As she'd done the previous day, she peered through the window. Jeb performed for a bridal party, his motions fluid. Whatever he'd said to some dark-haired chick, she was drooling over him. *If only she knew the real Jeb Carter.*

Did he see himself as a showman? He flashed his magnetic smile. She felt it again. The urge to be led in dance . . . not just any dance . . . *the* dance. A rite of passage dance? *Yes!*

She tried to recall the details of the legendary dance from a tale passed down by her grandmother. It all reminded her of her father and some of his spiels, enough to put her on edge. Even the memory of him dressed in a tux dancing with her at the Holly Ball wouldn't soothe her.

As soon as she entered, she caught Jeb's grimace. *What was that all about?* It bothered her more that Sally and Ted missed it.

She let some moments pass—ample time for Jeb to acknowledge her, approach her, and apologize.

She inhaled an aroma of cedar. Like the smell of her parents' walk-in closet. A feeling of home. Amanda worried she might loiter all day in the place. And what if she were to catch the scent of his lavender? That, she convinced herself, would cause her to flee.

Amanda glanced across the shop. Ted and Jeb stood side by side, chatting like old friends. Her spook-friend stood a few inches taller, like a pine tree next to an old-growth forest oak. Ted's not bad, but Jeb? A Virginia sawtooth oak!

She took to browsing the clothing racks, searching for a sports cap that could survive a storm.

Amanda felt taps on her arm and startled. It was Sally.

Her friend whispered, "We've secured a tour," and she was beaming.

Amanda kept her voice low. "Great. I love it. Now you'll get to see the jerk in action."

Sally swatted her arm.

Amanda's words came fast. "No need for me to linger. Have a great time."

She returned the sports cap to its hanger and exited. *It will probably be the last time I ever see him.*

Good riddance, James Carter.

Kat, Coffee, and Pie

Although the coffee shop was bustling, Kat recognized the woman immediately. Kat's habit was to provide a friendly greeting to all her customers, but in the case of the snooty, standoffish woman whom she figured was a New York socialite, she braced herself. Kat would feign politeness, but only to get business. This customer wasn't the type to be a regular weekend visitor. *Why waste my energy on her?*

"Good morning, Kat with a *'K'*. May I have a large mug of your *sailor's delight,* please?"

The unexpected greeting, tinged with an expected tone of uppityness, paralyzed Kat. She wondered if the woman had detected her previous mocking. How could she have learned the Kat joke? Told too many times? Certainly not with the tourists, the out-of-towners, the come-heres. It was a private little name she used with those she trusted. People like Jeb, and some of her more seasoned help. Her teenage summer staff? Never granted the privilege. She'd made one exception two summers ago, but it was with a niece, and she could only call her *Aunt Kat*. Even to Jeb's girls, she was known as Aunt Kathi.

The woman pulled off her glasses and revealed her eyes. They screamed a thousand words. The pain behind them was evident. A pleading to be accepted was another. Kat relaxed and couldn't contain a smile. "If I knew your name, it'd be on the house."

"It's Amanda." The lady returned the smile and cocked her head.

"One large sailor's brew coming right up, Amanda, and it's on the house," Kat responded gleefully, then asked, "If that's what you really want?"

"I do!" Amanda's tone was sincere. "More than you may think, but let me pay. I have another favor to ask."

"Okay." Kat fought back a sense of knowing. This was no New Yorker. She must be a local . . . a waterman's girl. Had to be. Either that, or the woman was military. She had the airs of an officer. No, the daughter of an officer. *Coast Guard? Navy!*

"Would you mind if I left a note for the Carters and a tip for Sierra?"

"Ahh. I heard you two got caught in that storm."

Amanda flinched and she restored her glasses.

"Why not just leave it with Jeb at the Shop?"

"He's too busy dealing with his morning tour," Amanda said unconvincingly.

"Do you know the saying, 'What doesn't kill you makes you stronger'? Maybe something your mother told you?"

Amanda nodded sheepishly.

Kat continued, "And then my mother would say something else, like, 'Look for the salvation that may come from a storm.'"

Amanda tried to hide her startle.

"I think it would be wrong for me to serve as a go-between. Why don't you drop it off at their house?"

Amanda's expression didn't reject the suggestion out-of-hand, so Kat added, "Since you've already been there, I'd be glad to provide their address."

Amanda turned reflective. "Yes. Thank you. It would remove any guesswork." Her voice remained tender. "Do you know where I might purchase a homemade pie this *morning*?"

Kat nodded slowly. "Jim's River Market in White Stone . . . less than two miles from here . . . best gourmet food around."

Amanda gave a small shrug like it was common knowledge.

Kat decided to play along with her ruse, and when she told her, "I'm not sure how *early* they open on Sundays, but when they do, you'll find our finest pie."

Amanda brightened.

Kat provided another tip; Amanda left practically skipping, coffee in hand, and drove off in a Jeep.

The picture was becoming clearer for Kat.

Did Isabella make a mistake or was she seeking my help?

White Stone

"A place where heaven and earth never agreed better to frame man's habitation." Captain John Smith

Amanda made repeated attempts to pay for her coffee. Kat refused, saying confidently, "Next time."

Why did Kat even think there would be a *next time*? Amanda exited the shop. *Oh well, on to White Stone.*

On their way down to the Northern Neck on Friday, Sally had asked about the origin of the town's name. Amanda gave her a history lesson. "The settlers named it for the white ballast stones the Brits dumped in the local waterways. They needed to make room in their holds for tobacco—Virginia's biggest export back to England."

"What'd they import?" Sally's voice toyed.

Amanda's face said, "We ain't going there."

Neither the town nor the bridge were unfamiliar to Amanda. Jim's was the unrivaled takeout eatery in the area. What she'd failed to remember were his Sunday hours. As a teenager, her family had been frequenter's of the deli. Her father spoiled her and her mother with Jim's oysters Rockefeller and gourmet pizzas for her girl parties.

The small town was another memory lane for Amanda. Not that anything happened in White Stone. For Amanda, it was a crossroads. Wherever she headed, she had to pass through White Stone. During the school year, it was a daily occurrence. She had to traverse the town to get to school, whether it be on the north side of Kilmarnock, or over the tall bridge to her high school on the Middle Peninsula.

The reason she crossed the river to the private school had nothing to do with segregation, but her mother's insistence that she learn how to sail. It was a strange request. She already assisted her father in the charter business and had become a Bay erudite. So why require it?

Her mother argued that she'd have a better chance at earning a scholarship to an elite university since so few young ladies sailed. She might even make it to the Academy.

Amanda had indeed received an appointment to the Naval Academy for sailing. She was a shoo-in, not only for sailing, but her grades were excellent and her father was an alumnus. It didn't hurt that she was a female, and her nomination had come through one of their U.S. senators. Her local congressman had begged the family to make the nomination, but the senator trumped his request. Had it not been for her mother's failing health, she would've accepted the appointment.

During another of her father's drunken bouts, he said, "Not only have you betrayed us, but the Old Dominion."

"Betrayal? How do you think I feel, Dad? And what does Virginia have to do with any of this?"

"Learn your history, Izzie!" They were in the den, and he swept his hand towards their book shelves.

She didn't hang around for his groggy lecture and stomped up the stairs to her room. She cried for some time, and later that evening, committed to Marymount University in Arlington, where she could be near her Aunt Nancy, taking advantage of a student-athlete scholarship for soccer.

During the summers of her high school years, Amanda explored what lay below the bridge using the data she'd extracted from Capt. Kip's logbook. Around the massive pilings that supported the sixty-foot tall span, she discovered productive flounder fishing holes. Her father exploited the information on his charter excursions. After the holes dried up, she learned, to her chagrin, that one of her father's clients had exposed her fishing hot spots on a fishing forum. It was a painful but valuable lesson she gained about protecting secrets.

Amanda pulled up to the curb and strained her eyes. A sign hung from the window. Jim's didn't open until 9:30 AM. The timing suited her. She had another errand to run—an opportunity to surveil her father's marina. Would he be at church? Maybe his fiancée sleeps over? The marina should be sleepy—the likelihood of attracting attention should be slight. *After all, I'm just a regular ole weekender enjoying the sights.*

CHAPTER 8

Marina

Amanda covered the eight miles to the marina entrance in as many minutes. She would've liked to have removed the Jeep's top, but considered it too risky. Off the main road, the entrance to the marina forked. To the right, the Marina House, the horse pasture, and the stables. The left fork led to the marina, Amanda's intended target.

She passed the main gate, and the pasture came into view, lush and green. Several horses were grazing. The Jeep rolled along as Amanda let her eyes wander, and then she slammed on the brakes.

"No!" *Could it be?* "Gusty?"

That was her horse in the pasture. *Gusty!* Her beloved Gusty! Amanda couldn't resist. She reversed the Jeep Wrangler and reentered, taking the right fork. She scanned her surroundings and parked by the barn. There were other horses—evidence that her father was renting stables. But there wasn't a soul in sight. She parked, careful to prevent being trapped in by another vehicle.

She got out of her Jeep and walked up to the pasture fence.

Gusty, the quarter horse, perked up his ears. Their eyes met, and he neighed and trotted over to her.

"Oh, Gusty!" Her legs could barely support her. She reached for his ears and put her arms around his entire head.

He reached for her shoulder with his muzzle and mouthed it.

"Ouch!" She stepped back and looked at him. He didn't come close to breaking her skin. "I guess I deserve that."

She put her head alongside his and held him while rubbing his ears. There were no more friendly bites. Tears of joy flowed freely down her face. "I suppose you could use an apple?"

At first, she headed towards her Jeep, but then saw the trees. "Well, you sure have grown up," she spoke to the three apple trees along the border of the property. The apples weren't completely ripe, but close enough. She gathered a handful of the colorful ones and returned to Gusty.

She held out the first apple. "Peace offering. Will you forgive me?"

He gobbled it up.

"It's not my fault, Gusty. He told me to leave. It's not my fault!" She fed him the remaining apples and continued to rub his ears.

She wiped her face. "I've got to go, Gusty. Are you okay with that? I'd really like to see you again, but things just aren't right with Dad. You understand that . . . don't you, boy?"

The horse neighed again when she returned to her Jeep. *Won't the horse stop!* A fresh bout of tears released as she pulled out from the paddock and returned to the marina entrance.

Amanda found the marina as expected—still. The serious anglers had left by dawn. The rest of the marina community was sleeping in. Her father didn't open up the pumps and the tackle shop until 11:30 AM on Sunday. She parked closest to the small but functional Marina Office. It was more of a shop than an office, its primary function to administer fuel sales.

She stepped up to the door and tried to open it. Locked. She cupped her face with her hands, blocked the sunlight, and peered in. *Nothing new.* The small shop was stocked with safety equipment that included flares, horns, rings, and a few life jackets. Her father provided basic fishing tackle necessities and carried bait in the freezer. A few water recreation items were kept on hand for the desperate boater, but his prices on them, especially the water tubes, were exorbitant.

The windows were cheap and thin and the large slider window was unlocked. Amanda inspected the marina for eyes, observing none but the squawking seagulls and two ospreys chasing a bald eagle threatening their young flyers.

She nudged the screen off its track, letting it fall to deck, then fastened her damp palms to the surface of the window and gave it a little push. Reaching her hand through the opening, she turned the doorknob.

She crept through the small store and into the back office. She stiffened. Her palms remained damp. Two pictures were on her father's desk. The first showed him at the helm of the *Queen Mary* with an unknown woman at his side. He was smiling and looked content. The second picture was of the same lady holding a crab pot full of blue crabs, the sunset reflecting off the woman's face—perfectly staged. She, too, was smiling and seemed content. They probably anchored the *Queen Mary* and steamed the crabs right on board—alongside a glass of wine. Maybe he proposed to the woman then.

The thought of the wine reminded Amanda to be on the lookout for her father's booze. When she returned for a brief visit during the summer after her mother's death, she'd found liquor in the shop. Her father had never been far from the bottle. When she also found it on the boat, they had words. She threatened to report him to the Coast Guard and have his license revoked. It was a horrid memory—one of the last things she'd said before leaving for good. The two had quarreled the night prior over other issues. The family legacy, for one. He still hadn't forgiven her for declining the Naval Academy appointment.

"You're throwing away everything we did for you!" he'd slurred, gesturing with a half-empty bottle.

She responded by blaming him for her mother's death—failing to demand that her mother undergo more invasive cancer treatment.

He ignored the accusation and snarled, "You're wasting your life up at that girls' school." Her father was referring to Marymount, but he hadn't realized that it was no longer an all-girls school. His sister Nancy had attended in the '70s, and that's what he remembered about it.

The insinuation hurt Amanda even more. It reminded her he'd taken no interest in her application, nor her freshman orientation, and for that matter, nothing about her first year. He came to none of her soccer games. He never asked about her grades or her degree choice.

He was focused on caring for Mom at the expense of anything

else, including her, his own daughter. Amanda proposed a gap year. She insisted they could share the burden. Her father refused. In honest reflection, her mother's desire was that she not put her "young, promising life on hold. Who knows, Isabel, I may be over this spell by December." She wouldn't be over it until her death in March.

The safe in the shop hadn't been moved. Amanda wondered if the combination had been changed. Sitting at her father's desk and using the numbers on his phone as a guide, she transposed "IZ-ZI-EW" into the six-number combination. She wiped her hands dry using a rag hanging from a wastebasket. A familiar clicking sounded as she spun to the left, to the right, and back again to the left. She pulled down on the lever. *Bingo!* In it, she found the cash purse, a few titles, and her father's pistol. But no ring!

Before departing, she grabbed hold of one of the pictures and eyed it closely. *Hmph*. She would have liked to have thrown it down and shattered it into a thousand pieces, but she restored it as found. It wasn't the woman in the picture who bothered her, but his wine glass. It appeared to be filled with sparkling water.

"I hate you, Dad!" she slammed her hand down on the desk. She felt the sting of tears. "No, Dad, I really want to love you . . . but I can't. I just can't!"

Treads gently sounded from the oyster shell drive from the nearby West property, enough for Charlotte Dandridge to pause on her side-entrance stoop. She'd just exited her home, stepping into the carport, on her way to church. The vehicle's engine's hum was barely discernible, but it was getting louder. Then it cut off entirely.

Her neighbor friend, Charley West, had been renting out stables on the adjacent property for as many years as she'd known him, and it wasn't unusual for locals to pull into the lane and then to the barn—but rarely on a Sunday morning. She didn't consider herself a nosy neighbor, but she couldn't help but notice the response of a particular horse. A Jeep was now parked by the barn, and a woman she didn't recognize exited the vehicle. The stranger walked up to the pasture fence, and the quarter horse perked up its ears. Not just any horse, and not a tenant horse. *The West horse!*

Charlotte stepped out into her yard where the view was better. She found a spot behind her wall trellis—a gift from Charley. Thick, scarlet-red roses climbed it, their color matching her floral print dress.

She fingered a small gap in a cluster of semi-double blaze blooms and peered through it. Without being called, the horse trotted over to the lady by the fence. The two were affectionate with each other, and the visitor knew the horse's name. Charlotte's mouth dropped.

She employed her lip-reading skills—a talent she'd acquired through her CIA case officer training. She was adept at it, even with the distance between her house and the pasture. The visitor spoke the horse's name repeatedly and quite emphatically, the emotional reunion, palpable.

When the horse finished chomping down several apples, the strange woman kissed him on the side of the head and returned up the lane.

When the vehicle turned back towards the marina, Charlotte reentered her house and commanded a view from a second-story window. Now it appeared the stranger was breaking into Charley's marina shack!

Charlotte quickly returned to her carport. She drove across both her and Charley's adjacent side yards, avoiding the noisy gravel. Arriving at the marina, she parked between two large sailboats on lifts and cut the engine.

The woman in Charley's shack had left the door slightly ajar, but beyond that, it was difficult to see what she was doing inside.

Charlotte dug through her purse and pulled out her smartphone. Charley's number was only a speed dial away. So were the police. But why make a scene? She doubted the woman was armed. Why not confront her? *No!* Trapping her could escalate the situation.

The air was heavy. Charlotte looked at her watch and blew out a breath. She eyed the yachts on either side of her. The hulls could use a fresh coat of paint.

There was movement again at the shack. Charlotte held her breath. It hadn't been five minutes before the intruder exited, shut a window, and re-inserted a screen into its frame. The twentyish-looking woman turned around, scanned her surroundings, and quickly departed. Charlotte noticed nothing carried out. *If she's a thief, she must've been disappointed with Charley's bait.*

The woman whizzed by in the Jeep. Charlotte released her breath and felt the slightest thrill. "I guess I'm still pretty good at this," she said. The Jeep's driver hadn't even glanced towards Charlotte's Ford Fusion sitting between the yachts.

Charlotte allowed several minutes to pass before she exited the marina. She came upon the same Jeep idling on the bridge at Foxwells. The driver signaled for her to pass, but paid no attention to her when Charlotte drove by. Charlotte, on the other hand, got a good look at the girl in the Jeep.

Charlotte was no longer asking, "Who just broke into Charley's office?"

The answer was obvious. Her foremost concern was what to do with the information.

Chosen

On leaving the marina, Amanda stopped on the Foxwells Bridge. Traffic was light and she had a few minutes to burn before Jim's would be open. She felt safe here, so she removed the Jeep's roof and stowed it. Below her, fish battered the concrete and splashed as they chased prey. She straddled over the passenger seat and leaned out over the rail. *Rockfish!* Her hands sweated. Where the trail-edges of the current collided twenty yards from the bridge, the stripers leaped out of the water.

She'd often fished here with her neighborhood friends. For many, less privileged than she, it was for sustenance. The tides funneled water under the narrow passage below the bridge, providing a smorgasbord for the predator fish lurking in the slipstream wash.

It wasn't long before a car approached from her rear—some sort of Ford sedan. Amanda extended her hand out her window and waved, paying no attention to the driver as the car passed around her.

The Hens' tour meandered in the distance, crawling at a snail's pace. A small smile danced across Amanda's face. She doubted they'd make it out as far as Little Bay before having to turn around. They'd yet to reach the war canal and she expected the Hens would crash at the first beach excursion. *Paddleboard Guy is going to have a hard time rounding them up.*

Sally looked like an Olympian compared to the younger women in the bridal-party. *At this season of their lives, shouldn't they be looking their best?*

The thought deserved a rebuke, and she erased the smile from her face, feeling as if she'd salted her own open wound. The women were enjoying themselves . . . celebrating life . . . immersed in healthy social interactions . . . preparing to celebrate a marriage. She felt all alone.

Dad did this to me.

Amanda grabbed her binoculars from the glove compartment and set them on her lap.

I'm not being honest. Her father had made attempts to reconcile. She'd ignored them. He would've come to her graduation, but she chose not to attend to avoid the *opportunity*—an opportunity for him. She, on the other hand, still celebrated by attending many of her friends' before and after-parties. Her Aunt Nancy offered to throw her a party of her own, but she refused. Amanda lived out the day on her own terms.

Amanda's memories came after her again, like the scampering crabs of the tidal flats bursting out of their sand holes. Her father hadn't exiled her horse. Gusty was in excellent shape. Someone had taken good care of him. The family dog was missing, but that wasn't a surprise. Tootsie, the chocolate spaniel lab, was twelve years old when she'd left.

Maybe her father had sent a letter about Tootsie's passing. If he had, she'd never opened it. Like all the others he posted, she threw them into the burn box.

Although Amanda hadn't read them, she suspected she was now discovering what might have been within them. She found that forgiving *herself* for shutting him out was far more difficult than forgiving *him. What did Dad lose?* She was beginning to understand. He'd lost his beloved wife, his dearest treasure, the one he'd chosen, desperately wanted, and cherished. *Mom was the girl he singled out from all the others.* He had plenty of options. Her mother told her so.

Amanda remembered a story her mother recounted as they sat together on the porch of the Marina House, waiting for her father to return from a charter.

"Won't you come sit with me, Isabel?" Her mother bundled under a blanket, but it was warm outside.

Amanda fetched her a hot tea and expected her mother to launch into a discussion about warm water versus cold. But she only wanted to speak about Amanda's father. Her mother's voice now continued to play in her head to the music of the chirping birds and the tidal current flowing below:

"I was out having dinner with my college girlfriends at the downtown waterfront in Annapolis. Your father entered the restaurant with a handful of his midshipmen pals and we locked eyes. His party sat opposite mine across the main aisle. My friends were chit-chatting and gossiping quietly in *girl-speak*. I knew what they were doing, but I wouldn't take part in the game. They were ranking the sailors across from us . . .

"He was dashing in his midshipman's uniform. The guy had promise. He knew what he wanted in life and was pursuing it. That wasn't the case with most of the other young men in my circle. He kept me paralyzed . . . stealing glances as they discussed their homework—thermodynamics. Funny how you remember little things like that. I was embarrassed. He singled me out amongst my friends . . . and your father *outranked* his companions.

"During the meal, I dropped my cloth napkin, and he reached over the aisle, snatched it, and wouldn't return it. He grabbed a spare clean one from his own table, pulled out a pen, and wrote a number on it. It was the number of the phone at the end of his hallway at Bancroft Hall, the largest dormitory in the world. He wrote *West* next to the phone number and handed it to me. He told me years later that he paid the restaurant for the cost of the napkin . . . at his insistence. I didn't call him for six months, but eventually got the nerve to do so. He invited me to the traditional Ring Dance. The rest is history."

"What history, Mom!" Amanda muffled her cry, encouraging her mind to remember.

"As the relationship progressed, I returned to your father's family home in West Point—Virginia, mind you—to attend his high school reunion. I always thought it strange that a guy born in West Point would attend the Naval Academy, and over the course of your father's career, he was often confused as being a West Point Military Academy graduate.

"I discovered my *Charles* was quite the guy in his hometown. I met many of his high school friends, his sportsmen, and even his academic teams. He was a scholar-athlete, much like you, Isabel.

Your father's guy friends approved of me, but his lady friends gave me the cold shoulder. Had it not been for your Aunt Nancy, I wouldn't have made one female friend in that town. They made me feel like I was stealing their hometown hero! They considered him to be off-limits. I never admitted to your father how flattered I was by his guy friends. 'Now, Mary, if this town idiot doesn't get a ring on your finger within a year, you know where to find me.' I left the reunion with no less than five phone numbers scrawled on either business cards or party napkins."

"After graduation, they shipped Charles off to Pensacola Naval Air Station for flight training. I had no ring. I hadn't fully accepted the difficulties of life as a naval spouse. He didn't relent in his pursuit . . . patient with me. When he sensed my inclinations had changed, he was prepared and returned one weekend as part of his training. He and his instructor, along with another student, were making a cross-country sortie, learning to navigate and land on unfamiliar airstrips. He managed to secure a solo. I boarded as a stowaway. How he pulled it off, I don't know. They were more relaxed about those things back then. Had he been caught, it would've been nothing more than a slap on the wrist. The other two aviators had been in on the plan. Typical of your dad, his proposal was well-planned and dramatic!"

"But how, Mom! What did he do?" Amanda now groaned from the Jeep, no longer able to remember. *Where did the ring come from?*

He'd chosen her mother. As their daughter, Amanda wasn't "chosen." A *child* was chosen, but nothing more. *My parents "got what they got" with me and did their best to raise me . . . but I wasn't chosen!*

Had her father wanted a son instead?

She wasn't the center of their marriage—just a by-product. *My mother was* chosen*!*

Amanda trained her eyes towards the party on the water—one girl was equipped with bright pink paddles. She sighed. *Oh . . . to be chosen.*

Amanda sighted the tidal-marsh inlet. The waters of the Bay sparkled beyond it. Ted and Sally were bringing up the rear of their entourage.

She eyed Jeb. Even from a distance, she could make out his

features and the smoothness of his motions. She pulled the binoculars to her eyes.

Paddleboard Guy seemed to play the role of referee, entertainer, and guide—all-in-one! The girls flocked about him and angled for his attention. He doled it out evenly, kept them happy, and maintained the peace.

She zoomed in on him. There was less sulking in his face. Sulk or not, she admitted to herself he was handsome. That tingly feeling shot up through her spine. Still, there was something else about him she couldn't put her finger on. *Why am I so drawn to him?* She let out a large huff. *This is ridiculous!*

If a girl paid too much attention to Ted, Jeb intentionally attracted her away with his flashy smile. He would engage in some chit-chat with her and then slowly and deliberately lead her to the front of the pack. Sally would regain her position, paddling alongside Ted as he trolled a line behind his board. In a span of minutes, Ted caught two fish and tossed them into the cooler. Sally was impressed, though Amanda didn't know what was being said, only that Ted was receptive to her praise.

A few girls removed their protective sun shirts worn over their bathing suits and swooned in after Paddleboard Guy.

How senseless.

"Is he so worth it to do something so stupid?" she whispered out loud, "Just to expose cleavage?" She shook her head. "Your skin shouldn't see the light of day."

Paddleboard Guy wasn't taking the bait. Amanda's heart fluttered. *Please, God, he can't be that genuine!* She stopped the feelings cold and returned the binoculars to their place.

Amanda wondered, if she was on tour, and Jeb flashed his phony smile at her, how would she respond?

I'd smack him in the face!

Blueberry Pie

Tires crunched on the pea gravel driveway. Ralph honed in on them above the whirling fans of his screened-in porch. It couldn't be Maria's minivan. He didn't expect her home with the girls for another hour, and besides . . . they sounded like wide truck tires, emanating from the front entrance of the Bay House where Jeb usually parked. *Didn't he head out for a morning tour?*

Earlier, Ralph had taken the girls to their Sunday school class while he attended his own class and made no plans to stay for the later service. There would be a guest speaker, and he always suspected that the pastor brought in inferior fillers for his own job security. In Ralph's opinion, they were all deficient in some form or another.

Maria joined the girls later to attend the main service. She'd come home raving about the message. She always did. He was content to attend the men's class. Ken was teaching a series on eschatology, end times gloom and doom. He expected Ken would throw the virus into the mix. Ralph had seen the trick used before, but it would still be interesting.

Ralph preferred to remain planted in his chair, savoring a rare quiet moment on the porch with his newspaper and a cup of coffee. He glanced up from the paper and relaxed his eyes. They swept a view like the hand of a clock turning back time. To his far right, his lagoon emptied into the mouth of Henry's creek. The surface was smooth today, broken only by fleeing shad. To his front, a flotilla of watercraft traversed Indian Creek. Sailboats, heading out for cruises. Motorboats, hurtling in after making early catches of Spanish mackerel and bluefish. Grandfathers, fishing with their sons, returning to their retirement homes on the water to recharge and re-emerge in a few hours, dragging tubes with their grandchildren in tow.

At eleven o'clock, his line of sight took him across Fleet's Bay to Windmill Point, nearly eight miles distant. To his left, as if beckoning the promise of youth and adventure, expansive views of the Chesapeake Bay—tugs pulling barges and other tankers coursing through the shipping channel. The osprey pair, which earlier in the summer had closely guarded the nest at the end of the dock, were now only periodic visitors. They'd successfully launched three chicklets this year. The first to fly did so by the Fourth of July weekend—typical.

Ralph glanced over his shoulder and peered back through the house towards the front entrance. A faint figure was leaving something at the doorstep on their porch.

He pushed up from his chair exhaling a heavy sigh and padded across the great-room. When he reached the etched-glass front door, he opened it and stepped out onto the stoop-deck.

The West girl!

She was pulling away in her Jeep. Ralph shouted at her over the din of the tires and engine. He hadn't planned it—it just burst from his lips.

Amanda's quick stop at the River Market proceeded uneventfully. A teenager was manning the register, and Jim and his wife were in the back. It was a swift purchase. Had either been at the front of the store, Amanda would've been nerve-racked, even with the goofy hat and glasses. She removed them on her way to the Bay House—her hair down and blowing in the wind. She crossed a small bridge and located the property's entrance, where she'd exited the day before with Maria. It was subdued—neither gated nor fenced, but certainly isolated and private—the sandy drive leading to the home spanning over half a mile.

She'd prepared a thank you note earlier that morning using the resort's complimentary stationery. She attached it to the pie's box and set it on the porch.

Dear Mr. and Mrs. Carter,

I would like to thank you for the kind rescue of my person from the waters of your Bay. I am deeply sorry to have put your granddaughter Sierra in harm's way. My actions were reckless. You have raised her well. She did an excellent job looking out for my safety. I wish I had been more careful with hers.

I found Nora to be another marvel. You should be most proud in both.

Thank you for the dinner. It was delightful, and the discourse that followed later with Mrs. Carter, engaging.

I would like to make restitution for the damage incurred to your beautiful Galleon. I'm to be blamed.

Sincerely,

Amanda

Why not mention the *Paddleboard Guy* father? He was despicable and didn't deserve recognition. Her feelings had changed only slightly since when the note was first written, but not worth the effort required to rewrite it.

"Miss West!" a voice shouted over her crackling tires in the gravel.

Amanda was in reverse and braked the Jeep hard, her head slamming against the headrest. Her heart pounded in her throat.

Ralph stood on the porch, waving enthusiastically. She hadn't expected anyone to be home. And certainly not to be called *Miss West*!

She cut the engine, stepped out of the Wrangler, and faced the man. She tried to conceal her trembling by grasping her hands around her stomach, but it leaked into her voice. "Good mor-orning, Mr. Carter."

It would've been impossible to run from Ralph. His smile enlarged his cheeks.

Her voice stuttered, "I . . . I've brought over a blueberry pie from

Jim's. S-sorry, I would've liked to have baked it myself."

His expression flattened, but his voice held some tease. "What happened to you calling me *Ralph*?"

Some heat returned to her face. "Yes—what happened to you calling me *Amanda*?"

Ralph clutched the pie-box like a prize. "Why don't you join me on the back-porch for a nibble and a good cup of coffee?"

Amanda eyed her note, still attached to the pie-box. Her heart stroked an abnormal rhythm.

She stepped onto the stoop-deck and reached for the stationery envelope affixed to the box.

His hand landed right on top of hers and the letter. "Not so fast, young lady."

She flinched, but then caught his eyes. They were playful. She wondered if he had a serious bone in his whole body.

His tone teased again. "I'd like to read it."

She sighed and dropped her shoulders. To have left it and run was one thing. But now . . . to face him while he read it? Her stomach churned.

She followed Ralph through the front door and into the kitchen. He reached to the upper shelf of a cabinet and pulled out a mug. It was decorated with colorful seashells and sand dollars. "Will this do?"

She nodded, and he poured a thick, dark coffee.

"Cream?"

"A little," she said, pinching her fingers.

Ralph spoke with the voice of a victim, "Maria typically dilutes my coffee with half a cup of water."

Her hand came to her mouth as she suppressed a giggle. She raised her mug in a gentle salute. Anything to regain her confidence.

Ralph led her to the screened-in porch carrying two small plates and the pie; he pulled up a folding TV table to fit between them and tossed his newspaper aside.

Amanda placed her coffee on the table and sat down. Ralph raised the note in the air. Her hands trembled, so she placed them in her lap.

Ralph eyed the pie but then reached for the thank you note. He read it to himself. The silence was so loud it was deafening.

Eventually, he murmured, "Mmm," and his eyes came up from

the stationary. "I noticed you didn't mention my son in your *kind* remarks." He showed no concern for his sarcasm.

She blushed. "No. I didn't."

He tapped on the stationery as if to punish it. "You've given Maria and I far too much credit."

"Oh." *I am a bad girl.*

"Yes. Our granddaughters are who they are because of James. Not us." He wagged a finger in the air, and his expression turned inquisitive. "I understand why."

Amanda stiffened. "Why what?"

"His behavior last night was atrocious . . . not like him." He shook his head. "I understand why, but I'd like to offer an explanation for his odd . . . and at times . . . rude behavior."

Amanda acknowledged him with a shy nod and turned her gaze to the water. *Heaven forbid he suspect I have feelings for his son!* Ralph wouldn't continue until she returned her attention to him.

"Actually, he's never rude. Last night was an anomaly, and I'm not apologizing for him." He shook his head again. "He needs to own up to it, but I want you to understand his demons. I think he's still dealing with PTSD."

This was a serious Ralph, a side to him she hadn't seen the evening before. She waited patiently for him to continue, but awkward moments prevailed.

Amanda hugged herself. "Why'd you call me Miss West?"

"Your features." He tilted his head. "You resemble your parents. I'm close with your father." He paused and his voice softened. "Maria and I also knew your mother."

Other than her Aunt Nancy, it was rare to speak with someone who knew her mother. But Amanda was in the Northern Neck now. Who wouldn't know her mother? She suppressed the pain in her throat and had no words.

Ralph broke the silence. "Jeb knows your father even better than I do."

"Oh," she said dismissively.

Ralph tried to read her, but she didn't give him anything but a blank stare, more out of fear of what she'd say unfiltered about Jeb. They'd be mean, vindictive words. Confused feelings she might share with Sally. But not Ralph!

Ralph served the pie and continued to explain the nature of the relationship while eating a slice. She'd lost her appetite, but still dabbled at it with her fork. A small morsel changed her mind. It went down smoothly with a slurp of coffee.

"Does your father know you're here?" His forehead creased. "He didn't mention your visit this morning."

Panic hit her. "No. And please, Mr. Carter, don't say anything." She leaned forward and lowered her voice. "I beg you to keep this in confidence."

He looked up at the ceiling towards a fan. "We can do that." His eyes came to her. "I believe your father would welcome you with open arms."

Her shoulders felt lighter. She forked her pie again. "Does your son know?" An edge crept into her tone.

"I doubt it. And I'd suggest you not say anything. Maria and I, of course, won't either."

Her breaths felt easier.

"Jeb's focus is on the business right now . . . trying to keep it afloat. Pun intended." Ralph cracked a small smile, and it slowly disappeared. "He hasn't healed."

She cocked her head. "I'm sorry." Amanda needed to remind herself that she was still angry with him.

Ralph's eyes softened. "You take so much after your mother."

"Thank you." Her mother was always gracious. A twinge of guilt tugged at her stomach. *Why don't I take after her? She could forgive anyone. When did I become so bitter?* Amanda put the brakes on the memory. She offered Ralph a hesitant, apologetic smile. When she spoke, the edge had left her voice. "I'm deeply sorry about the damage to the *Galleon,* and I want to make it up to you. It was my fault."

"It would've happened, regardless." His tone wasn't convincing.

"I don't think so, Mr. Carter. I saw very little damage to the boats at my father's marina." Amanda gestured with a hand in the creeks' direction. "And how about the boats nearby?"

"No."

She swept her hand towards the water views. "And neither do I see any holes in the screens."

"Good eyes, Ms. West. You'd make a formidable insurance adjustor. I won't be filing a claim. I know a glass guy who'll take care of it—far less than my deductible."

"I'll pay his bill."

"No, you won't." Ralph stiffened.

Amanda sighed, and her body surrendered. "What can I do to make this up to you?"

"Ahhh." Ralph nodded and narrowed his eyes. "I haven't thought about that, but when the time comes, I'll let you know," he said with a wink.

Some moments passed, and she raised her hand to her forehead. "You should know that I pushed your granddaughter well beyond her comfort level. I was thinking only of myself."

"Not all of it could've been foreseen. I wasn't worried nearly as much as Jeb. I expect Sierra will come around eventually." Ralph closed his eyes, and she wondered if he was silently praying.

"Thank you. You mustn't have any faith in me."

Ralph jolted and opened his eyes. Was it something she said? Or how she said it?

He leaned forward. "On the contrary, Miss West. I have an incredible amount of faith in you."

She drew back. It was the most absurd thing she'd ever heard. Secretly, she savored the compliment, even though she didn't believe it.

He raised his index finger as if measuring the wind. "With God in your heart, I have faith you'll make the right decisions."

Well, that declaration was even more preposterous. Ralph and Maria knew nothing of *who* was in her heart—who was in control of her life. She'd made no statement of faith the prior evening. Hadn't she nearly killed his granddaughter? If he only knew it was in order to sneak into her father's house . . . Wouldn't that say something about her faith? Her compulsion for the ring? Hate for her father? *How about that, Mr. Carter?*

Eeyore

Ralph finished a second piece of pie before escorting Amanda back to her Jeep. Another vehicle sounded in the distance.

She felt Ralph nudging her elbow, and he spoke, "Grans returning from church with the girls. She's going to rave about the guest speaker. Watch how she solicits the backing of my granddaughters . . . although I bet Nora fell asleep on her shoulder."

Ralph had said it all in a deadpan tone. Amanda didn't know

whether she would laugh or cry. He winked at her and she burst into laughter. What a release! He laughed too and this time she did cry a little.

Nora's squeal escaped from the minivan. *She must have recognized my Jeep.* It wouldn't be hard with its pink signage on the spare tire:

Sierra kept her enthusiasm in check. Nagging guilt punched into Amanda's abdomen again. *Sierra's more upset than I thought.*

Nora was the opposite. Her singsong voice floated out the moment the van door opened. She ran straight to greet Amanda, wrapping her arms around Amanda's waist.

As Maria got out of the minivan, her voice teased, "And what's this secret rendezvous with the mermaid, Ralph?"

The look conveyed much more, and Amanda understood—Maria would've known Amanda's mother and made the connection. Amanda approached Grans, and the two embraced. Amanda wiped a tear and quickly composed herself.

"Mermaid indeed! I caught her before she could escape. She left me a blueberry pie."

"That was kind." Maria's face brightened.

"Yes, *Maria*, I was trying to remember the last time my own *sweetheart* made me blueberry pie."

"What a coincidence, *Ralph*. That's just what I was thinking on the way home from church. I doubt my *sweetheart* could make pie, but I was wondering when he last brought one home for me."

"Mother's Day!"

"No, that was Jeb."

Ralph's face projected futility—he was out-manned four to one. He knew when to throw in the towel. Fortunately for him, Nora grabbed Amanda's hand and interrupted, "You can't leave now, Miss Amanda. We just got here."

She found herself back inside the house without realizing it. Sierra, however, remained silent and somber.

Maria offered Amanda lunch, but she declined.

Nora strolled by the kitchen island and eyed the remains of the pie. "Grans, looks like Gramps got into the pie . . . before lunch." Her voice turned deliciously sweet. "Shouldn't I have a piece with Miss Amanda?"

"If she gets pie, then I get pie," Sierra cried.

Maria rolled her eyes and barked, "Ralph, next time . . . hide the evidence!"

Ralph dropped his shoulders. His cowering was totally fake, and he winked at Amanda.

Amanda stifled a giggle and looked towards the girls. "How about I just sit with you while you eat? I've had my piece."

Ralph opened his arms in a wide *V*. "Hers was this big!"

Maria waved her hand at him and shook her head in disbelief. The girls giggled, and each put an arm around him. Amanda smiled, unable to stifle her amusement.

Maria gave her the evil eye. "You're encouraging him, dear." Amanda burst into laughter. Maria joined in.

This family is full of fun and joy! But how strange. How could Ralph and Maria be more akin to a comedy act when their son was . . . a party pooper! *I guess he got the Eeyore gene.*

"Best gramps in the world," Sierra said proudly and glanced up at him.

After Nora's eyes played with Sierra's, they danced towards Amanda. "We have some exciting news." Nora inched up in her chair.

While she continued to speak, Amanda tucked a loose curl behind Nora's ear and noticed Sierra brighten a little.

"We've been invited to serve as Eco-Tour Buddies on a cruise to Tangier Island!"

Amanda's insides warmed. *Buddies* typically referred to roles aiding special needs individuals in some activity. *My world!*

"How interesting. Tell me more."

Sierra settled back in her chair and wrapped her arms in front of her.

"We're taking a big boat!" Nora stretched out her arms for emphasis.

"How big?" Amanda let her eyes drift toward the ceiling, not wanting to appear too eager with Sierra watching.

Sierra dropped her arms and swung her left hand in front of Nora's mouth to quiet her. She spoke matter-of-factly. "Forty-eight feet. Certified for fifty people. It has a pilot house towards the bow with a head—"

"A head?" Amanda interrupted, fixing her sights on Nora.

"Yes, that's the nautical term for a bathroom on a ship," Nora said, pulling Sierra's hand down away from her mouth. "It has a roof that comes halfway down towards the stern . . . and it has a tuna tower! *You* can stay in the shade when it gets hot." The excitement in Nora's voice escalated. "But *we'll* be going fast, Miss Amanda. *We* won't be getting hot!"

The boat sounded just like Captain Kip's. It made total sense. He'd been part of the Special Angler program in the Northern Neck for years. And Tangier Island was only a short jaunt from his slip at Ingram Bay Marina.

Sierra dropped from her bar stool and headed to the sink. "The trip includes a walking tour of the island, fishing, and talks from a crabber and oysterman."

Amanda thought the girl was suppressing her enthusiasm, but that was okay. Their fledgling relationship was still on life support.

Sierra refilled her water cup, turned, and flashed a smile at her sister. Was that her way of granting Nora permission? Approval for what Amanda suspected might come? Would they invite her? She already knew she'd jump at the opportunity.

Amanda turned and looked out towards the water to hide her anticipation. She caught sight of Ralph holding an unusual expression but couldn't quite make sense of it.

Maria cleared her throat. Amanda still had her back turned towards the woman when Maria spoke, practically choking on her words. "The girls will escort several families having children with special needs on a specially designed tour of Tangier Island." She coughed again and explained how she'd run into the charter captain and his fiancée at church. The couple who'd extended the invitation. "The invitation was more of a plea for help. They have a way of overextending themselves."

The description rang true of Captain Kip, always overextending himself. How sad to learn he'd lost his wife. It was Captain Kip she'd first sought when finding her father drunk on his boat. Better Kip than an immediate report to the Coast Guard. He'd promised to keep a watchful eye on her father.

And Kip was safe. Like Ralph and Maria. He might figure out her identity, but he'd respect her privacy and the fact she'd returned to the Northern Neck.

"Oh, Miss Amanda, why don't you come with us?" Nora cried.

Maria sipped her tea and coughed yet again, but when Amanda peered over, she looked okay, just patting her chest and eyeing her husband.

Amanda turned around and faced the girl. "When?"

"Tomorrow!" the girls popped in unison.

Sierra showed surprise at her own exuberance and quickly knitted her arms.

Amanda gave Sierra a look that asked for her approval.

Sierra fought a reluctant, unforgiving face, but lost control, her lips curling upwards.

Maria coughed louder. Amanda frowned. If something was wrong, wouldn't Ralph come running? Or did Maria just have a sore throat?

The woman stopped coughing and her expression turned curious, like she was more interested in hearing Amanda's response.

Amanda kept her gaze on Maria, just in case, and threw some playfulness into her voice. "Well, I really do need to get back to work . . . and I didn't provide notification . . . but it does sound nice. I'll *so* be missing my friends at work . . ." She stopped there and gasped dramatically. "Will there be dolphins?"

"Yes!" both girls sprung from their barstools.

Amanda turned her attention to them. She tossed her hair back and slapped her sandal on the floor. "Well, that settles it. I'll go!"

Nora squealed and threw up her hands, spilling what remained of her drink. The girl's cheeks reddened, but Amanda squashed Nora's embarrassment with a laugh and was quick to grab a paper towel and clean it up. She then returned her attention to Maria.

The woman was frozen and appeared ready to faint; the blood drained from her face.

"Are you okay, Maria?" Amanda grasped the woman's hands, and Maria gently squeezed her hands in return, wearing a fraught grin.

Ralph stepped towards Maria. "She's fine," he answered, though his expression was one of concern. However, he wasn't looking at his wife, but at Amanda.

Concern for me?

Ralph turned from them all, hiding his face from his granddaughters.

It hit Amanda then like a tree falling squarely on her. Maria's coughing, Ralph's pinched expression. How had she missed the possibility?

She didn't dare face the girls when she asked, "What's the name of the boat?" As much as she tried to hide it, Amanda heard fear leak into her voice. She suspected her coloring was not that different from Maria's.

"The *Queen Mary* . . . Captain West's boat," Sierra said, like it was an obvious fact.

Amanda's stomach knotted in a thousand twirls. *My father's boat!* Why hadn't she seen that coming? The boats were nearly identical. It was Captain Kip who led her parents to the same custom yacht maker in Maryland. He advised them. The *Queen Mary* was an improved version of his design.

A swarm of butterflies invaded Amanda's gut, and her mouth went dry. They didn't need to know that she knew the vessel like the back of her hand. *But Dad! What about Dad?*

"Excuse me." Her back remained turned to the girls, and she continued a course right past Maria, out of the kitchen, and straight into the bathroom.

Amanda took some steadying breaths. She grasped the edges of the sink. In the mirror, Amanda looked as wan as Maria had. She couldn't blame the couple. They tried to warn her without alerting the girls. She felt vulnerable and naked. A feeling not so different from the one she experienced in the same room the night before.

Saving face with Nora and Sierra would be impossible. *Sierra doesn't deserve me bailing on her.* The idea made Amanda's head spin. All day on the boat? So near her father? Nowhere to hide.

Amanda cupped a handful of water and splashed it on her face. *For once in your life, Amanda, do the right thing!*

She brightened and grinned. Fake. *As fake as their father's plastic smiles.* She gave herself another minute to think. *If I do go, what might I discover about the fiancée? The ring!*

When Amanda reentered the kitchen, Ralph stood next to Maria, their backs to the sink. Amanda raised her cheeks a little higher, so they'd know she wasn't backing down. She stepped behind the girls on the stools and wrapped her arms around them.

"Thank you for inviting me. I'm looking forward to the outing." Amanda regulated her voice and impressed even herself with how well it concealed her anxiety.

Maria arched an eyebrow, in awe. Ralph gave her two thumbs up.

Nora looked up at her. "You're going to love the boat. And Captain West? He's a very nice man."

Amanda patted her back. "I'm sure he is." Amanda needed to restore her practiced smile, so artificial she suspected the kitchen light bounced off it.

"His fiancée is nice, too," Sierra said, and Amanda felt like she'd taken a sucker-punch to the gut.

"I bet. I can't wait to meet her." Amanda thought her voice sounded flat even with the fake smile.

She strode into the breakfast room and absorbed the panoramic view one last time. "Well, it's about time I get back to my friends." She reluctantly turned from the sight and faced the girls. "Anything I should plan on bringing tomorrow?"

"Sunscreen!" Nora cried.

Sierra abandoned her stool. A good sign she wanted to walk Amanda to the front door. "Don't forget your polarized sunglasses."

"You can count on it." Amanda nodded, thinking to herself, *some very dark ones.*

CHAPTER 9

Conforming

Jeb sized Ted up as a mild Jimmy Stewart, or even a young Tom Hanks. He was the type of guy that any classy girl would like to take home to visit their mother. During the excursion, Jeb treated him like a king—at first, only to add coals to the fire of his conflict with Amanda. As he observed Ted and Sally more, he was motivated simply by his admiration of both.

Sally was witty, but circumspect. He suspected Amanda told Sally her version of events from the prior day, but he didn't feel judged by Sally. Her open mind, and even a sense of approbation, encouraged him.

Ted was immensely humble and well-spoken, and if Jeb could help him in the way of this lady friend, he was more than happy to oblige.

Jeb outfitted Ted with one of the fishing paddleboards along with a pole rigged with a silver spoon, resembling a baitfish that Ted trolled behind his board. The scheme kept Ted to the rear of the entourage, while Jeb worked the Hens towards the front. Jeb was careful not to overbuild Ted's confidence and meek manner. He couldn't afford for Ted to lose his place—and that was to be segregated in the back of the pack with Sally.

Ted's competitive streak was obvious, and Jeb used it to exploit the situation. If Ted got too full of himself out in front with a Hen, Jeb paid additional attention to Sally. Ted would then slow down until Sally caught up, and Jeb tactfully moved back up to the convoy's head. The maneuver was seamless.

Jeb struggled to get his tour to move off the first beach. The bride with the pink paddle fell into his camp, so the rest had no choice but to be left behind or join them. The winds behaved, and their journey through the war canal was uneventful. Jeb told a few stories and also found a few moments to sidle up alongside Ted. This had a secondary effect of eliminating jealousies amongst the Hens as they all seemed to absorb themselves in rapt conversations—Sally included.

The bridesmaids squealed upon seeing the exclusive beach at Cedar Island. The bride gave Jeb a broad smile. "Thanks . . . good call."

He hung back as the women beached their boards and romped about. There were small tidal pools to explore and even a sand volleyball getup.

The leeward side of the island possessed deep anchorage, watercraft beaching their bows right into the sand. Anchors tossed onto the beach prevented the boats—twenty at least, saddled alongside one another—from slipping away. It was an electrifying party scene full of young life with numerous local high schoolers dominating the makeshift volleyball court and music blaring from a tiki hut. Many multi-generational families were present too—from the granddads to the grandkids.

Three teenage girls whisked in on jet skis. The ringleader was a cute little blonde, and the other two girls acquiesced to her. They could have just as well been on motorcycles. There was nothing inherently wrong with the girls. They each wore life jackets and operated the jet skis safely. They peeled their eyes to the action on the island as they approached. Jeb's guess? Looking for guys, and apparently, the boys they sought weren't present. Probably some high school friends. The three teen girls maneuvered the jet skis close together, had a few words—led by the blonde—then took off as fast as they'd come, shooting back towards the north.

One follower was a strawberry blonde, and it made Jeb think about Sierra. In only a year's time, Sierra would mix with this same crowd. He could already hear Sierra's voice pleading for a jet ski. With it, she'd have all the freedom in the world to go and come as she pleased.

He, of course, would say, "No." He'd make some feeble excuse that their budget was tight. Gramps would hear none of it. He never said "no" to anything for his granddaughters—within limits. A jet ski would definitely be within limits. Even if he had to purchase a used one.

Regardless of Kat's advice, Jeb was holding to his rules. She didn't see this world. *"Loosen the reins?" Really?* He wondered, would Sierra be a follower or a leader? *Look at the sway Amanda had on her yesterday!* Her high school years could be just as bad.

Erin never conformed. She was her own brand. Confident! Seemed to know exactly what she wanted out of life. Jeb's legs weakened, and he nearly fell down on his board.

Erin, why do I have to do this alone?

Lounge Chairs

Returning from the Carters, Amanda found Ted and Sally by the pool. They were seated in chaise lounge chairs with drinks in their hands, facing each other, and their knees nearly touching. Ted spotted Amanda before Sally. He sat upright in his chair, his attention leaping from Sally to the pool deck.

Amanda approached them with a wry smile. "Nothing wrong with squeezing a bit more together-time from the weekend."

Sally flicked at Amanda's leg. Ted sighed and continued to fix his eyes on the activity in the water.

"Before diving into a recap of our adventures, we need to talk logistics." Amanda regained Ted's attention. "My original plan was to drop Sally off at the Farm on my way home tonight, but I'll be staying on for another day."

"What a coincidence. I have a class there too!" Ted said, which Amanda already knew. "I'd be happy to take her."

Sally suppressed a smile.

Amanda glanced back at her. "Would you be okay with that? I know I promised to take you, and I still can, if you'd prefer me over Ted."

"No, no. I wouldn't want to inconvenience you, especially with this very capable fisherman at my service." Sally put her hand on Ted's arm. "What if we became stranded and had to fend for ourselves?"

"I'm pretty sure I can out-fish Ted, anytime, anywhere!" Amanda stood with her hands on her hips. "Are you sure, Sally?" She gestured at the man with a look of mock disdain. "You'd rather go with him?"

"Stop it, Amanda!" Sally shifted towards Ted. "I'd very much like to accept your offer. Don't pay any attention to the cocky *angler girl.*"

Amanda tilted her head. "Great. With that settled, I'd like to hear about your outing."

Ted's eyes bounced between the ladies. "Amanda, your friend here covered one of those bridesmaids in mud."

"What?" Amanda smiled.

"I don't know exactly how it happened, but when I looked back, Jenny, a bridesmaid, was covered in mud. Everyone else was in front of us and we were in shallow water where the bottom was that real soft mud. Next thing I knew—Jenny was screaming and whirling that goo back at Sally."

Sally sipped her drink and remained silent.

Amanda raised her hand. "You're not the only witness. I watched you from the bridge."

"You were there?"

"Not long." Amanda had seen enough to know Sally took exception to one particular bridesmaid that was flirting with Ted. She remembered Ted paddling past her, and the girl slipped behind Sally. "Maybe Sally was just a bit careless with her paddle?"

She'd seen Sally plant her paddle an extra six inches into the mud and lift it vigorously.

Sally finally spoke. "How was I to know Jenny was right behind me? Total accident!" she said in mock disbelief. "I hadn't realized it'd gotten so shallow."

Ted shook his head, looking incredulous. "Sally, had it been one scoop of mud, yes . . . possibly an accident, but you must've whacked her with five bucket loads."

"Did I, now?" Sally smiled wryly.

Sally's expression punctured the dam holding Amanda's pent-up tensions. She guffawed robustly, and Ted and Sally joined in. She didn't tell them what she'd observed Jeb doing to help relieve the friction between Sally and Jenny; he'd heaped his attention on Jenny, leading her to a deep water hole where she could clean off.

Still laughing, Amanda flopped down in a lounge chair next to Sally. She ordered a drink and played with her toes in the air. The Hens had fought hard against each other to win Ted's attention, but Sally had fought even harder and was rewarded. Ted was charming and easygoing, but wasn't aware of his attractive personality. Genuine humility. In all her meticulous planning, Amanda couldn't have foreseen the dynamic out on the water between the two, and the magic that was becoming Sally and Ted.

Amanda's paddleboard jerk was now Sally's angel and her esteem of Jeb grew more because of his ability to read a scene—his situational awareness. *Why would I think otherwise? How could he run his business without it?*

"Wow," Amanda spoke softly to herself. Her chest lightened. Jeb solved two problems. First, Ted's attention was removed from her. Second, Ted's intentions were now on Sally, and gladly received. Was that Jeb's apology?

Sally broke the silence. "Whattah you thinking, girl? You've been so quiet."

Amanda savored the moment of peace before dropping her legs to the teak lounge chair. "Nothing. Only that the man has problems. And whatever they are, they're not mine."

Sally reached for Ted's arm. "Who're we talking about now?"

Amanda shook her head. "I will demand he act civilly."

Now Ted eyed her.

"No, Ted. I'm not talking about you. Relax. You're fine."

"I know. I just think you've read *him* wrong."

Amanda eyed Ted. "So what, now you've got a guy crush on him?"

Sally's hand came down hard and flat on Amanda's arm. Amanda felt the sting, but she relished it. She knew Ted could be brutally honest. He was a geek, after all, and struggled with sarcasm.

Sally continued to glare at her, like a mother, demanding her child make amends.

Amanda's words lacked enthusiasm. "I'm sorry, Ted."

"You make it sound as if you'll see him again," he said.

"I meant to say *if* I ever see him again. I still need to pay Sierra's tip. I meant to pay it earlier when I visited the Carters, but I lost my mind."

He winked at her and dramatically pulled on his left earlobe.

"What's that supposed to mean?" Amanda couldn't hide her agitation.

Sally giggled.

Now it appeared Ted and Sally had their own inside jokes. She ignored them and let her mind drift. A young family was playing keep away in the pool with a Nerf football. *Sweet*. The father had teamed with his boy as his two daughters chased them down, crying, "Unfair!"

Amanda struck her forehead. "What was I thinking?"

Sally glanced at her. "Huh?"

Amanda's stomach knotted, and she felt lightheaded. "I can't do the eco-tour tomorrow . . . Crazy! Far too risky."

Sally drew large invisible circles with her nose. "Is this about him . . . her . . . or what's the youngest one's name?"

"Nora! No, it's not about Nora. This is about Sierra. The *jerk* won't be there."

Sally glared at Amanda. "Don't you be speaking that way about him, girl."

Amanda sent her gaze across the creek and shook her head. There was no point in responding and revealing the craziness of the bouncing pinballs ricocheting in her chest. Even if she tried, she'd sound like a blubbering fool.

Amanda caught sight of Ted's knowing look with Sally. They'd teamed up against her.

Sally's eyes softened. "How is it in just two days you're so mixed up with this family?"

"I don't know, Sally . . . I really don't know. This entire weekend has gone haywire."

"Maybe for you it has," Sally breathed in deeply, "but I've quite enjoyed myself."

Amanda caught Ted blushing.

She dropped her shoulders and sighed. "I can't do this. I should head home now."

"Oh no! You can't renege on those girls. This isn't just about you anymore." Sally turned to Ted with a pleading expression.

He leaned forward and was about to speak, but Amanda raised her palm to stop him. "Okay, okay . . . I got this. My remorse needs to be more than words. I have a promise to fulfill."

Although Amanda liked the way she sounded, inside, she was terrified.

"I'd advise that you not pay the tip," Sally said, looking very serious. Ted nodded in agreement.

"Why?"

"You'd be insulting the girl."

Amanda took a moment to think about it. They were right. Her intuition had been telling her the same. "But I promised."

"If you tip her with cash you'll devalue the relationship," Ted said. "She wants far more from you, Amanda."

"Like what?"

"Your friendship."

"But she's expecting a tip," Amanda argued.

"When you see her, just tell her you haven't forgotten and why you've withheld it. If she wants the money, she'll tell you. Be prepared to give it and walk away."

Ted was wise. It would be easy if Sierra only wanted the money, but she doubted that was the case.

Sally spoke her thoughts, "You could offer to take her shopping. The type she wouldn't want to do with her father."

"Do I now owe you a tip for your wisdom?"

"I got mine." Sally glanced at Ted. He didn't blush this time.

Amanda joined Sally back in their room while her friend packed.

"You're totally not yourself," Sally said, returning from the bathroom with her cosmetic bag.

"What do you expect?"

"No, not your dad stuff. We understand the stress you're under, but Ted and I picked up on something else."

"So you've been talking about me," Amanda snapped. "Is this how you two bond?"

"We couldn't help but talk about you. It's a side of you that we've never seen. And you should thank me I didn't raise the topic out by the pool with Ted." Sally's expression was serious, and Amanda heard the concern in her voice. "I have no desire to embarrass you."

Amanda gripped her sides. "Go on."

Sally looked up from her suitcase. "Why are you so afraid of this guy? He's definitely not a jerk, but you keep calling him that . . . and other things."

"Who, Paddleboard Guy?"

Sally slapped her hand on the bed. "Perfect example. His name is James Carter."

"So what."

"You're acting like a child. I've never seen you like this. Jekyll and Hyde. In Northern Virginia you're Amanda Mature West. Here? More like a twelve-year-old."

"Typical for an only child." Amanda grimaced.

"Well, you certainly fit the bill. Adult one day, spoiled baby-child the next."

"So, is that it? Are we done with your psychoanalysis?" Amanda narrowed her eyes hoping it would tell Sally to end it.

"No." Sally closed the distance and touched Amanda's hand. "I haven't even said the hard part."

Amanda drew a cleansing breath. Sally cared, and a properly received rebuke could only make Amanda stronger. She dropped her hands to her sides.

"We think you demonize things that scare you."

"We?"

"Yes . . . Ted only confirmed what I suspected."

"Which is what?"

"James Carter scares you."

Amanda cocked her head back. This was absurd, and Sally needed to know how crazy it sounded. "He scares me?"

"Here's the thing, Amanda. I think you're used to guys turning their heads for you, but they never grab your interest . . . but this guy and his daughters? They've lit a spark under you. But the thing is, he doesn't play like all the rest. And there's a risk he may not fall for you. But instead of stepping up to the plate and taking a swing, you disparage him."

Sally's words hit her like a thousand darts.

"Maybe it's a coping mechanism," Amanda admitted.

Sally straightened. "Darn right . . . and not a good one. But I understand. And with all this stuff going on with your dad, I get it. Just don't demonize that man."

"He hasn't played nice either."

"Probably just as scared as you, girl."

Amanda felt her shoulders drop. In her heart, she knew her friend was right, but there was no time now to explain how hard it was to be virtuous. Kind. At times over the weekend, she felt the entire world conspiring against her. Even the weather. And now, her closest friend had rebuked her.

Sally embraced her. "You're the most courageous person I know . . . to come back down here like this." Their eyes met.

Amanda nodded. Though Sally's words had pierced her soul, she knew her friend spoke the truth. "You're right . . . I can do better."

She helped Sally with her bags, accompanying her to the resort's circular drive. Ted was waiting in his car. He advised Amanda to wear a different shirt for Monday's outing and to change out the sunglasses. She would've preferred to shop at one of the thrift stores in town, but they were all closed on Sundays. He suggested the Walmart on the other side of Kilmarnock.

Amanda hugged her companions and wished them well for the week. Ted delicately reminded her again of the Iwo Jima story and to cover her butt.

As she waved her friends goodbye, her heart was filled with both joy and anxiety.

She was on her own now.

Walmart

Jeb pulled his truck into the parking lot of the Walmart just on the edge of town. He remembered the controversy the store created upon its arrival. Half the locals were happy for it, the rest were not. "It would be good for the economy!" the one half argued, while the conservatives suggested, "It'll change the texture of our town and hurt the small mom-and-pop shops." However, there was no stopping it.

Jeb didn't deny his hypocrisy. He'd been vocal about the evils of the Walmart while in the early planning stage but was now a regular customer. He was running low on a few supplies for his own tours, and with Caleb scheduled to fly solo as a guide in the morning, he didn't want to risk a shortage of sports drinks. The weather report predicted the standard fare of hot and humid.

Charlotte entered the double doors just ahead of him. Not surprising. *Likely running errands for Charley.* She was innocent, having transplanted to the Northern Neck after the controversy subsided. Jeb had gotten wind of their planned eco-tour for the special needs families. Probably shopping for drinks and snacks. Charley didn't typically supply drinks for his charter clients, except for emergency water. But tomorrow's activity was different. These weren't clients.

Charlotte had a bounce in her step. The tailored tour was their shared brainchild. Based on what Jeb understood, her involvement with Charley differed greatly from anything she'd ever done at the Agency. *I'm sure he put her corporate liaison skills to good use.* Jeb learned she coordinated the stations for each component of the tour, which included the museum curator on Tangier Island and several island watermen.

Jeb crossed paths with Charlotte in a grocery aisle. She was fixated on something—or someone—halfway across the store towards the women's clothing section. He preferred not to engage in chitchat. It had been another long day of an exhausting week! He was looking forward to a breather on Monday. But it would be rude to ignore her, so he forced a reluctant hello.

She turned around in surprise. "Oh—hi, Jeb. How are you?"

"Tired, ready to go home and relax." His voice conveyed the fatigue of having spent all day on the water in the hot sun.

"I bet. We're looking forward to having your girls tomorrow. Should be a great time." Her face brightened. "Any chance you might want to join us?"

Jeb's stomach tightened. "Ohhhh . . . they'd mentioned nothing to me." Another sign things were getting totally out of control.

Charlotte was apologetic, "Charley and I spoke with them at church this morning. They seemed excited." She touched his arm. "We'd really like you to join us."

The pain in his stomach intensified. "Don't tempt me. Paperwork day tomorrow. I'm buried in it." He eyed the cold drink section and fought back the temptation to grab a beer and down it.

Charlotte's eyes echoed her sincerity. "Your girls are growing up. Don't forget that. These years will be gone in a flash."

Her words slipped between his ribs, right to his heart. "I thought I said not to tempt me?"

"Tempt? I thought I was guilting you," Charlotte's tone teased. "I understand. It can't be easy running your own business, and I know you're in the middle of your busy season."

Jeb remembered something Charley had told him a year after Jeb had launched his business. The advice had consumed Jeb. "Just don't let the busyness of life take precedence over its beauty."

Charley also warned him about the principle of *little lasts*. "You'll never know when you've reached the *last* time they'll ask to be tucked in at night . . . or the *last* time they ask you to tell a bedtime story. The big lasts are easy, Jeb. Like a high school graduation. You see that coming a mile away and prepare for it. But the *little lasts*? Nah . . . you don't always see those coming."

Charley provided several examples and his regrets of not keeping track of the *little lasts*. Like the last time his daughter had asked him to dance. "Had I only known, Jeb." Even when she'd last held his hand. "Does Nora still ask?"

"Yes, but not Sierra. I don't have a clue when that ended."

"There you go, Jeb. That's my point."

Jeb could only hope now that Charlotte didn't suspect the tag-teaming effect of her words. There'd be no stopping her influence. Subtle as it was.

Charlotte's eyes drifted past Jeb and locked on something to his left. Following her glance, he saw who had captured her attention. There was only one person perusing the women's department. His eyes made a double quick pace back to Charlotte—no need for her to know he'd noticed.

The two continued a brief banter until Charlotte released him. Jeb was grateful for her consideration. He was ready to collapse. As he left her, he peeked back over his shoulder. Charlotte was stealing glances towards Amanda, like she suspected her of shoplifting.

Ain't it time to go home, city girl?

Persistence

"Daddy, why don't you come with us tomorrow?" Sierra started, rekindling the pain Jeb felt in his chest earlier. The family had just sat down for dinner. It was the girls' night to cook, with the aid of Grans. She kept it as simple as possible. Burgers with plenty of toppings.

He'd have a hard time saying "no" to them. Charlotte hadn't helped the situation. Jeb specifically blocked out one Monday a month to recharge, but he hadn't been strict about keeping the day free. A large extended family was in town for a reunion. They were willing to hang out through Monday for a tour, a party with a predominance of tweens and teens. "A lot of girls," the father told him.

Although Jeb spent ample time with his girls, the activity rarely centered on their interests. He loved the fact that they could participate in the business, but the outing scheduled for tomorrow was different. It wasn't about him. It was their project—their passion.

"What time do you head out?" he asked.

"The *Queen Mary* leaves the docks at 9:00 AM," Sierra answered.

"We've got a tour scheduled in the morning, but if you're willing to help get Caleb launched, I'll continue with you all to Tangier."

"Caleb?" Sierra bolted upright in her chair. "On his own?"

"Yes. I've been considering it. Now that *you've* led a tour on *your* own, I should give Caleb a shot—plus there'll be a bunch of tween girls tomorrow."

Sierra couldn't suppress a squirm, and her face reddened. Jeb hadn't intended to tweak his daughter. She wasn't jealous of Caleb. Just the opposite!

The burger and bun on his plate looked fine, but its allure evaporated. This was horrible. *Sierra has a crush on Caleb? Worse, Caleb's taken an interest in her?* Kat had mentioned the possibility only yesterday. He wondered what it would've been like to have had a boy, not in lieu of the girls, but a boy. His knees rattled under the table. *With the boy, I'd only be worried about the boy. But with this girl? . . .* All the boys!

Jeb grabbed his thighs and steadied his knees. "If Caleb does well tomorrow, I'll need him to take Saturday's tour too . . . I want to fish the tourney." He looked at Sierra. Her smile was forced. "When do you return?"

"3:00 PM," Sierra said with a blank face.

Jeb's voice wavered. "You still want me?"

"No!" Nora cried out. "I want to sleep in tomorrow!"

Jeb dropped his jaw in mock astonishment. "You don't want me?" A needle prick went straight to his heart. *Is this how it ends? Losing touch with my girls?*

Sierra's voice caught his attention, and her tone was stern. "I'd like to go with you in the morning and make sure Caleb gets the speech right."

He was pleased she'd gotten a grip on her emotions. He was missing Erin and wasn't prepared for the discussion he needed to have with Sierra. Erin would've done that, and she would've done it well. He found it strange that he could comfortably speak with Caleb about topics of the heart, but failed to do so with his own daughter.

"I'd be happy to bring Nora to the marina later . . . been some time," Grans said. "I can take pictures when you pull out."

Resolve set in. *No way are they slipping away without a fight.* "Okay, then it's settled. I'll go!" He shook his head teasingly towards Nora as if to say, "I'm going to get you for this." Then he leaned towards her, extended his hand, and gently flicked her bangs. He left his hand on the side of her face for a beat.

Jeb's appetite returned, but something else didn't quite feel right.

Not what the girls had said, but what they didn't say. He just couldn't put his finger on it.

CHAPTER 10

Monday in August

Second Thoughts

Amanda woke Monday to the music of Italian composer Ennio Morricone streaming from her iPad. She hadn't slept well, but at least the final few hours were deep. She rarely needed an alarm to wake her.

A pleasant dream had taken over, one she didn't want to wake from. In it, she found herself working in the Shop. As its owner! Sally and Ted were browsing through the racks of merchandise when a stranger entered. James Carter. He acted unusually nice as he sought Amanda's help with clothing recommendations. She had him try on several fishing shirts, pointing out when the duds matched his eyes. The girls were there too, helping her, but their role was murky, Jeb never acknowledging them as his daughters. All of it felt so warm, which is why she wanted to stay in the dream, hoping to see where it led. "Falls" from *The Mission* soundtrack was still playing when she realized it was only a dream. Cognizant, she'd loitered in it for the full duration of the opening track, "On Earth as It Is in Heaven."

Now, as the beating drums of "Gabriel's Oboe" played, reality hit her—her commitment to participate in the tour. Whereas her time spent immersed in half-sleep felt ephemeral, her heart now raced dangerously, so fast she worried she'd faint if she rose too quickly. Rays of sunshine burst past the curtains, and she covered her eyes. She let the softer notes of the song play on while she gradually lowered her hands and sat up in the bed.

The picture across the room, sitting on the desk, horrified her. The one with her and her mother, taken when Amanda was sixteen. They were arm in arm, like teenage pals. Could have been confused for twins, even back then. The framed photo was one of Amanda's most prized possessions, packed whenever she traveled, and it had always provided comfort. Not this morning . . . or last night before heading to bed. The music from "Ave Maria Guarani" increased her tension, so she turned it off.

How could she spend half a day on a cruise in such close proximity to her father?

She'd woken up twice during the night and rehearsed her cover story and the techniques she'd employ to keep him at a distance. Amanda prepared to deny, deny, deny. Mumble, mumble, mumble. He may not recognize her features when padded and covered, but her voice gave her serious concern. She stayed up watching a movie on the resort's cable TV. Amanda liked the way actor Marisa Tomei carried a heavy Bronx accent in the film *My Cousin Vinny*. She tried it. *Not bad*, she thought. Marisa Tomei it would be. Better than the mumble, mumble, mumble approach.

She'd even taken the precaution of adding a small foam pad at the top of her butt. Ted had loaned her his own home spun contraption with a slim nylon belt with a mesh pocket to hold multiple sizes of foam. On seeing the change, Sally yelped, "Girl, most women would pay good money for that look."

She fetched the pre-ordered continental breakfast waiting for her on the other side of her door. She had no appetite, but worried she'd develop seasickness on an empty stomach. Seasickness had been a rarity for Amanda, but she preferred not to take any chances. She tried the muffin, but the oils in it didn't sit well.

Amanda padded across the room and lifted the framed picture. She pulled her hair back and inspected herself in the mirror, the reflection looking more like her mother than her sixteen-year-old self. But for the mole above her lip. She covered it again in a thick layer of makeup.

What would her father see? A resemblance of himself in her? No! Only her mother saw those. *But those traits from mom?* Like her eyes? They'd explode before him like fireworks!

Why do it? Why take the risk? The ring? Not worth it! And to be trapped on the boat all day? Forget about it! But she could at least see the girls off at the marina.

Amanda fetched her new sunglasses off the dresser. A cheap purchase, but darker than the ones she wore Saturday. Would they stand up to the test? She didn't trust the image she saw in the mirror, so she pulled out her phone and took a selfie. They seemed okay. She only needed to resist the urge to take them off, like when she might want to rub her eyes. What if the girls needed her eyes—a glimpse into her soul? *Sierra must see my penitence.* And their father? *He won't be on the tour. But what if I catch him elsewhere and want to punish him with my eyes?* But he might intuit something else. A softening towards the man.

Amanda wrapped the picture in her pajama top and set the bundle in her weekend bag. As she headed towards the door, a recent memory hit her like a lightning bolt. She gasped. In the urgency of the impending storm and the crises that followed, she'd forgotten what she'd seen on her father's nightstand. That same picture! *How can dad be ready to remarry with a picture of Mom on his nightstand?*

And what would the fiancée think? *What's dad got himself into?* Not that she cared. Right? *I really don't care. She's his problem, not mine!*

Amanda quickly packed the rest of her things. Now, with a change in plans, she'd only lose a few hours of work this Monday. She'd search the Marina House as soon as her father's tour departed and hit the road after that.

She considered filling her coffee mug in the resort lobby. *Nope!* Kat's coffee would set her straight. One more splurge from the Yokel. She'd covered the entire weekend's expenses from the stamp money.

If in the event she were recognized at the marina by her father, she'd deny being his daughter. With several families expected to be on board, why would he want to embarrass himself? This was her worst-case scenario. She'd flee and deal with the aftermath later. No chance her father would corner her on the boat with all his guests. Mostly, Amanda suspected, her father would avoid shaming himself in front of Sierra and Nora. They seemed to adore the guy. *Why was that?*

Her chest weighed heavier than a millstone at the thought.

Rivah Boy

Jeb approached the town's speed zone and braked the truck gently. A cyclist rode ahead of them about a hundred yards from the Shop's entrance. Caleb. The young man was wearing the Shop's signature, bright blue sleeveless compression shirt. Jeb side-glanced at Sierra sitting shotgun. She straightened and sucked in a sharp breath. Caleb had already entered the Shop's driveway when she reached over the center console and punched a quick tap on the horn.

Jeb pursed his lips and eyed his daughter. "Now you're making me look bad."

Her retort came quickly. "Am not." Her nose squinched, much like her mother's, when Jeb would catch Erin sneaking back into the house after an impulsive purchase from a yard sale. A cute knick-knack or two, maybe spending a whopping five dollars. But Erin came back wearing an expression like he'd caught her with her hand in the cookie jar. Jeb loved that about her, the way Erin kept life fun.

Caleb was stowing his bike at the rear entrance as Jeb pulled into his spot. Sierra extended her hand out the window and slapped the truck's door panel. "That was me," she yelled with a dose of nervousness.

The young man acknowledged her with a small nod as he lowered his backpack off his shoulders.

Jeb tapped on Sierra's leg. "I was teasing."

She turned her flushed face to him. He reached for her hand. "I'm looking forward to our cruise with Captain West today."

"Thanks, Dad. I'm glad you're coming."

He released her hand, and she quickly exited the truck. She and Caleb were soon chatting at the Shop's back door. Jeb paused for a few beats and wondered about *little lasts*. How much longer would Sierra encourage him to join in her activities?

Jeb stepped out of his truck and approached Caleb. "You ready to run the show?"

"Yes, sir, Mr. Carter—ready to go!"

"I believe you." Jeb unlocked the Shop's backdoor, leaving Sierra and Caleb to enter. He returned to the yard, hoisted the paddleboard trailer, and lowered it to the hitch on the back of the truck. He didn't want to be hovering when Caleb debuted in the Map Room, rather, he vowed to lay low in his office.

On entering the Shop, he found Sierra planted behind the counter.

Jeb figured it wasn't his place to coach her on how to coach Caleb. *If she wants to hover, that's her business.* Jeb had an inkling Sierra wouldn't make Caleb nervous. He actually wished she would—it would help squash his concerns that Caleb reciprocated her feelings.

Jeb put his hand on the counter and eyed the young man. "I'll stay out of your way. Where's the map pointer?"

"Right here." Sierra was quick to pull it out from under the counter and hand it to Caleb, essentially declaring him the man of the hour.

Jeb controlled a smile, then did exactly as he had promised: he headed to his office and parked himself behind his desk. Papers cluttered his workspace, and he tried to concentrate on a bank statement.

He'd never given the reins to anyone. Although several teens had worked for him each summer, none had solely led a full-fledged tour beginning in *his* Map Room.

He leafed through a stack of bills. He struggled to focus and stood up. The urge to pop into the Map Room and correct Caleb or supplement the show was overwhelming. He took two steps to his door, stopped himself, and returned to his seat. *Why am I worried?* Caleb had seen Jeb do it so many times, and Jeb insisted Caleb perform a dry run. The young man was a natural, but once in front of the group, Jeb didn't know if the smooth Rivah Boy persona could hold.

Jeb still believed the teen ensemble, soon to arrive, was a good place to start. *He'll be a sucker for the flashing eyelashes*—young women just learning how to apply mascara.

Jeb recalled his first encounter with Caleb over four years ago. It was at a launch site on Carter's Creek in Irvington. The eleven-year-old was holding a snake and extending it towards Jeb. Caleb secured the head of the snake between the tips of his fingers, while its body wrapped around his wrist. Fortunately for Jeb, the tour group hadn't yet arrived. He was pulling the paddleboards from the trailer and setting them on the grassy area near the water's edge. It was obvious the boy was screaming for attention.

Jeb approached him. "Hi there, young man. I see you found my pet snake."

The boy threw his head back, and his eyes bulged. The snake's tail twitched.

"Would you please return him to the creek where he belongs?" Jeb tried to keep a straight face.

"Oh, yes, sir. I didn't know he was yours, sir!" The boy shot up tall.

"Well, he isn't." Jeb grew a smile. "But I really need him back in the water before my clients arrive." Jeb twirled his index finger circling near the snake's head, but kept his eyes on the boy. "What's your name?"

"Caleb Payne."

"Pleased to meet you, Mr. Payne. I'm Jeb Carter."

Jeb extended his hand, but thought better of it.

Caleb looked at the snake he was holding in his right hand and offered his left. "Glad to meet you, sir."

"What do you say we call him Henry?"

The boy turned the snake to look him in the eyes. He chuckled. "I think it suits him, sir."

Jeb noted the boy's manners. Although he appeared lonely, it was unmistakable he was reared well. "Are you from around here, Caleb?"

"Yes sir, right around the corner . . . Corrotoman Point."

"I know it. We paddle by the Point every now and again."

"I've seen your tours go by. I've waved. Have you seen me?"

Jeb's chest tightened. "Well, now that you mention it, yes." He recalled seeing a boy on the point. If Caleb insisted it was him, good enough. The gamble paid off because the boy brightened immediately.

"Caleb, once you've returned Henry to the creek, why don't you give me a hand? I'll even give you a complimentary tour with the group I'm leading today . . . assuming you've nothing better to do."

The boy's face brightened like it was Christmas morning, and he hustled to the water's edge where he released the snake.

While Caleb soaked in the attention, Jeb found him to be extremely helpful. Caleb was polite with the clients and informative, a mix between Tom Sawyer and Huckleberry Finn. He was also well-read. Someone at his home must have given him a love for reading, and Jeb found Caleb was accurate to a tee in his explanations of Bay marine life. He was comfortable speaking with adults, but Jeb suspected those influential adults in Caleb's life didn't explore the outdoors with him. Although Caleb lacked that experience, Jeb was glad to provide it, and because Caleb was precise in his descriptions, Jeb embraced the boy's *tag-a-longs.*

Accurate identification of the plants, fishes, invertebrates, birds, and other inhabitants of the bays and inlets was paramount during Jeb's tours. Caleb quickly earned Jeb's confidence in his ability to answer questions about the habitat and showed a keen sense when to point out its marvels, like the rays—southern stingrays, skates, and massive cownose rays—a mainstay for Jeb's tours. Nearly every tour came back with multiple sightings.

Caleb could also describe clouds. Jeb couldn't. He didn't admit this to Caleb at first, but played along. In time, Jeb learned how to describe the sky and all the different cloud formations, eventually teaching it to his girls. The clients coming from the burbs noticed the sky. He took it for granted, but they didn't. They weren't used to the expanse of it once on the water. Inevitably, rainbows would appear . . . full rainbows without obstructions. He explained that too.

Caleb often played the *sheepdog* role during tours. While Jeb remained in the middle of the pack, Caleb either raced ahead to guide the faster paddlers or stayed behind to pick up stragglers. If either mentioned a *Henry*, the other knew a snake had been spotted, and not to alarm the clients.

When a family was equally split between stronger and weaker paddlers, Jeb encouraged Caleb to venture ahead with the older kids—and more often than not, the father—into the small bays where they might catch a dolphin sighting. On several tours, Caleb guided them smack dab in the middle of a dolphin pod. Jeb cherished the stories they carried back, many claiming a once-in-a-lifetime experience:

"It swam directly under my paddleboard and was far larger than I expected."

"They would dive below me at the last possible moment!"

"I've never felt so vulnerable."

Although they were friendly, Jeb still feared the day a dolphin cow would upend one of his guests.

The drawback to splitting a family tour was that Jeb was often left with the mother who invariably believed it her duty to ask all sorts of personal questions about himself. He tried polite expressions that would tell them not to bother, because if they learned he was a widower, they all had either a sister or friend they insisted upon introducing to him. They also gave a sympathy tip. He hated those and simply passed the money to Caleb.

Over time, he planned ahead for those types of scenarios and wore his wedding band. They still asked questions, but mostly they wanted to know about his wife. He'd tell them all about Erin and never let them know she'd passed. Now with Sierra available to do tours with him, the problem was completely solved, his daughter running interference with the well-intentioned moms.

Caleb's high school football coach had him working out in the weight room, and the boy had grown to be a young hunk. At least that's what the girls were saying. Jeb noticed more of them loitering about the Shop when Caleb was on duty. On several occasions, Jeb heard them talking near the clothing racks, out of earshot of Caleb stationed near the Shop's front, and not realizing Jeb was toiling quietly behind his office door.

For the tween schoolgirls, he was the *attraction*. It was the age of social media, and all the tour groups were generous with their postings. A client tagged the Shop in a posting showing Caleb with a Hen's tour on the beach. The women surrounded Caleb in the photo. Not Jeb! And the bridesmaid titled the shot, *Rivah Boy*. Another responded to the post, claiming, "Our surfer dude!"

During the summer, Caleb grew his hair to shoulder length, and he tanned uniformly. He also had a slight southern drawl, and when paired with his good manners, it made him irresistible.

Caleb wasn't aware of these postings, and Jeb wouldn't make them known. His parents, whoever they were, kept him off social media. Jeb had considered developing a tour named the *Rivah Boy Eco-Tour* targeted towards young families. He mentioned it to Kat. "If Caleb is such a hit, why not capitalize on his popularity?"

She gave him an earful, and he dropped the matter.

Yes, Caleb's ready for this, Jeb thought as he tried to busy himself with papers. He wanted Caleb to succeed. Why be single-threaded?

A maxi-van pulled up to the curb, and one of the extended families piled out. *More than I could wish for—lots of tween girls!* He learned this family comprised ten children, only one of which was a boy. The Shop granted them the *mercy rule*, that is, Jeb stopped billing beyond five children. The lone boy was about Caleb's age—*I hope they hit it off!*

Caleb's spiel projected clearly into Jeb's office, "Good morning ladies and gentlemen, my name is Caleb Payne, and I'll be your tour guide for today's adventure."

He introduced himself to each of the adults—the mothers, fathers, aunts, and uncles—offering coffee and tea, always answering questions with a "Yes, ma'am," or a "Yes, sir." Jeb inhaled a relaxing breath, and he felt light.

Caleb doted on the tween girls, suggesting, "Miss, might you enjoy an herbal peach tea this fine morning?" For the teen boy, he stroked his ego by offering him the fishing paddleboard, suggesting he'd be a stronger paddler and could handle the extra weight. He received a dirty look from an older sister. "My apologies, miss, I'd be glad to put you on one of the fishing boards and help you feel comfortable casting from it."

Jeb rolled his chair to his office doorway. He spied Sierra, red in the face, like a teapot ready to explode.

He was heartened to hear Caleb explain a planned wardrobe change. A protective swim shirt to go under his vest, which Jeb knew to be adorned with the Shop's logo. Within moments, Sierra was ringing up sales.

What Jeb liked most about Caleb's Map Room presentation was his use of the word *adventure*. It was original, not something Caleb had picked up from Jeb. Caleb would take them on an adventure. No doubt about it!

Sierra, too, positioned at the shop's front, was hanging on his every word. Caleb promised he'd guide them to previously unexplored waters.

Although Jeb couldn't see Caleb, he stole a few glances of Sierra. It didn't matter. Her eyes were fixed on Caleb . . . or possibly the girls. She was indeed boiling over. Jeb suspected the girls were ogling Caleb. Sierra spoke their language and would understand what the parents were missing. Once Caleb's presentation was complete, and the younger girls made their way out the front door, Jeb faintly heard two of them say, "Oooooh laaah laaah." Probably cousins, each out of earshot of their fathers.

Jeb envisioned how all of it would transpire on the water. The tweens and their sisters of this large extended family would continue their unique coded communications. One might start, "Ooooh," and then another would respond, "laaaah," and then a few rhythms after that, a third would finish with, "laaaah." As the fathers were none the wiser, the cousins would bond through their silliness.

I wish I could charge for that!

Avoidance

Amanda entered the coffee shop to a much lighter crowd. She was limping and already feeling hot in her garb. No line had formed, and she wasn't worried about tripping again into the likes of the man, James Carter. He was absolutely the last person on her mind. At least, that's what she told herself.

Kat was working by herself behind the counter. Amanda took off her glasses as she approached. No sooner had she done so than Kat's hand came to her arm.

"You okay?" Kat's safe eyes glistened.

Amanda wondered if she'd burst into tears. She felt totally alone and her nerves were rattling every bone in her body. "Is it that obvious?"

Kat let go of her. "I'm on your side."

They were comforting words, and Amanda relaxed. "I'm supposed to be joining the girls on an eco-tour today."

Kat nodded. "I know. Sierra came in bubbling over with excitement." Then her eyes widened. "On the *Queen Mary*?"

"Yep . . . crazy, huh?"

"I'd say. But good on you, lady!" The pop of the door sounded. Kat's eyes left Amanda. Shuffling feet and a new set of voices behind her got louder. Fresh patrons. Amanda thought about coming clean with Kat. She had no plans to get on that boat!

Kat touched a finger to her lips and then tapped on her heart. "You can do it." She brought her hands together as if in prayer.

Amanda swallowed the lump in her throat and blinked back the sting of tears. "Thank you."

With her coffee in hand, she exited the Yokel and glanced in the Shop's direction. A large entourage was exiting. *That's a good sign*, she thought. Paddleboard Guy will be predisposed for the day. *One less distraction.*

Sierra's face was flaming red as she stood by the door on the front porch. She stuck her tongue out at some girls who were making their way towards their vehicles. *Wow! What brought that on?* A wave of compassion hit Amanda . . . similar to the ones she'd been experiencing with Nora.

The girl needs help. James Carter wasn't counseling her. That, or he's blind to it. If the man could only be civil, she was willing to give him some advice. Not that he'd take it. *He's far too proud.* What would she know about teenagers? *More than him.* She wasn't a mother, but she knew what it was like to be a teenage girl in the Northern Neck. *I owe that girl my life.*

Sierra hadn't taken her number, and Amanda resolved to give it to her at the marina. Even if she had to tell Sierra who she was and a brief explanation of why she couldn't join the cruise.

Amanda sat in her Jeep when she spied Jeb's truck pulling out of the Shop's driveway and towing the paddleboard trailer. He passed right by her, his head turned towards a passenger. Her heart missed a beat.

A maxi-van trailed the truck as they headed towards the intersection that led out of town. Sierra rode shotgun in the truck, her eyes on the visor-mirror. Curious. Why wasn't Maria taking Sierra to the marina?

She wondered about the man's values. James Carter didn't seem to have any—none that were important to her, at least. *He's a self-centered brat with a lifestyle business.* Living the good life at the expense of his slave daughters.

Sally's words from last night stung like a bee. *Is this what I do? Demonize people? Does he really deserve that?*

Amanda let several moments pass before making a U-turn and following the same route Jeb had taken through White Stone. She wanted one last chance to help Sierra.

She detoured down Mosquito Point Road to put some space between Jeb's truck and herself. There were several new houses—more like mansions—built on the bluffs overlooking the river. She would have likened them to Northern Virginia McMansions—7,000-square-foot houses on quarter-acre lots—but these custom homes were situated on large lots and designed to match the setting, not that different from the Carter estate. Apparently, the owners weren't concerned about the mosquitoes. Reaching a dead-end, she turned around and made her way back to Windmill Point Road and then down the peninsula.

She passed by the kayak launch not far from the marina entrance. A teenager was hoisting paddleboards off the Shop's trailer, but Jeb's truck was gone.

Amanda's gut knotted. Within minutes she'd see her father! Her palms sweated into the leather steering wheel cover. Her breaths came fast, and she opened the windows and inhaled the salt-drenched air. It was time for an attitude check. She resolved to robe herself with a detached and objective attitude to properly judge him.

Amanda found a parking spot as far as possible from *Queen Mary's* slip, but where she still commanded a clear line of sight. No one paid any attention to her as several families arrived in separate vehicles. Excitement hung in the air, and there was one man in the middle of it all. Her father! Gregarious. Greeting the tour party like the pastor of a country church.

Her heart pounded. She studied the ruggedly featured man as if he were a stranger. Ten years should have done some damage, but his skin was healthy, not the way an alcoholic's should look. The quick glimpse she'd caught of him on Saturday wasn't complete. A reckless lifestyle should've added twenty years, but instead, he looked far younger. Amanda clenched her teeth.

Her father engaged each family as they approached the boat and provided additional attention to each child with special needs. Not a side of him she remembered. Loving people. But now he looked natural. When Amanda viewed herself in the rear-view mirror, she saw a scorned woman.

There was James Carter, too. All chummy with her dad. Her father showed an understanding in each individual that Jeb didn't. Not that Jeb was inattentive; he just appeared lost. But her father? Found!

The man should be miserable! Instead of seeing a bitter face, she saw happiness, even joy. If their separation was the cause, why interfere? His life emerged better without her.

If her father discovered her, what would he see? Amanda tasted her own venom. Each breath felt tighter than the one before. The girls would notice her flaring nostrils. How embarrassing! Take the risk of joining the cruise today, and they'd unmask the wretch that she was.

Why not ask Maria to apologize to the girls for her? It was the only way. Sierra would have to understand, and through Maria, the full story would be told. Captain West was her father!

To think that she'd ever set foot on that boat again, her mother's boat? Never!

Her dad boarded the *Queen Mary* and marched to the helm. Jeb trailed behind him like a puppy on the heels of his master. Strange. Amanda looked over her shoulder towards Jeb's truck. The windows were up, and it appeared to be locked. Was he going? All the more reason to stay away.

Jeb's girls were angelic. Outgoing and sweet, pulling the special needs individuals out of their shells. And who'd coached them? Not Jeb, but her own father! A tidbit she'd learned from Maria.

Now Maria could tell Jeb and his daughters her saga, only after Amanda was safely back in Northern Virginia. She could hide from the consequences of the truth which would rip her reputation to shreds. Amanda was a fake. Every bad thing Jeb thought about her was true.

For the briefest moment, she summoned an ounce of sympathy for James Carter. Her chest squeezed a little tighter for the man who created a mass of confusion in her head and heart as he wobbled, trying to interact with the special needs community. An environment in which Amanda's father and Jeb's girls thrived. There, on the dock, James Carter didn't appear comfortable in his own skin.

Jeb wasn't acting or performing today. Her dad's second fiddle was on show for no one. Amanda could see Jeb's sincerity. A bit awkward, but genuinely interested in others. She watched as he introduced himself to several families and the effect he had on them. An effect that he couldn't see. The way they brightened. It was too hard for her to admit that he might be humble. There was a gentle nature about him. *But why do I pull out the worst in him?*

Jeb's movements elicited lingering glances from a few of the mothers. Studying him, trying to understand him. Amanda admitted she'd done the same, attempting to take the measure of the man.

When her father asserted himself with the entourage, Jeb hung back from the crowd, unwilling to draw attention to himself, yielding the stage to her father. Jeb absorbed the interactions, his face showing struggle at times when her father seamlessly engaged a Special Angler.

Amanda noticed a rail of a girl, possibly in her early twenties, eyeing Jeb. She appeared European and probably an au pair hired by a family to assist their teenage son who appeared to be on the autism spectrum. The poor girl seemed completely out of place and uncomfortable. She studied Jeb and her father, but mostly Jeb, and looked away whenever Jeb's eyes turned toward her. She was wholly mesmerized by him.

Is that the way I look at him? Studying him? She could hardly blame the girl.

While Amanda's father was quick to make the Special Anglers feel welcome and comfortable, he'd overlooked this young woman. Jeb didn't!

Although Amanda suspected Jeb failed to understand the aid's role, he noticed her and discerned she felt left out—not a parent or a sibling. Just the hired hand. When he approached her, she appeared star-struck, like Brad Pitt had just acknowledged her.

Jeb didn't pick up on it, but rather he took up a conversation with her, and provided his undivided attention. Nothing flirty. Only caring.

Her countenance transformed, as if he'd given her supernatural confidence. *What could he have said to cause that?*

The girl, who moved like a ballerina, had to return her focus and duties to her charge, but her eyes continued to linger on Jeb. He turned to other tasks, oblivious to her gaze.

That was the thing with Jeb. He oozed a subtle, sublime *wow factor*. It was clear as day! Like what a movie director perceived during a rising young actor's reading of a few script lines and realizing the person was a future star. One that would sell countless movies. A studio cash cow.

What appealed to Amanda more was that Jeb was golden on the inside. The part of him she'd stared into after he'd pulled her from the Bay.

Why is he awkward with me? Even brutish!

She worried that if she got anywhere near the boat, just to speak with Sierra, Jeb would distract her and derail her cover story. Would he feel obliged to introduce her to Captain West, her own father?

The sight of two large yachts departing the marina distracted the tour party. Even Amanda couldn't prevent herself from ogling the mini-ships, not so much for the luxury they afforded, but the thought of escaping on one as a stowaway.

Fingers tapped on the Jeep's glass, and Amanda jolted in her seat. She opened her eyes. *Maria!* Amanda sighed a huge breath of relief and lowered the window.

The woman's warm eyes faced her. "Good morning, dear. I was looking for Amanda. She drives a Jeep like this."

Words stuck in her throat. Amanda reached out her shaking hand and received Maria's grasp midway up her arm. "You scared the living daylights out of me," she finally whispered.

"You'll be fine." Maria's voice sounded reassuring. She gestured towards the vessel. Excited voices rang amongst the throng of Special Anglers. "Look at 'em. He's got his hands full. Your father won't have any bandwidth for you."

Amanda gulped, avoiding Maria's gaze. Amanda remembered her mother as a brave and calculated risk-taker. When Amanda returned her eyes to the older woman, she sensed Maria was reading her mind.

"Your father will be playing to that fiancée of his. This will be a big moment for the two of them."

Amanda liked the way Maria spoke with a hissing sound. As if Maria wanted the relationship to fail. *Why diss the fiancée?* Did Maria share her own concerns? Jealous for her own mother. Another reason to like Maria even more!

At the docks, Jeb shuttled ice to the boat's ice-chest, and then a petite, dark-haired lady directed him to fetch a picnic-sized cooler. Presumably full of drinks. Something her father never did . . .

provide drinks on board for the clients.

Her father became animated and began stomping his feet on the dock in front of the boat. He'd spotted a Special Angler with an Army hat, and even from this distance, Amanda could make out the slogan emblazoned on it. *Go Army, Beat Navy!*

"That just won't do, Jeremy!" he yelled at the boy, who laughed hysterically.

Her father crossed his arms and gave the boy a serious face. "I've never allowed a cap like that on my boat. I just won't have it."

A worried look took over the boy's expression, and her father's face turned playful, enough to put the boy at ease. He pulled off the boy's cap and rumpled his hair. It was a risky move, considering the boy may have had sensory issues.

"I'll make a deal with you, Jeremy." Her father waved his own cap in the air. Amanda knew it was the one with marina's logo on it, containing a caricature of the *Queen Mary* bursting from a wild surf, like it would jump right off the hat. "If you're willing to leave your hat here at the marina, I'll give you one like mine from the tackle shop."

The boy looked thrilled at the offer, and her father quickly led him to the marina store. They returned with the boy wearing a new cap; the boy yelling with excitement. Her father held the boy's Army cap in his hand and walked it over to the boy's parents. She suspected he would badger them about being Army fans. She could only confirm that they took possession of the hat and stowed it in their vehicle.

"I'm surprised you came," Maria said.

Amanda prepared to tell the woman the truth—she'd chickened out. She stared at her lap.

"I'll cover for you as far as the girls are concerned. Whatever you do today, I totally understand." Maria's words soothed her. Like the way her own mother helped overcome her initial fears of jumping off a diving board. Just enough space so she could muster the necessary courage.

Amanda spotted Nora looking in her direction. If Maria's presence provided a gentle push, Nora's eyes added a stronger pull. *I'm doing this!*

"Maria," Amanda's voice pleaded, "please stay with me until the last minute."

Maria nodded, and when she gently squeezed Amanda's arm, Amanda felt a jolt of determination radiate to her shoulders and chest.

Maria reached through the window with her other hand and touched Amanda's covered mole. "Nice touch."

Amanda raised a scarf over her mouth. "Just in case," she said, keeping her accent thick.

"Not bad. You sound like a New York Jew."

"Supposed to be Marisa Tomei. She's Italian."

"I had you pegged for Barbara Streisand."

"I'll take that as a compliment."

"It was. Another beautiful and talented woman." Maria shot a glance to the docks. "Now what's the worst that could happen? Your father recognizes you and showers you with love?"

"I doubt it, and I'm not close to returning the favor." Amanda tried to control her tone, but it was still bitter.

Maria frowned, but her eyes held understanding.

Amanda's father stuck his head out of the pilothouse and announced the final boarding call.

Amanda pursed her lips and blew out. It was time!

Maria grasped her hand as they walked to the vessel. When Maria pulled out her camera, Amanda used the distraction to board and bury herself in the group. Nora was quickly at her side, her arm wrapped around Amanda's waist. Amanda's trembling ceased. She likened the girl's effect on her to the balm of Gilead. Amanda still had thoughts of running, but her breathing relaxed. She could do this! With Nora.

Jeb passed through the families on his way from the pilothouse to the stern and unleashed the tie-down lines. When he turned around and caught sight of Amanda, a puzzled expression took over his face. She dared not meet his eyes, even from behind the sunglasses. He headed back into the pilothouse, shaking his head.

Amazing. How could he show a complete stranger—like *ballerina girl*—some attention, but wouldn't acknowledge her, a friend to his daughters?

He's got serious problems!

Cool as a Cucumber

Jeb saw her the moment he turned from tossing the last stern line to the dock. There was Amanda, sitting with Nora, cool as a cucumber, like she'd done nothing wrong. Everything was wrong! *What's she doing here?* This was to be a day to bond with his girls. And for his girls to aid Charley and Charlotte in their ministry efforts. Not to be distracted by the New Yorker!

What was he to say to her? "Glad to see you"? He wasn't. His girls would fawn all over her. Nora was already clinging to her! A complete dilution of their Carter family efforts to entertain and care for the other families.

Jeb remained silent, anger welling from his core. He entered the pilothouse and stood next to his friend, Captain Charley West. He needed a moment to get his bearings. The situation was doubly embarrassing since Charley would suspect him of inviting the woman. Positively the last thing he would've done. He thanked God she was covered and hideously dressed.

Jeb was already feeling lost and shameful. Two healthy daughters governed his world, and he was humbled. His girls were naturally communicative and not that different from their circle of friends—the ones from their small church and school community. So different from the group on the tour. These kids were all over the map. Some with speech impediments. One boy was extremely introverted and made minimal eye contact, like the process pained him. An older girl was impulsive, loud, and shrill. A teen boy repeatedly circuited the boat's back deck and stimmed with a spongy ball.

Captain Charley guided the vessel through the narrow channel leading out of the marina while Jeb could only stare blankly at the passing slips and the jetty. Charley and Charlotte had coached his girls for today's event, but they hadn't considered that he needed help too.

Jeb had prepared to apologize to Charley for his lack of understanding of the special needs individuals, but the image of Amanda, wrapped in Nora's embrace, irked him. And now he braced for an earful from Charley about it.

The *Queen Mary* rounded the tip of the Windmill Point peninsula and approached blue water, then Charley set her on a northeasterly course towards Tangier Island.

"Who's the *girl*, Jeb?" Charley's voice startled him.

Jeb wrapped his arms in front of his chest. "You mean that *whack* with the hat and scarf?"

He glanced over his shoulder. A gaggle had formed around Charlotte at the stern. Most eyes were riveted on her as she gave her orientation and safety speech for the tour. *Great*. No one took any interest in Jeb and Charley in the vessel's forward cabin.

"Yeah," Charley's tone accused. Exactly what Jeb was expecting. Charley would be less upset with the increased head-count and more concerned that the person they'd dragged along wasn't ministry focused.

Jeb tossed his hands up. "I had nothing to do with her coming."

Charley peered over his shoulder. Their view of her from the helm was mostly obstructed.

Charley creased his nose. "She looks familiar somehow," he muttered.

Jeb eased a side window open, and the air in the cabin moved. He let out a sigh. "I hope not. She's a nutcase. I think she's from New York."

Jeb stuck his head out the port-side window. The bow whispered as it sluiced through the water. *Intoxicating.*

"How's it she knows the girls?"

Jeb reluctantly pulled his head in and eyed his friend. "That's a long story. But believe me—you might want to avoid her."

Jeb peeked behind him. Amanda's back faced him, and her enormous hat flopped in the wind. Nora clung to her as they kept their focus on Charlotte, but they'd drifted closer to the cabin door. He flinched.

Not a chance she could eavesdrop over the roar of the engine. *Right?*

Jeb gestured with his hand, moving it up and down to tell Charley to keep his volume low.

Charley wrinkled his nose. "I have time for a long story. At thirty knots, we'll make the trip in forty-five minutes." His voice lowered. "If she's as crazy as you say, why's she hanging out with your girls? Seems creepy to me."

Jeb shook his head. *Here comes the trash talk.* Like the good ole times. The two could go at it for hours. This part of their friendship was like chicken soup to a winter's cold. He smiled and the captain returned it.

"Come on, amuse me, Jeb."

Jeb spoke from the side of his mouth. "Well, that's part of the story. Initially, she hit it off with Sierra and Nora, but mostly Nora. Then she had a falling out with Sierra. Fell within the good graces of my mom . . . and totally flattered my dad."

Jeb was surprised at his own amusement. What happened to being mad at the woman?

Charley seemed to soften, too. He chuckled.

"He can be a sucker at times."

"Right." Jeb twisted his mouth. "Like when he overpaid for the *Galleon* from the fine establishment of Charles West, chief proprietor of Windmill Point Marina?"

Charley flattened a smile. "Your dad got a great deal on that boat! There was a waiting list for it . . . would've made a pretty penny had I sold it to the next guy in line."

Jeb rolled his eyes, thrilled the conversation had veered from the woman.

Charley turned serious again. "So, how'd she flatter your dad?"

"She complimented the lines of the *Galleon*," Jeb deadpanned. *Move this discussion back to boats!*

Charley roared in laughter, and the *Queen Mary* lurched. He straightened up. "Jeb, you're too funny!" Charley strained to keep his hand on the tiller. "You mean to tell me that your *dad* . . . was over-flattered about a well-placed compliment on a boat . . . that *he* adores . . . for which *you* claim he overspent?"

Jeb turned his back on Charley and stared out his port-side window. He'd tossed Charley a softball, and his friend plastered it!

"It wasn't just that," Jeb whispered. She brought over a *blueberry pie* . . . specifically for my dad!"

Jeb's emotions surprised even himself. What prompted that? Her note? He'd stumbled upon it on his dad's dresser while helping search for his father's misplaced reading glasses. Jeb was too embarrassed to tell them. Not only because of the letter's content, but also because he lingered to read it—an invasion of their privacy. His father was right to have tried to protect him from it and the woman's manipulative ways.

How could anyone be that intentionally avoidant of responsibility? Passive aggressive, too! She owed Jeb an apology, not his father! It was as if the woman had pierced him with a spear and continued to twirl it in his stomach.

Charley stiffened and returned the vessel to its proper course.

"Oh . . . I see. This could be serious." He lowered his voice. "Is blueberry his favorite?"

"Yess," Jeb hissed.

Charley raised an eyebrow. "Homemade or store-bought?"

"Store-bought."

Charley shrugged. "From where?"

"Jim's."

Charley acknowledged with an understanding nod. "As good as homemade or better . . . does seem odd that a complete stranger could hit the ball through two wickets with your dad. Possibly a mere coincidence, but then again . . . possibly not." He glanced over his shoulder towards the stern.

Jeb's eyes followed, seeing only the top of Amanda's hat.

Charley continued, "Why don't you walk me through the whole story from the beginning?"

Jeb took a step back towards the cabin's rear and peered out through the open door. Amanda was sitting on a bench seat and settled into a book. The wind and the engine swamped the voices emanating from the back deck.

Jeb returned to the front. Charley was staring at him with raised eyebrows.

Jeb cocked his head and glared at Charley. "She ain't a Northern Neck girl, so you can forget about where you're heading with this."

Charley's eyes danced. "My mama said to keep away from girls who don't fish."

"Thanks!" Jeb exhaled. "About time you started speaking some sense today." Jeb leaned closer to Charley. "That woman back there is a loony and she certainly can't fish . . . shocked she even ate our fish at the Bay House." Jeb's words felt forced and disingenuous. She'd gorged on the mackerel like she hadn't eaten in a month. His mother had offered her a second filet, and she was quick to accept it. Later, she finished the rest of Nora's, saying, "I just can't stand to see fish wasted."

Charley nodded. "Good words, Jeb. Just make sure you're not missing something under that shell game she appears to be playing. You never know when you might happen upon a pearl."

Jeb dropped onto the padded bench seat. "I have no plans to replace the pearl I had."

Charley's smirk faded. "I didn't say that."

Jeb felt Charley's eyes, but he didn't return the gaze. What felt like bags of sand weighed down his shoulders. Eventually, the moment passed, and he turned back to Charley.

His eyes showed compassion. "That's not how I think of Charlotte. She's not a replacement for Mary. Life's moved on. Just like my Mary, I think Erin would want you to move on."

Jeb folded his arms. The playful banter was gone. The conversation's new direction made his chest hurt. He wanted to tell Charley to shut up, but he bit his lip.

"Look at me at sixty." Charley spread his arms wide. "I think I still have some good years left. I don't want to go it alone . . . and I'm not raising two girls."

Charley looked good at sixty—even buff. Jeb didn't feel the need to mention it to him. *Why stroke his ego?* He'd make a great AARP poster child. Charlotte had ordered fun T-shirts to commemorate the day, and Charley was busting out of his. "Thanks, Charley. I'm happy for you and looking forward to your wedding. Couple of months out, right?"

"Early November. Veteran's Day weekend. I'll be hosting some of my ole Navy buddies. Be sure to block it out on your busy calendar."

"Of course. I wouldn't miss it for the world. By the way, what's the latest on the prodigal daughter? Izzie . . . right?"

Charley's face fell. "That's the one." He sighed. "Thanks for remembering, but *not* something I wanted to think about today."

Jeb felt the pain from mentioning the girl's name wallop his own chest. Had he been subconsciously vindictive? He hadn't intended to hurt Charley, but it was obvious he'd hit a nerve like the center of a bulls-eye. At least now the focus was off Erin.

Jeb kept his eyes on Charley. He owed him that, to help Charley nurse out the more intimate thoughts. It's what their shared therapy sessions had taught them.

"I haven't heard a word. I think she's still overseas. The little I hear from my sister is that she's not taking it well." Charley shifted his footing. "If only she'd come home and meet Charlotte. She'd understand."

Some moments passed, and Charley's gaze returned to Jeb. "I think Izzie thinks like you. She may consider my fiancée a *replacement*, but I don't think your girls would look at your situation that way."

The weights still pressed down on Jeb. He stood, stepped to the cabin's rear opening, and eyed his girls. They were in rapt, spirited conversation.

"Nora was too young to remember much about Erin. Sierra might be different." His voice raised a notch. "But it doesn't matter . . . no prospects . . . there's nothing on my radar, and I'm not taking my boat to any new waters." *I wish he'd drop the topic.*

"Careful, Jeb." Charley's head snapped towards him. "It's times like these when a fish comes flying out of the water and lands right in your boat."

"Like Charlotte? Is that how it was for you?" Jeb's eyes softened. His peripheral vision caught the sight of Amanda's big sun hat. She was still reading on the bench seat and Nora was mingling with the others.

Charley's voice was light. "Yep. I thought I was just minding my own business with the marina. She retired nearby . . . used to vacation here. Threw herself into what we do here."

"And was there not a little coaxing of that fish to get it out of the water?"

"Maybe a little." Charley shrugged sheepishly.

They both eyed a sportfisher, trolling, heading from the north, and Charley maneuvered the *Queen Mary* to give them right of way. A few moments later, Jeb saw Charley twitch. Not quite like a Parkinson's twitch, but something else.

"What's wrong?"

"Nothing."

"Yeah, that's what I noticed." Jeb struggled to describe Charley's depressed but oddly hopeful expression.

Charley tilted his head back. "Huh."

"Don't take this as being rude, but I'm not getting a downer vibe."

Charley squinted and turned his face away. Jeb didn't mean to embarrass him, but Charley was fighting tears.

Charley faced forward again, fully in charge of his emotions. "You're the most perceptive person I know, Jeb."

"I try for my friends."

"Yeah . . . I haven't said a word to anyone, but yeah, I just sense something's happening." Charley's hand came to his chest, and he tapped it several times. "Izzy . . . something in my bones."

"Spiritual."

Charley's eyes widened. "Yeah . . . exactly." Then he gave some small head shakes. "I just don't know why."

"Maybe I should pray for you . . . for her. The whole situation."

Charley nodded, and his expression showed he was touched by Jeb's gesture. Whether or not God's hand was in it wasn't the point. This was about his friend knowing that he cared. He had no ability to intervene on Charley's behalf for his elusive prodigal daughter. He did, however, place his hand on Charley's shoulder and quietly pray. They didn't have long. A family from the back seemed ready to join them in the pilothouse.

It was time to embark on fishing talk, and Charley was ready to provide tours of his helm. A great distraction they'd both embrace, and Jeb readied himself to kick some fun into the day.

Flummoxed

As the cruise settled on its course, Amanda mingled with the Special Anglers and their parents, kindly aided by Sierra and Nora who made introductions. Nora's toothy smile won over everyone—even the European girl—and in combination with Nora's entrancing eyes, Amanda believed Jeb's youngest could get away with anything. *How does he handle that?*

Amanda pulled out a Wall Street thriller novel from her bag. She attempted to read it while sitting on the bench seat outside the cabin door—the best possible place to hide from her father on the boat and eavesdrop. She edged closer to the opening and turned slightly. She couldn't see her father, but with the shiny reflective bookmark Ted had loaned her, she could make out Jeb's reflection and the family of five he was greeting in the pilothouse.

"Hello again," Jeb said.

"Hi," the mother responded. She pulled her husband to her side. "This is the man I told you about. He rescued Winston out in front of the Yokel."

"Glad to meet you." The man extended his hand. "I'm Rod Peterson. Thank you for seeing after Winston . . . and for the cinnamon bun. I was such a louse, leaving Melinda to fend for herself."

"No, you weren't, Rod!" Melinda's hand went to her husband's shoulder. "Mr. Carter, Rod is a gem. He came back from the golf outing and took care of the kids so I could go shopping with my mother. My father loves to golf and has a hard time finding partners."

Jeb placed his hand on Rod's arm. "Please call me Jeb."

"Okay, Jeb. I'm glad you could see firsthand the challenges we face with a child on the spectrum. Your daughters are lovely, by the way."

Amanda closed her book and listened more intently. The voices coming from the cabin barely eclipsed the din of the engine.

"Thank you," said Jeb. "We're glad to be joining you today. It's been eye-opening. When I first met Winston, I hadn't even considered it."

Duh. So much this guy doesn't see.

Charlotte passed by Amanda on her way into the cabin. Jeb and Rod continued to converse while Melinda left the cabin, leading Charlotte by the arm to the stern. Amanda strained to hear their voices as the two stood with their backs to her.

Charlotte's voice was barely perceptible. "You looked embarrassed. Don't worry."

Melinda's voice carried better. "But Charlotte, that's not why I was embarrassed. Winston took off running in front of the coffee shop, but that wasn't it."

Amanda's eyes returned to her book. *Better if I tune them out.*

"Then what?" Charlotte's voice held some agitation mixed with curiosity.

"I was *flummoxed*." Melinda exhaled like she'd made a major confession. "Flummoxed by the man."

Amanda flinched. She glanced up. Charlotte placed her hands on her hips. "What do you mean, *flummoxed*?"

"He has a way about him . . . I can't put my finger on it. A strange aura . . . in a good and sweet way."

Charlotte nodded, and her voice teased in agreement. "Well, I don't know about that." She chuckled. "He certainly has a nature that adds color to life."

Melinda's voice was soft and barely audible. "He was totally innocent and did nothing forward. He came across as so strong . . . even chivalrous . . . but then, so sad. I felt the urge to wrap him in my arms."

Amanda rolled her head. *This can't be the same guy! James Carter?* "Hmph." It didn't matter what any of these people thought about Jeb. His being a friend of her father made it worse. *I can't trust him.* She side-eyed Charlotte. Probably the fiancée. *Another enemy!*

Amanda put her book down. Charlotte began working the back deck, ensuring everyone was well-hydrated and had ample sunscreen. For those who'd neglected to bring sunglasses, she pulled out spares. Several Special Anglers screamed excitedly. The polarized sunglasses enabled them to see a new world. Further water depths and vibrant colors. They coursed through numerous dolphin pods, and now the mammals were visible both in and out of the water. The pelicans were active, likely feeding on remnants of kill from the abundant Spanish mackerel frenzies. Several mackerel went airborne.

Anticipation prickled Amanda's arms. She stood, took a few steps to the starboard rail, and peered out over the water. Her heart raced, and her eyes rose to the fishing poles which hung neatly from the fiberglass ceiling. In the pilothouse, her father faced forward. Jeb's eyes peeled towards the school; he appeared ready to pounce. *Good for him.* She gently turned the spoon attached to one of the poles. The hook was clean and sharp. All the gear was perfectly staged and ready to be deployed. *At least he's got that right . . . but what are those two idiots up there thinking? How can they pass by these fish? These kids would love it.* She huffed and sat down.

Her father yelled out, "Charlotte!"

Charlotte's eyes cut to the cabin and took on a serious stare. She pointed at her watch. "Schedule to maintain." To those on the back deck, she said, "We've got watermen waiting for us. The crabber and the oysterman. Hopefully, we'll find these macks on the way back."

Amanda's stomach knotted. Charlotte's face resembled the woman in the pictures in the marina office, but she wasn't wearing a ring. Amanda looked for a ring-line, but that was absent, too.

Charlotte went into the pilothouse, put her arm around Charley, and offered him a bottle of water. It wasn't overly affectionate, but her father's response gave it away when he grabbed Charlotte around the waist and brought her closer. Amanda sent her eyes to the book, but she could no longer see the words. Her chest tightened and she tried to calm herself, remaining still until the pain numbed.

The tour group loitered at the starboard and stern handrails, still observing the surfacing dolphins. Amanda scrambled to the port-side bench and opened her book. Her bookmark mirror provided a view of the helm.

Charlotte gave her father a flirty pinch.

Amanda peered over the gunwale. Now her anger splashed about like the dolphins, pulsating in every part of her body.

Charlotte's voice reached her. "I had a strange conversation with Melinda a few moments ago."

The small mirror showed that when her father looked at Charlotte, the woman moved her focus port-side towards Jeb. Amanda couldn't resist the temptation to glance back over her shoulder. Jeb's eyes were on the horizon. Charlotte looked back at Amanda's father and passed a finger across her lips.

"Ah, yes." Her father nodded. "The power of influence is often stronger than the power of position, but a captain must realize he's still the captain, and he must . . . at times . . . pilot his own ship."

"What are you two jabbering about over there?" It was Jeb's voice, and he sounded as if he'd been daydreaming. Amanda doubted he'd picked up on anything the two had been saying. His tone was sad. Where had Jeb's thoughts drifted? And why should Amanda care? Was it a care for him, or rather, irritation? Irritation because Charlotte and her father teamed up on him?

"Only my glory days, Jeb," her father said in his fibbing voice. "I was telling Charlotte of my time in the Navy."

"You were a pilot, Charley," Jeb corrected.

"A fighter pilot." Charlotte squeezed Charley's arm and there was pride in her voice.

Charley smirked in Jeb's direction.

Amanda looked over her shoulder again, wanting to see Jeb's expression. Charlotte caught Amanda's quick glance, and Amanda froze.

Within a few moments, a woman stood in front of her. "I'm Charlotte," she said, "Thanks for coming out today." The woman's face showed a controlled smile. "I see you know the Carter girls."

"Yes, I'm Amanda." Her mouth was dry and she could barely speak. She remembered her faux Bronx accent. "The girls invited me. I'm still getting my sea legs." Amanda stood, carefully keeping her back towards her father.

Charlotte's eyes spoke a thousand things at once. They were deeply stern, but also understanding. "Why don't I take you on a walking tour once we arrive at Tangier? Those two up there can handle the Special Anglers and Jeb is especially good with kids."

Amanda remembered her discussion with Ted and her hasty verdict of the man who turned out to be James Carter. The man she misjudged in a blink. *Has he misjudged me?* She jettisoned the worry. What mattered now was whether she could trust the petite woman in front of her.

Don't overcomplicate it. Stay away from Dad and interrogate the fiancée. *A perfect opportunity!*

"Thank you, Charlotte, I'd like that." Amanda liked the way her words sounded, but the adrenaline pumping through her veins told her how far she'd pushed the limits. *Just find the ring, Amanda, and be done with it!*

Heart Strings

Amanda couldn't return to the book. She tried to relax while taking in the activity of the group. Nora held the hand of a girl as they stood by the safety rail watching the water go by.

Amanda gently tapped Nora's shoulder. "Can I meet your friend?"

Amanda had already learned quite a bit about the girl in Nora's grip. She'd met William and Sarah, the girl's parents, but she didn't need them to tell her Jeanette had been born with Down syndrome.

Jeanette was petite, strong-willed, and wore large glasses. Nora had served as her pal for the first half of the journey towards Tangiers.

Nora's nose wrinkled. "Why are you speaking so funny today?"

"Oh?" Amanda coughed and held her throat. She reached for her water and took a swig. She whispered in Nora's ear, "Does this sound better?"

A curious smile grew on Nora's face. "Yes, Miss Amanda, much better."

Jeanette was a cutie pie and had already taken a liking to Amanda's father. As she stood facing Amanda, the girl's eyes drifted into the pilothouse. She pointed. "I wanna go in there."

"You want to visit Captain West?" Nora's voice rose with

promise.

Jeanette responded with a firm, "Yes," and her eyes turned to the cabin's opening.

The two disappeared, and Amanda heard the doting voice of her father. Under her breath she murmured, "Oh brother." But then a pang of guilt bit her. *Why can't I let him be?*

William and Sarah found spots next to Amanda and sat down. She inquired more about their daughter. Jeanette was a *runner*. On a whim, she could be out the door and running to who knows where, darting across dangerous streets in suburbia. The parents on the tour understood this and other traumatic events. They'd maintain a lookout for her when at the marina. For a *runner*, adding water to the mix could be deadly.

On the *Queen Mary*, Jeanette had nowhere to go but to soak up the attention of the Carter girls, Captain West, and Charlotte. Her parents could relax and take in the day on the water, a far cry from their "loathsome government jobs back in DC." Amanda provided genuine empathy upon hearing their complaints, but she didn't dare reveal her own background.

She learned how the special needs parents used events like her father's tour to connect with other parents like themselves. They'd compare notes on schooling resources, long-term care, and daily ups and downs. Many accepted the fact that their children would never be fully independent, so they talked about who would care for their children upon their own deaths and how the care would be administered. They traded war stories regarding their estate attorneys—commonplace anecdotes within their community.

Amanda occasionally glanced behind her towards the helm. Jeanette clamored for independence. Amanda's father continued doting on the girl, and now she really flaunted it. William stood and made his way to the pilothouse entrance. It didn't sit right with Jeanette, and she looked back at him with an expression that said, "See ya, I'm with him."

Jeanette was with *him*. Amanda's father! Amanda's chest compressed as if yanked below fifty feet of water. *Whose decision is that?* Even if it was her's, and she could fix it, where would it lead? Pick up where they left off? She didn't think so, and her sense of isolation doubled.

Her father invited Jeanette to sit in the cockpit and drive the

Queen Mary. William stepped into the cabin and asked for a tour of the vessel's console, but his daughter forced him away. "You stay back there! This is for me and Cappin West."

He exited the pilothouse and shook his head in a mock show of disappointment.

When they arrived at Tangier Island, Jeanette didn't leave Amanda's father's side, holding his hand as they walked the waterfront lanes. Amanda appreciated the distraction the girl created. It reminded her of another young girl grasping those same big, powerful hands. They provided her security as they hiked, she and her mother with the man in between, along mountain trails in Maine cut into steep cliffs—beautiful views of the ocean, pounding surf below. The crashing waves sounded like thunder, and as she watched Jeanette and her dad, she felt her heart pounding as it did when looking over the cliffs. She worried Charlotte could hear it.

Tangier Island

Charlotte and Amanda were ushering the contingent from the small harbor towards the town museum when Charlotte asked, "Have you been here before?"

Amanda tried to ignore her, occupying herself by herding the lively group—some loud, looking all about, some quiet, staring only at their feet as they walked. She quickened her steps as she moved away from the docks, sucking in a heavy breath of salty air.

Jeb and her father stayed behind to secure the *Queen Mary,* Jeanette assisting them, declaring herself part of the *important crew.*

Who's Charlotte? Amanda glanced back and sighted the woman. Her father wore a puppy-face whenever he was around her, as if he would do absolutely anything the woman wished. *How does she hold such a grip on him?* The brunette wasn't unattractive, Amanda begrudgingly admitted. She oozed confidence and authority. *Dad's type?* The thought gave her pause.

Amanda noticed Charlotte's chic beige Bermuda shorts. Another tough admission? The woman commanded a decent figure. She didn't dress like a teen, *and definitely not like an old maid.* She wore a matching T-shirt like her father's, but hers was a tapered woman's cut. The finely knit cotton appeared much softer, and its heather-purple color accentuated her darker features. Yes, it was possible her father would find the full-figured woman quite attractive.

Before leaving the docks, Amanda overheard Charlotte tasking the trio to prepare the oysterman and the crabber for the second and third stations of the tour. *Odd,* Amanda thought, for her father—a man who'd held considerable rank and responsibility—to be taking orders from her. *Did Mom order him around like this?* If she had, it wasn't obvious. But then she remembered how often her parents communicated without words. It was one thing for her mother to have bossed him around. But this lady? The whole affair tasted like a fireball.

Jeb's docile behavior? Forgivable. He was just along for the ride and struggling to be helpful. *Too bad he can't be nice around me.*

But her father and his subservient attitude? Acting like Charlotte's lapdog. Amanda resisted the urge to grab him by his shoulders and shake him.

She felt a nudge on her arm. Charlotte had caught up with her. "Have you been here before? I wouldn't want you to miss the tour if you haven't."

Amanda smirked. The woman was still behind her and wouldn't see the expression; but then, before Amanda realized it, Charlotte was sidled alongside her, and the two bumped shoulders as they approached the island's museum—a converted bungalow surrounded by a white picket fence.

Amanda glanced at the older woman's face, deeming it full of thought and calculations.

Charlotte didn't need to know the whole truth. Amanda was interviewing the fiancée, not the other way around, and Amanda didn't want her words turned on her—after all, *Charlotte's probably some floozy, an executive assistant type . . . making a living by preying on vulnerable widowers.*

Amanda forced a breath through her nose. "Yes, when I was younger. I'll skip the museum. I doubt it's changed. The history certainly hasn't." She turned to Charlotte. "I'd prefer to walk."

She nodded and squeezed Amanda's hand as they stood by the front door of the museum. "Okay, we'll give the docent a moment to get started, and slip away."

Great! She doesn't have a clue what's about to hit her.

Amanda suspected the woman was cunning and possibly quite intelligent. Surprise? No. The exact traits she'd need to pull the wool over Amanda's father's eyes.

The museum's front entrance hadn't changed. Three small steps led to the landing. The decking had worn a little, and the vinyl siding was the same. Fresh white paint on the exposed wood fascia boards and deck rails gave the place a clean and welcoming atmosphere. The crab-shaped chairs and the large checkerboard table hadn't budged.

When the parents ahead of them eyed the three-dollar admittance fee, Charlotte spoke up. "We already took care of it. Just go in. Inez is expecting us."

The front door quickly opened, and the logjam on the porch landing dissipated. Amanda trailed Charlotte inside, but they stayed at the entrance.

The museum encompassed what once was the combined space of the home's living and dining rooms. Their group barely fit into the area, and the AC sounded as if it was on overdrive, laboring to keep them cool. Maps, portraits, and other nautical displays covered the walls, while several glass-enclosed stands protected other island artifacts. Several in the party streamed to the skipjack replicas resting on the stand tops, along with a wire-framed model of an iconic, stilted Chesapeake Bay lighthouse.

Amanda recounted to herself the many excursions she'd made to Tangier Island. It wasn't unusual for her father's clients to book the *Queen Mary* for just that purpose. She made use of her time by reading great novels and studying the sonar. When the clients disembarked for their village walkabout, she cherished the time playing poker with her father.

Now, the musty air rekindled a totally different memory—one with her mother and an extended visit they paid to the curator. The curator and her mother went at it for nearly an hour, debating the timings of Captain John Smith's exploration of the Bay. Amanda had always known her mother to be kind and gentle, but for some reason, she argued with a passion consistent with having a chip on her shoulder, like her entire identity hinged on the details. On their journey home, she only remembered her mother saying, "Too bad for her. Your father and I had a fine piece we would've donated." What the *piece* was, was never revealed.

Amanda felt a small jab at her ribs.

"Something wrong?" Charlotte asked.

She wanted to say, *Yeah, it's not every day someone pokes me*, but instead she fibbed, "No, no." She tapped her nose and whispered. "They probably turn off the AC at the end of the day."

Charlotte whiffed twice and nodded. "Yeah . . . gotta keep that air dry."

The docent waited for the group to settle in before she greeted them, "Welcome everyone to the Tangier Island History Museum. I'm Inez Pruitt, and I'll be your guide for today."

With that settled, Amanda braced. She knew the impending spiel and wouldn't blame the docent for forcing animation into her voice and mannerisms. After all, how many times could Inez present the same story and remain excited?

"Prior to 1608, our island was inhabited for centuries by the Pocomoke Indians, but when Captain John Smith arrived, he found it vacant. He named it and the surrounding islands, the Russel Isles, after the doctor on board his shallop—"

Alex, a Special Angler, interrupted her. "What's a shallop?" His tone was terse, and he never looked up from the floor.

Inez's eyes brightened in a way that said she was delighted the group was paying attention.

Alex responded before the woman could catch her breath. "A shallop is a small boat."

"Yes, that's right, young man. Thank you." Inez tried to make eye contact with him, but he continued staring at his feet.

Alex must have detected dead air, because he resumed in earnest, "Captain Smith and his crew employed a shallop to explore the Chesapeake Bay. It was smaller than the boat we traveled on this morning."

Stephanie, one of the Special Angler girls, yelped her delight. "Yay! We came on the *Queen Mary*." She spun around in a happy loop.

Amanda sensed satisfaction from several parents, who smiled and chuckled at the sight of the teen girl, not to mention Alex's grasp of the history trivia.

Inez continued, her tone indicating she wanted to get back on track. "Yes, I know your boat. Well known in this part of the Bay. The shallop would've been considerably smaller." She cleared her throat. "Not until 1713, when the Colony granted two patents to Elizabeth Scarburgh and Anthony West, was a reference first made in any land records to the name *Tangier Islands*."

Amanda's pulse quickened. How long had she been ignoring her West family history? She did it out of necessity—a survival mechanism. It came with the territory of rejecting her father, a thought quickly returned to the basement of her soul.

She wondered about her dad and James Carter. Where might their discussions go now that she wasn't in earshot of them? And what if Jeb had blown her cover? Described her features as he'd seen her on Saturday coming out of the water, mentioning her above-the-lip mole?

The docent continued her rote speech. "When the Crown issued the first patent in 1670 to Ambrose White, it was only referred to as 'an Island in the Chesapeake Bay.'"

"What's a patent?" Alex belted out again, his gaze directed towards the back corner of the room, like maybe he'd find a roach.

Before Inez had a chance to respond, Alex answered without looking up. "It's a colonial land grant, much like a property title."

She responded, "Yes, that's about right. You did your research."

"Yes I did, Mrs. Pruit. I always read before coming to museum."

"You're such a smart boy, what makes you think I'm married?" This time, Amanda heard some annoyance in Inez's tone.

"I searched the property records online. Mr. Isaac and Inez Pruitt own property 6526 Slater Lane."

The parents smiled, exchanging knowing looks with each other, and then with small nods in the docent's direction, tried to encourage her to continue.

"Okay, Mr. Smarty pants, can you tell me from those records whether I'm happily married?

Amanda wanted to scream, "No!" based on Inez's tone. Her husband was likely an old cuss, a waterman she'd mostly tolerated.

This time, Alex looked up. Not at Inez, but straight ahead, looking like a computer with its CPU on overdrive. Amanda worried the boy suffered a buffer overflow. He returned his eyes to the floor. "How do you know the Indians were here centuries before Captain Smith?"

Alex's question surprised Amanda, not so much for the way he recovered from an uncomfortable situation, but the question's content. How many times had she heard the docent's earlier statement and accepted it at face value?

"I suspect you know the answer to that too?" Inez's voice held a tone that mirrored Amanda's own curiosity.

"Archaeologists discovered huge grounds of oyster shells dated to time periods before 1608."

"Yes. Excellent. I think we'll move on." Her voice became perkier. "Our island became notorious during the War of 1812 when the British used it as a staging ground for raids and built an encampment they named Fort Albion. It sheltered 1,200 British troops."

"You didn't mention the slaves," Alex interrupted, and then said flatly, "The British granted freedom to the slaves who made their way to Tangier."

"Correct again," she stretched out her words. Amanda wasn't sure if the lady was keener to stay clear of the topic, or simply out-maneuver Alex.

Once again, Alex took advantage of her pause. He quickly steered the discussion to William Wilberforce and the absolution of slavery in the British Empire.

Finally, a parent intervened. "Do you speak *Elizabethan English* here?"

"The *Queen's English*?" The docent chuckled and acknowledged the parent with a smile. "No, I'm afraid that's a myth. Although our inhabitants maintain their own dialect, language experts consider it one of *American English*."

Amanda felt a gentle pull of her arm. "Let's leave this to the Carter girls," Charlotte whispered.

Amanda followed Charlotte out the door, but left with an urge to applaud the Special Anglers and the docent. They'd made what was typically boring, ancient history into a living, breathing experience. Behind them they could hear other Special Anglers getting into the mix, some seeking attention, and a lively discussion continuing.

"That big brute of a man, my fiancé, has some family history tied to this place," Charlotte's voice teased as they distanced themselves from the museum.

Amanda cocked her head. "Oh?" There it was again, a quickening pulse she couldn't control. Was it the mention of Amanda's family history? Or the way Charlotte referred to her father?

Amanda judged her parents as complete opposites. Her father? Type A and outspoken. Her mother? Quiet, introverted, and calculating. But when it came to history, they were joined at the hip, compulsively encouraging each other as if their identities hinged on it. To Amanda, they claimed, "It's more than Virginia history. It's the history of our nation."

Charlotte's voice returned Amanda to the present. "Charles and John West—his ancestors. I'm not sure which one . . . claimed four hundred acres on the Island in 1671, one of the original colonial patents."

Amanda halted and folded her arms. She sighted a gray pelican and drew in a deep breath. Would Charlotte know their West family story went further back, tied to the founding of Jamestown?

Charlotte stared at her.

Amanda sensed it. "Oh . . . I love the smell of saltwater air." She returned her eyes to the lady. "Brute?"

The older woman relaxed a bit. "The charter boat captain. He's a teddy bear. He tries to show a rough façade on the outside . . . sweet as pudding on the inside."

Charlotte's words paralyzed Amanda, and the woman's eyes probed. "Amanda, what's your relationship with the Carter family?"

Charlotte had yet to offer much about herself. As the elicitor, Amanda felt more novice than she wanted to admit. The conversation needed to be turned! She kept her tone as hum-drum as possible, hoping to bore the fiancée out of her mind. "I barely know them at all. I only met them this weekend."

"Huh . . . by the looks of it, I'd think you've known those girls all their lives."

"Nope. I booked a paddleboard tour with Sierra on Saturday."

"Sierra?" Charlotte raised her eyebrows. "I wasn't aware she gave tours."

The boredom in Amanda's voice vaporized and she couldn't hold back some emotion. "Yes, she's a wonderful tour guide and a charming young lady. Nora's another gem." She was about to mention Paddleboard Guy, but where would that lead? Her thoughts and passion crashed into one another like a riptide taking on a sandbar. She regretted mentioning the girls, and now her voice came out in a panic, "How'd you meet Captain West?"

Charlotte's brow wrinkled, and she exhaled a long breath, contemplating.

Amanda silently prayed that Charlotte would drop the Carter family discussion. Maybe Ralph and Maria were safe topics, but certainly not the son.

A soft smile came to the woman's face. "I retired to a home near the marina. We met at our local church." Charlotte slowed the pace of her words. "I didn't know how I'd take retirement, but I've settled into a lifestyle I like very much." Her eyes drifted. "Charley and I participated in a mission trip to Haiti, and that's when the sparks flew."

"First marriage?" Amanda struggled to conceal her skepticism and a look of disdain, expecting her father would be Charlotte's fourth marriage—minimum.

"Yes."

Amanda flinched and tried to cover it up with a fake stumble. She righted herself and forced a smile.

"It's my first marriage, but not my first love. Had I not been so married to my job, I'd probably be telling a different story."

Amanda's eyes widened.

The other woman continued. "I had plenty of suitors, but I kept getting promoted and shipped to far-flung locations overseas. I saw the divorce rates in my line of work and didn't care to become a statistic."

"What happened to the *first love*?" Amanda asked, honestly intrigued.

Charlotte gazed blankly down the narrow street. "We met in the late nineties. We were both back in the States completing *home* duty. John—military—worked in covert action and special ops. It was then I resolved to settle down. We agreed to start a family once we married, both in our mid-thirties. Then 9/11 hit. John accepted a special operation in Afghanistan . . . said it would be his last. We set our wedding date for April. He was killed during a firefight in January." Her sigh sounded as if it came from the gut. "I threw myself back into the job—my coping mechanism." She faced Amanda. "I was looking forward to life as a wife and mother."

Amanda grabbed Charlotte's hand. A thousand strange feelings hit her all at once. The woman standing in front of her was older, but how different were they? She waited for several long moments before saying, "I'm sorry."

It was clear the woman was fighting back tears. "Thank you." They resumed their pace and Charlotte's face lost its sadness. "Retirement's been an adjustment. I never slowed down, and I avoided all attachments. It was during Charley's offseason that we started to connect through several community activities. Our work with the special needs community brought us together. When we returned from Haiti, he began asking me to help him with his Special Angler outings. I pushed back, seeing he had plenty of teens needing community service hours. He kept insisting." Charlotte sighed. "Serving others is what drew us so close."

"How'd he propose?" Amanda asked, softly, desperately, still foraging for a reason to hate the woman. She remembered the ring and thought, *Hang on . . . stay on mission.*

"It was very romantic . . . a sunset cruise . . . nothing like how he proposed to his *Mary*—his first wife—but perfectly appropriate for our circumstances."

Amanda lost her focus and would've liked to slither under a rock—not expecting this woman to speak so respectfully of her mother.

"Charley knew that I'd taken up crabbing off my dock, so he offered to put my crab pot out one day farther near the edge of the channel. Later that afternoon, he took me for a cruise on the *Queen Mary* to retrieve it. He equipped the boat with everything we needed to steam the crabs and enjoy them aboard." Amanda stared into nothing as the woman continued. "I had wine, he had water . . . he served a nice cheese and some olives and a French baguette . . . perfect weather . . . soft light. He even brought candles."

Amanda froze, and she felt the color drain from her face. "I noticed you're not wearing a ring. Did he give you one?"

"No." Charlotte's tone was curt.

Heat shot to the roots of Amanda's hair. Of course the woman would say 'No.' To admit receipt of such a valuable heirloom would be treachery, and this woman was too smart for that. No chance she'd risk being seen in public wearing the ring.

"We'll be picking out matching wedding bands. That's enough." Charlotte's eyes reclaimed her pensive and calculating look. Her voice faked sweetness, "Amanda, I don't recall asking where you live or work. I know so little about you."

Amanda tensed. This was dangerous. She faced Charlotte and spoke the first thing that came to mind. "Do you find Jeb odd?"

Charlotte's face wrinkled, and she narrowed an eye. "No, maybe predictable, but not odd. Do you find him odd?"

"Yes." Amanda would have preferred to speak freely but why drag Charlotte into the conflict she had with Jeb?

"Oh," Charlotte responded with a tint of surprise. Charlotte's face screamed something else, but Amanda couldn't decipher it. "My interactions with the Carter family have all been positive. He and Charley are close." Charlotte's tone filled with sincerity, "He's a *good guy*, Amanda."

Amanda's emotions churned. For a brief moment, she felt as if she heard the words of her own mother.

Charlotte tapped Amanda's hand. "We need to return to the museum and escort our charges to the oysterman. Can you stay with me after that? Charley and Jeb can then take them to the crabber." Charlotte's tone became stern, "I'd like to ask something you *didn't* want to answer."

Amanda's insides erupted in momentary panic. She composed herself before responding, "Yes, that would be fine, but shouldn't we be with the group?" *Where's this woman taking this? I can't discuss work. It's classified!* But Charlotte was speaking a familiar IC language.

Amanda drifted to the rear of the group as Sierra, Nora, and the half-dozen families walked across town to the oystermen's facility, where the Important Crew waited.

Charlotte held Amanda's father's attention. He momentarily grabbed Charlotte's hand, spoke to her, and then he and Jeb led the contingent to the oysterman at the docks. Charlotte fell to the back, where Amanda was lingering. Charlotte signaled for her to follow.

Amanda relaxed out of view of her father, but her stomach sank as she faced Charlotte.

The two gained a safe distance from the group along a small lane before Charlotte resumed, "Amanda, you didn't tell me where you work, what you do, and where you live?"

Amanda licked her suddenly parched lips. "I'm a logistics officer."

"I know." Charlotte's eyes blazed. "I was the Station Chief in Rome when Tripoli Station was abandoned."

Amanda kept her eyes from acknowledging Charlotte. Her mouth was dry and her pulse, fast and irregular.

The woman continued, ". . . after the Benghazi attacks. I heard the story of what *you* and Jenny went through . . . and everyone else from Station." It was an allusion to the bloodied aircraft that returned to Tripoli, the one Amanda and Jenny had chartered to rescue the Benghazi Base personnel. Someone had even written a book about the catastrophe and turned it into a movie, but Charlotte's anecdote was not in the book.

"You know who I am? My name?" Amanda voiced skepticism. It was all she could do to conceal a consuming panic.

Fight or flight? The impulse gave her no comfort. To run would require her to return on the afternoon ferry to Reedville. She could avoid her father now, but he'd likely catch her at the Buzzard Point terminus.

Charlotte's tone welcomed a fight, "I know your surname, being the same as my fiancé. Need I go on?"

Amanda's heart rate doubled. She stopped and faced Charlotte. It wasn't anger after all. It was assurance. Charlotte was pleading to be trusted.

Amanda fought the urge to collapse. She exhaled and her body sagged. "How long have you known?"

"I saw you yesterday morning at the pasture . . . and then when you went into the marina office."

"I broke into it." Amanda straightened.

"I know, but I was trying to be diplomatic."

Amanda closed her eyes and shook her head. "Does my father know?"

"No!" Charlotte burst out. "I don't believe he's on to you. He mentioned to Jeb that something about you looked familiar, but Jeb thinks you're some *whack* from New York."

"He thinks I'm a *whack*?"

"Don't read anything into that." Charlotte became testy. "That man's fighting to ignore you with every muscle in his body."

Amanda covered her face with her hands. *What in the world have I got myself into?* If Charlotte had intended to loosen her up, the trick worked.

Charlotte continued, "Your father heard the story about the blueberry pie."

"Was that a giveaway?"

"I'm not sure. That seems to be a local thing. Jeb found it strange. You would've been better served if you'd gotten a cheap one from Food Lion."

Amanda grew a smile. "Yes, but I hadn't planned on coming out here today . . . and I certainly didn't plan on Jeb replaying the story to my father."

Charlotte clasped Amanda's hand. "What are you going to do?"

Amanda's voice cried out like a little girl, "I don't know. I'm not ready yet." Her tone became firm and sincere. "I like you. I want you to know that . . . and I appreciate your respect for my mother. I see *now* that my father is *not* the man I left here ten years ago."

Charlotte sighed. "He desperately wants to reconcile." Her eyes glistened. "I want you to reconcile. He's suffered long enough . . . You've suffered long enough." Charlotte's hand came to Amanda's cheek. "The same pain I see you suffering is how I felt after the death of John . . . and how I tried to compartmentalize that pain. You don't need that, especially since your father wants you back."

Tears trickled from Amanda's eyes. She needed to hate this woman, but now Charlotte's hands caressed Amanda's face. She saw sincerity in this woman's eyes. Love and understanding. Still, her stomach twisted.

"Amanda, I'll respect your wishes . . . to a point." Charlotte's eyes remained sincere. "If you want to hide yourself from your father when we get back on the boat, I'll honor that . . . and I'll do all I can to help you get back to Washington without his knowledge."

"Those are my wishes." She wiped her face and glanced up the alleyway. The oysterman had freed the entourage, and Nora was leading the pack with a boy her age, a brother to one of the Special Anglers.

Charlotte took a step back. "I understand. I can see that you've taken a lot in this weekend."

Does she know I snuck into the Marina House? It wouldn't take the professional long to elicit details from Sierra. *But what could she know about my search for the ring?* "It's been overwhelming, especially while trying to maintain cover."

"You've actually done quite well for yourself, especially for a logistics officer. Did you transfer to Ops after I last saw you in Rome?"

"No." Amanda brightened, appreciating the compliment from the senior officer. "The Benghazi experience was a blur."

Charlotte began to move, and Amanda joined her, maintaining their distance from the tour group.

"Yes, I understand that and why you wouldn't remember me."

"I was very junior."

"May I see your glasses?"

Amanda snorted a laugh. She reached for the stem of her sunglasses, removed them, and handed them to Charlotte.

Charlotte turned them around and chortled. She eyed the reflective mirrors on the inside corners. "Who taught you this trick?"

"A friend in the business." Amanda dished a flat smile.

Charlotte raised her brow. "Mirror tape from Walmart?"

Amanda chuckled with a nod.

"Have you been reading your father's letters?" Charlotte's voice became more serious, as she returned Amanda's glasses. "I noticed how surprised you were to see Gusty. You should've known from his letters that Gusty was being properly cared for."

"No, Charlotte. Please give me time. I simply want to work through this in my own time. I won't let this linger, but I do want to reconcile . . . when I'm ready. At a place and a time of my choosing."

CHAPTER 11

Catbird's Seat

For the rest of their time on the island Amanda was able to relax. Charlotte was true to her word and ran interference, always distracting her father when he neared. Given that he was so beholden to the woman, it made her task easy.

On their return cruise, Amanda waited till the last possible moment before boarding the *Queen Mary* and found a seat on the large cushioned bench adjacent to the pilothouse. With the boat now moving, she didn't need to think about her father. He was focused on his duties to carefully navigate out the harbor, and she knew Charlotte would keep him fully occupied at the helm, even if it required sitting on his lap.

The Tangier Island Marina slowly disappeared behind the stern. Nora appeared to have tired of the boy who'd taken a liking to her, and she now sat next to Amanda, her head resting on Amanda's arm.

Jeb stowed the vessel's dock lines, and loitered at the stern, staring at the trailing wake. Maybe he was sorting through his thoughts? *Readying himself to acknowledge me?* Had it not been for the fear of exposing herself to her father, she'd confront James Carter for his rudeness. She worried now that by not doing it, she empowered him.

He eventually turned around, making no attempt to look at her, and found the empty spot next to Nora. Amanda kept her eyes glued to the horizon.

Although the heat of the day had settled in, that wasn't the heat she felt. She was angry at him, unwilling to extend any excuse for his incivility, *especially in the Old Dominion!* The stop at the museum had reminded Amanda of that fact. How King Charles II of England, touched by the colony's loyalty during his exile, gave Virginia her nickname. He called Virginia "the best of his distant children," and sometime around 1663, elevated Virginia to a position of dominion equal to England, Scotland, Ireland, and France. *Jeb acts like a come-here . . . as if he was from New Jersey.*

"I think I deserve a hug from my baby doll," he said, breaking the silence after what felt like an eternity.

Jeb's hand brushed Amanda's shoulder as he put his arm around Nora, pulling Nora's head to his chest. He did nothing to increase his distance from Amanda, and if anything, he'd edged closer, causing Nora's hips to push against Amanda's legs.

What if I smell the lavender?

The parents were immersed in their own conversations and it was relatively quiet, but for the dull roar of the engine propelling them west towards the mainland. Jeb seemed to be on the verge of speaking to her. How might he react to her thick-fogged New York accent? S*hould I say something? If I could trust him, I'd just tell him.* She craved a magical knife to slice through the tension.

"You're hot and sweaty, Dad." Nora's head notched up a bit.

"Me?" his tone mocked disbelief. "I think it's you, precious."

Amanda was afraid to look over, certain Jeb's eyes bore down on her. And now she felt like a hypocrite, judging him for not acknowledging her. But here she was, frozen in place, unable to turn her head.

Amanda's father's voice bellowed from the cabin, "We need someone to man the tower!"

A wild sensation ran through her body. The call to the tuna-tower meant one thing. They were on the prowl for mackerel schools.

Jeb rose immediately. Only then did Amanda take a real breath.

He assisted his girls and several from the group—those who weren't afraid of heights—up the ladder and onto the platform. Amanda stood up and headed to the stern. It provided a better view of the tower, but she risked detection by her father every time she peered over her shoulder. Fortunately, he remained focused on the sonar.

The climb up to the tower had been daunting for most of those with special needs. Once on the platform, they gripped the safety rails, their fists clenched tight. Their eyes were wide with awe. The views were spectacular. It was her favorite spot on her father's boat. Back then, she referred to it as her parents' boat. After all, he'd named it after her mother.

Guilt ate at her as she lingered at the stern. *Maybe I should give Jeb and his daughters some space?* She'd attracted considerable attention from the girls all day. Amanda glanced up towards the tower. The three actively engaged with the Special Anglers, and she ached with some regret. Had she misread the oddball? *Maybe he's not as self-absorbed as I assumed.*

Shortly thereafter, the group started pointing in the distance. Sierra stood near the tower's console and Jeb passed her the radio's microphone. Her voice boomed over the radio, "Schools of macks at two o'clock, Captain!"

"Any birds?" Amanda's father responded on his radio.

Sierra was ecstatic. "Yes, the Spaniards are jumping clear out of the water."

"Roger . . . changing course. Please ask your dad to ready the rigs."

A shock ran through Amanda's body. How many years had it been since she'd heard her father signal a crew for battle? She tightened the grip on the handrail, resisting the urge to yank down the poles hung from the weather-roof.

A queue formed at the top of the ladder, and Amanda moved quickly across the deck to assist. Several were shaky as they descended. Jeb tried to encourage them. "Good things await for those who get down safely."

"He's right. You can do it." Amanda stood at the ladder's base and placed her hand on their calves halfway down.

She considered helping Jeb as he came down, thinking it would break the ice, but then stepped back from the ladder and removed her sunglasses. Their eyes locked momentarily. Jeb offered her a nod. She didn't know what to make of it. When he tried to walk by, they brushed shoulders, and the contact felt forbidden. She stepped out of his way, her cheeks warmer than before. He headed off without saying a word and began deploying the trolling gear.

Catching Sierra halfway down the ladder, Amanda said, "Can you show me the ropes up there . . . how do you spot the fish?"

"Sure!" Sierra glowed and returned up the ladder. Amanda quickly followed.

Once resettled on the tower, Sierra said, "Just look for jumping fish." Sierra pointed as another mack leaped out of the air. "See that?"

"Yes!" The view was magnificent. Amanda felt sixteen again, a breeze clipping by her as she held the rail and faced the bow. She fought the impulse to remove her hat and the rest of her getup. She was lost in a peaceful time. Days spent on the *Queen Mary*, eyeing her father's clients below, fighting fish, and directing him to the thrashing schools. Nothing gave her more pleasure than "commanding the tower" as if she was queen of the realm—the skies and the seas and all that lived in them having to obey her every command.

With Sierra distracted, Amanda worked her way over to a plastic cap that was affixed on top of the roof directly above where her dad was sitting at the helm. Prior to her father installing a radio on the tower, he cut through the ceiling below and fitted the hole with a PVC pipe. The contraption enabled communication between the tower and the helm without yelling. Most thought it was an appendage to support an antenna. Her dad had likely forgotten all about it. Amanda unscrewed the cap and let it hang from the pipe. She stood close to it and listened. If he detected the cap's absence, he'd already be screaming up through the pipe, but he didn't. He was hollering at Jeb to get more lines in the water.

Amanda stepped to the rail facing the back deck. The anglers were jittery with anticipation as four lines were being pulled behind the boat—ready to cut right through the school of fish. Goosebumps hit Amanda too.

It was a convenient spot to have a conversation with Sierra. With their backs turned to the pipe, her father would hear nothing.

She was also enjoying the view of the guy manning the rigs. Even serving as a mate, Jeb's motions were like water coursing through a slide—controlled and elegant. She'd never danced on the tower, but in that moment it's what she felt like doing.

Amanda glanced at Sierra and played dumb, "What's that shiny film on the water?"

"It's an oil slick," Sierra gestured. "When the macks slash the bunker, it releases the oil. It tells you the bigger fish are feeding!" Sierra hadn't finished her sentence before several lines went down.

Jeb assisted the anglers to reel in the beautiful fish while Nora and Charlotte led a chorus of cheers. Amanda longed to take part in the fun, but that just wasn't possible.

As the excitement spread, her torment increased. Charlotte snapped pictures of the anglers pulling their fish out of the water. Each catch held vibrant colors: teal-green backs inflected with silver and distinct elliptical goldenrod spots.

Jeanette's voice echoed through the pipe, apparently still keeping company with Captain West.

Nora and Charlotte headed into the cabin. They encouraged Jeanette to leave his side to reel in a fish. She wasn't budging.

Charlotte returned with Nora to the main deck, and Nora pulled on Jeb's arm. "Daddy, Jeanette needs a little coaxing. We want her to catch some fish."

"Yes, Jeb, she needs some encouragement," Charlotte added.

Nora returned to the cabin, and Jeb's eyes followed her. He yelled toward the bow, "Miss Jeanette, I'll be a better man for you than that ole geezer, Captain West." He beckoned with his hand. "Why don't you come back here and fish with me?"

Amanda could envision Jeanette's face: looking up, pursing her lips, and squinting. The young woman had become her father's darling. Nora escorted her from the main cabin, where Jeb drew her out by constantly changing his facial expressions—mixed in with a good dose of charm. He showered her with attention and explained the fishing rigs and how he would assist her at the right time. She was sold!

The right time came quickly when a rod twitched, and with bursts of unbridled encouragement, Jeb assisted her in landing her first mackerel.

Her father's cry reverberated through the pipe, "Are you trying to steal my girl, Carter?"

Sierra turned around, looking for the source of the voice and then stuck her head down through the rail and peered into the starboard side window. It satisfied her curiosity.

"Wasn't too hard, Captain West!" Jeb returned the volley.

Amanda's dad batted back, "Did you remind my *girl* that it was Captain West that put you on those fish?"

Jeb turned to Jeanette and sweetly asked, "Have you left Captain West for *me*, or the *fish*?"

The question flustered her nearly to the point of tears, but she gained her composure, raised her eyes, and said, "Let me think." She paused with her finger on her nose. "My teacher told me if someone asks me a hard question, I should take my time . . . and think about it before answering."

Amanda glared down at Jeb and spoke under her breath, "What an idiot. What was he thinking?"

But then she saw Jeb fighting back tears, and guilt poked her again like pins.

He responded in the most tender of voices, "Oh . . . I'm sorry, Jeanette. I didn't mean to tease you. Will you forgive me?"

Jeanette tilted her head and paused before saying, "That's okay, Captain Carter."

Amanda's father spoke resentfully, "What's the guy doing back there?"

Jeb's returned a look that said, "I got this."

His eyes. The thing Jeb did with his eyes! The effort required to dislike him was becoming insurmountable. *Don't fall for it, Amanda!*

"Jeanette," he said, "why don't you call me *Mate* Carter. I'm serving as Captain West's *mate* today. "

Jeanette looked up innocently. "Okay, Mate Carter . . . I have an answer to your question."

Jeb was on his knees, his face only inches away from hers. "I'd love to hear it."

"I *want* you both and I'd like to keep fishing."

Amanda felt another needle poke her as she realized Jeanette just spoke Amanda's own thoughts. Amanda didn't long for her father. She needed to be angry with him. *I don't need Paddleboard Guy either!*

Jeb scanned up towards the tower in her direction, and she quickly turned her back to him. She took a few deep breaths and wrapped her cheeks in her hands. *I'm not sixteen. Back on mission, Amanda! The ring. Focus!*

"We need to be on the lookout for dolphins." Sierra's command brought Amanda to her senses.

"Why's that?" Amanda answered, grateful for the distraction.

"The macks will panic and stop feeding."

"Well, until then, I have another question for you. This morning at the Shop . . . why were you sticking your tongue out at those girls?"

"Who told you that?" Sierra said with a look of alarm.

"Nobody. I saw you when I walked out of the coffee shop."

The panic was now in Sierra's voice. "Does my dad know?"

"I doubt it."

"I was mad. Those girls were ogling *my* Caleb."

"Oh. That would explain it then. I'd be mad too. I might've wanted to scratch their eyes out."

Sierra smiled. "Yes, that's exactly how I felt."

Amanda grasped Sierra's hand. "Does Caleb know you *feel* this way about him?"

"I don't know. I've said nothing to him."

"But, Sierra, you referred to him as *your* Caleb. Does he believe that you *two* are an *item*?"

"I don't know, but he's very kind to me and Nora. We're good friends and we all get along."

"But you'd like it to be more than just friends?" For a moment, Amanda heard her own mother's voice in her own.

"Yes. He's *my* Caleb," Sierra insisted.

"Well, may I give you some advice?"

Sierra raised her eyebrows. "Are you going to say anything to my dad?"

"No, you don't have to worry about that. I don't recall speaking but a few words to your father in the short time I've known him."

"Amanda, I wish you'd get to know him."

Why would Sierra say such a thing? She even looked embarrassed for Amanda.

Amanda let the moment pass and then asked, "Does this mean you've forgiven me?"

Sierra tilted her head and several moments passed before she said, "Yes."

Amanda fought back tears. She stepped towards Sierra and hugged her. "Thank you . . . This is all I hoped would come from this day."

When Amanda stepped back, she discovered she'd startled Sierra with her affection. "What I did was very wrong, and I knew better. I wanted your forgiveness more than anything."

"I'm not sure I understand." Sierra's voice was tender, but uncertain.

"I know, but sometime in the future I might be able to explain to you what really happened on Saturday. For now, please trust me. I was wrong in what I did."

Sierra's face was still confused. "Okay."

"I haven't forgotten your tip."

"Aww, don't worry about it."

"I have worried about it. I can pay you now in cash if you want it."

Sierra's brow furrowed. "Why have you been worried? Are you broke?"

Sierra's sincerity hit her funny bone, and Amanda muffled her laugh to avoid drawing attention to themselves. "No silly. But I'm not saying I'm rich either. I have a decent job and I can pay a sizable tip, but I don't . . . how can I say this . . . I don't want to put a price on our experience." Amanda wanted to tell Sierra far more. It was their shared experience and one that cemented a bond between them; but without a foreseeable future, why say that?

The girl nodded her understanding, and Amanda let a few moments pass. "I'd suggest you don't mention your feelings to Caleb."

"Why?" Sierra frowned.

"You have the home-field advantage."

"What do you mean?"

Amanda kept her eyes on the school of mackerel as the vessel made a wide circle. "What I mean is that these girls flirting with *your* Caleb are all out-of-towners. They'll see him for one day, and be gone the next. You're not going anywhere. But you don't need *him* to ever suspect that you're within his grasp."

"Are you saying that I should play hard to get?"

"Not exactly. As painful as this may sound, you need to take the long-term approach."

The girl's brows furrowed.

Amanda asked, "Do you want to go to college, Sierra?"

"Yes, I want to become a doctor."

"Okay, then, do you eventually want to marry?"

"Yes, and I want to have children." Sierra ignored the schooling fish.

"Alright, well, at what age do you prefer to be married?"

"When I fall in love," Sierra spoke in a tone full of innocence.

Amanda blinked—she hadn't expected that and wasn't prepared to go into all the complications of an early marriage. But now, what if it happened to Amanda? If she fell in love? There'd be no excuse!

But it ain't happening . . . no worries.

She mused about the man below her, her father. Was he preventing it? *Blocking my path?* She glanced to the stern and eyed Jeb. She was afraid to admit to herself what she thought about him.

Sierra continued, "I'd like to get married when I finish college."

"Okay, then you'll be about twenty-two years old. I assume you'll do med school while married?"

"Yes . . . ?" Sierra stretched out her response.

Amanda figured she didn't know about the additional years of *med school* and wasn't about to embarrass her. "Well, that's a long way off. So you'll need to plan on keeping this *fish* . . . Caleb . . . on the line, nibbling for many more years." *She won't be able to grasp the futility of an intimate relationship at such a young age.* She resumed, "But your emotions are telling you, you should have *him* exclusively for yourself *now*."

Sierra looked out over the water, staring at nothing in particular. The two silently panned the horizon for dolphins. Eventually, they spotted a pod in the distance and warned the back-deck crew. By the time word had made its way to Captain West in the pilothouse there was no time to avoid them. Like clockwork, the mackerel stopped feeding.

Sierra looked at her watch. "I doubt they'll go back."

"Why? You want to stay on fish?"

"Charlotte will hold to the schedule." Sierra sighed.

So, Charlotte does run the show. The arrangement was growing on her. *Probably why Dad's staying sober? A point for the fiancée.*

"I don't blame her. Some of these parents will be driving back to Northern Virginia tonight . . . she'll want to avoid burning them out."

Amanda kept a keen eye on the rigs and planers deployed behind the boat. She wasn't pleased. *Dad's lost his tactical fishing edge.* For a moment she thought about screaming down through the pipe, "What are you thinking? Lost your mind?"

The catches slowed, and Amanda broke the silence. "Sierra, you need to stay ahead in the count. You want to always be in the catbird's seat."

"Huh?"

"Oh, I thought you played softball?" Amanda couldn't mask her surprise.

"Yes, I do, I get it now." Sierra tapped her forehead. "When I have more balls than strikes."

"Yes, that's right. If you're the batter, and Caleb is the pitcher, you don't want to get behind in the count."

"Right. I think I understand."

"When you're ahead in the count, you have more options."

Sierra nodded, "I can choose to bunt, maybe . . . take a risk and chase a wild throw."

"With the chance you might smack it for a homer!" Amanda grew a self-satisfied smile.

Sierra tilted her head. "I never realized how softball could teach me how to deal with Caleb."

Amanda wondered what it might be like to be a mother. *Would I be able to give advice like this to my own daughter?* Looking down from the tower to the main deck, she gazed at Jeb manning the rods. *Am I ahead in the count with this guy?* It was a crazy thought. *Paddleboard Guy hasn't even entered the ballpark, much less thrown a pitch.* Or had he? It didn't matter—more crazy thoughts—her long weekend was nearly over. Her only concern now was disembarking the *Queen Mary* without being recognized by her father.

The fishing concluded, and Jeb stowed the gear. He disappeared into the pilot house. Several voices echoed out of the pipe. *Good, they'll distract Dad at the helm . . . they'll tempt him to spin fishing tales. No question he'll entertain them.*

She and Sierra descended from the tower. It would be a good time for her to mingle with other families on the back-deck.

Amanda tensed, readying herself for a race to her Jeep upon arrival. The thought of never seeing her new friends again was unbearable.

She spoke to Charlotte and all the families and apologized in advance for her impending abrupt departure.

Lastly, she spoke to Sierra. Amanda's words came fast, the only way she could hide her emotions. "I need to say my goodbye to you and your sister now. I need to hustle back to Washington this afternoon. Please thank Gramps and Grans for me and let them know how much I appreciated all our time together."

Sierra's countenance fell. "But . . . but . . . when will we see you again?

Amanda looked away to avoid the girl's teary eyes. "Sierra, I really don't know . . . I really don't know."

Amanda fought her own swell of tears as Sierra turned from her and headed into the cabin. It would be too much to speak directly with Nora. That would only create a scene. *I'm such a coward.*

The vessel made its final approach to the marina, hugging the red channel marker to her starboard.

Amanda watched as Sierra wrapped her arms around her father's torso. He was immersed in conversation with Amanda's father and Charlotte. Amanda removed her eyes from the scene. No reason to listen in, either.

She grabbed her bag, careful to keep her back to her dad as he backed the boat into the slip. Amanda shared a knowing look with Charlotte just before jumping to the dock and dashing for her Jeep.

She unlocked it with her key fob on the run and climbed in. Within seconds, Amanda started the engine and shifted it into drive. It lurched forward. She glanced out her driver's side window and sighted Sierra running down the dock.

"Amanda! Amanda!"

Amanda wondered if her heart had just split in two. *How could this be so painful?* She jammed on the brakes and threw the Jeep into park.

She looked beyond Sierra to the *Queen Mary*. Her father remained distracted by the tour group. Her eyes returned to the girl. "Yes, dear! Yes, dear!"

Amanda got out of the Jeep and embraced Sierra.

With tears streaming down her face, Amanda nudged Sierra away, still holding on to the girl's shoulders.

Sierra's eyes glistened, and her voice held cautious optimism when she asked, "Why don't you join us for the fishing tournament this weekend? We'll be hosting two Special Angler families on board the *Galleon*." She threw back a wisp of her strawberry blonde hair. "There'll be lady anglers too."

Amanda cocked her head and her mind went blank for a moment. Her heart skipped a beat. "Does your father know you're inviting me?"

"*I'm* inviting you!" She rubbed her foot in the gravel. "Gramps will be the captain. We don't need my dad!" Her voice softened. "Gramps and Grans like you. Please come."

"Oh, well, I wouldn't want to push your father off the boat."

Sierra's eyes pleaded. "For Nora."

Amanda felt as if a lead slug had shot straight through her gut. *Why did she have to mention Nora?*

"Sierra . . ." Amanda pulled back a few loose strands of hair from Sierra's face. "I need some time to think it over." She pressed her fingers into her own forehead. "Why don't I call your Gramps and Grans later in the week? After I've had some time to think things through?"

Her words seemed to satisfy Sierra, a glimmer of hope shining from the girl's eyes. And for Amanda who felt much better than the thought of never seeing them again. The fear of discovery had distracted her from a wrenching pain she couldn't explain . . . and it all had nothing to do with her father.

The two exchanged numbers and Sierra freed her.

Shakes

Jeb was in the pilothouse when Sierra rushed into his arms. Apparently, Amanda and Sierra had settled their earlier rift. Jeb didn't want to dig deeper. It was pointless to pry. Sierra was ratcheting down her emotions like a clam.

He was still holding Sierra firmly when Charley spoke.

"Jeb, please let your dad know I'm going to need some help with this weekend's tournament. We're hosting more Special Anglers. We've overbooked." Charley's eyes focused on the narrow channel leading into the marina.

Charlotte placed her hand on Jeb's arm. "If you could take a couple of lady anglers and their fathers, we'd be much obliged. We have a pair that would be perfect for you and the girls . . . experienced with great sea legs."

Jeb shrugged. "I'll pass it on to my dad. Sounds like fun. I've enjoyed this. Depending on how things went today with Caleb, I'd like to get him to run another tour for me."

The boat edged into the slip, and before Jeb could tie it down, Amanda was gone. *Good riddance*, he lied to himself, suppressing the pain in his chest. Soon after, Sierra wriggled free like a champagne cork.

Jeb watched Amanda from the corner of his eye when she slipped away. He breathed a sigh of relief and wondered, even hoped, it was the end of the interloper; her extended weekend in the Northern Neck finally ending. And the last thing he needed was Charley and Charlotte picking up on his angst towards the woman, spinning visions of romance out of thin air. He didn't need his girls suspecting anything either. Still, Jeb knew he'd stolen too many glances at Amanda all day.

Why get involved? Amanda continued to scare him. It helped she'd hid her eyes from him for most of the cruise. When she'd pulled her glasses off—just once—he went weak in the knees. At a different stage of life, he might've welcomed such a feeling. But not now! Not when his focus needed to be on the girls and protecting the memory of their mother.

When they'd arrived at Tangiers and Amanda limped away with Charlotte, he'd struggled to believe it was the same woman he'd pulled from the water on Saturday—the one how took his breath away.

The woman on Tangier was distressed. *What had Charlotte done to her? She's hiding something!* But he also felt drawn to her, nearly succumbing to an impulse to rescue her.

He believed it was fair game to ridicule the woman in front of Charley, but on the other hand, a sense of duty gripped him to protect her from the shame of some deep-seated pain. He was grateful Charlotte seemed to have come to her aid.

On their departure from Tangier, after resolving to say something nice to Amanda, he'd seen Nora cuddled alongside her. His pulse lost its rhythm. *Nora needs mothering.* Something he dared admit to himself. When he settled cozily on the seat right next to them, he whiffed the lady's tropical scent. That didn't help either.

The fishing action that ensued was a godsend, and Jeanette, a wonderful diversion. It helped his family fulfill their purpose for the day. To have been further distracted by the woman would have betrayed Charley and Charlotte's efforts.

Charlotte sidled up to him at the dock and brought him back to the present. Together, they observed some goings-on between Sierra and Amanda. He looked at Charlotte. "What's that all about?"

She poked Jeb in the chest where it already hurt.

"More than you need to know right now," she said.

"Huh?"

Charlotte's eyes glared at him, "Yes . . . just leave it at that."

His girls said their goodbyes to all their new friends and loaded into his truck. They headed to the Shop, but Caleb was gone.

He grabbed his daughters by the hands and walked down to Kat's. He released Sierra's hand before he knocked.

Kat threw the door open. "Jeb Carter, you're no longer welcome here!" Her body slumped with fatigue. "This was supposed to be my day off."

Poor Nora. Her eyes widened. Sierra stiffened. They tugged at Jeb's arms as they stepped back from the entrance. He wasn't about to budge.

Kat winked at the girls. "Why didn't you tell me that Sierra's *Rivah Boy* would attract over two busloads of diners?"

Jeb caught Sierra's blush.

"My staff called me at home in a panic." A smile crept up Kat's face and her voice became very Southern. "Had it not been for your two sweet girls . . . no, I wouldn't have opened these doors to you, Jeb Carter."

It wasn't long before they were holding milkshakes.

"Was his sandwich ready for him?"

Kat faked irritation. "Apparently. I heard you ordered it in advance. He came over after his tour with a boy from that family in tow. He'd barely taken his first bite before a dad popped his head in the door with a few of his girls."

Jeb pantomimed Caleb holding the big Reuben, wiping the drips oozing down the side of his mouth.

His girls giggled, and Kat continued without taking a breath. "There were at least thirty of them when I arrived, and I'd swear a bus was sitting out front." She turned genuinely serious.

"That would be a maxi-van," Jeb deadpanned.

He eyed Nora and wrinkled his nose. She burst into laughter, some of her milkshake escaping through her nostrils. He quickly reached for a napkin and dabbed her cheeks.

"This is no joke, Jeb. More than just one large family!" She sighed. "The entire extended family—many who hadn't even been on *Caleb's* tour." She shook her head in wonder. "The grandfather arrived and paid a bill well over six-hundred dollars!"

"Yep . . . I would expect nothing less from my man." Jeb sat up a notch.

Kat shook her head in dismay.

Jeb grabbed Kat's hand. "Hey, I never thanked you for looking after Nora on Saturday."

Kat tilted her head back. "Huh?" She picked up Nora's soiled napkin from the counter.

Nora's sweet voice chimed in, "Daddy, I manned the Shop on Saturday."

"I know . . . with Caleb. You came here before he arrived . . . right?"

Nora raised her chest. "No, Daddy. I ran the shop by myself."

Jeb flinched. "Alone?"

"Yes, Daddy. I wanted to make Miss Amanda proud."

Jeb flexed his jaw muscles. Kat's expression told him to take deep breaths, to not spoil the moment, and he preferred not to give Kat an argument point in her favor.

As soon as the girls entered the restroom, he spoke up. "I can finally put the woman's intrusion behind us."

Kat leaned against the counter looking vexed.

"Things went too far, Kat . . . I've got to take all this in baby steps."

His friend remained mum . . . and oddly guarded. Before Jeb could press her, she left to clean up.

He let a few moments pass, shrugged, and found a nearby table.

Except for Sierra's strange emotional state, the news about Caleb couldn't have been any better. Jeb and his girls enjoyed Kat's specially made milkshakes on the house, the big "CLOSED" sign on the front door providing a fitting exclamation point on their day.

Slam dunk for the dad!

Bills

On his return to the Bay House, Jeb plowed into his paperwork with more energy, recognizing the time with the girls had been well spent. Erin would've been pleased. In moments like these, her sweet voice echoed from the past, "You chose wisely." But now, in his home-office, he still needed to pay the bills.

"Daddy, are you busy?" Sierra broke the silence.

Jeb turned calmly around in his chair and faced her. "Yes . . . but not so busy I can't talk with my daughter." His voice was soft, his thoughts still lingering on Erin. Sierra's green eyes kept him there.

What Sierra had to say was serious. It had to be. She'd maneuvered around the inquisitive ears of her sister who sounded as if she were still on the first floor.

Sierra wheeled an office chair from the corner and settled into it before saying, "How old do I need to be before I can get married?"

He arrested his surprise. This was a conversation he'd always hoped to have with her, but it had eluded him. "Sierra, are you asking me how old I will *require* you to be before you marry?"

Sierra's brow wrinkled slightly. "Yes . . . and no."

"Forty or fifty," Jeb teased.

She smacked her hand down on her armrest. "I'm serious."

"Okay, I'll consider allowing you to date at thirty. How does that sound?"

Her eyes pleaded, "No, Daddy, really."

Jeb maintained his poker face. "This is about Caleb, isn't it?"

Her eyes tightened, shifting to the clutter on his desk, and then the built-in bookshelves behind him. Finally she spoke softly, "Yes."

"Sierra, I realize you're not comfortable with this, but I'm glad you're talking with me about it. Promise me you'll always do that. I don't have your mother now to help me, so I'm it." He flattened his lips.

"How'd you know?"

Jeb raised an eyebrow. "Last night at the dinner table."

Sierra dropped her elbows to her knees and rested her chin in her hands. "Amanda says I need to stay ahead in the count."

Jeb dropped his head and shook it. *Her again?* He chuckled, mostly to give himself more time to think. "Well, that's some interesting advice." He sucked in an exaggerated breath. *Am I to thank Amanda for this?* Helping him break the ice on the sensitive subject? *Preposterous!* Guilt prodded him. *Why couldn't I say one kind word to her all day?* He hid a shudder.

Jeb knew that there'd be subjects that should be addressed with his blossoming daughter, and only hoped that Grans had taken the initiative. "What does it mean?"

"Well, you know . . . like in softball."

"I don't play softball, so I don't know what it means." His mind battled between the vision of the woman he'd sat next to at dinner against the sight of the woman on the Tangier tour. Sierra's features reminded him of Erin adding to the confusion.

Sierra's voice teased, "Daddy, it's the same in baseball."

Jeb creased his brow. "Oh, right? But how does it apply to your situation?"

"I'm going to stay one step ahead of him."

He cocked his head.

"Like in chess. I'm going to think things out four or five moves *ahead* of him."

Jeb sat back in his chair. "Did you get all this from the crazy lady?"

"No, only the part about staying ahead in the count and something about being in the catbird's seat." Sierra scrunched her nose. "And I don't think she's *crazy*. She's nice."

He felt Sierra's eyes search his face. "I think you take after your mother. That's the way she was with me, always a few moves ahead." He gently nodded. "You've received some good—"

He caught himself. He didn't dare credit Amanda with "good advice." "I hope you stick with your plan going forward."

Jeb thought he was handling this smoothly, but in truth, it was a revelation about how the opposite sex dealt with his kind. Was the out-of-town stranger taking this approach with him? *I haven't entered this game! But why do I feel drawn to it?*

He plunged straight ahead. "I don't want to see you bleeding out your emotions where everyone can see what you're thinking and feeling."

Sierra's eyes widened and she tensed, fighting tears.

"That was harsh. I'm sorry. Harsh, but honest. Your mother would have handled this. Found a gentler way to say it."

Sierra nodded and wiped her eyes. "You would've been standing next to her."

It was the greatest thing Sierra could've said. *To think we stood as an allied front. That's how she remembered us. God in the middle of all of it.* "Yeah, but she would've slapped me good." He let a small smile escape.

She couldn't hold back a laugh.

Some moments passed. "Aunt Kathi said something too, at the Yokel . . . It bothered me. What if Caleb had been around?"

"Yes, I saw your expression. You shouldn't be shy in saying something to her about it. She'll understand and protect you."

"What about you, Dad?"

"What do you mean?"

"You . . ." Sierra edged her face closer. "What about you?"

His heart pounded erratically. "Me?"

"Yes, you Dad."

"I don't know what you're talking about."

Sierra was earnest. "Your heart, Dad."

He tapped his chest. "My heart's fine." He wasn't very convincing. He placed two fingers on his neck, looked at his watch, and counted. "Sixty beats a minute. I'm in great shape." He forced a smile, concealing the fact his heart rate had jumped to over eighty.

She continued to glare. "You know what I mean. Are you ever going to remarry?"

Oh, she said it! Why did she have to ask? Jeb stared past her for several moments before answering, "It's complicated."

"What's so complicated about falling in love? Doesn't that just happen?"

"No—" he stumbled on his words. "I mean yes, but in my situation . . . it's complicated. I have you and Nora. We have values to uphold . . . your mother and I."

"Mom's dead, Dad."

Jeb rotated in his chair, away from his daughter. His eyes stung, and he felt his chest sink to his knees. He sucked in deep breaths.

Stemming his tears, he returned to face her and smacked his chest with the palm of his hand. "She's not dead here."

Sierra's eyes glistened, but her tone had some edge to it. "I didn't say she was."

"I lost her and I can't afford to lose you, too."

Sierra wiped her face. "Dad."

Jeb closed his eyes. After several moments, he felt her arms around his neck.

"Look at me," she said.

He opened his eyes to find her green ones looking into his soul.

Her tone was soft. "You're not losing anybody . . ." Then she teased, "and besides, you said I couldn't start dating till I was thirty."

Jeb folded his arms. "I know how we agreed to raise you . . . and I'm going to stay on course." Uninvited, Amanda's face flashed in front of him. Her goofy hat and oversized sunglasses. *I certainly wouldn't want a woman like that gaining influence over my daughters. An urbanite . . . already filling the girl's heads with wild thoughts.* "No one should interfere with that." *I doubt the woman has any morals.* "If ever I do fall in love again, mark my words, it'll never be with that New York lady whatsername."

Sierra's tone was flat, "I wasn't asking about her. It was a general question."

"Oh." Jeb flushed. He thought about Nora and the affection she had for Amanda. The image of Amanda and Nora sitting next to him on the *Queen Mary* blazed in his mind. But two days before, when Amanda stormed the Shop, she pushed him to the edge. He'd nearly exploded, tackled the floozy, and carried her out.

Ditzy? No! There was a real soul behind her enchanting eyes. When he'd pulled her from the water on Saturday, her eyes were inquisitive. Reading him. Absorbing him.

Crazy, mad woman when she came into the Shop. Possessed! Infuriating! She'd given him no choice but to fight back. But at the Bay House and on the tour? Intuitive and intelligent.

"Daddy . . ." Sierra's voice softened, and Jeb startled.

He strained to regain focus. "Yes?"

"How will I know when I fall in love? Like, how was it with you and Mom?"

Jeb rubbed his forehead and squeezed the bridge of his nose. It was a fair question. *I need you, Erin!* In all his power, he wanted to get it right.

"When you're truly in love, the reality of the situation is better than your dreams." He nodded several times. "That's how it was with your mother. She was better than my wildest dreams. And I felt she loved me just the same." His eyes drifted beyond her, to where he could see the sky. "To love someone so intensely, and feel loved in return, there's nothing better."

He returned his focus to Sierra. She was smiling so brightly it chased every shadow from his heart. Maybe, just this once, he'd hit one out of the park

The two continued along for some time as Jeb moved off the topic, fumbling his way through, offering his fatherly advice. Sierra asked about the implications of med school, which he explained. Jeb suspected Sierra was holding other secrets, but he chose not to probe. He was making progress. Two steps forward, one step back.

Amanda had set him back. But she was behind him now. Sierra had given him permission to crack open his heart.

Permission was one thing. Having the willingness to charge ahead was altogether different. *Maybe a dating app? Winter would be a good time for that.* Another wild thought hit him. The pursuit! He'd never pursued a woman. With Erin, he only had to breathe. He'd never gone to the plate and risked being struck out. Rejected. Erin had practically demanded he propose to her. There was no question she was going to say "Yes!"

Jeb leaned back in his chair and closed his eyes. An awkward silence—but for a ceiling fan—enveloped the space for nearly a minute.

"I have a confession, Sierra." He sat up straight, faced her.

She blinked and fidgeted in her chair as she waited for him to continue.

"I've attempted to mold you and your sister to be like your mother." He searched her face. Her eyes narrowed. *She agrees.* "I've been wrong. You're not your mother and were never intended to be. You're your own person." He spoke softly, "I'm sorry."

Tears formed at the corners of her eyes. She stood, closed the distance between them, and wrapped her arms around him. "No, Daddy. You're doing your best. I know that's all you want for us." Words wouldn't come for Jeb. They were stuck in his throat. Instead, he let his tears speak for him.

CHAPTER 12

Cable

Amanda had already downed two cups of coffee by 9:00 AM Tuesday morning. The weekend had left her exhausted. By 1:00 PM, she was mostly caught up on her primary duties: procurement, tracking, and delivery of specialized tech-ops equipment to local and far-flung locations around the world. A whole different ball of wax from a typical logistics job. At the Agency, she employed cover mechanisms for the procurement, taking initial receipt of the equipment at various CONUS nondescript Agency buildings. She did all of it well and could do most of it in her sleep.

She spent her lunch break in a chat session with Sally, who was still at training. Sally's whirlwind romance with Ted wasn't waning, and Amanda got an earful.

"You need to slow down!" Amanda advised.

"Don't worry, girl. I got this," was Sally's response.

Amanda typed feverishly, describing her clash with the fiancée and explaining her ties with the Agency. After closing the chat session, Amanda decided to investigate Charlotte. She only had her first name, but she had a location and a time: Rome Station, 2012. It didn't take Amanda long to identify the Rome Station Chief at that time, Zara T. BERRYCLOTH. The name was a pseudo, so Amanda performed a lookup to discover the real name: Charlotte F. Dandridge.

She persisted with additional searches on any cable that referenced BERRYCLOTH before her conscience pricked her. Her inquiries were expanding well beyond her authorized uses of the Agency's secure cable messaging system. Amanda sighed. The archaic system for exchanging messages between Headquarters and its stations and bases had barely changed since the '80s. The history of sealed diplomatic communications went back ages. When Amanda trained newbies, she'd make excuses for the system, but would also retell some history of secure communications, like the orders provided by King James to the Virginia Company. "A physical wax seal confirmed not only the source of the orders, but their authority."

The cabling system she used now to inspect a message from Madrid Station had similar features. Multiple layers of encryption added authenticity and legitimacy of a source—fully vetted and trusted—*information collected by our own Agency officer!*

Amanda clicked all the obvious links on the message, some producing ominous pop-ups, telling her she wasn't allowed to view the cable. The notifications issued email addresses for further inquiry with an organization in the Counter Terrorism Center (CTC) and the Counter Intelligence Mission Center (CIMC).

Strange, she thought. *Those organizations are mostly unrelated.* Regardless, the sensitive content was being compartmentalized. *Better to stop now before I get in trouble.* Since she usually spent so much time in the messaging system, who'd suspect her inquiries were outside her official duties?

What struck Amanda as being odd was the cable she tripped upon was fairly new—May. *Why would a recent cable reference Charlotte if she'd retired several years ago?* And one that came from Madrid!

Caroline was talking to a colleague when her computer chimed. She turned around. A pop-up flashed in the middle of her screen. It deserved some attention from the astute analyst who worked in the CIMC. At least her boss thought she was astute, as noted in her annual performance review. Caroline's motto? *Fake it till you make it.*

Caroline navigated to her email inbox and selected the message associated with the alert. She skimmed it and learned someone had been attempting to access a "cable of interest"—one from Madrid Station she maintained in a highly sensitive case file. She rarely chased these down and was about to ignore it. *Always a reasonable explanation*, she thought, access granted in nearly every case.

"Wait a second," she spoke softly. *That cable!* She remembered it. A very strange cable. For good measure, she clicked on the alert link, and it displayed the details of the cable in another window on her screen. She quickly scanned it and scrolled to the bottom. *Yes, this was the one!* She absorbed the last paragraph. It still made her head spin. It was personal! She wondered if anyone else at the Agency could read between the lines and interpret it that way.

Am I it? For such a time as this?

Via the Agency's Person Finder web-app, she entered the person's pseudo-name, seeking to know more about the individual who'd attempted access. The tool displayed the employee's organization within the Agency. *Why would someone in the Directorate of Support care about this cable?* Especially a deployed logistics officer in the DS&T?

She picked up her secure phone and started to dial the officer's number, but paused. *Better to address the individual by true name. More professional.* She launched the pseudo-name lookup tool, pasted the fake name into it, and clicked the decipher button. Caroline gasped.

Amanda I. West!

Caroline's phone—sandwiched between her shoulder and cheek—fell and boinked on her desk. She grabbed her purse, took two steps away from her cubicle, and stopped. *Oh darn!* She retraced her path and returned the phone to its receptacle. Scurrying out of the SCIF, she headed straight for the elevator. She felt a blast of heat when she exited the building and continued briskly towards her car. She would've run, but that would've attracted notice.

She opened her glove compartment and pulled out her smartphone. "Drat!" The car was burning hot, and her smartphone had shut down. After starting the car, the AC kicked in. She held the phone in front of a vent and waited a few minutes before attempting to power it on. When it did, she was ready to hit the speed dial but paused. Caroline dropped the smartphone in her lap and placed the car in reverse. Maneuvering out of the parking lot, she exited the guarded compound putting it behind her by several miles. Better not to place this call from the cell-tower adjacent to her secure facility. Even a novice in her field would suspect that several foreign services monitored it, collecting selector meta-data from the personal cellphones of those who worked at the compound.

Satisfied her smartphone had jumped to another tower, she dialed using her hands-free system. An excited voice blasted from her car speakers. It was a voice she'd known all her life.

"Caroline!"

"Mom, what's going on?"

"Huh?"

"Mom, you know something. Something's going on. Something's happening!"

Her mother sounded tentative. "How do you know?"

"I've tripped up on something here at work . . . something that I can't talk about."

"Okay . . . then yes." A deep breath came through, followed by her mother's resolute voice, "There's been movement, but not how I would've expected. Possibly strange and beautiful."

"What?" Caroline glanced in her rearview mirror. The highway's right lane was open, and she merged into it. "Mom, hang on. I need to find a place to park."

Caroline took the next off-ramp and pulled into a fast-food joint. *Strange and beautiful?* What was her mom talking about? "Okay, you have my full attention. Tell me all that again."

"I can't say. I'm keeping my distance." Her mom's tone was stern. "Caroline, we must be careful not to interfere."

"Interfere with what?"

"Something's happening with your brother."

Caroline flinched. "Well . . . what I've learned has nothing to do with him."

Her mother spoke slowly and thoughtfully, "Hmm . . . I'd like you to join me here on Saturday."

"I'm busy," Caroline's response came out like a shot and her chest tightened.

Her mother's words fired back at her with the same tempo, "Change your plans, please. I only need you for a few hours in the afternoon."

"Mom, it's a three-hour drive under the best of conditions." Caroline softened her voice. "It will upset the girls if I don't stay for the night."

"They don't need to know."

Her mother's tone told her everything she needed to know. She spoke through clenched teeth. "Fine—I'll toss all my plans out the window." Should she tell her mom about having to cancel a date? *No!* It'd invite a thousand probing questions.

She pulled out of the parking lot and found the highway entrance ramp toward her building. "Mom, what do I do with the information?"

"Given you haven't told me what you've discovered, how am I to advise you?"

Caroline rubbed her temple. "Ahhh . . . well, at least you've confirmed one thing."

"Dear, use your best judgment. We're trusting you in times like this. You must abide by the laws of the land."

"I think I have some leeway here."

Encouragement broke through in her mother's voice. "Well then, do what you must do."

Caroline sighed deeply. "Thanks, Mom. I'll see you Saturday."

She could trust her mother. Wisest person she'd ever known . . . next to her father.

Letters

By Wednesday night, Amanda could no longer delay the inevitable. Her father's letters. After all the years of depositing them in the *burn box*—a leftover shoebox—she hadn't burned them. She found it within a larger box containing some of her cherished college textbooks. They weren't textbooks exactly, but great classic American novels—several titles from James Fennimore Cooper. *Deerslayer* had strongly resonated with her. The tale of Tom Hutter and his daughters, Judith and Hetty, was reminiscent of stories her mother had told her as a child. For some reason, she sensed the novel was more like a parable describing her own identity. She wouldn't mention this in class, but she'd talked about it with her Aunt Nancy, who wouldn't dissuade her from thinking differently. She, too, had heard the tales in her childhood taught by her own mother.

Amanda committed herself to read all the letters in the order he'd sent them—but not all at once. She pulled them from the shoebox and carefully tore open their envelopes. The yellowing paper only reminded her of how long she'd avoided them. With so much to absorb, she took her time.

In the first several letters, her dad wrote of his own shame. Amanda discovered that he too struggled to forgive himself. He begged for her forgiveness, and said he'd prefer to do it in person if she'd give him the chance. He asked this not for himself, but for her own healing. Helping her to heal would be easier, he explained, compared to his struggle to forgive himself. In one particular letter, she learned he'd found a solution—he forgave himself by accepting someone else's forgiveness (and it wasn't hers). She blinked at the thought and felt a trail of tears burn a path down her cheeks.

She was sitting on her couch when she read about his Alcoholics Anonymous sessions and his participation in a grief counseling group. He mentioned the support he received from another widower, an accountability partner, but he didn't mention a name. She pulled the Kleenex box closer.

She studied letters in which he cited her soccer games. Nearly every game! *How can that be?* At first, she assumed he'd found the school's website and links to the streaming content from the games. Tears continued to spill, and she wiped those that had fallen onto the letters. In one letter, her father referenced an incident that occurred at halftime at an away game. It was her senior year, and the referee had pulled Amanda behind the bleachers—away from all cameras. As the captain, she'd been instructed to get "her girls under control." The game had gotten feisty on both sides. Aunt Nancy hadn't attended, and Amanda had never told the incident to anyone. *He had to have been there!* There was no other way. She pressed the letter to her chest and closed her eyes.

Other comments in the letters pointed to the same conclusion. *He'd gone to my games!* Deep, gut-wrenching sobs exploded from her center. Dropping to the floor and cradling her knees, she rocked.

The pain of her father's words in the letters made her cringe. How had she grown to hate, with venom building year after year? Her stomach churned.

Twice, while reading, she'd nearly vomited. The letters scattered about on the floor tortured her, each reminding her of the grim fact. She couldn't rewind the clock.

The truth came at her like a freight train, each letter another box car of reality. Her father was eloquent, sincere, wise, loving—

everything he'd been to Amanda before the decline of her mother's health. He was healed!

Amanda finally reached her limit. Her body felt vacant, and she set the letters aside. She donned her running shorts, shoes, and her dainty holster. The August light faded as she took to her well-lit neighborhood streets. She wanted to regain some semblance of who she was—equal parts strong, independent, and resilient, not the wretched daughter who'd thrown out every olive branch that came her way. She could muster no anger towards her father . . . only toward herself for ignoring him and stealing his joy.

The one thing Amanda couldn't do before going to bed?

She couldn't face herself in the mirror.

A double-wrapped manila envelope sat on the seat of Amanda's office chair when she arrived at work Thursday morning. It was impossible to miss, labeled with large red ink:

TOP SECRET—Isabella West EYES ONLY

Her stomach tightened. She picked it up and placed it on her desk. She'd come hungry, looking forward to breakfast in the cafeteria with Sally. Now her appetite vanished.

Beads of sweat formed on her forehead, and she mopped them off using the cuff of her blouse. No one at the Agency had ever addressed her as *Isabella*. Only someone in Security would have access to her given name. The system only revealed the initial *I*. Additional alarm bells pealed. The envelope showed her true surname, a violation of the Agency's security protocol for preventing disclosure of undercover officers. *Who delivered this?* Inquiring among her office mates would only bring unwanted attention to the envelope.

Amanda walked down her office corridor and located a red Expo marker resting on the dry-erase-whiteboard shelf. She returned to her desk and drew over the lettering, fully obscuring her name.

She pulled a pair of scissors from her desk drawer, cut off the envelope's top, and emptied its contents onto her desk. Two sheets of paper were stapled together, a sticky note affixed at the top of them. The note was scribed in the same red Sharpie ink:

Isabella, it's High Time you claim what is rightfully yours!

Amanda leafed through the papers. She quickly deciphered that she was looking at the cable from Madrid Station. The cable for which she had no prior access and one that came to her attention via her online queries regarding Charlotte. She scanned through it but couldn't find any reference to Charlotte. It was a weekly report coming from Madrid Station's counterterrorism liaison officer and her Spanish intelligence counterparts, the CNI.

She returned the document to the envelope and placed it in her desk drawer. She breathed steadily. She wasn't going to be in any trouble. If anything, the person who passed her the cable would be in trouble. Her appetite returned. The mystery could wait. Coffee and a breakfast sandwich with Sally now held her attention.

By late afternoon, Amanda pulled out the envelope from the drawer. The sticky note had the same effect as before, and she fought back trembles. She carefully reread the cable. This time, she noticed a small comment left at the end of it. The author of the cable, a CT officer, provided what appeared to be no more than an afterthought in her weekly report. It made reference to several long-lost artifacts, and of all things, an English artifact! *A tiara? Crazy odd!* Amanda pressed her fingertips to her temple. *Why in a CT cable from Madrid?* She reread the analyst's comments at least ten times. *And why linked to Charlotte?*

Amanda rotated in her chair and scanned her nearby cubicle spaces. Taking a breath, she stood holding the papers. She walked along the hallway, down two rows, and stopped in front of the shredder. It hummed smoothly until she guided the manila envelope containing the cable into it. The rough grind of the sharp teeth tapered off, and she exhaled a deep breath. The last of her father's correspondence beckoned. It was time to head home.

By Thursday night, Amanda had read through all his letters. She found nothing in them that dissuaded her from her probing incursions, especially since the Madrid cable. Her father was one thing. Charlotte was something else altogether—and any mention of her was notably absent in her father's letters.

She thought about the girls. There might be a significant age difference, but Amanda believed she'd gained a friend in Sierra. Maybe she could be a big sister to Sierra? They possessed a common bond, each having experienced the loss of their mothers. *It would've been nice to have had a sister*—a younger sister Amanda never got to know, lost through one of her mother's miscarriages. *Mom always told me I was her miracle child.*

Thinking of Nora, she bit her lip. The girl radiated contagious light. The feelings she had for her were far more complicated. Nora's innocence! She felt a stirring in her heart that nothing else could touch.

Amanda struggled with the convoluted thoughts she had towards Jeb. Sierra hadn't mentioned him as being part of the tournament crew. He'd have tour bookings most likely. *He's intriguing—an enigma.* His eyes, his voice, his movements. The thought of him being anywhere near her was frightening.

She closed her eyes and saw an image of her father. Jeb stood behind him. She reached for her father's shoulder, attempting to push him aside, but her dad wouldn't budge and blocked her view of Jeb's face. *I suppose James Carter is off limits*—not the right time for adding that mysterious man to the mix. She opened her eyes as anger flooded her veins. *The ring!*

Maybe her father was keeping it in a safe-deposit box at the bank. But that made little sense, since he owned a very solid safe. *There has to be another safe!* She felt it in her bones. Saturday's tournament day would provide the perfect cover for sneaking back into the Marina House. She could drive down at daybreak.

The ring was atypical and nothing like a traditional diamond engagement ring. Its beautiful gem appeared emerald in the light and ruby-red in darkness. When she'd asked about the gem type, her mother prevaricated. The gemstone was rare. The local jeweler failed to hide his gasp when she and her mom visited his shop to have a pendant repaired. He pointed at it. "The gem's cut looks very aged. Extremely valuable . . . but that's not what's so striking here."

Just before her mother pulled her hand away, he pointed at the red stones intermixed with the radiant white diamonds that surrounded the gemstone. "This can't be what it looks like." He shook his head, and then nodded as her mother's face remained stern and serious.

He asked if it was properly appraised for insurance—resulting in her mom becoming short with him and promptly concluding their business.

"Good luck," he yelled sarcastically as they walked out the door. "You might want to try Lloyd's of London."

Her mother would rarely wear the ring in public thereafter, but Amanda specifically remembered her mother wearing it the day they went to lunch at the retirement center and on a few other rare occasions. For everyday activities, her mother wore a decent wedding band and told her, "It's sufficient."

Amanda closed her eyes and raised the ring, visualizing its maritime and astronomical symbols. She assumed it was *Naval* tradition, but as she got older, she paid closer attention to the rings of the spouses of her father's Academy alumni. All traditional, and most with massive diamonds. When she eventually questioned her mother about it, she only indicated it was a family heirloom. Amanda neglected to ask, "Why the symbols? Which family?" She'd assumed it had come from her father. Her mother told her, "Hopefully, one day, you'll wear this ring. In *time*, dear, in *time*, you will understand."

Had she made the statement in a generic sense, telling Amanda she would one day wear an engagement ring . . . any ring . . . or specifically, that ring? The last time she'd seen it was at her mother's interment. Somber, dark-suited men opened the casket a final time for her father and her to say goodbye. He removed the ring, and Amanda never questioned him about it.

She thought about a college friend who, upon the death of her grandmother, was given an heirloom ring that went back generations. Her friend was speechless upon hearing the news. *She'd been chosen!* The ring could have gone to countless other relatives, but the grandmother chose her to receive it. Wasn't that what Amanda's own mother had said about the ring? *I'm an only child . . . doesn't that make me chosen?*

Amanda arrived for duty Friday morning to find another envelope waiting, resting ominously on her chair. It was labeled similarly and sent a chill up her spine. She wasted no time in opening it. Within it, she found a basic Intelligence Report, one that an analyst would assemble from multiple sources. It was short and to the point. It stated that a previous Agency retiree, one Charlotte Dandridge, maintained a close and continuing business relationship with MI6, the UK's version of the CIA. Other details in the report were redacted.

Amanda clenched her teeth. There was one and only one explanation. Charlotte wasn't being honest about her motives; she was playing her father. Amanda had seen enough of the report and shredded it immediately.

She was desperate to return home and inspect the ominous letter scribed in calligraphy. She recalled the similar reference to "High Time" and performed a quick Google search on her low-side computer. She viewed the term's definition: "a long-awaited event, an appropriate time, or past the appropriate time." Was that what the author of the letter was telling her? That she was overdue in reconciling with her father?

Her search also resulted in a reference to a Kacey Musgraves song. Reading the lyrics to *High Time* caused Amanda to silently weep at her desk, especially the lines about *missing one's roots* and *returning to the old me*. The strangest coincidence of all was to find the song on YouTube showing a picture of Kacey wearing a tiara.

Was there more? Like maybe a direct warning about Charlotte? The words from the letter came back to her now like strobing lights, even the misspelling of the word *rightfully*:

"It is High Time you claim what is just and rightfally yours. Time is of the essence."

Amanda did the simplest thing that came to mind, writing the letter sequence (ignoring the spaces) down a numbered column on a sheet of paper. The letter 'C' for Charlotte appeared on row sixteen. 'H' appeared on row twenty-two. She stopped there because the combination of the numbers formed the year 1622. It was the year of the Jamestown massacre in which 347 settlers were killed by warring Powhatans. If ever there was a warning about Charlotte, this was it!

There would be a change of plans.

Whatever you want, Charlotte, I won't let you get it!

Parents' Meeting

Jeb returned home Thursday night after attending a meeting for the upcoming soccer season for the girls. He hated those meetings. It was always the same old stuff, and at the meeting, he wasn't paying attention—until he learned he'd become a coach. The commissioner had asked for volunteers to handle an additional team, and Jeb hadn't stepped back quickly enough like the other parents. Pangs of guilt gnawed at him. He couldn't decline. After all, it was for his girls—an activity that didn't center on him. What Kat had lectured him about.

That's okay. The parenting phase with Sierra was now all about coaching. His authoritarian relationship with her was over, whether he liked it or not. Nora was different. She still needed mothering. Seeing the way Nora responded to that woman from New York reinforced it. *Why can't Mom fulfill this role?*

Another thought hit him . . . with the loss of Erin, Sierra had been stepping up as a quasi-mother. *Explains why she's so mature . . .* Her childhood, stolen.

Had there been a real, doting, compassionate figure for Nora, it would've lessened the pressure on Sierra. *Could Sierra ever regain some childhood?*

Jeb lay in bed, thinking about his motives for moving his family to the Bay House. *Who wouldn't want to live on the water in the middle of nowhere?* But that was from his perspective. As a kid, he only vacationed on the water and could never get enough of it. For his daughters, this "small town" life was all they'd known.

Kat's counsel rang in his ears as if she were standing in his bedroom: "Jeb, you're going to push her out if you don't back off a bit! She needs to see the rest of the world." He didn't want to push Sierra away. *Help me, Erin, I'm begging you!*

Jeb wondered about Charley. *Didn't he lose a daughter like that? Whoever she is . . . off in some far-off distant land.* With his wife Mary out of the picture, did Charley smother her? *Is that why she ran? Am I doing the same?*

Jeb committed himself to the tournament. He was confident in Caleb's ability to conduct a Saturday tour, but he still had to decline a booking. It was a sacrifice, especially on a high-demand weekend, but he knew how much it meant to the girls and his father. They were looking forward to hosting the Special Anglers, and his dad would need the help.

And how about Caleb? He was becoming more like family. If

there had been room on the boat, Jeb could've shut down the Shop for the day and invited him. *Money ain't everything.*

Jeb didn't deny that there might be more to his decisions than met the eye. Pride motivated him as much as the other virtuous intrinsics. Charley had needled him with texts all week, suggesting Jeb was afraid of the competition. Jeb believed Monday's outing on the *Queen Mary* had sparked it. It must have reminded Charley of their days together before Jeb ventured out to do his own thing. *He needs to get over it!* Was that it, or was something else getting under his skin?

The tournament was about honor. *If Charley wants to duke it out with me, it'll be on the water. Saturday! Just you and me, Charley. Head to head.* Queen Mary *against the* Galleon. *West vs. Carter. Forget about everyone else.*

I'll show you who's King Carter!

CHAPTER 13

Captains' Meeting

Amanda arrived at the Captains' Meetings unannounced. It had been a few years, but she knew the forum inside and out. As a young girl and a teen, not only had she participated in the tournament every year, but she also volunteered at the meeting. After all, the Little League was the beneficiary of the fundraiser and she'd been active in softball. She expected to find Sierra and Nora there, doing exactly what she'd done then—selling raffle tickets.

In some ways, the meeting was a bit like church. Greeters positioned themselves outside the Hayden building, which shared the same compound as the ball fields. It was a steel-constructed building with a kitchen in the back and ample open space for a hundred souls. The tournament would cram in double that amount for the meeting. They greeted nearly everyone as *Captain*.

"Welcome, *Captain.*"

"Good to see you tonight, *Captain.*"

"Good luck to you tomorrow, *Captain.*"

"Hey *Captain*, don't forget to buy a raffle ticket."

They'd filled the parking lot with their pickup trucks. Amanda inspected for a rare sedan—a telltale sign of a newbie. It suggested the boat owner perched his vessel on a lift at his private dock, risking the perception of flaunting one's waterfront. The captain would recognize the mistake and return subsequent years in a pickup truck. Amanda's Wrangler wasn't totally foreign. Thanks to its towing hitch, it garnered little notice. She herself would attract minimal attention too since several captains came with their gals and many of the team compositions were family affairs, some intentionally scheduling reunions around the big tournament weekend.

Tom Girrard stood at the entrance to the Hayden building. He managed a local funeral home, and Amanda suspected the Little League secured him again as the tournament's master of ceremonies. For a person who dealt with death during most of his waking hours, he had a wicked sense of humor and would keep the assembly in stitches. He knew nearly everyone and would spare no one a joke at their own expense, especially previous tournament winners.

Although nothing stated any requirement about donating winnings back to the Little League, most of the winners did so. Winning was more about bragging rights. Tom knew all the history, and if a greedy captain returned in a subsequent year, Tom would call out the generous captains in order to shame the greedy. It worked. Amanda had seen it play out time and time again.

They treated the optional $100 entry Calcutta differently, administered outside of the "official" tournament. Typically, the pot would climb well over $5,000. It was where the big boys played.

Amanda waited in her Jeep for several minutes. She didn't really need to go in. She just needed to connect with Ralph and the girls. Let them know she'd arrived. Secure tomorrow's game plan. *This is crazy!* Possibly the riskiest setting of any she'd attempted incognito. *Why do it?* Undoubtedly, her dad would be inside, too.

She spotted his pickup truck. The fifth-wheel style for pulling heavy trailers and the marina's logo emblazoned on the doors. She bit her lip.

This is for those girls! Her heart raced. *Ralph and Maria too.* Some of the sweetest people she'd ever met.

She scanned the parking lot, wondering if they'd come in the minivan. Ralph had no shame and wouldn't think twice about driving to the meeting in it with his granddaughters. It would definitely be the only one. And there it was.

He'd parked close to the entrance. She silently thanked God that Jeb's truck was nowhere in sight. Her heart found its natural rhythm.

Tom acted as the chief greeter, likely working his hit list for the heckling to follow.

Amanda checked herself in the mirror. Some color had drained from her face. She wore her grunge get-up with the large dark glasses, but in place of the enormous sun hat, she wore a sports cap with the Shop's logo, providing enough cover to her hair without looking out of place at a fishing tournament. "Not bad," she said to herself. She carefully tucked a few wisps of hair under the cap.

A large team with kids piled out of a crew-cab pickup truck near to where Amanda was parked. *Perfect!* The family wore specialty T-shirts made up for the occasion with their boat's name on them—*Reel-Em-In*. She stepped out of her Jeep and slipped in right behind them. Straggling along for a few steps, she maneuvered herself into the middle of the pack, in lock-step with one of the mothers. Amanda kept her head down as she approached the door, but Tom was true to form. He addressed her as *Captain*.

Did he see me when I got out of the Jeep? A shiver passed through her, and she was afraid to look up. She mumbled back in her thickest faux Bronx accent, having spent a good hour of her drive that afternoon practicing Marisa Tomei again. Would it fool him? Either way, she wasn't stopping for chitchat. If Tom discovered it was her, he'd call out the *Legend*, the West girl—his nickname for her—the only youth angler to three-peat in the tournament and then go on to win Lady Angler honors her first eligible year at sixteen.

She didn't see Tom's eyes when she neared him, but she felt them. What if he'd seen hers through the glasses? A few more steps and she was past him. Tom worked on his next set of arrivals directly behind her. "Good evening to you, Captain. Sure looks like the weather is shaping up nicely for y'all tomorrow."

"Smooth and flat . . . smooth and flat." The captain sounded giddy. "Just how we like it."

Tom continued to engage the team, and she exhaled a huge breath.

She strode several steps into the large assembly hall and scanned the room. It was a madhouse and already overflowing beyond its capacity.

It didn't take long for her to find her father. He sat at a table near the front, close to the makeshift stage, opposite where she'd entered. Perfect. She took another deep breath. She'd maintain her distance while he schmoozed with other charter boat captains and worked potential customers. She expected him to be engrossed in a protracted fishing tale or griping with a colleague about proposed changes to the fishing regulations.

She located the girls near the entrance, not far from her. As predicted, they were selling raffle tickets. Her chest tightened. *I shouldn't distract them.* Not yet, at least.

Nora raked in the dough. There wasn't a captain in the house that dared turn her down, her sweet pleading voice and endearing eyes wouldn't let them. Amanda silently laughed. The cash bucket brimmed over, and Nora chased down some loose bills—mostly twenties—scattered on the floor.

With her back turned to the far end of the auditorium, Amanda lowered her glasses and let her eyes fall upon the girls. They came running and some more bills spilled from Nora's pail. This time, after Amanda squeezed Nora closely, she helped her pick up the cash.

Ralph was soon at her side and acknowledged Amanda with a fat grin. "I guess you'll be doing some fishing with us tomorrow?"

She restored her glasses; Ralph would understand. She hugged him and took a deep breath, then she whispered in his ear, "My Dad's alright. I'm the problem. Just give me time, Ralph."

The dark sunglasses were a lifesaver. Tears welled in Amanda's eyes. The confession itself surprised her. Something about Ralph pulled it out of her. The man was full of love and understanding. *What if I'd been his daughter*? How different life would've been. *Ralph accepts you as you are. Warts and all.*

He stepped back from her and nodded. "You just do what you need to do . . . in your time. Maria and I will continue to respect your wishes." Then he grabbed her arm. "And we're praying for you."

A lump filled her throat. His eyes were so full of compassion. The thought that Ralph and Maria would pray for her. *How kind.* She struggled to speak. "There's so much I didn't know."

She glanced over her shoulder. The girls were focused on their duties, and Nora would soon return, eager to impress Amanda with her ticket sales.

"No worries. We'll need to depart by six." His eyes sparkled, and excitement filled his voice. "You know where to find the *Galleon*."

Amanda wiped her face under her sunglasses and roamed a bit with the girls, avoiding contact with everyone else. She recognized nearly half the crews in the crowd. *Good people*, she thought, and she longed to greet them, hug them, and talk about how they'd all grown and where their lives had taken them. *In time, in time.*

She bought twenty dollars' worth of raffle tickets from both girls and then meandered by the registration table. A pile of orange-colored flyers caught her attention, and she grabbed one. She retreated to the back corner of the hall and began to read it. Her heart raced, and she had to brace herself against a wall. The floor shifted and her legs nearly went out from under her.

She tried to continue reading the flyer, but her eyes twitched. The sweat from her palms discolored it, and her breathing turned erratic. The adrenaline that pumped through her veins was a mix of fear and anger, and this time, then anger wasn't directed at her father.

Amanda moved quickly across the room and found Ralph. When she reached him to tell him she was leaving, her mouth was so dry she could barely speak.

The meeting was well on its way when Jeb arrived. He finished a late family tour—an afternoon picnic excursion to Cedar Island—one in which they'd encountered dolphin pods in Little Bay.

He found his father and the girls huddling in the back. Their faces were serious when he approached them, and Sierra and Nora acted a bit standoffish.

"What's up?" he whispered. "You seem mad."

Sierra only shook her head. "Nothing's wrong, Dad. We knew you'd be late."

Jeb hugged both his girls, searching for a clue, forcing them to wiggle from his grasp. Tom was in the middle of his rules spiel, and Jeb braced for a barrage of well-placed jokes capitalizing on his own tardiness. If not for the threat Tom posed, he was more intent to focus on his daughters and extract a confession—whatever it was they were hiding.

Less than thirty seconds passed before Tom erupted with a sarcastic laced greeting. "So good to have you join us tonight, Captain Carter." Tom moved his eyes to the rest of the assembly. "Hey folks, you know what the trouble is with being punctual?"

Jeb, thinking it would be better to play some offense, yelled back, "Nobody will be around to appreciate it!"

It was a mistake. Tom tilted his head, letting his eyes dance around the room as a sinister smile grew on his face. The longer Tom continued to stare at the crowd, the laughter grew. Everyone knew what was coming.

Jeb wanted to kick himself for starting the fight. He felt the hundreds-plus pairs of eyes landing on him. Now he'd be forced to answer questions regarding rules that Tom had previously explained.

Tom straightened himself, and everyone in the assembly hall quieted below a whisper. "Jeb Carter, Northern Neck's most popular *eco-tour guide*, can you please explain the prize we will award to the top *female* angler?"

Jeb didn't miss the slight—the way Tom enunciated "eco-tour guide." Most everyone else in the room would pick up on the subtle jab too.

Jeb crossed his arms and put some snap into his voice, "Yep, this area's top *skinny-water fishing guide*." He extended his arms wide and eyed the anglers. "Big fish . . ." He placed one palm close above the other. "Small water." They'd know he wasn't exaggerating. During the summer, his paddleboard and kayak anglers out-fished the big boats nearly every day of the week.

A generous supply of heckles and catcalls dwarfed the room. Jeb notched another point in Tom's favor. *Why am I falling into his trap?*

Tom pivoted his body back and forth like a robot letting his eyes pan the house. "And your answer to the question, Mr. Carter, for the benefit of all who arrived on time?"

Jeb had enough. He searched for his girls. Nora had made herself small and was hiding behind his dad, who was now pinching the bridge of his nose. Sierra turned her back to him and whispered to a friend from her softball team. *My own family keeping their distance as if I'm a pariah.* He chuckled to himself.

Jeb faced Tom and said with exasperation, "First place in the Ladies Division and two hundred dollars . . . just like it's been every year."

"*Bzzzzzz*," Tom blurted over the microphone. The group burst into robust laughter, but they were becoming restless.

"Jeb, let me explain this *again.* This is a last-minute rule change this year. We will crown the top *female* angler Queen of the Bay and award her the Lady Mary Boleyn Tiara." Tom took an exaggerated breath. "Now, Jeb, I'll give you a second shot at this, but worded differently." His eyes scanned the rear of the hall and found their target. "If your beautiful daughter, Sierra, catches the top fish, what will she be awarded?"

Jeb glanced over his shoulder. Sierra's cheeks had reddened.

Tom's out to trick me. She's not eligible for the Lady's Division . . . only the Youth Division.

Jeb placed his hands on his hips and faced Tom. "Assuming we don't submit her fish into the Grand Prize Division, she'll win the Youth Division trophy and the two hundred dollar prize." His voice was overly confident and no sooner than his words left him, he cringed.

"*Bzzzz* . . . Jeb, I'm only signaling half a buzzer on that one."

Jeb exhaled a sigh of relief, but now he was curious and not at all embarrassed.

Tom eyed his crowd. "Is Jeb right?"

Half of the anglers seemed to agree with him, the rest were shaking their heads.

Tom continued, "Okay, I'm glad we're going through this again because many of you still don't get it." He pounced his palm on the small podium as if ready to preach a fire and brimstone message. "Jeb's right. Sierra may only enter her fish in the Youth Division—the Grand Prize Division—but not both! And not in the Ladies Division, since she's fifteen years or younger."

Jeb glanced at Sierra. The flush in her face was gone, and now Tom had even her attention.

"We're treating the Queen of the Bay like a Calcutta."

Jeb was careful to avoid confidence in his voice, "De facto entry and no additional fee?"

"Correct!" Tom raised his fists in triumph. "Great point, Jeb. We treat it like a Calcutta, but it's not the cash Calcutta. Now, Jeb, I assume the *Galleon* has entered the cash Calcutta?"

Ralph yelled, "Absolutely, we're not cheapskates like Clay Hollander."

All eyes in the auditorium found Clay, a local marina owner, who'd failed to enter the Calcutta and forfeited the large purse. The group roared in laughter, most knowing the story. Hollander's seven-year-old daughter had caught the tournament's largest mackerel, but could only claim a Youth Division win. Not only that, the fish bested any in the tournament's history, just shy of the State record. It would have earned a $25,000 bonus. Clay had punished himself over the years. Jeb sighed relief. The attention was now off of him. *Thanks, Dad!*

Clay's boyish face showed his embarrassment and Jeb flattened his mouth, not desiring to pile on the poor fella.

Tom squeezed his nose, a good sign he wouldn't harass him either since Clay's marina hosted the weigh-in.

Tom's focus came back to Jeb's side of the room. "Thanks, Ralph. So, assuming Team Galleon enters Sierra's fish in the Youth Division, she'd win that prize, the $6,700 dollar cash Calcutta, and be crowned Queen of the Bay. The tiara is awarded to *any female* who submits her fish in either the Lady, Special Angler, or Youth Divisions! Does everyone understand this now?"

Tom inspected the faces—good enough. He needed to dismiss the meeting and get the antsy teams out the door; chores remained those who needed to dress up their rigs for the morning.

As the crowd dispersed, Jeb met with Charley and his father. They looked over their shoulders. No one paid any attention to them as they remained huddled, hammering out details for Saturday and a joint strategy for the tournament.

The girls mingled with their other friends who'd been selling T-shirts and raffle tickets for the Little League. It had been a good night. Most of the shirts were gone. Saturday's weather forecast was promising, resulting in many late entrants, mostly smaller boats . . . and one very unusual entry.

The Mate

Saturday morning, Jeb sprung from his bed like a jack-in-the-box. His 5:00 AM alarm had yet to go off, and the house was eerily silent. Normally, he'd hear the Bay lapping small waves against the riprap, the crickets in the tall grass, or the screaming green tree frogs which fastened themselves on the windows. This dawn, not a sound.

He rarely had problems falling asleep. But last night the demeanor of his girls, his father, and even his mother had bothered him. They seemed to keep some distance from him. Charley had continued to egg him on too. Maybe that was it? Jeb didn't consider himself to be hypercompetitive. A knot formed in his stomach. *Was my behavior so bad that the girls felt ashamed of me?* He knew better than to let Tom get under his skin. *I was just playing along.*

He didn't appreciate becoming the center of attention—definitely not his style. And the captains' meeting felt strangely different. He couldn't put his finger on it; something was looming. He could see it in the faces of the other captains, all strangely jittery. It reminded him of the way large dark schools of silversides looked before dashing en masse under his paddleboard. The women at the meeting acted the most unusual, whispering, sometimes craning their necks, as if on the lookout for a country mega-star.

Jeb showered and dressed quickly. His focus was clear, but his insides were a jumble of nerves. He'd never taken the tournament so seriously. It had always been about the time with his father, his girls, and occasionally other siblings and friends. All for a good cause. Today was no different, and Jeb tried to convince himself that with the Special Anglers joining them, it would be even better. But something else was at work that he couldn't deny. The atmosphere of the morning itself held that same palpable feeling of electricity.

The coo of a dove sounded, the first note to play in the new day. It wasn't long before other creatures joined the orchestra. Jeb likened it to the feeling in a theater just after the lights went out and the movie's big score reverberated ever so softly.

Jeb tapped on the door of the girls' bedroom. Sweet snores answered. He set a portable speaker in the hall and left it to play the opening music of Jurassic Park. It seemed to fit the strange morning's mood.

A water-valve screeched, coming from the direction of his parent's master bathroom. A good sign. His father would be out soon to join him, and his mother would rise to rally the girls.

Jeb headed to the *Galleon* to assemble a few more mackerel rigs, grateful for an excuse to expend his nervous energy.

Evidence of an orange orb danced near the horizon, teasing a warm glow. Boat engines roared faintly in the distance, marking the early risers. Tournament teams making speedy escapes from the creeks towards big water. A shot of adrenaline splashed through Jeb's chest. Those vessels were likely running to the Eastern Shore side of the Bay. Saltier water over there, a magnet for mackerel.

Jeb lowered the *Galleon* into the creek. He was stowing his bags when his father arrived at the end of the dock. Jeb looked up at him. "Is she fueled up?"

"Good morning to you, too." His father's tone sounded like Jeb had insulted him.

"Sorry . . . yes . . . good morning, Dad."

"Of course the boat's filled up." His dad tossed up his hands and dropped them. "It's tournament day after all . . . game on!"

Jeb wrote it off. His dad would understand, and if his old man failed to see the nervousness bleeding out of him, Jeb would've declared him legally blind. Jeb glanced at his watch. "Where are the girls?"

His father responded without a hint of urgency, "Maria is getting them all set. They were sitting down to breakfast when I walked out."

Jeb's skin crawled. Typically for a tourney, Jeb knew him to be jumpy and barking out orders. *He's being too casual.*

If his father wouldn't be edgy, then he would. Jeb readied himself to spring from the boat and chase the girls out of the house.

Moments later, Nora popped out the side door running with her bag in hand, her hair tossing back and forth.

Jeb blew out heavily. "Finally."

She arrived in front of the *Galleon* out of breath and tapped her grandfather's hand. "Grans says to tell you the water pump died." It wasn't uncommon to have the water pump falter to nothing more than an overloaded circuit-breaker.

Jeb shook his head, and then his stomach churned on seeing his father nonplussed by the news.

His dad's cell phone rang. It was his mother with the same bad news, and his dad hustled back to the house.

Crunching tires sounded from the driveway, but Jeb stayed focused on the job at hand—powering up the vessel and all its high-end electronics. *We're not expecting anyone? Right?*

All the fishing gear needed to be stowed and perfectly positioned for quick access. Jeb was leaving nothing to chance. If a line tangled, clippers needed to be at the ready. Jeb understood the necessity for keeping the lines clean of tangles while pulling them behind the boat during a fish frenzy. If you were sloppy, tangled your lines, and failed to replace the knotted rig with a fresh one, you wouldn't catch fish. Game over! No one would accuse him of being a sloppy angler today.

His father returned with his shoulders slumped. "Son, you're going to have to go on without me. I've gotta take care of this water situation for Maria. It doesn't appear as simple as the breaker." He shook his head and delivered an exaggerated huff. "I may even need to call a plumber."

Jeb felt like a balloon ready to burst. "How's that gonna work?" His voice exploded, and he threw up his hands. "Drive and mate at the same time?"

Ralph stood still, and his arms were straight down his sides. "I've found you a mate." His father acted nervous and confident at the same time.

Jeb rolled his eyes. "Who? Can he meet us at the marina by 6:30?"

"No." Ralph's tone was matter of fact. "*She*'s here and ready to go."

Jeb glanced towards the Bay House. Sierra was coming, and . . . *wait . . . is that the whack? Couldn't be . . . Where's the goofy hat?* They had bags in hand. Amanda's breathable white shirt covered a brightly colored halter top. Combined with her cargo-style shorts, she looked like she was modeling fishing apparel. *What a joke!*

"Dad . . . no! You can't be serious!"

His father stepped closer to the craft and lowered his voice. "Jeb, you need to make the best of it. The conditions look good."

The knot in Jeb's gut gnawed even more. He glanced again towards the Bay House. The shorts Amanda wore looked like a brand he sold at the Shop, and she looked better in them than the models.

His dad wasn't finished. "You're taking the tournament too seriously. This should be about the Special Anglers."

The last thing he needed right now was a lecture. "Charley's taking it seriously, and he's still angry that I bailed on him to start my business. He's in it to kick my butt, and he already said so in as many words. He's been texting me all week!"

His dad shook his head. "I wouldn't worry about it. Make it a fun boat ride. Charley's softened up—seems like Charlotte filled the gap." His father gave him an expression he couldn't interpret. "Look, if I can get the water fixed, you can swing back around and pick me up. But if you get on fish, don't detour!" His voice became stern. "Promise me you won't leave feeding fish on my account."

This made no sense. Why would his father so quickly surrender his most cherished day? "Dad, just call the plumber and let him take care of it!"

"I'm not going to abandon your mother!"

"Come on, Dad. She can handle the plumber." Jeb regretted his response because his dad's expression told him he'd crossed a sacred line, disrespect towards his mother. Embarrassed, he turned from his father and found some gear needing to be stowed.

His head was still down in the cockpit when he heard Sierra's voice from some distance away. "Daddy, Daddy, look who's come!"

He glanced up. Sierra and Amanda, linked at their elbows, were approaching the foot of the dock.

Jeb turned to his father and grimaced. He spoke quietly, "Yeah, Dad, look who's come . . . seriously, you can't do this to me."

"I heard that!" It was Amanda's voice.

He raised his head. The woman had just stepped onto the dock—fifty yards away. *Wow! She has good hearing.*

Jeb wondered if the wind had carried his voice, but there was none and the water was dead calm. Perfect fishing conditions, sultry with a slight overcast.

"Son, this will be a lot harder on me than you." Jeb's father adopted a forlorn look—one Jeb now suspected he'd staged. "I've been looking forward to this much longer than you have."

His father's suggestion that this woman would help mate was outrageous. The Special Anglers were going to create enough work for two of them—he and his dad. Heat ran up his face to his ears. The *Galleon* wasn't like Charley's boat—a specially designed wide-berth vessel that could comfortably accommodate large parties of anglers. On the smaller *Galleon*, Jeb was prepared to man the lines while his father expertly drove the boat, chasing mackerel schools. Now he faced the challenge of doing it all himself, and along with his girls, entertaining the Special Angler families. Though a friend of his girls, Amanda was dead weight and would take up valuable space. *One more person I'll need to entertain. Worse, she'll be in the way.*

Nora handed him her bags along with his portable speaker, turned, and took off running towards Amanda. Jeb eyed the speaker and the song list still showing in the queue from the Jurassic Park album. He selected "The Raptor Attack" and kept the volume low. His breathing relaxed.

Jeb covered his face, exasperated, and peered out between his fingers as the woman walked up the dock with Sierra. Her stride was as he remembered it from their first encounter. Confident and pushy. *Where's the limp?*

Jeb turned to stow Nora's bags. The woman's steps grew louder, and then two simultaneous thuds rattled the decking. He jolted, nearly hitting his head against the roof overhang. He turned around, and the woman's bags were practically at eye level with him. That and her toned, athletic legs.

He eyed her belongings. One was a gym bag, and the other appeared to be her lunch satchel. He was afraid to look up, but he finally craned his neck and faced her. Her eyes glared down at him as if expecting him to offer a hand, assist her into the boat. He remembered her eyes, too. *Careful.* He worried he'd get lost in them.

Jeb folded his arms in front of his chest. *If she's a proper mate, she won't need my help to board the boat. But who am I fooling? She's no mate.* He gave her a lopsided grin.

She returned it along with a sarcastic tone. "Nice music."

Jeb lost his balance and took a step back. *A small wake must have rocked the boat.* Though the water was flat.

Her eyes showed vulnerability. *This would be a lot easier if she'd hide them behind her sunglasses.*

She wore a sports cap with his Shop's logo embroidered on it, and he wondered when she'd bought it. Now he wanted to hide.

Amanda clamored over the gunwale, and his father quickly stepped forward to assist her. Jeb caught a look from him and real shame hit the core of his bones.

Sierra glared at him from the dock. "Daddy, you're not being nice. You haven't greeted Amanda."

He extended his hand to Sierra, but she refused it and climbed on board, her chin raised higher.

He squared up facing Amanda and offered a firm handshake. "Welcome aboard, *Mate*!"

He regretted it.

Her steady and serious gaze, vulnerable and so near his face, nearly knocked him off his feet again. He caught her scent. Tropical. This was the beauty he'd pulled from the water a week ago—the one who'd sat so close to him at dinner that he'd been fearful of her touch. Not the woman from the Tangier Island tour. And not the bossy woman who'd barged into his shop.

She eyed one of his trolling rods already in its holder and fingered the line. She moved around the boat and touched other rods as well, along with Jeb's rigs. She brushed her hand past the net and then lifted the lid to the large fishing cooler. *Probably looking for soft drinks.* She said nothing, only a slight nose wrinkle. He wanted to say, "Not happy with my ice selection?" but kept his lips sealed. Hanging under the gunwale, she grasped the de-hooker. Not a chance she'd know the purpose of the tool. Finally, she faced him again.

"You keep a tidy ship, Mr. Carter."

"Argh," he said under his breath. *She has no idea!* For good measure, he said, "That'll be *Captain* to you, *Mate*."

She flung her hair and turned from him in a huff.

Jeb shrugged and eyed his dad, hoping for some sympathy. Understanding from his girls? Forget about it!

I'll tolerate her today for nothing but the distraction of her stunning looks . . . absolutely nothing under the hood with this crazy woman!

Bag of Tricks

As the *Galleon* got underway, Amanda's appearance changed. She donned a loose-fitting checkered-blue blouse that she tied at the front, a pair of large goofy glasses, and an oversized sun hat. She stuffed the sports cap with the Shop's logo back into her bag. *What a relief!* Her wearing it played with his emotions. If her intent had been to warm him up, it had that effect on him like steroids.

Jeb suspected she wasn't into high finance after all, but a glitzy model from New York needing to conceal her identity from paparazzi. Probably a relationship gone bad. *Explains the pain in her eyes.*

He chuckled under his breath as Amanda struggled in vain to keep the pretentious hat on her head. It didn't settle quite right until the *Galleon* came off plane and they headed into the narrow channel leading to Charley's marina. She dug into her bag, pulled out something concealed in a plastic grocery sack, and handed it to Sierra. Retrieving another item from her bag, Amanda inserted something in her shoe. She tried to be discreet, but Jeb was having a hard time keeping his eyes off her. She'd transformed back into the Whack.

"What's in the bags, *Mate*?"

"Mind your business, *Captain*," she snapped, punching his arm lightly. "I need to run into the restroom when we arrive."

A shiver ran up his spine and he rubbed the place where she'd hit him. He widened his eyes in a playful expression to exaggerate his injury.

She eyed him curiously.

Only half serious, he said, "Well, as my mate, you need to help me tie down the boat before you take off."

He didn't expect her to do it, but when they reached the dock, she expertly employed hitch-knots on the cleats. Jeb raised an eyebrow.

She glanced back at him and then hurried off. For a moment, he actually thought she'd stuck her tongue out at him.

"You know, we have a head on the boat," he yelled as she raced to the marina's bathhouse.

She gestured with a dismissive wave without turning around.

He shook his head. The door had a combination lock, and the marina only provided the combo to those who leased slips there. He readied himself to provide it to her.

She tapped on the number pad and entered immediately. "Hmph," he grunted. *What do you know?*

Sierra ran off, right behind Amanda, but headed to the *Queen Mary*. Amidst the chaos of Charley, Charlotte, and the first mate assisting their guests on board, no one noticed Sierra accessing the large fish cooler on the stern, which Jeb knew was already filled with ice.

Charlotte approached with two young women at her side. "Jeb, I'd like to introduce you to Sarah and Tasha."

"Howdy, ladies." Jeb saw their faces brighten as they eyed the boat. "Welcome aboard the *Galleon*."

Nora was at his side and shy handshakes were exchanged.

Sierra raced back to greet Sarah and Tasha. The older girls, whom Jeb assessed to be his Special Anglers, continued to gape at the boat. Sarah was loud and gregarious; Tasha, quiet, but smiling. All of it gave Jeb a good feeling about the day. These two young women were troopers. Now, he only wished his *mate* would fall in line.

Two men trailed the ladies with bags in hand. Charlotte introduced the fathers, Chuck and Rob.

"Glad to have you joining us. I'm Jeb. These are my daughters,

Sierra and Nora." Jeb waited for the girls to exchange handshakes before continuing. "We have another member of the crew serving as my mate," he said, providing the men knowing glances. "Gentlemen, I'll need a lot of help today. You'll understand this better when *she* returns."

Jeb felt a slap to his arm. Sierra stepped forward and faced Chuck and Rob. "Amanda's my friend and she's very nice . . . she just doesn't get along with my dad."

"Teenage volunteer?" Rob asked. "Nothing wrong with that."

"Nope, that's not it," Jeb said, sporting a fake smile.

"Well, I hope she can fish?" Chuck scratched his forehead.

Jeb shook his head. "I doubt she's ever touched a fishing pole her entire life." He paused for effect. "We'll be leaving the rigs to the menfolk."

His daughters quickly bonded with Sarah and Tasha. Sierra provided a tour of the *Galleon's* features with particular mention of the head. Their faces were aglow, providing plenty of *oohs* and *ahhs*, especially towards the *Galleon's* impressive sonar and the radar console.

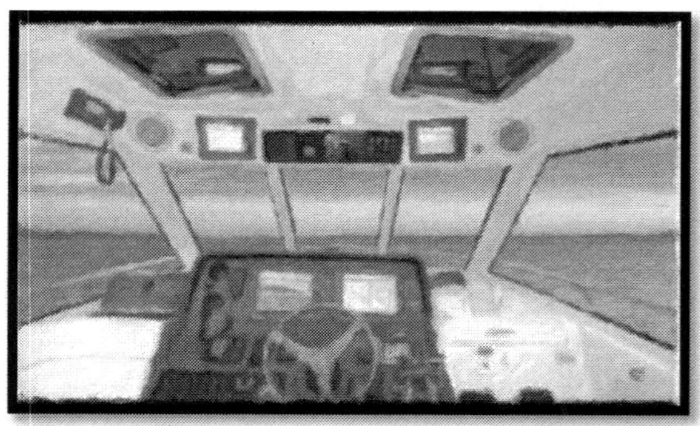

Jeb observed the *Queen Mary* and her crew, settled and ready to depart. He offered to take their team picture from the dock, if only to delay them. They had three Special Angler families on board. Charley promised that he'd stay in communication with the *Galleon* and that they'd stay within view of each other while on the water. Charley played it up as "us against the fleet," but Jeb wasn't buying it. He'd mated for Captain Charley enough to understand his competitive streak. He might appear all flowery on the outside, but in reality, he'd be plotting.

Jeb threw up his hands. "Sierra, would you mind fetching the mate? We need to get going."

Charley yelled, "We're leaving, Jeb. My crew's ready to go. I'll hit you up on the radio." He rolled his eyes. "Your mate's not my concern. Who'd you get, by the way?"

Jeb set his coffee mug down and snapped a crew shot of the happy anglers using his smartphone. "I don't really have a mate. We're waiting on the Whack. Didn't you see her when we pulled in?"

"No. Did she drive in?"

"No, she came with us on the *Galleon*."

"Roger that. Not my problem! We'll see you out there." Charley turned and entered the boat's cabin. A few moments later, he stuck his head out of the helm's window. "Gotta get 'em early. That's when the bite will be. Mark my words."

Jeb turned, looking for Amanda, then heard the Caterpillar engines throttle. Charley raced the large *Queen Mary* out of the marina like a bat out of hell, and the wake it created tousled the *Galleon*.

Only the *Queen Mary's* stern was in view when Amanda reappeared, not even a little winded. She stood before him with her hands on her hips.

"What are you doing, Mate!" Jeb vented his anger. "They've taken off and we're sitting here waiting for you. If you're going to be the mate, start acting like one!"

She covered her face, turned from him, and stomped to the *Galleon*. The eyes of the entire crew were on them.

Chuck pulled Jeb aside and whispered, "Girlfriend?"

Jeb lost his mouth of coffee. Recovering, he spoke softly into Chuck's ear, "Definitely not my type." When he boarded the *Galleon,* Amanda's countenance had completely flattened. A double anchor settled in his stomach. He was grateful he'd skipped breakfast, otherwise he would have puked it. Even his coffee didn't feel right.

Once underway, he glanced back toward the stern. Amanda sulked while sitting on a bench seat. When he caught her eyes, she glared daggers at him. It was so painful that he preferred she throw them.

Sierra was doing a good job helping situate Sarah and Tasha when the boat rose on plane and began to skip across the water. Jeb eyed the speedometer—over 50 mph.

Jeb poked his head outside the pilothouse. Tasha and Sarah's eyes were enormous. Chuck held his daughter tight. "You two okay?"

"Yes!" Sarah screamed with delight.

"I'm not sure they've ever gone this fast on the water," Rob said.

Jeb kept a steady hand on the helm. "Good. Do we need to slow down?"

"No!" cried Sarah.

"Tasha . . . you okay?"

She pumped her fist. "Go fast, Captain Carter!" Her smile grew larger.

Jeb beckoned Amanda to join him in the pilothouse. She threw her head back and nearly lost her hat. She eventually joined him in the isolation of the small enclosure but huffed her resentment.

He was afraid to face her—her glasses were off.

With a sincerity that pulled the anchors in his stomach, he said, "I'm sorry, Mate. You didn't deserve what I did back at the marina."

Amanda pursed her lips—*better on her than Julia Roberts.*

She seemed to pause until he regained his composure. "And exactly what is it you did at the marina?"

He picked up on what she was doing, trying to further bait him, anger him again—lure him away from a sincere apology. He stuck to his guns. "I've let the competition get the better of me, and took it out on you in public. That was uncalled for. I was wrong."

Amanda hugged herself and turned her back to him.

It made it easier that he didn't need to face her. "I get it you're mad. I started this off on a bad note. But the girls were really looking forward to this . . ." Jeb hesitated, then plunged ahead, ". . . and it appears now they were looking forward to you being here." It was the hardest of all the admissions. He'd been duped.

The next set of words came easily to him, "Will you forgive me?"

She didn't budge.

"Hang on everyone!" He cut back on the throttle and the Whaler fell off plane, screeching to a halt—if ever a boat could do such a thing. It produced a large bow wake. He stepped to the rear of the pilothouse and stood in the doorway looking out towards the stern.

"Crew," he started. He already had everyone's attention but for Amanda—still sulking. He waited another moment until everyone reclaimed their seats and braced for the wave. "I owe you all an apology for my behavior . . . the way I've treated my mate. I've been a jerk. I'm sorry."

They were wide-eyed and facing him.

The wave hit and shook the boat. He turned to his daughters. "Girls, I've been taking this all too seriously. Will you forgive me?"

Nora jumped up from her seat and grabbed his waist. "Yes, Daddy."

Sierra remained frozen. Her eyes drifted to Amanda and returned to her father. Sierra nodded ever so slightly.

Jeb took a half breath. Pressure squeezed around his chest. *She wants proof.*

Rob spoke up. "Hey . . . don't feel bad on our account. You have our permission to take this seriously. Our girls have done plenty of fishing. This tournament is a whole different animal."

Jeb was grateful for the man's efforts, a nice deflection from the conflict. "Thanks, Rob. I'll consider it, but I need to tone it down."

Chuck shrugged.

Sarah cried out, "We want to win!"

"Yeah!" Tasha joined in.

Sierra squeezed his hand. When he glanced back towards the pilothouse, where Amanda remained, open-mouthed, she quickly looked away.

He returned to the helm. "Alright then . . . Hold on everyone!"

He glanced back, satisfied the crew was secure, and pressed down on the throttle. The force of the acceleration pushed him against the pilot's stool. Screams of excitement came from the crew at the stern. Even Jeb couldn't suppress a few goosebumps.

Amanda's back remained turned to him. He leaned close to her and whispered, "How'd you know the combo to the bathhouse?"

She whipped around and faced him. Her tone was flat. "Where are we going?"

Jeb tilted his head. "I need to chase down the *Queen Mary*. I have no idea where they've gone."

Her arm flung across his chest and she pointed to a spot on the electronic GPS chart, "They'll be here."

He jolted. "Why?"

"Trust me." Her face was serious. "Captain West will want to run the southern edge of that channel on an incoming tide."

"What?" Jeb widened his eyes. "My mate speaks fishing language?"

Her eyes barely softened. "Don't ask," she said sternly.

Jeb didn't and figured he might as well placate her and get it over with. *After this, she'll no longer be a bother.* He turned the *Galleon* to the south. He glanced at her. "I liked that cap you were wearing earlier."

"Me too," she said softly—even a bit of sweetness in her tone.

He caught her slight smile as he fell back into the raised helm seat. He felt ten pounds lighter.

She dispensed with the sun hat, goofy glasses, and the loose shirt. She combed her hand through her hair and re-donned the Shop's sportfishing cap. He could barely breathe as he snuck glances of her, the beauty at his left, the rising sun bouncing off her face.

Sierra entered the cabin and pulled out the binoculars. Within a few minutes, they acquired a visual on the *Queen Mary*. Jeb didn't acknowledge Amanda's tip. *It's going to empower her.*

"Humph." Amanda left him for the stern to engage with the Special Anglers and their fathers.

Jeb noticed the natural way she connected with lady anglers and how quickly they accepted her.

He couldn't *help* but notice.

Nutcase

Jeb worried. Amongst her other intrinsic traits, the woman kept demanding his respect—requiring standards of behavior that were ingrained in his own psyche. Lessons his father taught him. In word and deed—how his dad treated Jeb's mother. He'd failed miserably and was drained. Drained from wasting his energy trying to dislike the woman to the point of treating her unkindly.

Why do it? Why keep lying to myself? Simple. The flip side of the equation was a slippery slope.

"Mate!" he yelled.

"Yes, *Captain*?" was Amanda's sharp response, tinged with sarcasm.

"I'll need you up here to help drive the boat. Sierra can assist you with the controls. I'm going to start rigging up."

"Yes sir, *Captain*!" Jeb noticed her wink at Rob and Chuck.

"Hey, Mate, where's Jimmy Stewart this weekend?"

"Who do you mean?"

"Your significant other."

"Oh him! The tall sexy guy." She'd bumped his shoulder as they passed and their eyes met. She moved on and took her position at the helm. "He's a real mover and shaker, Captain . . . but nope, not here this round."

"Working some big deals, is he?" Jeb pulled the first rod from its holder and deployed its rig into the water.

"Yes! Working a deal with my best friend Sally. I believe I owe you thanks for that."

Jeb's tongue tied. He busied himself setting a planer running behind the boat.

"Is he your agent?" He wanted to ask about her modeling agency directly, but feared if he was wrong, she'd take it as a compliment.

"My agent?" Amanda chuckled. "We don't have agents in my line of work . . . just officers."

Jeb wrinkled his brow. "Oh." *Maybe she's in high finance after all.*

The boat slowed.

"Sierra, see that our mate holds our speed at six knots!"

"Got it, Captain," Amanda growled back. "I know how to read a speedometer." Her tone then lightened. "I'd suggest we start below five knots. If the blues begin mangling the lines, I'll speed up."

Jeb's jaw dropped and he avoided looking at her, instead peering over the water.

"Are you okay with that, Captain?" she teased.

Jeb looked at her, his mouth still half open. "Yes, Mate."

Rob whispered something to Chuck.

Jeb brushed by them and spoke softly, "Secrets, gentleman?"

Rob opened up his palms. "What's up between you two?"

"Nothing!" Jeb barked.

"But is she right, Captain?" Chuck asked.

Amanda yelled without diverting her attention from the sonar, "Let the fish be my answer!"

Jeb doubted she understood a single pixel on its screen. He waved his hand in her direction and spoke barely above a whisper, "I suspect she's being coached by Sierra."

Amanda didn't flinch. "Am not . . . Captaahn!"

"How is it you have such great hearing?" Jeb yelled with genuine curiosity.

She pointed into her ears. "I've never worn earbuds." She glanced over her shoulder and gave Jeb a lopsided smile. He flustered and nearly tripped.

He placed his hands on the gunwale and pulled in a few deep breaths. "Nora, are you keeping an eye on the *Queen Mary*?"

Amanda continued to needle him with a persnickety smile. He tried to ignore her and yelled, "I want to know when they start catching."

"Yes, Daddy. Sarah and Tasha are helping me." Nora's tone was doubly sweet.

Jeb poked his head through the doorway of the pilothouse. Amanda and Sierra's attention was fixed on the *Queen Mary* as if expecting a train wreck.

Amanda pointed out the fish marks on the sonar. "We should be on some bigger pods shortly!" she glanced over her shoulder. "What color are your spoons, Captain?"

"Silver. Some with chartreuse and hot pink flashes. Why?" *Does she really know what she's doing?*

"Captain, you need to switch them out with gold-colored spoons," Amanda spoke with too much confidence. "Use the silvers for bright light situations."

"You're crazy!" Jeb yelled at her.

He turned to Chuck and Rob and whispered, "Cuckoo."

"Humor me!" she cried.

"Captain, why don't you just switch out a couple?" Rob suggested. Chuck shrugged in agreement.

It wasn't total mutiny, but close. *Time I take a different tack with the woman.* Regain control.

Jeb exaggerated his movements like a marionette while he pulled in lines. At first Sarah and Tasha looked at him oddly, like they couldn't make out heads-or-tails of who their captain had become. He gasped, shook, and gave them his shock-face, the one that said, "You don't believe?"

They howled in laughter.

He locked eyes with Amanda. She gave him a dirty look.

Jeb froze. His marionette face said she'd hurt his feelings.

Nora spoke in a nervous jitter to no one in particular, "Daddy's being funny."

He replaced the silver spoons with the gold-colored ones, and Jeb returned them to their mounts. On each rod, he released the lines and set the planers. Within seconds of setting the last one, the tips of both poles yanked down. Jeb jolted and peeked over his shoulder.

Amanda missed it. *Thank God!*

Jeb turned around. "Fish on, fish on!"

When Amanda shot a look back, Jeb tightened his face.

Sarah cried, "I got it!" She rushed forward, and Jeb handed her the first pole.

Jeb raced to the other side of the boat. "Tasha, you take this one!"

Amanda's hair flew as she rotated at the helm. "What rigs, Captain?"

Jeb wouldn't look at her and kept his voice subdued. "Doesn't matter, Mate, just keep driving the boat." He waved at her over his shoulder. "You're doing a fine job right where you are."

Jeb bounced back to Sarah's side, reached over the stern, grabbed Sarah's leader line, and in one smooth motion, pulled her fish straight from the water and into the cooler. "We've got everything well under control back here."

Tasha and Jeb made quick work on hers, too. Rob and Chuck exchanged looks of disbelief—Jeb more worried about his diminishing fishing reputation. The same two rigs with the gold-colored spoons were reset and returned to troll behind the *Galleon*. When the tips of the poles bent down again, Jeb signaled for quiet. They landed two more macks and threw them in the cooler, but all the females on the back deck screamed even louder than before.

Amanda glanced back at him, raising her sunglasses and lowering her chin.

He ignored her and hastened to re-deploy the rigs.

"They've got one!" Nora yelled as she pointed towards the *Queen Mary*.

They were close enough to the *Queen Mary* to hear the cheers from their crew. The anglers were scrambling about on their back deck. Charley's voice blared over the radio, "Skunk off the boat. How about you, *Galleon*?"

Nearly ten seconds passed before Jeb yelled towards the front, "Mate, you need to answer the radio! We're busy back here. You know what a *skunk* means, right?"

Amanda froze with her hand in the air, nearly grabbing the microphone.

Jeb tossed another fish in the cooler.

Sierra grabbed the microphone. "Four in the cooler, *Queen Mary*. The skunk's been long gone from the *Galleon*."

Jeb stepped into the door of the cabin.

Captain Charley's voice broadcasted over the radio, and his tone was serious. "Careful on your comms, *Galleon*. Lots of ears listening out here today."

Amanda grabbed Sierra's hand. "Most of the teams will recognize the *Queen Mary* from a distance, and possibly even the *Galleon*. We need to be careful not to let the other boats know we're catching."

Sierra nodded and returned a bright knowing smile, then activated the microphone, "Roger that, Captain, dolphins everywhere."

"Nice," acknowledged Charley.

Jeb stood alongside Sierra and Amanda. "Smart," he said. "Charley will appreciate the disinformation." Sierra stood taller.

Something wasn't right on the *Queen Mary*. Jeb grabbed the binoculars. George, the first mate, had tossed their first fish into the oversized cooler. Now, he screamed as he looked down into it. Mayhem ensued.

"Captain!" he yelled from the stern, raising a banana. "What's this?" Every pair of eyes on their boat fixed upon it.

Without asking for them, Amanda yanked the binoculars from Jeb. She took a look and passed them off to Sierra.

"Captain West is charging to the rear of the boat," Sierra said. Her voice became nervous. "He's screaming, too."

"Jumping up and down?" Jeb asked.

Amanda spoke with unusual disdain in her voice. "He's having a temper tantrum."

"He's dangling something in front of their faces." Sierra burst out laughing and then covered her mouth. "He's confronting every single member of the crew . . . even Charlotte!"

Amanda smiled.

Jeb didn't need the binoculars. He'd sped up a notch and brought the *Galleon* in a little closer. "He's inspecting for guilty consciences."

Charley waved the disdained object of fishing lore in each face. He wasn't satisfied—there were no giveaways.

Jeb glanced behind him. Two lines twitched. He returned to the back deck and put the poles into the hands of the Special Anglers.

"Jeb Carter, Jeb Carter, I know what you've done!" Captain

Charley's screams barked over the radio, sounding convincingly angry.

Amanda and Sierra were frozen, staring at one another.

"Hey," Jeb yelled with a rod in his hand, "is anyone going to answer the *Queen Mary*?" He was dealing with repeated hookups on the gold-colored spoons. Jeb flashed a look of disgust and made his way to the front.

Amanda cringed and seemed more than happy to relinquish her seat at the helm. She still managed to nudge Jeb as she passed him and vacated to the back deck. *She's guilty,* Jeb thought, . . . *but darn cute.*

Jeb grabbed the radio and engaged the mic. "Charley, what are you talking about? I'm busy fishing over here. "

"Who put the contraband on my boat?" Charley shot back.

Jeb glanced back towards the stern where he found Amanda. She'd plopped down in a corner covering most of her head. He glared until she acknowledged him, masking her guilt with a funny face.

He snapped his attention to the *Queen Mary,* now at their port side. Charley's entire crew, a dozen in all, faced the *Galleon;* Charley dramatically tossed the banana towards it.

Jeb radioed back, "I know nothing, Charley . . . I had nothing to do with it."

Jeb scanned his crew, most with bewildered faces. Rob seemed to understand.

Amanda stood, dusted herself off, and faced Tasha and Sarah. "It's a superstition that goes back to the 1700s. Many cargo ships were lost at sea with bananas in their holds."

His mate returned to work tending the rigs, but when Jeb caught Amanda's attention a few moments later, he raised an eyebrow. She doused him again with her silly face. Jeb just shook his head, trying to bury his own smile.

Sierra was standing next to him, and it was obvious she could barely contain herself.

"Was it you?" he asked. "Who put you up to this?"

Amanda was laboring to hide a mischievous grin. Jeb felt the last of his defenses melt away. But then she started digging through one of her bags.

"What are you doing, *Mate*?"

"I'm switching out your planers. They should be painted black. When the sun starts to shine, these silver ones are going to scare away the mackerel and attract the blues. The lines will be butchered in no time with *yours*."

"Oh," he responded, dumbfounded. He offered no resistance while his *mate* switched out the planers. Chuck and Rob were getting the hang of landing the fish and were keeping the girls busy. As the Special Anglers caught fish, Jeb dashed back to capture pictures of the anglers posing with their prizes.

He eyed Amanda, "What are you doing now, *Mate*?"

She raised her head from the cooler she was using as a workbench. "I'm switching out your cheap leader lines with fluorocarbon leaders. The fish will see that cheap stuff you've rigged."

Jeb bit his tongue. A few minutes passed, and he yelled back, "What else do you have in that bag, missy?"

"Mind your business, *Captain*!"

Amanda's eyes sparkled. *She's in heaven.* She inched forward with her small fishing bag holding it like a Christmas stocking.

He peered into it. Jeb moved his jaw, but no words came.

The bag was filled with multicolored spoons, planers, fishing line, inline sinkers, and all sorts of other mackerel rigs, even a floatable pull-behind hot-pink birdie.

"When the light comes out, we've got to go with this one," Amanda said, pulling a Drone pink-flash spoon from her bag. "The only ones I see on your boat are these cheap Clark spoons."

"What's wrong with 'em?" Jeb felt docile and raised his hands. He didn't know whether to whimper or argue. "We're still catching . . . more fish than I can count."

"Yes, we're catching, but only half of what we *could* be catching."

Jeb flung his head back and set his eyes on her. "You're a total nutcase. An absolute nutcase. Do you know that, Mate?" Regardless of his words, there was no way to conceal his admiration.

To Jeb, nothing was more attractive in a woman than *spunk*! And with her eyes so yearning, he turned his back to her.

CHAPTER 14

The Bet

More hair loosened beneath Amanda's cap as Jeb watched the marvel work. She'd been managing the back deck for a good half hour after switching out the lines with her own rigs. The cooler was brimming over with fish, and Rob prepped another cooler to handle the overflow.

When Jeb had offered to show her how to release the lines, set the drag, and dehook the fish, she sent him an icy stare.

What did she really know about fishing? Especially this unique style of trolling? If she failed to set the planer correctly with the lines at their proper distance behind the boat, all of them were bound to tangle into a jumbled mess. Instead of fighting her, he pulled his line clippers from his pocket and waved them at her. "Just in case, Mate."

Amanda pursed her lips. "Like I said, Captain, it appears you run a tight ship . . . and don't worry, I won't tangle the lines." She turned and the ends of her hair slapped him in the face. A moment later, she faced him, appearing a little hurt. "And besides, if I do, I'll clean 'em up myself."

He left her to her own demise, but defeat never came. When she'd haul in a mackerel over the stern, she acted like a chef in a Japanese steak house, twirling the dehooker as if it was a baton, adding dramatic flair to the release of the fish from the lure and into the cooler. Rob and Chuck turned wide-eyed at her display. Jeb said nothing, but was glad to see Sierra take an interest, letting Amanda instruct her on the technique.

The fishing had waned, and Jeb glanced back. Amanda wore a stern, studious expression while peering out over the water. He refocused on the sonar, searching for bait pods. After a long moment, he heard her scream, "Captain, your angle is wrong!"

"What?" Jeb infused a playful snap in his voice. *Will she pull another rabbit out of a hat?*

Amanda grimaced while maintaining a grip on a pole that was secure in its rod holder. "Your approach angle to the underwater ledge!"

"What are you talking about, *lady*? Look at that line." Jeb gestured to a port-side pole that twitched. "Fish on!"

She jumped to the other side of the boat, pulled the rod from its holder, and handed it to Tasha. "We should have fish on at least half the lines right now!" Amanda helped Tasha land the fish, and then she was at his side. She pointed at the sonar screen and images of bait balls. "The bait is running in this direction."

She had brushed into him and stood close. He picked up the scent of coconut oil and struggled to focus on the sonar screen. Jeb took a deep breath. She nudged him and pointed at the screen. *Humor her again?* Why not? It cost him nothing. After studying the screen, he shook his head. "How in the world do you make that out from the screen? You're crazy!"

Amanda bumped him again with her shoulder as she turned to face the stern and spoke loud enough for everyone on the boat to hear her. "Yes, you already called me a *nutcase*." She put her grip on the wheel. "With that now established, let me drive the boat."

Jeb glanced at the crew. They were all staring back at him. He assumed the fishing had slowed for the last hour due to the tail end of the ebb tide. He nudged her hand aside and gripped the wheel with both hands. "You're crazy!"

"You're being childish. Let me take over the helm, *Captain*."

Jeb grunted a pirate's "Argh." He exhaled through his teeth. "Suit yourself, *Mate*. Do you know what you're doing? Hang on, I've got a better idea." He glanced towards the stern. "Sierra, come up here, please!" Once she arrived, Jeb continued, "Please straddle alongside the mate. Make sure she doesn't do something stupid with the controls."

Sierra smiled wide. "Like throttle it up when you're leaning over the stern?"

Jeb headed out the door. "Exactly! I'm grabbing my life jacket."

"Oh, Dad, Amanda would never do anything like that," Sierra

said seriously.

"Yes, she would," Amanda said. "Get your butt back there, Captain, and be prepared to catch fish!"

Nora gaped in disbelief. Jeb rubbed her head on the way out the door. He whispered, "Don't worry honey, she's all bark."

When he looked over his shoulder, Amanda's back was turned, but Sierra's mouth hung wide, too. After he caught Sierra's eyes, she grew a warm smile.

Amanda flipped her hair over her shoulder and glanced at him, but he quickly moved his attention to the men.

Chuck and Rob were whispering amongst themselves about "more fireworks." Jeb wasn't sure what to think about that, but if the fireworks continued to entertain them, he'd do his part. After all, it wasn't work. Only pure joy. Toying with his mate felt completely natural.

Jeb kept his voice low, "My apologies for my nutcase mate, gentleman. I'm going to humor her this one last time to shut her up." He formed his hands into a bullhorn and placed them around his mouth. "Ladies and gentlemen, we'll resume catching fish shortly after we give our first mate a turn at the helm."

Rob and Chuck snickered. Rob's tone wasn't very convincing when he said, "Captain Carter, hope you won't be eating crow."

Jeb flinched. "Not a chance! We'll lose a couple of minutes in our pursuit, but we'll have peace for the rest of the day."

Rob suggested, "Betting pool, anybody?"

A howl came from the pilothouse. With one grip on the wheel, Amanda waved a twenty dollar bill with the other. "Three hookups on this turn!" she yelled.

"Fine, I'll take that bet!" Jeb yelled back at her, dismissing her with his hand.

"I want twenty dollars for every additional fish, Mr. Carter." She glanced back, and Jeb caught her playful look.

Jeb could in no way fold his hand. He steadied himself. "I'll take that one too, Mate! And that's Captain Carter, to you . . . Mate."

"All the same to me, Captain. I like easy money," she said, and proceeded in her approach across the ledge. Five lines went down and the sixth pole on the port-side stern twitched. Once the team had hauled in the fish, she demanded that the sixth line be inspected. Jeb retrieved it and hid his gasp. The line showed marks, clear evidence it had been bitten off. He tried to hide it, and she stormed to the stern, minutes of bickering ensuing between them.

When Jeb finally relinquished, Amanda declared she didn't want his money. Jeb waved his hand back at her. She rolled her eyes and tried hiding her face.

One that lit up with a smile that couldn't be contained.

Leroy's Gulch

Something wasn't playing right between two of Jeb's starboard lines. He could tell by the way the tips of the poles twitched. He reeled one in to discover a rat's nest of fluorocarbon fishing line and the rigs of both poles globbed into a jumbled mess. A mental error!

Jeb cursed under his breath and realized his mistake—both lines had been set at an equal distance behind the boat. He shot a quick glance towards the front. There was his excuse. *Her!* Thus far, he didn't believe Crazy Lady at the helm had spotted it.

He wasn't prone to cursing and was grateful the Whaler's sluicing through the water masked his mutterings. It made him even madder that he'd done it. Not the snafu . . . but the cursing! Now he was angrier at his own bubbling temper.

He pulled out his snips, and in less than a minute, cleaned up both rigs and restored them to the water. The leftover fishing line danced about on the deck like tumbleweed. He fell to his knees, scrambling to gather all the loose-ends. While still on his knees and out of view of the woman, he eased up the lid of the fishing cooler and slid the jumbles into it.

"Uh oh," Rob said.

Jeb was in the push-up position, ready to raise himself from the deck, when he caught sight of Amanda's legs practically touching his nose.

"Whatcha doing, Captain?" she said, her voice sassy.

He pumped up and down a few times and for good measure let out a large breath. "Just a little exercise between hook-ups."

"Hmm."

Jeb looked up to see her eyes narrow and her nose tighten like she'd got a whiff of a dead animal. He raised himself.

She lifted the cooler lid with her pinky. "What's this?"

The jumbled ball of cord was now inches from his face. "Wow!" Jeb forced his surprise and scanned the crew. Everyone was bearing down on him. "Looks like our fish puked up rigs from another boat."

She shook her head with a look of disgust. It softened, and he felt like her toy. "I expected you to blame me," she said. He knew she was referring to her driving skills.

"I'm not naive. You would've grabbed my ear lobe and dragged me to the GPS console. The track line would show us on a straight course."

She flinched. Maybe she'd understand now his mean ways were behind him. She pulled off her sunglasses, which worried him, suspecting she'd want to intimidate him. That, or she wanted a better read of him. "So exactly what is the problem?"

You are! Everything about you. "I suspect the sun's gotten the best of me today."

She flashed a playful smile before spinning around and returning to the pilothouse.

Jeb rubbed his chest trying to dampen an onset of an arrhythmia. *That can't be healthy.*

After another half hour of catching, Sierra found her way next to him on the back deck. "Dad, I think you're wanted by the Cap— . . . I mean . . . Amanda. At the helm."

"You mean first mate?" Jeb glanced over his shoulder. Rob and Chuck were doing an adequate job handling some lines and aiding their daughters in catches.

"Yes, Daddy. She needs to speak with you."

"Why doesn't my first mate just yell at me? She's been yelling at me all day."

"Daaad."

Jeb bobbled his head again like a marionette and made his way toward the pilothouse. Nora, Sarah, and Tasha burst out laughing. He continued as if being pulled by the strings straight to Amanda's side. He glanced at Sierra. It took her a few moments, but she eventually laughed at him too when he contorted his face.

He worried about Sierra. Sometimes she took life too seriously. Was she really to blame? Maybe it was true. He'd been sucking the joy out of life since Erin's death.

He raised his head near Amanda's face as if hoisted up by guide strings, his leg still dragging a good ways back. "Yes, Ma'am."

She slapped his hand and giggled.

He jiggled his head and bounced his shoulders like the

marionette.

At the stern, Chuck was keeled over and shaking uncontrollably. He stomped his foot, too. It was infectious and the girls couldn't contain themselves.

I guess I got 'em.

The humor was feeling better and better. How many years had it been since he'd laughed like this with his girls?

"Stop it!" Amanda covered her mouth but her giggle escaped. Before he attempted another antic, she cut him off with a serious tone. "Captain, I think we're going to need to do something different." She shook her head and wiped tears from her cheeks. Her beautiful mole was breaking through a small touch of makeup.

"How so?" Jeb echoed her tone.

She burst into laughter again. "Here, take the wheel. I can't stand it any longer."

Jeb laughed some more until she calmed down. Whenever he'd give her his serious face, she'd break up giggling again and slap his arm.

Is that what girls do these days? Slap guys around? He didn't remember Erin doing it.

Amanda tried to speak between laughing snorts. "All these fish are about the same size. Everyone else is likely catching the same."

Jeb cocked back a little. "And your suggestion?" He braced for her command. His serious expression wasn't fake, and that seemed to settle her.

He thought about torturing her some more. A forehead wrinkle would do the trick. He couldn't get enough of her laugh, but he remained poised and claimed a silent victory.

Her eyes needled him and she waited a few seconds before continuing. "One last *Hail Mary* along the ledges of *Leroy's Gulch*. We'll have time for about an hour of fishing if we pull up lines now and make a run for it."

Leroy's Gulch—a sixty-foot hole by the underwater asphalt pile—wasn't notated on any chart. The locals knew it by that name. *Not an outsider!*

Jeb gazed deeper into her eyes. *Who is this woman?* So caught up in the day's activity, he hadn't considered how Amanda knew so much about fishing. And her devilish sense of humor, the way it played to his. He was simply enjoying her—afraid to call her by her name, for fear of being woken from a dream.

"Where're you from, *Mate*?"

Amanda froze as fear painted across her face. She stared straight ahead. Several moments passed before he bumped her on the shoulder.

She continued to ignore him, so he dropped the matter, placing his focus on the sonar screen.

She eventually turned towards him, tapped him on the hand, and spoke softly. "Let's just focus on the fishing, Captain. There'll be time for that later."

Amanda wasn't telling him something, but he didn't mind. He liked the idea of *later*. He nodded. *Surely the girls will invite her back to the Bay House.*

Amanda resolved she needed to explain everything to Jeb. His parents already knew the truth. *Why hide it from him? I've been too obvious—reckless!* How could he not notice the game with the limp? *I'll tell him tonight when we return to their place . . . clear my conscience . . . possibly explore other feelings.*

That morning, when she'd first arrived at their estate, she wasn't prepared to see Jeb because Ralph and the girls had never mentioned him. His comment when she stepped onto the dock galvanized her. It was time to stand up to the chauvinist bully, James Carter. And then he played the song from Jurassic Park. *He was worse than a bully!*

She didn't miss Jeb's humiliation in front of Ralph. But Jeb was only remorseful for having violated a code of conduct. *At least he recognized it!*

Jeb was likable, and she wanted to like him, but how could he be so mean to her and so nice to Ted and Sally? *What's he afraid of, anyway? I don't bite.*

She wondered whether he was a *Judas* or a *Peter?* In her book, Judas had only remorse without repentance. Peter repented . . . like her own father. His letters and his life now showed sincere contrition. But Jeb? Simply caught in the act! Like Judas. Causing Jeb to appear small compared to her dad.

She thought Jeb had been petty, but creative with his opening musical score. Was that a sign that beneath it all, he really cared? Her feelings somersaulted when she stood close to him. His lavender scent slowed her a beat, stimulating her to realize Jeb was cornered, his family teaming up on him, including her unexpected participation.

But why does he work so hard to bring out the worst in me?

When they neared her father's marina, Amanda wanted to slug Jeb in the arm like she would've hit her father, but she pulled back at the last moment. She couldn't corral the anger that had so easily empowered her—feeling as if she'd been exposed to kryptonite. The only person standing in the way of Jeb . . . was Jeb!

She continued to make excuses for him, but then his words really hurt her. Like when she'd come from the marina's restroom. To add insult to injury, he played the score from the movie Jaws. The cruel joke was obviously at her expense . . . with people she hadn't even met.

And to scold her in full view of the crew, *what a jerk!* His harsh words rewound the clock, back to the horrifying ordeal in the guest room at the Marina House, when she'd been bludgeoned by her own father's words. She'd looked to the *Queen Mary* as Jeb yelled at her, and this time, it was her father fleeing, not her. She wondered if her father, if he'd known, would have protected her from the horrid man. Mr. James Carter.

She had nowhere to run but to the Marina House. She thought about retreating there and calling Ralph and Maria. They'd understand. But the girls and the Special Anglers? She'd be letting them down!

Ralph's words came back to her, "Jeb's got problems . . . just try to understand." *Not my problem!*

But Ralph's advice gave her pause, and she resisted her instinct to flee. *Who doesn't have problems?* And those early pokes? A defense mechanism? *To make me irritable and unlikable?*

There was a fierceness about Jeb that Amanda believed was anger, but maybe there was something more. When he'd come for her and Sierra, he hadn't lashed out or embarrassed his daughter—he'd jumped into the water and hugged her. Intense and desperate. Something sad.

And could she fault him? How was he to know she was hiding from her father? She wasn't acting like herself. *Would Jeb know that?*

Although Jeb's harsh words had rekindled a familiar anger, when he apologized, he'd pulled the rug out from under her, infusing new anger. She was angry that Jeb had dared steal her own.

All the nerve to ask for her forgiveness! Isn't that what her own father had been seeking? Forgiveness was a slippery slope. If she could so easily forgive Jeb, might she do the same for her father? *I'm not ready for that.*

Something else gnawed at her. Jeb and her father. How they were spun from the same cloth!

Jeb's eyes, from that point on, were always soft. But also confused! The girls' pull on her had weakened through the day. *No, that's not it.* Nora continued to stir a place in her heart that nothing else could touch. She admitted the girls' gravity hadn't diminished at all, but rather, *his force had grown!* She felt like she was spinning in an orbit around him.

Why does he stand so close to me? Or am I standing close to him? Their faces nearly touching. Brushes from his elbow, his smell, and his antics. He began playing music to her tastes and taking an interest in her preferences—virtuoso performances by the Three Tenors and Andrea Bocelli. He played Bocelli's duet with Celine Dion—"The Prayer." And then Katherine Jenkins' "I Believe." He played the theme song for *An Officer and a Gentleman*, "Up Where We Belong."

Could he know what he's doing to me? He was playing for the entire group, right? Music was her love language, and she felt like a wad of putty in his hands. *Was it his too?*

His daughters adored him as he karaoked on the back deck or from the helm. If he would've extended his hand for a dance, she would've thrown herself at him. She envied his daughters when she saw them dance with him between catches. He danced with Tasha and Sarah too . . . *but never me. I'm just the mate.*

His girls seemed utterly confused. *I suppose they'd never seen their father flirt.* She worried Sierra would blame her for it.

Please, God, show her I'm not at fault. She doubted God would answer that prayer—egging Jeb on in equal measures.

She snapped to and gripped the helm wheel tighter.

I've lost all control!

A Storm and a Fish

Amanda turned her focus to the sonar and driving the boat. This was their team's golden opportunity for landing larger mackerel. It was also prudent to turn down the heat with James Carter. She figured, *I'll keep 'em fishing back there, and we'll stop tangling up here.*

From their screams and hollers, she knew they were catching and resisted the urge to glance towards the back deck, fearful she'd lock eyes with Jeb and be unable to let go. Sierra was more involved with the fishing now—a positive development. She deserved her father's attention, too much of which had been going to Amanda. Sierra had ceased asking for Amanda's advice and now sought it from her father. She also stood in the center of the boat, obstructing Amanda's view of Jeb. *Clearly, the girl wants to put a stop to this!*

Amanda used the moment to snap a picture of the ongoing action and text it to Sally. She added a message, "Did I tell you I was back in the NN this weekend?"

"No you didn't you crazy girl!"

They texted back and forth a few times before Sally dropped off without any explanation.

Amanda jolted when Jeb suddenly appeared next to her in the pilothouse, waving his smartphone. He turned it in her direction, gesturing to an alert from his radar app. "It's brewing just beyond the horizon," he said, and she knew he was referring to a storm.

He pointed at certain traces on the vessel's radar console, further indicators of what lay ahead.

A tingling sensation hit her. *Was it him or something else?* Maybe both!

She fixated on the radar screen and then gestured at it. "They're right here, Jeb. We've got a huge school of fish five miles out." Amanda kept her tone more professional, done with the flirting, and also tired of calling him Captain.

Why can't we be a bit more personal?

"How do you know?" His tone was business-like as well. More respectful, like she was his equal.

"We've got birds feeding!" She tapped excitedly on the radar screen.

Jeb rocked his head, but she sensed resistance. Their commotion in the helm caught the attention of Chuck and Rob who quickly joined them.

"We don't have time," Jeb said.

Ridiculous! "The storm is a good forty-five minutes out."

Jeb twitched. He gazed blankly towards the horizon, his eyes hollow. He remained silent.

She nudged him. "Jeb."

He stirred, and their eyes met. His were still vacant. He mumbled at first, as if escaping a bad dream. Finally, his voice cleared. "I think it's about time to turn in. We've had a good day."

Was this evidence of what Ralph had warned her about? His PTSD? Did his clients ever see this side of him? The ruddy man who could strike the most confident pose as if being pulled off the cover of an outdoor magazine. That feeling of sympathy returned, like how she'd seen him on Monday, trying to adapt to the Special Anglers. She was proud of him now. Jeb had been an incredible host to Sarah and Tasha, becoming their friend.

Amanda eyed the other men. Chuck shrugged. Nora was taking a nap, but Tasha and Sara were perky as ever. Sierra had the look of a caged tiger. Amanda pushed the throttle forward a notch. She kept the *Galleon* on a direct course towards the bird flock.

She let some moments pass before facing Jeb. "Captain Carter, do you want to win this tournament or not?"

He froze again.

She wondered what he saw in the storm . . . *any storm . . . just like a week ago.* She turned to Chuck and Rob with a faint smile. "Let me talk with him for a moment." They got the hint and exited the pilothouse.

Amanda spoke softly this time. "Are you okay?" The man was trembling.

Jeb grabbed the console's grip hold. It steadied him. "No, Mate, I'm not." His tone echoed her kindness and his eyes fell on her. "I'll let you pull the lines for one good turn, and then we're heading for the barn. I'll work the lines. You drive the boat into that school." He handed her his phone. "Here, pick something from my playlist."

Amanda stared at it. *Maybe he wants me to program my number into it.* Presumptuous, maybe—but it's exactly what she wanted to do.

She waited until Jeb left the pilothouse before touching the phone's screen. She spoke to herself, "Just choose a song, Amanda . . . and make it good!"

A backdrop image appeared showing Jeb's face flush against that of a beautiful woman. Layered, strawberry blond hair fell about the woman's face—one that looked eerily familiar. *Is that his girlfriend?*

She selected a song and started it. Amanda was about to set down his phone, but stopped herself. She opened his phone's camera-roll instead. *Just a quick glance.* She found plenty of pictures from his tours, but not the lady in his phone's background image—not until she reached photos taken nearly five years ago.

"Oh, God!" Her stomach dropped to the deck of the boat. The camera-roll showed pictures of Jeb and the woman scuba diving off a catamaran in a tropical location. It looked familiar, too. She exited the camera app. *Should've been obvious!* Sierra closely resembled the woman—how Sierra might look in ten years. *I guess he didn't want my number!*

She glanced back. Jeb and the crew were busy with catches—big fish! They were all hollering like mad. Even Nora was up from her nap and landed an enormous one. Jeb was twirling her about and yelling, "I think you've caught a winner, Nora . . . I think you've got a winner!"

The song ended and Amanda selected one by Rascal Flatts, "Bless the Broken Road." It was sentimental, powering her through the early stages of conflict with her father. She'd held out hope back then that they'd mend things, but the flame died. Today she had new hope for her and her father. Genuine hope. He'd paved a path for her. *I might not be ready to take it yet . . . but soon enough, I will.*

The first notes of the song played, and Amanda fought back tears. She saw her father's face.

Suddenly, Sierra was at her side. She quickly grabbed her dad's smartphone from the console and stopped the music. Sierra's eyes were wide with alarm.

Amanda gazed at the girl. "What did I do?"

Sierra took a deep breath and was trembling. "Amanda, why don't we pair your phone with the speaker?"

Amanda glanced towards the stern. Jeb, his shoulders shaking, was gripping the gunwale with both hands. Rob, Chuck, and the rest were oblivious, dealing with fish on the lines.

"Quick . . ." She handed her phone to Sierra. "Do it!"

Sierra paired it in seconds. Amanda selected a waltz from her playlist—a recent live recording from Vienna, Austria. She looked back at Jeb. Rob attempted to pass Jeb a water bottle, but he was rubbing his eye with the back of his hand.

Sierra raced back to him. "Daddy, it's a waltz. Amanda's playing a waltz for us. Won't you dance with me?"

Jeb grabbed a towel and wiped the sweat from his face. Amanda suspected it was more than sweat. The water bottle was in his hand now, and he polished it off in two long gulps.

Amanda had always wondered about the man and whether he could waltz. Would he know classical dances?

Chaos surrounded him, but Jeb danced with more elegance than she could've imagined. Occasionally he would grab a fishing pole and pass it to one of the girls, all while he continued to dance with Sierra. Nora switched out with Sierra, and he led her just as beautifully.

The sting of tears hit Amanda's eyes. Jeb was so graceful. And not that different from her own father. She thought about what it would be like to be in her father's arms for a dance again. Her desire for reconciliation swelled within her soul, her heart racing.

Maybe Jeb will ask me to dance.

Instead, he screamed from the stern, "Mate, you need to start pulling in the lines. Now!"

Amanda flinched, shocked by being taken from her longings and also by the radar. The afternoon storm was coming upon them much quicker than expected.

Nora and Tasha pulled in fish exceeding twenty-four inches. Amanda's determination surged.

"Captain, we need a big one for Sierra! Five more minutes, please. The storm will go to the west of us," she yelled back at him.

"Pull 'em in!" Jeb's manner was serious. "I'd like everyone else to take shelter in the pilothouse! Sierra, take the helm!"

He was soon at Amanda's side. She felt a nudge at her elbow. "Thanks for the waltz." His eyes were the warmest she'd ever seen them.

"I'm sorry about the song."

His voice turned tender. "No worries, Mate. How could you have known?"

"Yeah . . . but will you tell me about it someday?"

Jeb gazed off towards the horizon. "I need you to bring in the lines."

She argued for one last fish for Sierra. He responded, "Mate, I haven't seen you land *one* fish today." His eyes were soft and burning with intensity at the same time. "Help me bring in the lines now and I'll save one for *you*."

She nodded and dashed out with him to the back deck. They worked together and quickly brought in the lines—all but one.

The dark sky unleashed the rain. She and Jeb returned to the pilothouse where the rest of the crew huddled. The windows were barely cracked open, and it steamed. She couldn't help but be jammed up beside him, her chin at his throat.

She spoke quietly, "Captain, would you mind turning off the sonar and the radar?"

He stared at her. His mouth moved, then froze.

It was a crazy idea. Maybe she was about to earn another tongue lashing from him. At a time like this, *turn off the radar? What was I thinking? He won't understand.* As if the prior weekend's storm hadn't been enough for him.

Just as she placed her hand on his arm, he turned from her and flipped a couple of switches. The electronic screens blackened.

A long moment passed before his eyes returned to hers. "Are you happy now?"

"I was going to apologize," she whispered.

He shook his head, eyeing the horizon. "It's okay. We've got this."

She stayed silent.

"You think the sonar scares the fish?" he asked.

"Not just that," she said.

Jeb's eyes narrowed. "What?"

"You must learn to sense the fish and how they feed below us in the trench."

He smirked. "You're crazy . . . and don't think you can make this about me!" He raised his hand, ready to wave her off, and then he closed his eyes. His look turned serious.

"Don't tease me," she pleaded softly. They'd caught the scrutiny of Rob and Chuck.

He opened his eyes. "I'm not, Mate."

Amanda stiffened. The mocking she expected didn't come.

Jeb made a sweeping turn away from the storm and back to the north. He gazed right into her eyes, "I'm fairly confident we can outrun the squall." His tone was full of intensity, without anger.

Is he feeling what I'm feeling? The electricity in the air. He'd taken the bearing of a Spanish bullfighter and thrust his hands upwards. "We need some music. Music to attract a big fish for our mate. What do you say, guys?"

Sarah hollered, and the other girls joined her in a cheer for a song.

Jeb yelled out, "Let me see that phone of yours, Mate."

She handed it to him, and he poked at it. His eyes sparkled. "Opera, right?"

She danced her eyes back to him. He made a selection. Notes played from *Nessun Dorma*, an aria from the opera Turandot by Giacomo Puccini. It sounded like music from Phantom of the Opera. How ironic. It was she who wore the mask.

Jeb directed the crew to be quiet, and he closed his eyes again. He steered his hand flat in front of him like he was visualizing a bobsled run down an icy track.

Amanda closed her eyes; her breathing slowed. The music took her to another world—a time before her mother's passing. When life seemed perfect.

Some minutes passed, and the dull hum of the engines went silent. She felt the *Galleon* slow.

The baits will be falling deeper. Brilliant!

He reignited the engines and the *Galleon* lurched forward.

"Fish on, fish on!" Sierra screamed.

Amanda glanced back. Dark storm clouds backdropped the lone rod's isolation. The rod drove down hard, not popping up as it did with the other fish—it flexed downward and twitched violently.

"Okay, Mate, go get it! This one's yours!" Jeb nudged her, and electricity went right through her.

Did he feel that?

She clutched Sierra's hand and stepped towards the door. Jeb seized her other hand. "Sierra, take the helm!" Jeb stared back at her, "Mate, to the deck! You promised to bring it in!"

Nora, Tasha, and Sarah were all cheering as she tried to resist him. He wouldn't let her go. She worried he was going to pick her up and carry her if she didn't obey. *I'd like that. Take me away.*

The rain came down in sheets, and the music's tempo increased towards its climax. Jeb grabbed the pole from its holder and placed it in her hands.

She stomped her feet as the torrent washed over her face. "Jeb, I really don't need this fish."

She felt his arms around her waist and she stopped breathing. She closed her eyes for several long moments as his arms remained wrapped around her sides.

A snap sounded. She looked down to discover that Jeb had fixed a rod holder about her waist.

Jeb's voice woke her. "What are you doing, Mate? If you don't tighten the line, you're going to lose that fish."

She cranked in the slack. "Let one of the girls have it!"

The climatic notes of *Nessun Dorma* trembled through her. *Does he even realize how romantic this song is? A story of a princess and secrets . . . all tied up in a name?*

"They've caught enough fish for one day! I want to see *you* catch one!"

"It's big, Jeb!" She set the bottom of the pole into the holder, held the pole tight with her left hand, and used her right hand to alternate between reeling and wiping her face.

"I know. Reel it in! I need to get this boat home!" He was silent for several moments and spoke again in the sweetest voice she'd heard all day, "You know, *Amanda*, I think you're *alright*."

"What'd you say?"

"I said, 'I think you're *alright*.'"

"No, what you said before that!" she screamed over the rain, the wind, and the triumphant music.

He came to her side. "Just land the fish, Amanda!"

He was afraid to touch her—fearing another zap of electricity. Or whatever was going on between them. Pangs of guilt pierced through him. *I let my hands linger around her slender waist too long.* He had to tighten the harness. Right? *What would the girls think? I've betrayed them and their mother.*

She looked into his eyes. "You hear that, *James*? You did it again." It was her soft, feathery voice, the one she used with Nora. Her wet hair seemed darker now, some strands stuck to her reddened cheeks, and her eyes captured the blue charged bolts dancing on the horizon. She looked more stunning than she had all day.

"Yes, I know."

He pointed beyond the boat's stern where the fish surfaced. "Pay attention. I'll be more careful in the future. Just land that fish!"

She did.

CHAPTER 15

Indian Creek

Boats, big and small, of all makes and models, made their approach to Indian Creek. Jeb eyed the horizon. He could see for miles. Nearly all were on plane, coming from the north, east, and south, many high-end center consoles with T-Tops specifically designed for trolling. Some had colorful wraps around their hull with glossy photos of their sponsors and dramatic visuals of fish leaping, lures hooked to the mouths. Several large Chesapeake-styled deadrise vessels hammered through the water, mostly charter boats like the *Queen Mary.* With dormant winds, excluding the storm, most angler teams stretched out their fishing to the 3:00 PM lines-out-of-the-water deadline. Now they were racing in to meet a 4:00 PM weigh-in deadline. If anything had ever created an eclectic boat parade, this was it. Many of the boats hosted families and friends, and for most, it was the climactic end of traditional summer.

Jeb had seen it all before. There was some real *eye candy* in this year's tourney, even a million-dollar-plus Viking that edged in front of him at the mouth. Looks could be deceiving. He recalled participating in a rockfish tournament on the Potomac only to have a guy in a seventeen-foot jerry-rigged dinghy take home the goods. He was fairly certain the captain collected more winnings that day than he'd invested in his boat.

Jeb knew who the pros were in this contest. He didn't care about them, except for one. The conditions were nearly perfect for small craft, with minimal chop, and the high-end *Galleon* possessed no significant advantage over them except their tactics—that is, the *lady's* tactics. Had it been a windy day, the small crafts wouldn't stand a chance. Many of the locals were competitive. But today he didn't care. This day had turned personal.

Everyone else on the *Galleon* cared about winning, but not Amanda. She grew fidgety and tense. *What would she know anyway about a small town tourney?* Her interest in the tournament had waned on and off during the day, but certainly not the fishing. The act of fishing consumed her. She didn't leave a stone unturned in *Galleon's* tactics, possessed by perfectionism. When he lightened up, enjoying his girls and their guests, her intensity increased and filled the void. But now? Something else was gnawing at her.

The tournament was old school. It hadn't adopted a professional live leaderboard like others in the area and those featured on the cable fishing networks. The weigh-in status was to be communicated over VHF mobile radio channel sixty-six, but it never was, or if it was, you rarely heard it. They tasked a kid from the Little League to do it, but once the frenzy of the weigh-in began, no supervision was provided to monitor those call-outs. The only reliable way to know what was happening was to place a person on your *pit crew* at the weigh-in station to monitor the old-fashioned whiteboard for updates and communicate the standings back to their team on the water. On this day, it was Ralph, and Jeb overheard him speaking with Sierra on his smartphone.

"Hi, Gramps. Who's leading in the Youth Division?" Sierra set the phone to speaker mode.

"Boat number twelve at one and a half pounds," he responded.

"How about overall?"

"Top aggregate weight in first place right now stands at seven-point-one pounds."

Jeb ignored the chatter. Most of the serious contenders, beginning to queue at the Chesapeake Boat Basin, hadn't weighed-in. The *Galleon* was still fifteen minutes out, entering the mouth of Indian Creek—over a half mile wide—behind a line of equally spaced boats skipping across the surface. Their crews waved towards the shorelines. *Odd.*

Jeb glanced at the boats beyond his stern. Similar gestures from them, too. *Who does that?* He shook his head. *Who are they waving at?*

Nora cried out to the Special Anglers, "That's where we live! The Bay House!"

Jeb's mother was on the dock, her arms outstretched above her head, slowly waving. Jeb would have confused her gesture for a distress signal, but her tempo was steady and elegant.

From the water, the setting was majestic. Nearly every boat in the long procession, their captains driving like idiots, acknowledged his mother. To the *Galleon's* portside, they did the same for another person on the opposite side of the creek from his mother. A lady stood at the stern of a majestic sloop facing her. The large sailboat flew an unusual flag. Jeb didn't recognize it as a local boat. The name on the stern—*Santa Margarita*—was barely visible. Both ladies waved gently, acknowledging the armada of fishing boats. *Strange,* he thought, *the sloop's probably on a Bay cruise . . . come in for fuel . . . waiting for all us crazies to free the channel.*

"Daddy, Grans sparkles!" Nora yelled.

Jeb didn't dare risk removing his eyes from the train of boats beyond his bow. They were humming along at over forty knots.

Nora's voice cried out again, "Tasha, Sarah, look at my Grans!"

The girls began passing the binoculars around. He stole a glance at his starboard side. It was true. Something was reflecting the sunlight near the top of his mother's head.

Amanda had her head down and was digging in her costume bag. He braced himself. The princess, mermaid, or whatever she was, would likely transform herself again into the kitchen maid. He breathed a deep sigh.

Only a few boats had come in early, the advantage being that the time of weigh-in served as a tiebreaker. Jeb didn't care but to beat one boat, and he predicted the vessel was ahead of him, possibly having already weighed in.

"Daddy, why don't you pass them?" Nora yelled.

"Bad style, sweetheart. If they were poking along, then I'd consider it. If I go around them now, they won't like the wake I leave behind."

"But, Daddy, I see Peyton and Parker on that boat. I want to beat them," Nora persisted.

"What size is their fish?" Jeb played along. The twin boys were dead ahead, standing and facing them from the stern of their father's twenty-three-foot center console.

"I don't know."

"Well, go ask them."

Nora yelled out from the bow of the *Galleon*, but the wind and the engine's roar drowned her voice. She raised her hands to approximate the length of her fish. They responded, gesturing to show a fish a few inches larger. Nora spread her arms wider, which was reciprocated by the twins, the game continuing until each reached the extent of their wingspans. Nora returned to the console. "Daddy, don't worry about passing them. I think their fish is bigger than mine."

"We'll know before long, dear. The fishing tales end at the weigh station."

Amanda was at his side. Ugly sweatpants were now covering her gorgeous golden legs. "Jeb, I think we've got a good chance of winning!" The excitement in her voice was muted, almost fake.

"Outright . . . the Open Division?" he asked with obvious skepticism.

"Yes."

"It's a four fish aggregate."

"So what? Combine my fish with the two top Special Angler fish . . . we'd have a real good chance!"

"Darn right!" He attempted to read her face. "And Nora's fish?"

Her expression was sheepish.

Jeb relaxed, and it came out in his eyes. He suspected that Nora's fish, their second largest, would definitely take them over the top. Amanda understood, and it heartened him. *She'll be smart not to cross that line with me.*

"I'm not submitting your fish to help us win the Open Division, Amanda, and I won't sacrifice wins for Sarah and Tasha either . . . not to mention, Nora gunning for a Youth Division win."

"But, Jeb," her tone was full of pleading but lacked sincerity, "don't you think we'd all rather have a team win than individual wins? You could even submit Sarah's fish in the Ladies Division and score a win there."

"She's won that division twice. Once here and once at Bay Bash.

You deserve the recognition that comes with a Lady's win, and besides, even if we win the Open Division, most of that money is still going back to the Little League. To be honest with you, I only care about beating Charley West head to head in the individual divisions. I'll let the chips fall where they may in the Open Division."

Amanda's brow furrowed. "Why is it so personal? What's he done to you?"

It really wasn't any of Amanda's business, but since she didn't know the guy, it was probably safe to just tell her. "He's proud and won't admit he's mad at me."

"So this is how you bicker?"

"Yes, exactly." He smiled mischievously. "Did you even meet the guy on our Tangier tour?"

Amanda quickly replied, "I only met his fiancée on Monday."

That's right. He didn't recall Amanda ever venturing into Charley's pilot house all day. He sighed a deep breath. "Only two boats in this entire seventy-six fleet are dealing with our calculus."

She nodded. "I know." Judging from her exasperated tone, Jeb worried he'd spoken down to her. "The *Queen Mary* and the *Galleon* are the only boats that fielded anglers in every division."

He didn't like that she placed Charley's boat before theirs, but chose to soften his approach. "Thank you. So you understand?"

She nodded.

Had she really grasped all the rules? *Yeah, she can fish.* But would she have studied the rules?

Jeb checked his watch. They were cutting it close. "I noticed Charlotte bringing in a few, so they might be competitive in the Ladies Division. I assume you saw their youth anglers?"

Her voice stumbled, "Yes."

Jeb faked some anger. "I'd like to smash him."

Amanda turned from him, pouty. She hugged herself and tensed. A stabbing pain went right to his heart.

The fact that Amanda's fish helped his cause was a consolation. *She may have been my enemy this morning, but now I'm flying around in her orbit . . . enjoying the freedom of saying her name—a name that should be announced to all at the awards ceremony! . . . Who cares if she's from New York!*

Sierra dialed Charlotte using his smartphone. "How'd y'all do,

Miss Charlotte?"

"Oh, hi, Sierra. Where are you?"

"Approaching now."

"We had a good day . . . a wonderful day." Charlotte sounded joyful before Charley's voice dominated from the background.

"Careful, Charlotte. That'll be Jeb phishing. Don't give up any secrets."

She came back on the phone. "Ignore him, Sierra. We've weighed in . . . but it doesn't matter. Our Special Anglers had the time of their lives. We all did!"

Jeb grabbed his smartphone, and his voice was light. "It was a good day here, too, Charlotte. Charley's right. Don't say anything more. I'll let our fish speak for us." He handed the phone back to Sierra. He wanted to tell her about the mate dropped from heaven, but the boats converging on the approaching queue distracted him.

Jeb glanced behind him. Only a handful of watercraft trailed them. He checked his watch again as they passed the red channel marker. Thirty boats were lined up ahead of them, waiting their turn to weigh in as if at a drive-through. This one just happened to be on the water at the end of a large dock.

Barely a minute later, an air horn sounded from where the scoreboard was situated on the dock. The four o'clock deadline! Sierra high-fived Jeb, and he wiped his brow.

"I could have blown by all those boats," he said, looking at his daughter. "We didn't have to make it this close."

"I know. But you've kept the peace."

He loved this about Sierra—always seeming to discern between good, better, and best behavior.

Amanda's voice floated in from the back deck, petitioning Rob and Chuck to convince Jeb to go for a boat win. They were siding with him!

Amanda reentered the pilothouse and stood next to him at the helm. Fear had overtaken her. It was the same expression he saw on Tangier Island when she hid behind the Special Anglers. She'd also reverted to her *goofy* look, throwing on the loose shirt and the big hat in place of the sleek sports cap. She'd replaced her fishing glasses with the oversized model and was limping; she'd pulled from her bag what he now figured was an orthotic device and had already inserted it into her left shoe.

"Jeb, will you be taking us back to the Bay House before the awards ceremony?" Her voice shook and her chin quivered. "I need to get my Jeep."

"I don't think we'll have enough time for that. The awards ceremony will be right here at the Boat Basin. We can't risk being late. It'd be an insult to the Little League."

She cracked a grin. "Are you holding me hostage?"

Jeb felt weak in the knees and he flickered a smile. "Yes." He dreamed of a light snack with her afterwards at the Bay House . . . *Maybe the girls will invite her. I expect we'll be celebrating a huge win . . . decompress from the day . . . she should share in the afterglow.*

"I really don't feel comfortable about submitting my fish in the Lady's Division," she said, irritated. "Nora has a fish that might win."

Jeb frowned. *That makes little sense.* "Nora's fish is going to the Youth Division, fifteen and younger. She's not eligible for the Lady's Division, remember?"

She nodded reluctantly. He resisted the urge to wrap her up in his arms. *Maybe that's all she needs.* Someone to help her get to the root of her fears. But that would be wrong. *Just because it feels natural doesn't mean it's right.*

"Listen, Amanda, you've bossed me around all day. I'll grant that you've mostly been right all day too, but I'm still the captain and I'm putting my foot down on this. Can't you see I'm just trying to be gracious?"

"I do. I'm sorry, I really do, and I appreciate all you've done. I'm sorry, but I just can't explain right now how difficult . . . how very difficult this will be for *me* . . . if that fish wins. Why not pass it on to Sierra? Guarantee a Youth Division win."

He desperately wanted to remove her sunglasses. "Simple. Sierra didn't catch it." Judging by the snag in her voice, he was certain she was shedding tears, but nothing dropped to her cheeks.

When he placed his hand lightly on her face, touching her mole, she startled and her hand came to her cheek. He wanted to tell how much more beautiful she was without the makeup, but now he felt like he'd crossed a line.

Jeb pulled the boat up to the weigh-in station at the dock, and no sooner had he done so, Rob and Chuck submitted the fish from the stern without discussion. The transaction with the weighmaster was complete in a matter of seconds. Receipts showing the weights of the fish were returned, and the tournament officials shooed off the *Galleon*, clearing the way for the few remaining boats in the queue.

For Jeb, it was a relief—the decision yanked from his hands. And even better, the tournament officials were still gawking at Amanda's fish. He glanced at her.

Her face was ashen.

Broadway

Most of the teams hung out at the marina following the weigh-in—parties breaking out amongst the boats tied off to the docks and nestled in vacant slips. Jeb and his crew were no exception. He prepared his portable speaker and chased down the *Queen Mary's* crew to join them on the dock for a celebration.

It was a simple tournament, run efficiently, and there was no reason to delay issuing checks, trophies, and cash. These were honest folks, and it was nearly impossible to cheat in a Spanish mackerel tourney. The Waterside Grill, adjacent to the marina, awaited the teams. Registration included free meal tickets for a buffet of roasted chicken and barbecue, so many would attend—winners and losers. Why waste a solid meal? For most, it was a consolation prize.

Charlotte grabbed his arm and beamed at him. "You know how much these Special Anglers like to dance, don't you?"

"Yes . . . I noticed."

"Jeb, what's that spunk in your step? You really did have a good time?" Charlotte's eyes dug deeper.

Jeb forced the smile off his face. "I don't know what you're talking about, Charlotte."

She burst out laughing and gripped his arm. "Nice try."

He spun up "I Gotta Feeling" on his speaker, and within moments, he had both crews out on the dock dancing. He twirled his girls around and stole glances at Amanda. She remained in the *Galleon's* pilothouse with her head down. When she did look up, he'd tease with a face that said, "Come dance with me."

She didn't budge, and the hurt in his heart doubled. It was obvious she wanted to join him, but couldn't. The fear painted across her face stopped her.

Jeb queued up another song. The Special Anglers and his girls were fully engaged, and he returned to the *Galleon*. Amanda's eyes, full of yearning, came right to him when he stepped onto the boat.

"How can I help you?" Jeb said. The desire to help her was so strong it both shocked and scared him. Like the drive that possessed him to protect his own daughters. Even how he'd cared for Erin.

Amanda looked towards the activity on the dock near the *Queen Mary*. She dropped to the floor of the boat and kept her back up against the gunwale. "Can you sit down for a minute?"

Jeb nodded. "Of course."

He found a spot on the boat's deck opposite her and sat down. She pulled off her sunglasses and their eyes met. He noticed she'd concealed her mole again with makeup. He wanted to say it was God's mark but feared she'd be offended. Amazing how this woman struggled with self-esteem.

"How did you do it?" she asked.

His brow furrowed. "Do what?"

"Apologize."

Jeb folded his arms. There was more he wanted to get off his chest; he needed to apologize for his behavior from the previous weekend but worried he'd make an excuse for it based on Erin's birthday. He'd take care of it later, at the Bay House, and let some moments pass.

Amanda's face held so much pain.

He broke an awkward silence. "You want my advice?"

She nodded and sniffled.

Jeb ran his hand through his hair. "Do you mean, how do I say it?"

"No. I heard what you said."

"What? Act like a jerk?"

"You're no jerk, James Carter." She wiped the back of her hand across her cheek. "This morning. After we left the marina. Where did you get the guts to apologize?"

Jeb laid his hands flat on the boat's deck. "To be honest, I didn't really think about it."

"How can you say that? You must've felt something. I can't believe it wasn't hard for you."

Jeb tilted his head and looked off into the distance. "Okay. I was thinking about you and how I would've felt if someone did that to me . . . like if Captain West had dressed me down in front of one of his charters. Back when I worked for him."

Amanda flinched. "Did he do that?" Her voice was sharp and insinuating.

Jeb shook his head fast. "No. I was just using that as an example. And besides, he's quick to forgive and clean his slate."

Amanda's eyes widened, and he continued. "I also thought about my girls and how I'd hurt their friend. And it was getting awkward for Chuck and Rob. I needed to free everyone."

Now she tilted her head.

"Yeah. I felt like I'd imprisoned our entire crew."

"We gelled after that."

Jeb threw some force into his voice. "Yeah . . . but it doesn't justify my actions . . . a team building technique?"

"I didn't mean it like that."

"I know. But I just wanted to make it clear. I'm ashamed of what I did to you."

Amanda's eyes glistened, and she remained silent.

He kept his eyes locked on hers. "You struggle to forgive—don't you?"

"Thanks, Jeb." Her words came fast, and her voice was dismissive. Amanda raised her chin slightly and peered over the gunwale. "I think they need their DJ back."

He glanced over his shoulder. “Yeah. I’ll go spin up another tune for ’em.”

He stood and reached for her hand. She rose, and they came face to face. She smiled, but it was only a mask for her growing anxiety.

He kept his tone soft. “You never answered my question. It’s hard for you . . . isn’t it? To forgive?”

This time, her eyes didn’t leave him. She massaged her throat and after several moments, the words finally came. “Yes, Jeb. In spades” She was fighting back tears.

“Well, here’s some more advice.” Jeb didn’t want to push it, but Amanda’s eyes encouraged him. “Forgiveness is about freedom. I wanted to free you and the rest of the crew. I didn’t want to leave you bitter.”

She looked up the creek and dabbed away some tears with her palm. “Hah . . . I was ready to run.”

“I’m sorry.”

“I know.” Amanda pushed her hair back under her hat. She clutched his arm. “And how about you? Freedom for you?”

He wrinkled his brows. “Huh?”

“Yeah. Have you ever thought about how forgiving someone frees yourself?”

Jeb took a step backwards. “Not really.” *What’s she talking about? Is this about her or me?* Her words settled like rocks in his stomach.

“I should get going.” He stepped up and onto the dock, hesitated, then glanced back at her. “I think you’re right. I enjoyed the day, Amanda.”

Her eyes said the same.

He extended his hand towards her. “You coming?”

“No. Go ahead. I need a moment.”

Jeb scanned the *Queen Mary*. Several sets of eyes were on him. Mostly Special Anglers edgy for another dance.

Throughout their mini-party on the dock, Jeb grasped the hope that lay before him—not the awards ceremony, but time with Amanda afterwards. *Who is she?* He felt more and more like he knew her. *Maybe she’s a movie star? Nah, that can’t be.* Sierra, or anyone else on the boat, would’ve put that together.

Then he solved it. *Broadway!*

He remembered Sally belting out tunes on their tour and during his mini-karaoke session on the beach with the Hens. *Definitely Broadway material.* That was Jeb's nickname for her, *Broadway Sally.* Amanda had only hummed melodies while on the *Galleon* . . . but she knew all the great music. Cultured. *Maybe she worried her voice would be the giveaway—we'd all figure out who she is.* The local girl that made it big time! *She has style too—like her friend Sally—when she isn't making herself look hideous.*

As the music played, he sang along, "*Tonight's going to be a good, good night.*" His feelings were mixed about her being a *Broadway* star. *Way out of my league.* But it relieved his conscience. *I'll have betrayed no one. My girls and I have made a valuable friend.* Nothing more and nothing long term could ever come of it. Safe! Amanda will be good for a few free tickets every now and again. *No wonder she didn't want to dance with me.* What if I stepped on her toes? *Her insurance probably restricts her from dancing with lowlifes like me.*

Receipts

The gong of a ship's bell sounded and the dockside parties disbanded, everyone streaming into the grill. Fishing stories from all the teams replaced their trash talk from the night before, with anglers waving their yellow receipts from weigh-in. The scales didn't lie, but nearly every team had a story of the winning fish that got away.

"We had this thing in the bag, but for Daniel and Brian that beat our fish off with the net."

"We'd have won, but David, who was driving the boat, kept causing our lines to tangle."

"Ron slept in late, and we missed the early run."

Several teams complained about late starts due to engine or electrical issues. They all believed they should've won, but for one minor glitch or another, they were all just out of the running. "Next year we'll get 'em." Even in defeat, these people were eternal optimists. The leaderboard showed three different instances where the tie-breaker rule had to be invoked, and for these anglers, the *what ifs* were the most painful.

Jeb knew the feeling. So many near misses with his dad. But today? He thought about the start of it—a nightmare. But then Amanda turned it into a pleasant dream. He wanted to pinch himself ten times over.

Tom Girrard found him soon after Jeb's crew had made it through the buffet line.

"Well done, Captain Carter! We're going to get the awards ceremony started shortly. Since your *Galleon* has so many individual wins, would you all mind postponing your team pictures till the end?"

Jeb carried lightheartedness in his voice, "No problem, Tom. Makes sense."

"Jeb, another thing, we need the last name of your lady angler. The form only shows the initial *W*."

Jeb wiped some chicken grease from his mouth, stood, and shook Tom's hand. "The *W* stands for *Whack.*"

Tom's brow wrinkled. "You can't be serious?"

"I am serious. She's a Wondrous Whack who knows how to fish." Jeb filled his voice with playfulness, but realized he didn't actually know her surname; in fact, he hadn't provided her name on the registration. His father had!

"Hang on, Tom. I really don't know her last name." Jeb glanced over his shoulder. *Where is she, anyway?*

"Jeb, she'll be the last one announced for an award. Just get it to me before we present her awards." Tom glared at Jeb. "I won't call her a *whack*!"

Jeb dove back into his meal, surprised at the intensity of his appetite. *Relaxed. Finally!* He raised his head several bites later. Tom was tapping on the microphone. Many were still finishing up their meals and starting on dessert. The individual divisions went five deep, and he started with the Youth Division. While most of the *Galleon* and *Queen Mary* teams sat in close proximity to each other, Amanda stayed in the back of the restaurant, away from the stage. She didn't eat—Jeb periodically caught sight of her and gestured with his fork. He preferred his team together, but nothing would convince her.

He walked back to her, concerned. "Amanda, have I offended you? Are you still upset with *me*?"

She lowered her glasses, and their eyes locked. "No, Jeb. Nothing like that. This has nothing to do with you." Her voice trembled and Jeb felt that ache in his heart again.

He stood close to her with his back to the stage and spoke soft but stern, "Is there anything I can do to help? Do I need to beat up someone here for you?"

Amanda cracked a small smile, but then it flattened. She grabbed his wrist and spoke softly, "Pray for me."

"Forgiveness . . . our previous conversation?"

"Yes. I need to do the right thing—grant freedom." She wiped some tears.

"You've got some ex here . . . don't you? I told you, I'd take care of that."

"No! Do what I said. I'll be fine."

"I care." He touched her shoulder.

Her glasses came back up. "Don't worry about me . . ."

Jeb caught Charlotte's eye. She was sitting with Charley and her team of Special Anglers. She walked back towards them.

"Jeb, why don't you let me handle this? I know what's going on."

"You do?" He turned to Amanda.

She hid her face from him.

"Yes." Charlotte's tone was firm, and she gently grasped Amanda's arm and led her to the ladies' restroom.

Jeb raised his arms above his head and dropped them limp to his sides. Exasperated, he returned to his team's table. By the time he got there, Tom had already gone through the Youth Angler Division, except for first place.

"Now, folks, here's a boat you'll be hearing me announce repeatedly tonight. First place in the Youth Division, at two-point-one pounds, goes to Nora Carter of the *Galleon*, captained by her father, Jeb Carter! Congratulations, *Nora*! Come on up here, gal!"

A shot of pride rocked through Jeb's body. His eyes followed Nora as she gaped on her way to the stage, glancing at Peyton and Parker as she went. She stood with Tom to wild applause and received her trophy plaque, rod-n-reel combo, and her award check.

Sierra appeared jealous, and Jeb was thrilled. *She's acting like a sister . . . not a mother!* Eventually Sierra's expression became one of sister-pride and she cheered effusively.

Nora was mystified as she eyed Jeb, then she searched for someone whom she couldn't find.

Where's Amanda!

He glanced back just as Amanda stepped out from the ladies' room. She pumped her fist violently in the air and she yelled, "You go, girl! You go! Team Galleon!"

He tapped his chest. Warmth filled his soul, and he turned his gaze to Nora. She was beaming. Jeb glanced back again towards the bathrooms. Amanda had disappeared.

The applause spread. The Special Angler ladies began to chant, "*Galleon*, *Galleon*, *Galleon* . . ."

Jeb gave Charley a look and mouthed, "That's one." Jeb was tempted to perform a small celebratory dance with Nora when she left the stage, but instead spoke to himself, "James Carter doesn't gloat."

Tom announced the results of the Special Angler Division, the *Galleon* picking up third and first place for Sarah and Tasha. The *Queen Mary* picked up second, fourth, and fifth.

The chants resumed. Jeb signaled the peace sign to Charley, and mouthed, "That's two."

Tom then went through the Ladies Division awards but held back on first place. He worked his way through the Open Division. Charley shook his head derisively.

Jeb assumed Charley was mocking the *Galleon's* absence in the Open Division.

Is that really it?

When Tom arrived at first place in the Open Division, his voice exuded thrill. "And the winner of this year's Open Division is the *Gall*—" He cut himself off and paused for good effect. "Oh no, folks, it's not the *Galleon*. It looks like Captain Carter didn't submit his best fish in the Open Division! Had he done so, they would've taken first." Tom tucked his arms in front of him and rocked from side to side. "Who's cheering *Galleon* now?"

The joke at the *Galleon's* expense stirred the crowd even further, especially Sarah and Tasha. Half the crowd was booing the *Galleon*, while the other half picked up the chant. Charley's crew shouted for the *Queen Mary*.

"The Open Division winner goes to Captain Charley West of *Queen Mary Charters* with a total aggregate weight of eleven-point-nine pounds. Congratulations, Charley. Let's get your team up here and take some pictures!"

Jeb inspected Charley on the small stage with his team. Charley forced a smile. *Not like him.*

The revelers knew what was coming next, and both the *Galleon* and the *Queen Mary* teams chanted. Tom looked over at Jeb, who slapped his head. *The name!* Jeb spun around, looking for Amanda. He tapped Sierra on the shoulder, and she raced to the back. Jeb faced Tom and shrugged. There was really nothing more he could do except make things worse—Charlotte was on the task. He was in just as much anticipation as Tom to learn Amanda's identity, ready to do his own Google search if he didn't recognize the Broadway starlet's name.

He clamped down on his lip. If he had taken just one picture of her using his smartphone, he could've searched with only her face. Too much to ask of Rob or Chuck, even though they'd taken numerous pictures. *Why was I so afraid to take her picture?* His stomach ached at the thought.

Tom stalled, stretching out his words. "Folks, before we present the last three awards, we just want to thank all of you for your participation and to all the volunteers who helped make this event such a success . . ." He tried to keep it up for a long minute, but the chants drowned him out. His face reddened, and he began to sweat.

Confession

Tom's voice and the raucous cheering and chants reverberated right through the walls of the bathroom. Amanda doubted any eavesdropper would catch anything of what she needed to say to the woman who'd just entered.

Amanda pivoted and faced Charlotte with only inches between their noses. She removed her sunglasses. Her boiling anger spilled out. "Why have you been spying on my father?"

Charlotte took a step back, and her eyes enlarged. "Really?"

"Yes."

"How'd you get wind of that?"

Amanda expected denial from the woman, but Charlotte's quick admission forestalled a brawl. Still, Amanda kept an edge in her tone. "Does it matter?"

"Not really. What matters right now is that you reconcile with your father."

Amanda felt the fire release from her eyes. "Why would you be working with MI6 against my father?"

"I'm not." Charlotte folded her arms in front of her chest. "I was . . . but not anymore."

"I don't believe you!"

Charlotte shrugged and pointed at the door. "Well, if you want to talk with my previous handler, he's sitting out there on his boat, still tied up to the dock. The guy is stone drunk."

Amanda flinched. "What?"

"Yep . . . broke off my contract back in May. They're still mad about it."

Amanda shook her head in total confusion. "Does my father know?"

"Yes . . . but how can you prove I'm not lying?" Charlotte stood rigid.

Not in a thousand years had Amanda expected the forthright confession. *Am I walking into her trap again?* Charlotte needed to run, not her. And what right had Charlotte to be heated with her?

"Here's what I suggest." Charlotte rubbed her hands together. "You face your father now and learn the truth before I have a chance to talk to him," her voice was sweet until that point and then became angry, "or . . . you can step outside and talk to my ex-handler." Charlotte shook her head. "Now, if you decide to take option number two, you'll blow your cover and your career."

Amanda looked away and ground her teeth. It would have been easier if the woman had just screamed, "Checkmate!"

Charlotte closed the gap between them and grasped Amanda's hand. "I have a third option for you."

Amanda shook and offered a feeble hand.

Charlotte lowered her voice and spoke firmly, "You don't have to do this if you're not ready. I'm not lying, and I want you to trust me. I can walk you out of here right now . . . get you back to your Jeep . . . and you'll be on the road to DC in no time."

Tom announced Nora's name, and Amanda summoned her last vestige of courage to vacate the restroom and cheer for her. She was careful to cover her eyes with her sunglasses. Jeb looked at her from his seat, but it was Nora's adoring eyes that forced a torrent of tears, and Amanda raced back inside the ladies' room.

Charlotte was still there, and Amanda fell into her embrace unable to prevent her tears from flowing onto the older woman's shoulder.

The door opened and Sierra appeared, her eyes soft and wide.

Amanda lifted her head from Charlotte's shoulder. "Thank you. I need to do this. I might as well get this over *now* and put it behind me."

Her gaze moved to Sierra. "It's time I do this."

Sierra's face remained full of concern and confusion. "What's wrong, Amanda? They're ready to announce your awards."

"Nothing's wrong, dear. It's alright. I'm just being shy." Amanda wiped her tears. As much as she wanted to explain it all to Sierra, the moment was gone.

"They need your *name*." Sierra handed her a pen and a notepad. "Your *last name*!"

Time stood still. Amanda stared at the girl and her arms shook. Sierra was a blur.

Amanda felt Charlotte's hands gently come to her face. Finally, Charlotte's eyes came into focus.

"Shall I?" Charlotte asked.

Amanda nodded, and Charlotte jotted a name on Sierra's notepad. Within seconds, Sierra was gone.

Amanda removed her glasses and the obnoxious hat. She sniffled. "I'm hot."

Charlotte closed her eyes, intertwined her hands, and rocked them prayerfully.

Amanda ditched the ugly sweatpants, and Charlotte opened her eyes.

"You may want to remove your shoe insert," Charlotte said.

Amanda snorted, and Charlotte was quick to join in the laughter even while she cried. Amanda didn't doubt the woman's sincerity. Other things still bothered her, but nothing compared to a severed relationship with her father. A father she knew loved her and wanted her back. Who craved her return long ago. If only she could run straight into his embrace. Now!

But first she had to face him. Amanda thought the laughter would have relaxed her, but now panic set in. The small restroom began to spin and her heart raced so fast she worried it might break. *Breathe, Amanda, breathe.*

Amanda felt Charlotte holding her hands. The room stopped spinning.

Queen of the Bay

Sierra raced by her father towards the stage and delivered the notepad to Tom. Jeb glanced back and still didn't see Amanda.

Sierra returned to the rear of the restaurant, and Jeb followed her, stopping outside the ladies' room door. "Is everything alright, Amanda?" He tapped gently. "Are you okay? They're ready to hand out your awards."

She was crying. "Yes, Jeb. I'm coming out."

What's going on?

"Go, Jeb," she yelled. "I told you, I'm coming." There was another sob. "Tell Tom I'm coming."

Jeb faced his daughter, her confusion mirroring his own. Amanda was his friend now, and he couldn't mask the pain lodged deep in his gut.

He returned to his team table and signaled two thumbs up in Tom's direction. Chuck and Rob were equally bewildered. Sarah and Tasha were caught up in the crazy chanting.

Tom wiped his brow and his voice boomed over the loudspeaker, "Okay, folks, our winner in this division is a bit shy, but we've got everything in order now."

The chanting continued and got louder. Jeb detected a serious development as he caught Tom's eyes, and figured he did, too. Charley was getting redder and madder, and it was made worse by the chants for his own *Queen Mary*. Why the Little League restored the Queen of the Bay Division this year, Jeb didn't know, but he remembered the history of it. *Charley's in a world of hurt.*

Charley was out of character and it wasn't helping that Charlotte was no longer at his side. He'd fought back his emotions and anger all day—flipping out over the banana, but Jeb doubted that's what was eating at him. Everyone on the boat would think Charley was playing around. Only Charlotte understood. Charlotte would've shown him the flyer from the Captain's Meeting. He would've discovered they'd brought back the Queen of the Bay Division. He'd have woken up angry and stayed angry. *I'm sure Charlotte did all she could to ease his grief and lighten the pain.* When laughter erupted on the craft, she'd get him to laugh at himself, and play along. It seemed to have worked . . . *until now!*

He's not hearing Queen Mary in the refrain. He's only hearing her name. Mary! Mary! Mary! From their grieving therapy sessions, Jeb remembered this history. *Mary*, Charley's wife, had won the award during its inaugural presentation. Out of respect for Charley and his wife, they eliminated it. It was the last summer of her life, and she'd gotten Charley to take her out on the *Queen Mary* during the tournament. It took all her strength to attend the awards ceremony, but she did.

What Jeb suspected was grating on Charley's nerves even more, was that the *woman* who'd won—Amanda—was an outsider, some *floozy* from New York. Someone with no sensitivity or understanding of his grief.

I kept telling him she was a whack . . . this woman about to unseat his own Mary!

Jeb recalled the picture of Mary that Charley kept at his console. *When did he remove it?* The woman with beautiful blonde hair and enchanting eyes.

Tom's voice boomed out, "The winning Lady Angler has also taken the Calcutta for the *Galleon*!" He was working to regain his composure and was waving the stack of bills. Jeb sensed he was stalling. "She hauled in a monster five-point-one pounder . . . Jeb, why don't you come on up and fetch your money?"

Jeb looked for Amanda, but didn't see her. He dashed onto the stage and snatched the wad from Tom's hand.

Tom gripped his arm and whispered, "Jeb, I need you to quiet your team down. It's out of control."

Jeb faked a smile.

"No, I'm serious. You need to settle your group."

"I understand . . . I do." Jeb nodded.

Jeb gestured to his team to settle down, but it riled the rest of the teams even more.

Tom continued and kept his words slow, "Folks, the top fish in the Ladies Division takes two additional honors. First, the fish submitted by this angler—" He stopped and looked at the notepad.

Tom's jaw dropped. Maybe Amanda was some starlet after all. But it was more than shock. His countenance looked like Sierra had delivered a tornado warning.

Something else wasn't right. If Amanda was famous, Chuck or Rob might have known, but they hadn't said anything.

Her laugh? Where had he heard that laugh? Something about her eyes, too. *She resembles someone.*

Tom pulled out his handkerchief and wiped his face. He began to put it away, stopped, and mopped himself again. "Before we call this lady to the front, we need to roll out the red carpet." He was losing his enthusiasm, and chants filled the void.

Jeb peered over his shoulder. Charlotte and Sierra stood outside the door with their thumbs up. He took a deep breath. The tournament volunteers quickly unfurled a crimson indoor-outdoor-carpet. They pulled a costume tiara from the awards table.

Tom's voice was serious and emotionless. "I need to also add . . . that in the long history of this tournament . . . no boat has ever captured the top honors in all three individual divisions."

It was a huge gaffe, his comments riling up the crowd further. It didn't help that most of the crews were half drunk.

Charley, trying to regain his composure, raised his hand extending his index finger to show his first-place finish. It energized Jeb's crew even more in their "Sweep! Sweep! Sweep!" chant.

Jeb shrugged his shoulders and closed his eyes. Charley's angry expression hit Jeb like a Mack truck. It matched Amanda's. Her infectious laugh? It was Charley's laugh! The eyes and the hair? Charley's Mary! The lips? Those were her own—a divine blend from both parents. *Oh, God!*

Tom's voice hesitated over the speakers. "Ladies and gentlemen, can we all now give a round of applause to . . . Amanda . . . uhhh . . . White Stone's own . . . *Isabel* . . . *West*! Winner in the Ladies Division and . . . our own . . . Queen of the Bay!"

By the time Jeb opened his eyes, it was too late. Charley's fist sailed towards him.

Charley's swing merely glanced across Jeb's chin, as Charley had tripped over a chair coming after him. His large hand grasped the collar of Jeb's fishing shirt and Charley wound up for a another blow.

"For the honor of my *Mary*, how could you do this?" he screamed. "Of all people, Jeb Carter, how could *you* do this?"

Jeb braced for the blow and glanced away. There was Amanda. She'd just stepped out of the ladies' restroom. Their eyes met for a brief moment and she shrieked. Jeb looked up into Charley's face, but it was frozen—his eyes locked onto Amanda's.

The throng gasped in unison. Confusion filled the room like smoke.

"Izzie?" Charley's fist was still in the air.

Jeb lost his voice. *How'd I miss it? Izzie! His daughter!*

How many times had Charley talked about his Izzie during their grief counseling sessions? *I've been a fool! . . . I deserve Charley's blow.* But it wouldn't come—the fist fixed, as if held by an angel.

Charlotte rushed forward and grabbed Charley's arm. He loosened his grip on Jeb's shirt.

The father's eyes wouldn't leave his daughter's.

Amanda kept her eyes locked on Charley as she went to the front, her hand clasped in Sierra's. Fully composed she graciously received her awards. She hugged the shell-shocked funeral director as he continued to wipe his face. Amanda turned slowly to the crowd. To Jeb it seemed she saw only one face—her father's. She paused for a moment, then bolted from the stage into Charley's arms and wept.

CHAPTER 16

Jeep

The awards ceremony wrapped up quickly. Everyone gave Amanda and her father space. Jeb gathered what remained of the *Galleon* and *Queen Mary* teams and took pictures, but his heart wasn't in it.

For many of the Special Anglers, it was both somber and joyful. They struggled to understand what they'd experienced mixed with the emotions of a victorious day.

Amanda's Jeep was still in the driveway when Jeb returned to the Bay House. A heaviness settled in his stomach. Only once in his life could he recall such a feeling. The day Erin called to tell him she couldn't join him for a concert at an amusement park. They were only fifteen, and it wasn't Erin who called. It was her mother who called Maria. Only after his mother had taken the call was Erin put on the other end of the line to speak with Jeb. Her demeanor was strange, and she didn't sound sick as she tried to reassure him that everything was fine. The call left him confused and heartbroken. He still attended the concert with other friends, but he was despondent and had a dreadful time. Within a week, all was patched up. Only years later, when they were in college, did she explain she'd canceled because of her period.

The mood was subdued at the Bay House. What Jeb envisioned as being a "good, good night" turned out to be a "bad, bad night." He'd cracked open his heart, believing he'd betrayed Erin, and then felt like he'd been dropped off a cliff. His girls asked all sorts of questions, but he had few answers.

Not long after arriving home, he received a call from the

Lancaster County Sheriff's Office. "Hey Jeb, it's Bo."

Jeb knew what was coming and didn't hide his anger. "What do you want?"

"You doing okay?"

Jeb scampered to the privacy of the upstairs office. He certainly didn't want his girls hearing this conversation. "Bo, I know that's not why you've called, so why don't we just cut to the chase?"

"You don't have to be so rank about it. I'm just following procedures."

"And?"

"The office needs to know if you'll be filing assault charges against Charley?"

"You've got to be kidding me! He missed."

"No, he didn't. I saw it. A huge waste of our tax dollars for him to have lost his cool like that."

Jeb knew Bo was referring to Charley's officer training at the Naval Academy. "Why not just kick 'em while he's down?"

"So, are you?"

"Yeah, Bo. I'm filing charges." Jeb huffed his exasperation. "Tell 'em I'm filing against Charley West for a *lame* assault attempt. Is that in your code? That's all it was. Lame! Go tell 'em that!"

"I can't tell them that."

"No! You tell them that. If Charley had really intended to hit me, he would've hit me! He needs to be charged with a lame attempt. There's gotta be some law against it. Lameness!"

"Okay, I think I got it, Jeb."

Jeb liked Bo, but he was too worn down to explain it to the officer.

Charley had been quick to apologize to him. He'd probably made the call with Charlotte in the seat next to him and Amanda in the back. And Jeb understood the intensity of what happened, never seen him so cross in all the years he'd known him. What Charley wanted was a brawl behind the restaurant. Something that would have released the horrible pressure built inside of him. The two would have hit the deck, tousled, and Charley could've explained. And Jeb would've nursed him through it. But now the poor man was humiliated. Jeb knew Charley's next call was to the tournament organizers. Jeb hoped the whole ordeal would blow over quickly. But one thing was for sure. No one would ever forget what they'd seen!

They ended the call, but Jeb knew he'd need to make things right with Bo in the morning. No doubt Bo would be stopping by for a visit.

Jeb retired to the breakfast room and collapsed in his favorite wicker chair, shell-shocked. His mother took over, explaining to the girls what had happened between Amanda and her father.

Sierra sat on one of the bar stools. "But, Grans, why did she come down here in disguise?"

Maria set a small bowl of vanilla ice cream topped with blueberries in front of Sierra. "I won't hazard a guess. I think we'll all learn the truth *in time.*"

"Will we ever see her again?" Sierra pleaded.

Jeb folded his arms.

His mother pointed at Sierra's dish and glanced at him, but he shook his head. "I hope so." His mother's voice was the only one with any cheer. "If she heals over the lost years with her father, she'll be down here more often. She might even attend church with him."

Jeb watched his father through the evening. Ralph remained unusually quiet and careful with his words. There had been an elevated discussion between his parents back in their bedroom, but he didn't know what they were discussing. One thing was obvious—his father held shame. But as for his mother, her disposition left Jeb mystified.

"Mom, don't you think I should drive Amanda's Jeep back over to Charley's?" Jeb didn't conceal his sadness. "She left her keys in it."

The sight of Amanda's Jeep hollowed Jeb. When did he last feel so empty? It was an awful place to go. *Erin's death?*

The thoughts confused him.

Regardless, he still wanted to see Amanda, and now she'd been taken away from him. *Ridiculous. How could I feel this way? . . . Contempt for her at the beginning of the day . . . and now this.*

Perhaps the longing had nothing to do with *Amanda. This is about* Erin. His breathing slowed. *I've swapped my feelings for one to the other . . . plain and simple!*

"Jeb, I don't think that would be wise." His mother turned to the sink. "We should take it as a good sign that we haven't heard from her . . . We don't even know whether she'll be staying at Charley's toni—" His mother stopped, grabbed a towel, and wiped tears from her face. "I meant to say she may be staying in her *own* home tonight . . . the Marina House is *her* home." His mother's voice broke. "She's come home."

Jeb wondered whether his day with Amanda was a mirage. If that were true, why were his girls so sad? It had to be real! Sierra could barely raise her eyes from the floor, and both girls were quick to head off to bed. He joined them in their bedroom.

"I promised your friend I would pray for her," he said to them.

"Our friend!" Sierra snapped.

Jeb steadied himself, placing a hand on a bed post.

Her tone remained sharp. "She's not your friend? Are you going to be mean to her?"

"Hey!" He grasped her hand. "You know me better than that. I'm only confused." His voice softened. "I just don't know what to call her." How would he tell them the earth had come off its axis? Or worse, the reality of Amanda was better than a dream. "And another thing . . . I will never be mean to her again . . . ever!"

Sierra drifted back into her pillow.

Nora reached for him. "What are we praying for, Daddy?" Her voice was lyrical. It reminded him of Amanda's voice and how she served the Special Angler ladies.

Jeb blew out a breath, wondering how much he should tell them. Not that he knew any more of the story than they did. How could he explain how Amanda toyed with his heart?

"That God would give her power to forgive and ask forgiveness of her father," he said. But to himself? *Help me forgive . . . Did she use me, God?*

Nora wrinkled her brow. "What's so hard about that?"

Jeb marveled at her sincerity.

"It'll be hard for Amanda, Nor," Sierra spoke firmly.

Jeb eyed his older daughter. "Why would you say that?" Sierra seemed to know more than he did. Now wasn't the time to ask her about it. Not in the presence of Nora.

Joy swelled in his heart. Sierra was remarkably discerning. And Nora? She always thought the best of a person.

"I don't know." Sierra wrinkled her nose. "Something about her makes me think it'll be tough."

He wouldn't name what Sierra perceived—pride. Now he felt

guilty for thinking it. And who was he to judge? The vice had crept around him all day: feeling the need to perform for the Special Angler families, having his fishing acumen tested by Amanda . . . He was grateful now that he stopped fighting her.

Better now that he lead his girls in prayer. Which he did. Then he kissed them good night.

Mariner's Compass

Amanda's mind swirled with questions. At Saturday daybreak, she'd dedicated herself to a mission: the development of a concrete plan of how and when she'd reconcile with her father and confront Charlotte. But when Jeb entered the picture, he complicated all of it, causing her to lose control of the situation. The last thing she ever expected by the end of the day was to have it play out in front of the entire town. Charlotte understood, took the reins, and expeditiously shuttled them back to the Marina House.

As Amanda predicted, forgiving her father wasn't as hard for her as asking for his forgiveness. She wanted to word it just like Jeb had said it to her. It didn't happen right away. Maybe her dad needed to be reminded of all the pain he'd put her through first. Charlotte stood by as referee. Her father rarely became defensive, but when he did, he caught a glare from Charlotte. When he acknowledged the hurtful things he said and asked for forgiveness, Amanda forgave.

The poison her father's words once held was gone, and Amanda was convinced they'd lost their ugly power over her.

Amanda wondered if Jeb would really pray for her. It was nearing midnight, but she still couldn't muster the courage to say it. To ask her father to forgive her. To free him . . . and herself. He didn't seem like he needed to be freed. He wasn't holding any resentment. But that wasn't fair. Amanda knew she played a part in the conflict. Seizing bitterness like a treasure. Exploiting it for self-righteous anger.

Charlotte suggested they call it a night. That's when Amanda spoke up. "Wait. I have something else to say."

Charlotte's face showed concern.

Amanda eyed the older woman. "No, Charlotte. I'm not taking this backwards." Amanda rose, placing her hand on the kitchen counter.

"Daddy, you need to hear what I need to say. What I should've said years ago."

He stood up and faced her. His eyes were vulnerable, and he looked like someone had kicked him in the ribs a hundred times.

"I've been proud and bitter, holding anger in my heart that I should've let go a long time ago." She swallowed hard. "My pride kept me from releasing it . . . releasing you." Her resolve wavered, and she sniffled.

He stepped forward, clearly wanting to hug her.

"No!" she said, as she held up her hand. "I'm not done." Tears fell and her shoulders shook.

He waited, and then she continued. "Daddy—" She drew in a deep breath, her voice trembling. ". . . will you forgive me?"

When he approached this time, she didn't stop him. His arms wrapped around her. Her sobs came hard in gasps, and he tried to steady her, stroking her back.

She regained her composure and looked at him. His eyes were full of tears and she pushed back from him. "Well, are you going to answer me?" She softened the words with laughter.

He nodded slowly. "Yes. I didn't need you to ask . . . but yes, I forgive you."

"I know." She choked. "You've been patient and kind. I needed to say those words." She grabbed another tissue and wiped her eyes. "Do you understand, Daddy?"

He only nodded, trying not to sniff, and eyed Charlotte. She stepped towards them and Amanda reached for her. She pulled Charlotte so close their faces touched and Charlotte's warm tears trickled down Amanda's cheeks. Her father wrapped his arms around them both, and they stayed that way for a long time.

They broke for the night, and Amanda padded up the stairs to her room. She would've fallen asleep quickly, but for suppressed thoughts of Jeb that now bubbled to the surface. It surprised her the girls were not first in her thoughts. How had he become so dominant? *What happened to his daughters . . . our burgeoning friendship?*

She felt like she lived a lifetime all in one day with him. Under the shadow of impending paternal conflict and her focus to protect her cover, she realized the stronger aspects of her personality went unbridled, exposing much of who she was to Jeb. She melted at his mischievous looks and glances, and he wasn't afraid to spar with her. *No one has ever stood up to me like that man . . . James Carter.*

Her eyes were still puffy when she woke up and made her way down to the breakfast room. She found her father sitting at the table, reading. "I thought you'd be going to church," Amanda said, airing some testiness in her tone. She still wanted to search the house.

"I thought I'd skip it and enjoy breakfast with my daughter." His eyes warmed her insides. "I have a charter this afternoon."

Her tone was still irritable. "What's for breakfast?" She opened the refrigerator.

"Anything you want, dear."

She snapped her head away from the refrigerator and eyed him, his tender reply surprising her. "Do you have any fresh fish?"

"Yep."

"I mean something from yesterday."

Her father spoke like it was a simple fact, "I know what you meant."

She moved across the room and settled in front of him. "So you didn't give it all away . . . to the Special Angler families?"

"Nope . . . saved a few. But I've got an even better surprise."

She couldn't contain a smile but curbed her curiosity for the moment. "I want to prepare them . . . with Mama's recipe."

Her father nodded gently and stood. "I'm sorry, Izzie . . . I'm so sorry."

"Stop it, Daddy. You've said it enough and now you're just making me feel guilty. I'm still angry at myself and I'm sick of us apologizing." She exhaled a cleansing breath. "I'm ready to live again." She took a step closer to him and nodded. She felt fresh tears stinging in the corner of her eyes. "I want to live."

He drew near, and she buried her head into his shoulder as he wrapped her in his arms. "Yes . . . let's start living."

After nearly a minute, she spoke. "I'm through with all this crying." She stepped back from him and wiped her face with her oversized night shirt. Her tone turned accusatory. "Were you coming to my games?"

He nodded slightly. "I couldn't come to all of them, but yes, quite a few."

Curiosity rushed through her. "How'd you do it?"

"Hey . . . you're not the only one in the family that knows a thing or two about disguises."

She teased with her smile. "Trench coat?"

He guffawed. "Changed it up here and there, you should see my hat collection." He stepped out of the breakfast room, headed to the laundry-pantry room, and returned with a large mackerel.

"Daddy, that's not my . . ."

"It is! Tom brought it over this morning while you were still sleeping. Their way of apologizing for bringing back the Division."

"Water under the bridge."

"Yep, but I'd still like a picture. Why don't you get your tiara and I'll take one out by the dock?"

Amanda answered by dashing up to her room and returning with her tiara. At the dock, with the water in the background, her father took pictures with their phones. He also took a couple of selfies with just the two of them.

"Let me go take care of this fish," he said.

"I'll be right in, Dad. I just want to fire off a pic to a friend."

A few steps into the yard, he turned around holding up her fish. "How you'd catch it, anyways? Did someone finally teach Jeb Carter how to fish?"

"No, Daddy. That one was on him."

His brow wrinkled and he didn't respond, turning from her and continuing to the house.

Amanda selected a picture from her camera roll—one of herself holding the large mackerel—and texted it to Sally.

"Whoo-hoo!" was Sally's response. Amanda noticed her text exchange with Sally from yesterday, when Sally had gone silent.

When Amanda returned to the house, her father handed her a glass dish containing her mackerel filets. He cocked his eyes. "How is it you connected so easily with the Special Anglers?"

She put her hand over her mouth and turned away. She kept her back to him as she spoke. "Just one more thing I stole from you . . . we hosted Special Olympics basketball tournaments at Marymount. Each of our sports teams adopted one of theirs for the event. I loved 'em."

She turned and faced him. His eyes were soft when he said, "I would've come to your graduation."

She put her palm on his cheek. "I know, Daddy."

He reached for her hand and clasped it between both of his. "I have something for you, Izzie."

She stiffened and dropped her hand.

"Something I've been wanting to give you for a long time. I'll be right back." He left the room, his pounding steps charging up the stairs.

She went to work on the filets, scrounging for spices, onion, and fresh garlic.

He returned holding a small, narrow, rectangular wooden box large enough for a necklace. She eyed the maritime engravings on it and noticed an unusual clock symbol. Everything about it looked ancient. "This was your mother's. I'd planned to give it to you at your graduation."

"Dad!"

He jolted. "What?"

She pushed out a big, deep sigh. "Do we need to keep going back?"

"Oh . . . I'm sorry."

"I told you . . . the word *sorry* is no longer allowed in your vocabulary." She eyed the box and teased with her eyes. She extended her hand. "What is it?"

He pulled the box back a little. "Not so fast, young lady." He gently lifted the lid and displayed a beaded choker and a necklace of jade, with a fiery blue sapphire enclosed in a dry mariner's compass.

Amanda drew a deep breath. "Daddy!"

She fingered the compass and brought it close to her face, eyeing the intricate mechanism—a freely pivoting needle floating on a pin encased in a tiny box with a glass cover and a wind rose.

"You said you wanted to start living." He raised his brow.

"Okay," her voice became girlish. "I like this type of living." She cupped it in her hand. "This is exquisite."

He placed it around her neck. She returned to the fish with a jump in her step.

When they sat down to eat, she asked him about Charlotte and her intelligence entanglements. He confirmed Charlotte's story. Amanda wanted to know why. Why had he attracted interest from a spy agency such as MI6? "Dad, the UK is an ally . . . a Five Eyes partner."

"Yes, I know that." He spoke with no concern in his voice.

"But then, why? It makes no sense."

Her father wrinkled his brow and clamped down on his lips.

She asked, "Did Charlotte tell you why she was doing it?"

"She doesn't know."

Amanda jolted slightly and leaned into the table. "But you do?"

She gazed into her father's face. It held an understanding smile—a smile she hadn't experienced in far too long. It gave her a good feeling, from the tips of her toes to the top of her head. She felt the urge to pinch herself, and then a pain of remorse settled in. *I lost ten years with him!*

After several moments holding her gaze, his eyes drifted downward towards the necklace and he spoke. "In *time*, dear, in *time*, you will understand this."

Amanda crossed her arms. *Mom used to talk like that.* She considered asking him, but thought better of it. Talk about her mother and the past was still bittersweet, and right now, she wanted to savor the promise of the future. Today was not appropriate to ask him about the ring, either. She didn't want her motives questioned—not by him, or even herself.

After breakfast, her father left to run the charter, and Amanda headed upstairs to shower. She pulled her prize tiara from the dresser and set it on her head, surprised by its weight. With all the craziness from the night before and the quick pictures with her father, she hadn't noticed how truly remarkable it was. *Amazing for a costume tiara!* She got a good look at herself in the mirror. Her eyes were less puffy. She massaged the necklace. Diamonds surrounded the sapphire. She felt like a million dollars.

Choker

The Jeep was still in the driveway of the Bay House when Jeb awoke. He had tours to conduct and needed to get yesterday's events out of his mind. He hadn't slept well and upon sight of the Jeep, his melancholy returned.

Jeb's heart began to race. *We packed a lifetime into a day.* He recounted his many confrontations with Amanda and their resolutions. Her lopsided grin on the dock? *How could a girl be so cute?* Although they bickered, he couldn't help but adore her. He stood his ground and was glad for it. When he acquiesced, it went to his credit and benefited his team. Twice he'd lashed out at her in anger, but she understood him and forgave him.

Jeb completed his afternoon tour, grateful to have slogged through it. He wasn't himself and only hoped he'd concealed the laborious effort required to endure both of the day's tours. When he returned to the Shop, the Jeep was street-parked out front. His chest pulsed. Amanda was on the Shop's porch, comfortably swaying on its swing.

Their eyes locked and held. He stopped the truck halfway up the Shop's side entrance, his heart still thudding hard against his ribs. Who cared if he blocked someone? A shy smile played at the corner of her lips and her mole was showing. He hopped out before his heart caught up and strode across his hardscape. By the time he reached the porch, he wondered if his feet had ever touched the ground.

She wore a global map of the world shirt with cut-off jeans and her eyes were radiant. These weren't the eyes from the previous week, or even from yesterday. The anger was gone from them now, and he thought she was ten times more beautiful.

Her hair flowed from the back of her sports cap, the one with the Shop's logo, and his heart did a double beat. Her shirt hung out behind her in a stylish way and wrapped around her neck was a most unusual choker. A compass dangled from it. If not for the sapphire in the middle of it, he would've thought the beads mixed in with the jade were American Indian. Possibly even pre-Columbian. Similar to a piece his mother owned—*a family heirloom,* she called it.

He reached the top of the stairs, and she stood. His eyes bounced from hers to the mysterious compass rose covering her breastbone. He felt weak in the knees and barely breathed. Silence remained between them for some time but for the necklace, as if it spoke for them.

Amanda finally stirred. "Jeb, I want to apologize for being dishonest with you."

His heart sank. Not what he'd hoped to hear. His body tightened, and he looked down—*were her feelings for me a mirage? I misread her!*

He gave it another moment before answering, "How's that?"

"I was dishonest by concealing who I am from you. I used your daughter to search the Marina House under false pretenses."

He glanced up to see Amanda's brow knitted with confusion and couldn't hide some anger in his tone. "I don't know what you're talking about. You never lied to me. I don't see a point in your apology." He'd fallen for a girl named Amanda, her name part of the attraction. Not Izzie! *What do I call her now?* She wasn't apologizing for the subterfuge. How could he explain it to her? *Too risky!*

"We should've never left the Marina House with the storm approaching. I was afraid to face my father."

Jeb swallowed hard. "Sierra should've known better."

"She did!" Amanda huffed and stomped her foot on the porch. Her eyes were passionate. Her teasing smile was long gone, and she grabbed Jeb's wrist.

A shot of electricity went straight through him, and he tried to breathe normally.

"I didn't tell her it was my house, and I pushed her away from it despite *her* warnings. I'm to blame."

He folded his arms. Amanda's eyes were winning. He swayed his head and looked past her. *She doesn't know the full extent of the danger they were in.* He bit his lip.

"The lightning?" she said, as if pleading. "I've never seen anything like it."

Jeb nodded. "It was an unusual storm."

She let a smile grow. "*Amanda* is my name. I began using it when I left here and started college. I've used it ever since."

Jeb blinked. Her face offered a ray of hope. He needed a moment and dropped his glance to the porch decking. He exhaled softly and returned his eyes to her. *The dream's alive.*

Now he regretted pulling his arm from her. Then something she'd said hit him. "You snuck into your *own* house?"

She nodded mischievously.

Jeb howled in laughter. *She is a crazy woman!*

She wasn't laughing and he worried he'd hurt her feelings. *Not again.*

She fought back a smile.

The real problem? *I'm crazy about her.*

His voice softened, "How'd it go with your father?" It felt strange not to call him *Charley*. *Her father!*

"Things went well." She sighed. "Thanks for asking. I'm about ten pounds lighter from all the bawling last night."

"Sounds like you may be dehydrated. How about a sports drink?"

She laughed.

Jeb continued, "We wanted to return your Jeep last night, but my mother advised against it." He refused to say it was he that really wanted to visit her.

"Thanks. We were still hashing through a lot of raw emotions." Her voice became dreamy. "Only this morning did we begin catching up from the past ten years . . . we've barely scratched the surface."

"I can only imagine."

Her eyes softened. "I'm headed back, Jeb . . . before I get too tired. I'm returning in a few weeks to visit my father and I wanted to ask you something."

A tingling sensation ran up the back of Jeb's neck—*maybe this will be an opening.* "Okay," he allowed.

"I'd like to continue visiting with your girls. I may have been dishonest in how I represented myself, but I was never *dishonest* with you in how I feel about them."

She paused and took in his eyes. He was more than happy to give them. *How about me? How do you feel about me?*

"I'd love to teach them how to ride and even come to their weekend soccer games. They'll always be welcome at my home. I still owe Sierra her tip, too, and I'd like to take her shopping."

The tingling thrill was gone, and he arrested a look of disappointment crawling across his face.

Wait a minute, this is still a step forward. "I'm sure *they'd* love that." He eyed the slats on his porch, took a few long breaths, and returned his eyes to her. "When I said I thought you were alright, I meant it."

When Jeb arrived in his truck, Amanda fought every muscle in her body to keep from running off the porch and into his arms. She remained on the swing and practiced controlled breathing. When he approached, and she finally stood up, a chill ran from the rear of her head, down her spine, and all the way to her toes. Jeb's eyes spoke volumes about a possible future. And now, what was standing in her way?

Too fast? The thought crossed her mind. *I need to rebuild with Dad.*

Jeb seemed to pull back, too. She was hoping for more from him, wishing he'd responded, "*I'd* love that."

And the thought that James Carter would have feelings for her? Not a chance. She suspected he'd been married to a goddess. *And I'm no goddess!* Her head was swimming, and the answer it provided was simple. She'd swapped the longing feelings for her father to Jeb. Her father loved her—she had no doubts. But James Carter? Does he even like me? *Let it be about the girls . . . Be patient.*

"Will you allow Sierra to lead a tour again?" she asked.

Jeb flinched.

Amanda knitted her arms in front of her. "Would you like a lecture from an over-controlled daughter?"

"No." Jeb's answer was quick. Some moments passed, and a smile played on his lips. "Yes, ma'am."

She dropped her arms. "Let's save it for another time."

He nodded, and his eyes fell to her neckline to the sapphire and the compass. He touched his own chest. "Amazing . . . the shirt, too." There was something more in his expression—an inquisitive look.

"Hah . . . found it in my closet this afternoon." Then she patted the necklace. "College graduation present from my dad today."

He nodded, and his smile was warm. "Isabel West is a beautiful name. Would you like me to call you that?" His voice was bright and hinting at a future.

"Thank you, James Carter. I'm fine with Amanda. I'll be back down for Labor Day weekend. I'll stop by then . . . and yes, I'll take you up on that sports drink."

Jeb retrieved it and walked Amanda to her Jeep. He didn't hug her, though it was exactly what she wanted from him. He did, however, politely open the door for her, grasp the door's frame where the window had been lowered, and wish her well.

Epilogue

A knock sounded on Charley's front door before he heard it open.

"Anyone home?" a familiar voice bellowed.

"No!"

Her steps padded in his direction. "Where are you?"

"No one is busy in his office."

He stood, and within moments, a woman appeared in the doorway. It was Nancy, his oldest sister. She beamed a smile at him like she'd just won the lottery. She pranced a few steps and then came right at him for a hug. "We've been missing you."

"I haven't gone anywhere." He smirked. "Good to see you, Sis. So what brings you to these parts?"

"I need you for a quick errand."

"What makes you think I'm available without any notice?"

"Well, are you available?"

"No, I'm booked to show a yacht at 10:00 AM. The customer wants a test sail."

"No she doesn't."

"Huh?"

"Exactly. We made that appointment."

"We? I don't like the way you said *we*."

"Right. Exactly. This isn't a personal call. Business. But when we arrive at the bank, it needs to look like it's personal. Brother and sister stuff. Family trust paperwork."

"Oookay."

"Can you just return to whatever you were doing?" she flung her hand at him dismissively.

He felt like an eight-year-old, being bossed about by his older sister. He didn't move at first, and became the target of her scowl. It was one thing to be bossed around by the Lady, but in his own house! Now he felt like a dog, tucking his tail between his legs, and he begrudgingly returned to his office. He heard his sister head back towards the kitchen and then the side entrance. Another woman's voice was heard entering and the two greeted each other like schoolgirls; then, their voices turned somber and hushed.

"Let's make it quick, then you two can get on your way." It was the voice of the new arrival.

"Have you ever been here?"

"Never inside. Not like this."

"Follow me."

Their scampering steps sounded throughout the house and even to the second floor as they moved briskly. The visitor kept gasping in awe. He suspected she was pausing in front of his furniture.

Their steps padded down the stairs and came in his direction. As they traversed the hall, he heard the woman say, "This place is better than the National Gallery."

"Amazing, isn't it?" Nancy said.

"Beyond my expectations. She was the greatest. How fortunate to have had such a conscientious caretaker." No doubt, these were kind words spoken about his late wife.

They passed by his office and he realized then they were heading to the den, saving it for last. His chest squeezed horribly tight. Even if he attempted to spy on them from his office with the door open, he couldn't see them. The business in the den could only mean one thing. A beloved aspect of his former life was about to be ripped out from under him. He fought back the urge to scream bloody murder and race into the den. This was his house. His property! What right did they have to barge in like this? He threw his hands behind his head and breathed deeply. He heard the women coo like doves after a few minutes of being in the den and then he heard the stranger being shuttled out through the same doorway she'd entered.

When Nancy found him several minutes later in his office, she was holding an ornate wooden box with fanciful maritime etchings. The sight of it sliced into him like a dagger straight to the heart.

"Do you want to see it?" her voice was sweet now.

"No."

"I understand." She let a few moments pass in silence. Her eyes showed understanding. "It's nearly perfect. The years haven't done any damage."

"Great." Like she thought that would bring him comfort.

She touched his arm. "Are you sure? This may be the last time you ever see it."

"So, you're taking it," he accused.

"*We're* taking it and I need you to carry."

"The box?"

"No. Your heat."

He jolted.

"Okay, yeah. Overkill. We're hiding it in plain sight." She reached into his trash bin and pulled out a few loose papers. Draft invoices. "Do you need this?"

"Uh, no, that's why it's in the trash."

"Just checking. Sometimes I use my trash bin for extra file space until I'm really ready to shred it."

"Hmmm. You're weird. I've always felt that way about you. Take what you want."

She flashed a crooked smile he remembered from their teen years. It had nearly every guy on the block flocking to her. "I need a couple of manila envelopes. One large enough for the box."

He gestured towards his office supply cabinet. She moved towards it, opened the door, and found his shipping supplies.

"Let's ride in your truck. It won't take long," she said.

"Wonderful. Like the good times."

Her eyes brightened. "Yes, like the good times," she said slowly. "Are you sure you don't want one last look?"

"I'm fine. I only care for one memory of it." *The memory of it on her hand. My Mary!*

"She was the best, Charley. You know that."

That was all he could take. His eyes gushed and she was quickly at his side, wrapping his head in the crook of her arm. Several moments passed, and he composed himself.

"I know this is painful, Charley, but I need to say something else."

He looked up into his sister's face, her eyes showing tremendous care. He nodded slightly to let her know he could handle it. He had a strong inkling as to what she was going to say, so he hinted at it, suspecting they'd violated the sanctity of his bedroom. "The picture."

"Yes, Charley. The one on your dresser."

"I'm not throwing it away."

"Of course you're not and I'd never suggest it."

"Your advice?"

"I wouldn't dare give it and I'm not qualified. I haven't been through what you have. But let's face it. You have two bright lights shining in your life now."

"Charlotte's been shining for well over a year."

"I know. So don't mess that up."

"I won't. You've given me an idea. I'll take care of it this week. Before Izzie returns for the weekend."

Her eyes moistened. She grasped his hand. "I'm so happy for you both. She'll understand."

"Thanks." He inhaled like he'd just reached a Rocky Mountain summit. "I don't want to confuse her about my intentions towards Charlotte."

She grasped his hand and pulled at him. "Come on. You drive. We need to leave the phones behind. Mine is still in the car."

He grabbed his keys and eyed his phone on his desk. She held both manila envelopes. One contained some of his office trash. The other? The most priceless artifact he'd ever set his eyes on. "Where are we going?"

"The Center."

He was dumbfounded and didn't hide it from his expression as he opened the passenger door of his truck for her.

After he got in, she continued, "It must be moved for safekeeping. We call it pre-positioning. Certainly you must understand this."

Charley felt a small spark, like the first crackle of kindling igniting deep within his soul. "It's been so many years." Nancy was alluding to sacred traditions he'd practiced as a young man.

"Trust us. We know what we're doing. Centuries of lessons learned."

"Meddling?" The question scared him, worried he was about to take a shot across the bow.

"Do you remember our ski trips in the Rockies? Those mountain passes?"

"Yeah." Charley glanced down at the marina as they passed. Everything was in order.

"What did you see on either side?" she asked.

"Huge slabs of wind-shaped snow cresting over the ledges."

"Exactly. Snowpack sitting on top of nothing."

Charley zoned out. It was too painful for him to admit his past failings. "I'm not sure I know what you're getting at except for an avalanche." His emotional state tapped his energy, leaving little to solve her riddles.

"We understand the danger . . . stronger snow overcoming weaker. One wrong step and this becomes a tragedy. For us all. For them? Irrevocable damage." She adjusted herself, pulling a grab handle. "We can't have that. Nothing must startle them."

He shook his head, exasperated. "You're still losing me." His thoughts drifted to a memory of skiing with his family on a glacier in the Swiss Alps.

He was driving out of the main gate now, and she snapped her fingers in his face. "We need the birds to come together naturally."

"Hmmm." Now she really did have him confused. *Better to just play along.* "But what's wrong if they're carried by the same wind . . . or nudged into the same ocean current."

"Okay . . . but nothing more. And most of all, let that current be God's making. Not yours!"

"And if this fails?" *When will she clue me in?*

"Our line is lost. This can't go on indefinitely. The Realm will move on."

He slumped.

Her words snapped, "But you must consider what's best for *her*. Shouldn't that be your first priority?"

"Yes. Of course it is." Putting *her* first made sense. Izzie meant everything to him. But *him*? He wasn't sure.

"Then don't worry about the ring."

His insides churned on their drive to the Center and even though he had a thousand things to say, mostly in protest, they spoke little. He helped Nancy from his truck when they arrived, and they entered the Center, first passing the on-duty guard, who barely took notice of them. They approached the reception desk. The woman behind it was sorting mail. She swiveled in her chair and caught his eye with a knowing look.

"Hi, Dorothy. We just need to visit the bank. Do I need to sign in?" he asked.

"Oh no, you're fine. If we can't trust a captain in these parts, who can we trust?"

"Awww . . . thanks." He slapped his hand to his chest.

His sister flashed Dorothy a smile as big as the sun, but didn't speak. Nancy took his hand and tugged him along, already two steps ahead, heading past an open-aired assembly room housing a grand piano. A long corridor led them to the bank's satellite branch—hosted by the retirement center for the convenience of their well-moneyed occupants.

Upon entering the small bank office, they approached the chest-high reception desk. He spotted another familiar face and cheated, noticing her nameplate before saying, "Good morning, Glenda."

Her expression showed she recognized him, too, but he could tell she was struggling to identify his sister.

To Glenda's left was the walk-in safe, partially opened. A waist-high gate separated them from the iron-cast door.

Nancy stepped forward. "Good morning, Glenda, we'll need access to safety deposit box 210."

The receptionist gaped. Whether or not she recognized the lady at his side, he didn't know, but he could tell Nancy's magnetic smile worked magic.

"Okay, that particular model requires three keys. Mine here . . ." she raised an odd-looking key, "and two others."

He reached into his pocket, found his key, and raised it. Nancy was already dangling hers.

They followed Glenda into the walk-in safe and she inserted her key into the center slot of box drawer 210 and rotated it. A hard click sounded. She turned around. "I'll leave you to it," she said, and left the space.

"You're not locking us in, are you?" Panic filled his sister's voice.

"No, just giving y'all your privacy." The teller pushed the heavy metal door to where he could barely see a sliver of the outside world.

Nancy's face turned white. "Let's make this quick," she said.

"Not much has changed I see." His poor sister was hyperventilating.

"Shut up and do your part." She'd already inserted her key into the second lock. A click signaled the mechanism's release.

He'd only meant to tease her about her claustrophobia. Making her mad may have helped take her mind off the tight space.

He inserted his key, and when he turned it, the box slid free.

Nancy kissed the manila envelope that wrapped the jewelry box, and gently set it into the drawer.

"Open that for me." She gestured towards the envelope in his hands that contained his trash office papers. While he pulled back the clasp and opened the flap, she pulled a small black device from her front pocket and dropped it into the envelope.

He tightened his brows. "Is that a beacon?"

"Yes."

"Why not put it in the other package?"

"We did."

He flinched. "Oh, of course you did." Who was he fooling? She was a professional and had the resources of a small nation at her disposal.

"Not nearly as obvious and almost impossible to detect."

"I hope you didn't damage the box."

"No, we added a fake bottom to it," she whispered.

He gave her the envelope and she laid it on top of the other one. She pushed the drawer shut and eyed the closed metal door with discomfort. He felt his eyes moisten. He needed more time to say goodbye to the heirloom, but Nancy continued to blow large breaths, and he was surprised she hadn't already passed out. Reluctantly, he reset his side of the lock, and after she set the one to the right, she rushed out of the vault breathing heavily. The receptionist returned shortly with her key and secured the center mechanism.

He joined his sister moments later in the parking lot. She was still breathing hard, but her color had returned. "Everything set?"

"Yes. Glenda wanted to chit-chat, but I covered for you. You know you're not the first one to run out of there like that."

"Thanks. Barely helps." She sucked in a large breath. "Okay, I need to get you to your appointment."

"I thought it was a ruse," he said, arriving at his truck and opening the door for her.

She climbed in and turned towards him. "It was, but you still need to meet with the woman about the yacht. Make it quick. Instruct her to climb aboard. Don't ask questions. She may ask you a few mundane things about it. Play along. Pull your key from your pocket and set it on the console. When you see that she's taken it, you'll know the appointment is over."

"Turn in my key?" He felt as if he'd been knifed in the chest.

"Yes. I'm sorry.

"Will I know her?"

"It'll be difficult to recognize her with a mask and scarf. Don't give her a hard time about it. Make it quick and let her be on her way. I suspect she's already taken on fuel at your pump."

Silence governed several miles. It was a kind gesture by his sister as he tried to collect himself. Things had seemed bright with the return of Izzie, but today was a setback.

Nancy's voice woke him from his melancholy. "You've been a great sport today, Charley."

"Like I had a choice?"

"Of course you had a choice. Free will. And by the way, which one of us was carrying?"

"You have Mom's domineering eyes . . . so I'd say you held the firepower."

"It goes with raising so many boys."

"You know I would've liked to have had more children." The hollow sensation in his chest continued to weigh him down.

His sister jolted. "Of course I do, but God gave you and Mary other gifts." She narrowed her eyes some. "You and Mary were in the right place at the right time under the right situation to pull off what you did. So many—who will never know the extent of your service—owe you a debt of gratitude." She nodded enthusiastically. "And I appreciate the way you created family and relationships right where you were . . . along the way . . . and even now at this time. My boys still talk about their wonderful visits with you all at the Marina House."

"They're welcome anytime."

"Be careful with that invite." He knew she was referring to the older boys who had growing families of their own.

"Their visits slowed."

"I know. We all wanted to be careful to avoid inflaming the tension between you and Izzie. They adore you both and still worship the ground tread by their Uncle Charley."

"I'm rarely on terra firma."

"The seabed supports the water the *Queen Mary* rides upon."

"So my reputation isn't soiled with them?"

"It never was."

"Why? Didn't Izzie talk?"

"Not with them. Kept it to herself. She spoke with me, of course, but she wasn't going to tarnish you in front of her cousins."

Charley's eyes moistened. "If you think it would help them, I have no qualms explaining the wretch that I was."

"Was?" There was some tease in her voice. "How about Jeb Carter?"

His shoulders tightened. "You heard about that?"

She snorted a laugh. "Not from Izzie." A chuckle took over. "Are you two okay?"

"We're fine. I apologized. He apologized . . . and then he threatened to file charges on account of me throwing an inaccurate punch . . . something like that."

His sister covered her mouth, but a robust burst came through. "You're kidding, right?"

"Jeb and I are fine. It was a wild moment. I've never had so many emotional knives flung at me at the same time from so many directions."

"And Jeb understood that?"

"He understood some of it. Far more than everyone else at the grill . . . but not all of it."

"And Charlotte?"

"She knew enough to diffuse it."

"Gotcha . . . but of course she doesn't know all of it. Please consider how that may change."

Charley side-glanced his sister. They were passing over the Foxwells Bridge and he spotted Jeb and his small fishing tour off in the distance making their way out of Windmill Point Creek. "I don't understand."

"Good," she said in the brightest tone she'd used all day. "That's exactly how this needs to work."

"What are you talking about?"

"We're not talking about it, Charley. Please trust us." She gently slapped her hands on the dash. "No, please trust God in this. We are trusting Him. We only ask you to do the same."

Made in the USA
Columbia, SC
16 February 2023

93fded68-9896-4e4c-a829-03f6859e28edR01